AT HOME IN ENGLAND

Reconfiguring Identity through Memory in Select Novels of Kazuo Ishiguro, Hanif Kureishi and Romesh Gunesekera

GURUDEV MEHER

ATLANTIC

PUBLISHERS & DISTRIBUTORS (P) LTD

ATLANTIC
PUBLISHERS & DISTRIBUTORS (P) LTD

7/22, Ansari Road, Darya Ganj, New Delhi
Tel.: +91-11-4077 5252, 2327 3880
E-mail: orders@atlanticbooks.com
Web: www.atlanticbooks.com

Published by Atlantic Publishers & Distributors (P) Ltd 2024

Printed & bound in India by Atlantic Print Services

Perhaps the self-same song that found a path
Through the sad heart of Ruth, when, sick for
home, She stood in tears amid the alien corn.

—John Keats, "Ode to a Nightingale"

Foreword

Dr. Gurudev Meher's book titled *At Home in England: Reconfiguring Identity through Memory in Select Novels of Kazuo Ishiguro, Hanif Kureishi and Romesh Gunesekera* is a treatise on the notion of 'home' that has undergone radical transformations, particularly with the advent of the postmodernist concepts of the fluidity of space and time. A renewed definition of home becomes both essential and contingent in a cosmopolitan diasporic scenario where the shift of space is a conspicuous phenomenon, and along with this spatial shift, we witness the concomitant reconstruction of cultural memory and identity. Combined together, memory and identity become constitutive forces that offer immanent materialities for the reconstitution and reconfiguration of home in diasporic spaces that are alien to the immigrant communities who have left their originary locations. In this scenario, home becomes a fluid and fluctuating category and remains no more confined to a rigid, inflexible spatio-temporal milieu; rather it becomes a perennially re-constructible entity whose constitutive components are emotions, sentiments and retentive cultural memories associated with the original home-spaces. Therefore, 'home' attains the qualities of transcendence over the conventional, binding grids of space, time, nationalities, territories and boundaries, and thus, attains the qualities of extensive spatio-temporal adaptability in diverse cosmopolitan scenarios. Home, in this ever-shifting, postmodernist and diasporic world, is transformed into a non-spatial and fluid dimensionality which is subject to multiple reconstructions through the fluid materialities of the immigrant's deep-seated memories and unexpressed desires engraved in the past.

In this context of renewed and radically redefined concept of home, Dr. Meher's book fundamentally carves a narrative that foregrounds the home's categorical defiance of the conventional, old, rigid, holistic and totalising models of historical representations, and its attainment of non-linear and non-chronological spatio-temporal fluidity in manifold trans-national, cosmopolitan imbroglios. The theoretical framework that Dr. Meher has developed in his book encompasses a broad spectrum of problematics associated with diasporic homing practices; his narrative addresses questions like ethnic and cultural dislocation, the dissolution of boundaries across national territories and frontiers, the obliteration of barriers between indigenous 'home' spaces and alien, trans-national spaces, the progressive proliferation of porousness and permeability between reclusive cultural domains, the reconstitution of home in the immigrant's mindscape laden with forlorn memory and desire etc. But, the fundamental point of assertion here is that the home is no more a tangible and physical embodiment inscribing a finite, immovable and quantifiable space, but rather is an exclusive mental category that is subject to multiple shifts, substitutions and reconfigurations across indefinite spatio-temporal axes and coordinates. The texts that have been undertaken by Dr. Meher are carefully chosen in a way that they would be able to elicit—through their strategic, fictional manoeuvres—the imaginative 'home-making' experiences of diverse, immigrant communities, emanating from countries like Japan, Pakistan and Sri Lanka. It goes without saying that these are the nations whose immigrants have constituted the highest diasporic population across the globe and, thus, Dr. Meher seems to have judiciously picked novels of Japanese, Pakistani and Sri Lankan authors so as to offer a larger, broader and more inclusive perspective on diaspora studies. The authors chosen by Dr. Meher for his critical analyses are Japanese-British novelist Kazuo Ishiguro, Sri Lankan-British novelist Romesh Gunesekera and Pakistani-British novelist Hanif Kureishi who offer to their readers variegated and kaleidoscopic spectacles of the immigrant communities' 'home-making' endeavours.

To make apt critical analyses of the mentioned works in the said context, Dr. Meher has made profuse use of the theoretical templates provided by Homi Bhabha, Paul Gilory, Stuart Hall, James Clifford, etc. who have theorised, in their respective, significant ways, the notions of hybridity, 'third space,' acculturation, multiculturalism, etc. which are extremely relevant in the context of the diasporic displacements and their summative replantations in an alien soil. The theoretical templates provided by these postcolonial/postmodernist thinkers have facilitated the comprehension of the evolution of mutated identities of the immigrants in ambivalent, cosmopolitan spaces in which they are posited after their collective migration from their previous ethno-cultural spaces. Applying these theoretical modules, Dr. Meher has successfully analysed pertinent diasporic contentions like the gross disruption of a single, monolithic and dominant cultural narrative, the dismantlement of the occident/orient binary, the dissolution of the notion of a sacrosanct, inviolable and monocultural rootedness, etc. which have evolved through the accretion of the immigrant communities' new, homing experiences. By dint of such critical inquiries, Dr. Meher has astutely cartographed the evolution of new composite cultural formations, proliferating hybridisation of identities, cross-cultural negotiations in the diasporic melting-pot, non-linear amalgamations of diversified spaces and times in this new 'mise en scene' that repudiates the rigid spatio-temporal determinism of historical and cultural constants. It hardly needs mentioning that these are the crucial issues and contentions that are both necessary and contingent to the notion of diasporic 'home-making.'

In the light of the above discussions, I vouch for the fact that Dr. Meher's book shall be a significant contribution to the existing scholarship on diaspora studies for its detailed and nuanced exploration into the idea of 'home-making' that is intimately connected to the lived experiences of many immigrant communities, especially those hailing from the subcontinent. In this book, Dr. Meher offers solid and sufficiently viable arguments backed by compact theoretical postulations and fitting textual elicitations. The book is replete with novelty of ideas; it bespeaks relentless scholarly pursuits made by the author and elicits an immense sincerity of approach. I wish him all the luck for the massive success of the book in terms of becoming a pioneering work in the field of diaspora studies.

Sambit Panigrahi
Professor of English
Ravenshaw University

Preface

'Home,' in the present cultural configuration of the world, carries multiple shades of meaning which can no longer be reduced to its conventional conceptualisation of fixity, security and boundedness. The postmodern notion of home moves beyond its material counterparts and embraces a dialectics of fluidity and movement, seeking to evolve a constructed locus of home in its plurilocal, multidimensional manifestations. When the 'homing desire' of the individual is allied with a deep feeling of loss and sadness, and the idea of home is entangled with a sense of irrevocable displacement, home ceases to be a place anymore, and becomes an emotion. Home, in this sense, transcends the physical limits of fixed boundaries and nationalities, and is metamorphosed into a non-spatial entity, spawned by the silenced memories and unspeakable desires of the past. The narrative of dislocation, in fact, replicates multiple homes in the diasporic imagination of the immigrants which makes the boundary between home and away a permeable and porous one, for one's home is not situated outside one's self but becomes an indispensable part of it. Our fate, therefore, is no better than that of a snail who tends to carry its home on its head wherever it moves.

This model of diaspora connotes a condition rather than being definitive of a community. This condition not only displays a strong proclivity towards multiple journeys and localisations but also exhibits a subversive impulse of disrupting the boundaries of the binaries. It perpetuates a differential redefinition of cultural accommodation and syncretism, filtering out the pitfalls of essentialism and stereotypical reductionism.

Cultural memory, in this narrative of reclamation, plays a pivotal role in reconfiguring the identities of the individuals, retrospectively rendered through the fragile fragments of a dynamicised memorialisation, bringing about a symbiotic confluence of the time past and the time present which helps evolve a reconfigurated version of identity in the discourse of home and belonging.

Cultural theorists such as Bhabha, Hall, Said, Gilroy, Clifford, Cohen and others seek to evolve a mutable conceptualisation of identity that is keen to disrupt the narrative of a dominant culture, introducing a fluid hybridization of the discourses of cultural purity and rootedness, to creatively reconfigure the discourse of dominance and resistance in the framework of transactive cultural encounters.

England, in this densely diasporising world, connotes a diverse, cosmopolitan nation in which diasporic themes and experiences turn out to be the most informing elements to an understanding of the contemporary English literature. It has been the 'home' of many diasporic authors and individuals whose narrative voices are vital in moulding the British cultural space and identity, adding to its complexity and negotiative rhetoric of diasporisation. Authors such as Kazuo Ishiguro, Hanif Kureishi, Romesh Gunesekera and others form a rich galaxy of diasporic writers in the literary scenario of Britain, migrating from the various parts of the world. These writers, albeit nourish a connection with their respective homelands, feel themselves utterly at home in England, searching and forging new modes of belonging to be identified with.

In their fictional manoeuvres these writers seem to suggest that feeling at home is essentially a subjective and culturally determined link to the imaginary, and that the memory of home is recreative of the inner poetry of the private self which is evoked by emotion and not by factual recollections. Identity, in the framework of the novels selected for consideration in this book, becomes an unsettled entity marked out by the discontinuities of time and space, whereby, through the ambiguity of displacement, the diasporans are able to reconstruct the inner landscapes of their minds to perpetrate their sense of belonging, disrupting the idea of bounded rootedness and homogenised belonging.

The rhetoric of diaspora then involves forging new narratives of belonging which seek to accommodate the migrant's position more appropriately than the older totalising or holistic model of representations. The diasporic subjects do not have to secure their 'roots' in a fixed place, a nation or an ethnic group, rather they must ceaselessly devise for themselves itinerant cultural 'routes' which take them emotionally to multiple places and into contact with different groups of the populace, establishing new connections between past, present and future without presuming a linear, continuous movement through time and space.

This book, thus, is an exhaustive attempt to cartograph and recapture the diverse dimensions of 'home' in the contemporary glocalized world in general and England as a specifically diasporic point, in which these writers are extraordinarily attentive to the reconfigurement of their cultural identities through the fragile fluidity of an ever vibrant memory, in the narrative of the sequestered self, in an alien ambience of apparent cultural fragmentation and dispersion.

Gurudev Meher

Contents

Chapter 1
Introduction: Theoretical Background and Scope of the Study

> "Home is where your feet are, and may your heart be there too"
>
> —Uma Parameswaran, "Contextualizing Diasporic Locations"

> "... We will not be capable of reclaiming precisely the thing that was lost; that we will, in short, create fictions, not actual cities or villages, but invisible ones, imaginary homelands, Indias of the mind."
>
> —Salman Rushdie, *Imaginary Homelands*

The notion of 'home' is as old as the history of human civilisation which over the course of time has assumed new dimensions in fiction written in English by the new diasporas in the West. Congratulatory claims have been made in favour of the epistemic centrality of the diasporic positions which is viewed as a universal ontological condition, dismissing all fixated paradigms of rootedness and stable territorialities. There is, therefore, an immense critical investiture promulgated in the reassessment of our understanding of home and belonging, locating them in the amorphous topography of mind which is based on the individual's lived experiences and relationships rather than monocultural, rigidified locationality.

Diasporic identity emerges as an unsettled position whose features are flexible enough to accommodate its adoptive strategies in the West between a number of intersecting discourses, locations and belongingness. The diasporic subjects feel a constant urge to reconstruct their own image of the homeland, creating an imaginative space for themselves, which is essentially linked up with their history, culture, memory, and tradition. It involves the reconfiguring of the inner landscape as the repressed memory of the past is viewed as an underlying condition of the nostalgic drive in the reinvention of an imaginary homeland. The diasporic subjects are continually faced with the problem of recollecting, rewriting and restaging the fragmented shadows of a long-lost past. Thus, attempts are made at tracing, retaining, re-examining, and reconfiguring one's roots in the cultural space of an alien ambience.

This study is an attempt to map the different modalities and complexities related to the idea of 'home' that is formed in the mind of the diasporic subjects and their representations in fiction focusing on the concept of identity as hybrid, fluid and fragmentary, enacting the eternal drama of re-inscribing, restructuring and restaging an incommensurable presence in the vast spatial dialectics of the mind.

The diasporic identity carries with it an ambiguous condition of ambivalent possessions and belonging, resulting in the ideological struggles of these individuals in the structuring and restructuring of their contesting diasporic positions and their reimagining of 'home' and 'homeland'. Hence, this study aims at foregrounding the significance of diasporic representation in England, relocating the process of self-actualisation in an adverse environment with fundamental concern over the notion of 'home' as an emotional construct spawned by the threads of memory and desire while exposing the intrinsic insubstantiality of all homes and homemaking projects.

This research would attempt a postcolonial and diasporic approach to critically explore the intricacies of 'home' and 'homeland' in the identity formation of diasporic subjects, highlighting memory as an important quotient in the reconfigurement of emotional spaces in the diasporic imagination and their representation in novels written by

Asian diasporas in Britain. The study proposes to deconstruct the stable, fixed, essentialised concepts of memory, identity and ethnicity in the differential dialectics of diasporic possibilities, taking recourse to the concepts such as ambivalence, hybridity, fluidity, performance, in-betweenness, etc. in the discourse of diasporic power relations.

For this purpose, some fictional works of three diasporic authors such as Kazuo Ishiguro, Hanif Kureishi and Romesh Gunesekera have been analysed and discussed. The trio, albeit, hail from different countries of origin, happened to be settled making England their permanent home, and significantly contributing to the growth and development of contemporary British literature. Since it is not feasible to evaluate their entire oeuvre in this study, a selective in-depth study has been attempted by taking two novels from each author for consideration that are critically recognised as diasporic texts. Although, Ishiguro has authored many novels till date, I find two of his novels—*The Remains of the Day* and *When We Were Orphans*—immensely valuable for my purpose which have become increasingly popular since their publication and in these two novels the concepts of home, identity and memory are explicitly worked out and exploited. Similarly, I select the first two novels of Hanif Kureishi—*The Buddha of Suburbia* and *The Black Album*—for my study because these are the works in which Kureishi is elaborately involved in exploring the multiple modalities of his 'cultural home,' exposing the insignificance and irrelevance of the fixed, stabilised and essentialist conceptualisation of home and identity in favour of a hybrid, non-monolithic, cosmopolitan culture, feeling utterly at home in England despite being occasionally subjected to racial discrimination. Further, some of the fictional works of Romesh Gunesekera are highly conducive to any diasporic study and thus for my present research, I am inclined to choose two of his best known novels—*Reef* and *The Sandglass*—in which the protagonists are forever suspended between alternating desires and locations in the quest for their identity and belonging, reconfiguring the inner landscape of their questing minds.

In all these novels, England serves as a common location or setting for almost all the protagonists and characters and therefore the focus of this research is mostly on England as a land of new belonging rather than the originary, native land of identification.

Furthermore, my research does not follow an overtly inherent rhetoric of diasporic reclamation through which the diasporic subjects seek to nostalgically nourish images and ideas of the homeland as a survival strategy as reflected in most of the diasporic texts, but the ways they challenge the spatio-temporal cartographies of these fixated entities, forging and reinventing new homing possibilities in an alien land of fragmented affiliations and shifting identifications. There is, therefore, a continued emphasis is sustained, in my study, on the theoretical frameworks developed by Homi Bhabha, James Clifford, Stuart Hall, Avtar Brah, Paul Gilroy, et al. where the focus is rather not on the 'roots' or originary location, but on the 'routes' or itinerant fluid locations, marked out by movements and lived experiences of the present. Hence, terms such as fluidity, hybridity, heterogeneity, fragmentation, in-betweenness, plurality, ambivalence, translation, permeability, reconfiguration, re-invention, reconstruction, etc., become watchwords to my purposeful analysis of the conceptualisation of 'home' and 'identity'.

****

In the world of increasing globalisation, 'home' carries multiple shades of meaning and is far from being a simplistic notion of rootedness and belonging. The shifting nature of home and identification has replaced the conventional conceptualisation of fixed home. The idea of home turns out to be a semiotic site where one negotiates the fluctuating images of the past with the conflicting realities of the present. The ceaseless movements that inform the lives of the diasporic individuals tend to loosen the sense of coherent identity and holistic communities in which stable, consistent, essentialised notions of identifications are openly questioned and contested. Questions such as what is home? Where is it? How does one's identity change with changing places? What defines one's identity? Is identity bound to a specific territoriality or can it be reconfigured with the existing memory in relation to the lived experience of the present locality?—are some of the key inquiries which problematise the concept of home in diasporic studies.

In explicating home, therefore, in the specificity of diasporic subjectivities, one must attend to the factors associated with nation, space and integration. The diverse connections and movements across the world have made our society densely diasporising which point out to the ways in which "the experience of space is always socially constructed" (Gupta and Ferguson 11). The manner in which people feel at home essentially relates to their feeling of rootedness to a particular locality and the connections to other places which are nourished through social networks and sensory environments. 'Home', then, is defined as several sites of sensory connections and dwelling places, both past and present, in the course of a person's growth and mobility in terms of travel, transition and memory. It can be described both as the actual place of residence carved out through lived experiences and the metaphorical space of individual attachments and belongingness. The discourse of home indelibly involves the discussion on identity and belonging which can be reconfigured with the concurrent existentialities of the diasporans, perpetually balancing and reconciling the global with the local, the personal with the political, and the feeling and inwardness of 'here' with 'there'. The study thus seeks to chalk out these spatial, temporal and emotional connections the immigrants foster and sustain in the creation and cultivation of their disparate homes away from their actual homes.

The notion of home conjures up an emotional territory which the diasporic individual seeks to belong. It is implicitly structured as "a purified space of belonging in which the subject is too comfortable to question the limits or borders of her or his experience" (Ahmed 339). The narrative of dislocation, in fact, replicates too many homes in the diasporic imagination of the immigrants which makes the boundary between home and away a permeable and porous one for one's home is not situated outside one's self but an indispensable part of it. Home, in diasporic discourse, thus designates an intricate, complex experience of belonging, characterised by a plurality of identification—a constructed location challenging the idiomatic of fixity, boundedness and nostalgic exclusivities. The intersectional space between diaspora and the place of origin are forever infested with an undercurrent of ambivalence and split perception as the diasporans are torn between disparate experiences of homes and contrastive affiliations.

Scattering or dispersion leads to a splitting sense of the home in which "a fundamental ambivalence is embedded in the term diaspora: a dual ontology in which the diasporic subject is seen to look in two directions—towards a historical cultural identity on one hand, and the society of relocation on the other" (Ashcroft, Griffiths and Tiffin, *The Post-Colonial Studies Reader* 425).

Home is a place created out of connections, collective memories and perceptions that solidify one's sense of identity and nativity, registering a feeling of nostalgia when dislocated. It performs a historical function, collectively contributing to the personal memories and collective myths. It involves a fellow-feeling among the members of a specific locality experienced in an indigenous space of belonging and proceeds with a stabilising rhetoric of progressive ideologies. However, the ease of movement and economical fulfilment thrust the lives of the individuals into a permanent flow when a certain degree of instability naturally comes to be associated with the idea of home which is progressively redefined as a space resulting from multiple journeys across the globe.

The concept of home is contributory to the general understanding of diaspora. The cultural identity of the diasporic individuals essentially relates to the plurality of homelands which is characterised "not by essence or purity, but by the recognition of a necessary heterogeneity and diversity" (Hall, "Cultural Identity" 56). Diaspora identities, with their varied notions of home and belonging, "are constantly producing and reproducing themselves anew, through transformation and difference" (Hall, "Cultural Identity" 56). The diasporic homes are thus continually constituted and reconstituted with the shifting configurations of identity and belonging and its informing elements.

Accordingly, most of the diasporic narratives incorporate a nostalgic recreation of the past through shared memories. The physicalities, peculiarities, histories and myths associated with the homeland leave an indelible mark on the collective memories of the diasporans. These shards of memories may not be a pure embodiment of the past but serve as reflecting the manner in which they are fluctuatingly modified to make sense of the existing conditionalities in a new alien ambience. The revitalisation of fluxing, disintegrated sets of images of the homeland moves beyond the fixated geographical boundaries, effectuating the emergence of a new communal reality, constructed through a universal, globalising sense of belonging which scrupulously distances itself from absolute national prejudices. As a result, "homeland had become a homing desire and soon home itself became transmuted into an essentially placeless, though admittedly lyrical space" (Cohen, "Solid, Ductile and Liquid" 3). Home, as a native land of identification and an imagined community, is thus deconstructed into non-monolithic, non-absolutist properties, highlighting the interactive or transactive encounters between cultures and communities. The poetics of homeland, in this globalising space, demonstrates the corrosion between the native land and the diasporic individuals as it turns out to be highly pluralistic, diversified and hybrid in a range of transcultural possibilities.

Home is, therefore, not rooted in a physical specificity, but it transcends the imagined boundaries of a nation-state beyond its material counterparts. The increasingly diasporic contextualisation of the nation-state has problematised the concept of home which rather draws attention to the essential instability of home as a signifier. Home can no longer be a normative point—homological and exclusionary—but a discursive position which can be reconfigured with the shifting conditionalities of existence and presence. James Clifford, thus, attempts to redefine diaspora with the epistemological shift of focus from originary homelands to the reconstruction of multiple homelands. Clifford's rejection of the doctrine of origin or return is significantly a liberating move as it takes diaspora away from the reductionary dialectics of the homeland and the ideology of nativism and essentialism. The idea of 'return to the homeland' and 'ethnic purity' as formulated by Safran, for example, have been co-opted in Britain by the right-wing reactionary nationalist discourses. Enoch Powell maintains that Englishness connotes a specific inherence of race and the aim is to keep English cultural identity within England's national boundaries. Powell's conceptualisation of racial purity is apparently motivated by his assumption that every racial presence has a nation to belong and that the national space of England is being contaminated by the infiltration of the outsiders who migrate to England and make England their home. It is precisely this sort of essentialist representation that this study attempts to work against. The various minority groups in Britain, including the second and third generation descendants of migrants, have significantly contributed to the creation of a diasporic space within Britain which challenges the exclusionary reductionism of nation, culture and belonging, rejecting the nationalist myths of homeland or originary identification. These diasporic articulations favour multiplicity and diversity which are reaffirmed by stigmatising the oppositions between binaries implicit in the essentialist narratives of home. Racial or cultural difference, in this sense, is not mere 'otherness' and 'displacement' and is never absolute but interpretative. Meaning can only be deciphered though difference. It is "infinitely dispersed, indefinitely deferred. In [Derrida], what is displaced—dispersed, deferred, repressed, pushed aside—is, significantly, still there: *Dis*placed but not *re*placed, it remains a source of trouble, the shifting ground of signification that makes meaning tremble" (Bammer xviii).

Stuart Hall in his paper, "Cultural Identity and Diaspora," asserts that cultural identity is always in the process. It is never complete and endlessly on the move. Cultural identity is dynamic and contested and is articulated through the relation of power, practices and experiences in the society. It is not predefined and ahistorical, transcending territory or culture. Hall seeks to re(theorise) cultural identity, taking recourse to Lacan's theory of enunciation, which suggests that the speaking subject and what is spoken do not coincide. Identity is not to be viewed as an essence but a certain positioning in a discourse and this representation is again conditioned by the position of the spoken form. This interpretation is highly complementary to the purpose of this study as it seeks to reject the legitimacy of the hegemonic nation-state laying claim on a fixed, clearly demarked self-defining home. Hall dismisses the claim of culture as an ontological primordial home which can be recovered by looking back to the place of origin or pure ethnicity and highlights the local or historical contextualities in the formation of cultural identity. Hall conceives the presence of a 'New World' across the globe which is the meeting ground of different cultures of the world—a negotiated space—"the place of many, continuous displacements ... the signifier of migration itself" ("Cultural Identity" 52). It is the continuous negotiations and mediations between cultures which evolve the distinctive cultural identity of the 'New World' diasporic communities. It points out to the deferred, disseminated positionality of all cultures admitting differences, discontinuities and hybridity into its supposed framework of originality or essence. Diaspora becomes a signifier for new possibilities informing the cultural homes and identities of these diasporans. Hall thus attacks the linear, unitary model of diaspora proposed by William Safran, claiming that "diaspora does not refer us to those scattered tribes whose identity can only be secured by some sacred homeland to which they must at all costs return.... The diaspora experience as I intend it here is defined, not by essence or purity, but by the recognition of a necessary heterogeneity and diversity" ("Cultural Identity" 52-53).

Analogously, Paul Gilroy employs the spatio-temporal image of the 'Black Atlantic' to suggest the indeterminacy of cultural home in non-absolutist terms. Gilroy's metaphor of the ship serves as a microcosm of the entire cultural configuration in motion, between the continents, which steers our attention away from the originary 'home' or 'roots' to what he claims as the dynamism of 'routes', a transnational dialectics of interconnectedness traversing the cultural or territorial boundaries of identification characterised by "flows, exchanges, and in-between elements that call into question the very desire to be centred" (*The Black Atlantic* 190). Gilroy questions the very essentialist notion of home which, far from being a stabilised location, is "marked out by flows" (Gilroy, "Diaspora and the Detours of Identity" 328), suspending cultural identity to an indeterminate space, always in flux, under construction and incomplete—a never ending 'process' than a finished, always already 'product'. Construction of such replicated 'homes' is valorising in the sense that it enables the dispersed diasporans to reconfigure their cultural roots, challenging the originary myths associated with a particular community or ethnicity. Homi Bhabha, in this context, coins the term, 'dissemiNation' which conveys the idea that the 'nation' is already contained in 'dissemiNation' and hence it exposes the frivolous insubstantiality of nationalistic representation, privileging cultural boundedness and common origins to the exclusion of difference or otherness. This idea of Homi Bhabha resonances with Rushdie's concept of home as a "scattered" entity (*Imaginary Homelands* 17) which cannot be actuated through space or time. The evolvement of terminology such as 'scatter' and 'dissemiNation' is indicative of a shift of focus from the firmness of 'roots' to the fluidity of 'routes' which unsettles "the ideological manoeuvres through which 'imagined communities' are given essentialist identities" (Bhabha, "Dissemination" 300). Construction of diasporic home, then, is forever deferred in a transnational hybrid space existing as a perpetual tension between 'roots' and 'routes'.

In course of time, identity which is associated with a certain sense of collectivity begins to be linked with a place, a language, an ethnicity and a culture which has been severely criticised in the framework of contemporary critical theory. Identities, according to the contemporary cultural critics, are not bounded by a place, language ethnicity or culture. Rather than being a fixed entity, it emphasises the process of eternal transformation utilising the resources from history, language and culture:

> Though they seem to invoke an origin in a historical past with which they continue to correspond, actually identities are questions of using the resources of history, language and culture in the process of becoming rather

> than being: not "who we are" or "where we came from", so much as what we might become, how we have been represented and how that bears on how we might represent ourselves. (Hall, "Who Needs Identity" 4)

Moving away from the conceptualisation of identity to identification, Hall stresses the non-monolithic image of identity which is established through the inclusion of differences and by addressing the informing otherness. In this continuous process of 'suturing', the focus is shifted from maintenance of boundary to its summative erosion. Boundaries are significant not in the sense that it is a prime marker in the poetics of inclusion or exclusion but that it turns out to be increasingly porous and permeable. Differences still continue to exist, but are transacted across and between cultures rather than subsumed through assimilation or acculturation. Diasporic homes are thus built, un-built and re-built through the process of negotiation, using the existing cultural resources to reconfigure its informing elements in relation to the present contextualities of time, place and situation. For Avatar Brah, the diasporic space is replete with the genealogies of journey which are combined with those of staying whereby the boundary line between journeying and staying becomes intertwined and blurred. The confluence of such diverse narratives captures the tension between national and transactional, self and other, originary and diasporic.

Salman Rushdie, Stuart Hall, Homi Bhabha and others have emphasised the fluid structure of 'home,' referring to the concept of hybridity, to signalise the evolvement of a new, mixed and dynamic culture as movements and flows across the world have been intensified, keeping pace with the postmodern upheavals in the contemporary world. Rushdie, in *Imaginary Homelands*, posits that "the great possibility that mass migration gives the world" results in a "newness [that] enters the world" due to the "mélange, hotchpotch, a bit of this and a bit of that" (394). When migrants move, from their homeland to another land, they not only carry their home culture to the host land, but in the process introduce new features of the host country to their own existing set of cultural referents. The transactive encounters between different culturalities accentuate the formation of new cultural spaces resulting from the localisation of global culture and the globalisation of local culture, which is called glocalisation by the globalist theorists reflecting a reciprocal rhetoric of mutual influences and relationships. Hall points out that identities are about interrogations, about the resources of history, language, and culture. Far from being situated in an essentialised root, cultural identity is an evolving process which is constantly subject to the endless discursive play of history, power, and discourse. Identity, therefore, is mediated through different representations such as language practice and projections, memory, fantasy and so on. This diasporic space exists as critiquing the rhetoric of return to the homeland or reclaiming an ancestral past because identities emerge from these split narratives as imaginary constructions, yet inevitably politicised in a range of influential relationships. Thus, reclaiming one's identity entails a subversion of the constraints of identity politics. The new space generated from these cultural transactions allows the diasporans to use their own languages, to recover their own histories and to reconfigure their new roots. Migrating from one spatial geopolitic to another also involves a migration from a certain psychological, emotional and mental context to the other. The diasporans, with this physical and metaphorical dislocation, have to relentlessly condition themselves between the ambivalent feeling of homeliness and homelessness, inaugurating a sense of loss through their multiple movements in the act of reclamation. Because it is an impossibility to reclaim what is lost, the diasporic subjects are left with "not actual cities or villages, but invisible ones, imagined homelands" (*Imaginary Homelands* 10).

****

At this point, I must attend to another important concept that is particularly relevant in the discussion of home and identity, i.e. cultural memory and its connection to the summative identity formation of the diasporic subjects. Memory, both individual and social, plays a pivotal role in the self-actualisation of identity. Memory is defined as the building block, the backbone of identity. Its contents are invested with multiple perspectives, thoughts and emotions of the person in the act of remembering which inevitably includes the feeling that the present recollection must be a re-experience of something that have occurred before. Memory, thus, serves as a mediator between the past and the present. Memory is considered as the foundation of personal identity which is constructed through the ceaseless transactions of the present with the past and anything which seeks to damage it poses a threat to the image of the self. It is a means to overcome the limitation of essential human condition by empowering the past to reappear in the present despite its temporal and spatial distance. Dorothee Birke astutely observes: "In order to answer the age-old question 'Who am I?' we more often than not look to our past and fashion a narrative for our lives. By comparing our present selves with the selves we remember, we experience ourselves on being in time—an experience which is crucial for our sense of self" (2).

Nicola King in *Memory, Narrative, Identity* suggests that the late twentieth century witnesses an increased focus on the discourse of memory as the new generation and national movements put more emphasis on the memories of oppression or marginalisation after the painful atrocities experienced in the two World Wars and the recurrent insistence on the fragile power of memory also marks "a renewed desire to secure a sense of self in the wake of postmodern theories of the decentered human subject" (22). Autobiographical or individual memory provides the person with different visions and perspectives of the world to make sense of the past experiences. Being the prime agent in constructing a coherent life story, the individual secures a sense of continuity in time and space which becomes part of his/her conception of authenticity or fulfilment of identity. By recovering memories in the fabric of a narrative, the individuals can connect themselves to the larger society around them as we tend to "organize our experience and our memory of human happenings mainly in the form of narrative—stories, excuses, myths, reasons for doing and not doing and so on" (qtd. in Birke 3). Through these "incessantly readjusted memories" (Lowenthal 199), the individual succeeds in forging links of continuity amidst the anarchical elements of the mind, foregrounding some and excluding others, moving from perspective to perspective to creatively construct a coherent narrative totality from the existing threads of memory. Life, which is made out of memory, then itself is a creative construction as Jerome Brunner claims: "The self is not an entity that one can simply remember, but is, rather, a complex mental edifice that one constructs by the use of a variety of mental processes, one of which must surely be remembering" (41). Similarly, Daniel Dennett in his book *Consciousness Explained*, puts great emphasis on the narrative proclivities of the individual memory whereby, in the impulsive act of story-telling, people convey their feelings and thoughts, reshaping the modalities of the past experiences. Dennett, however, relies largely upon animal imagery and construction metaphors and the manners the protective layers of the organisms are used to perpetuate the sense of identity as self-shaping elements of human thought—the power of the narratives to refashion individual identity in these 'web of discourses':

> The strangest and most wonderful constructions in the whole animal world are the amazing, intricate constructions made by the primate, *Homo Sapiens*. Each normal individual of this species makes a *self*. Out of its brain it spins a web of words and deeds, and like the other creatures, it doesn't have to know what it's doing. It just does it. This web protects it, just like the snail's shell, and provides it a livelihood, just like the spider's web and advances its prospects for sex, just like the bowerbird's bower. Unlike a spider, an individual human doesn't just *exude* its web; more like a beaver, it works hard to gather the materials out of which it builds its protective fortress.... This 'web of discourses'...is as much a biological product as any of the other constructions to be found in the animal world. Stripped of it, an individual human being is as incomplete as a bird without its features, a turtle without its shell. (416)

According to some theorists, memory is compared with history and psychology because people remember past incidents which have become history, but it also pertains to the psychological working of the individual mind. Holtzman opines that "memory ties anthropology to history, and in a different sense psychology" (362). Construction of memory is an ongoing process and can be reshaped and reconfigured with the shifting contextualities of the present reality. It is not a literal recreation of the past events, but instead a process of ceaseless construction, a reproduction of the past realities to cater to the requirements of the present. Endel Tulving claims that "memory is the present conscious awareness of an event that has happened in the rememberer's own past" (3). Memory, therefore, is a self-conscious awareness which explains its vital connections to identity. Devoid of memory, human beings have no goal to achieve, no direction to move forward, no ability to decide a course of action or to conceptualise the world around us. Our capabilities to learn from past mistakes and to grow as individuals are largely dependent on our memories. But memories are unreliable and are subject to suppression, distortion and falsification in a range of productive possibilities:

> ... memories are not accurate historical accounts of events as they happened at the time of encoding, but rather a reconstruction based on a number of affective and motivational factors. Memories are contaminated with information from similar events and so change over the years as we encounter new experiences. What we remember about an event depends on when and for what purpose we are remembering, reflecting our beliefs about ourselves and the world at present. Thus memory is continually reprocessed and reinterpreted with changing contexts and perceptions. (Feigenbaum 14)

The ability to identify and recall the past thus gives meaning, purpose and value to the individual existence. Self-continuity primarily depends on the function of memory, and recollecting past experiences connects us with our previous selves, however, disparate we may since have become. As Lowenthal aptly observes: "Those who bring more of their past into their present thereby both confirm their own identity and enrich the present with the past's amplified residue" (198).

The poetics of identity formation or socialisation, therefore, seeks to conceptualise memory as one of the indispensable parts of self-actualisation and situates it within the framework of human action and understanding, providing a solid emotional basis for the individuals to account for human behavior. Memory and identity thus change in course of time and far from being fixated, become representation or reconstruction of realities which are subjective rather than objective phenomena of the collective unconscious. Memory, however, involves indirect, second-hand accounts of the past events which is 'history' and 'history' in turn relies upon the eyewitnesses and other people's accounts and recollections that is memory. We tend to view other people's memories as history, as something that is empirically tenable, as we often verify our own individual accounts. The connection between memory and history then is a dialectical one, each influencing the other, reshaped by each other, blurring the boundary line between the known and the unknown, the self and the other, the story and the history.

Conversely, Maurice Halbwachs, in his seminal work *Individual Memory and Collective Memory*, argues that there are no authentic individual memories as such, since all memories are collectively formed in a specific society or culture. Halbwachs emphasises the social role of memory as a collective process because the individual's mind is organised and saturated by a social process; it perceives and remembers within the outline of a given social context and therefore "no memory is possible outside frameworks used by people living in society to determine and retrieve their recollections" (43). The individual memorises by placing himself with the larger perspective of the group and their viewpoints and group memory manifests and exacerbates itself in the fragmented memories of the individual lives. So, how we view or evaluate things today can be understood within the always-already model of our old memories, which by degrees adapt to our present perceptions of the world. As collective memory is inevitably a reconstruction of the past in the light of the presence, we seek to preserve and cherish the memories of our lives which are continually produced and reproduced. It is through the evocation of such memories that "a sense of our identity is perpetuated" (Halbwachs 47). Thus, memory in general and individual or private memory in particular, are recreated through social interactions in which particularly specific interpretations of things and events are reflected, demonstrated, negotiated, shared and contested, leading to a fluid dynamics of representation in the manner we define ourselves, the world and the others. From this perspective of collective memory, it is crucial, at this point, to examine how the memories of the displaced individuals, who live through multiple journeys and migrations across the globe, have been reconstructed in the fictional projections accomplished by the diasporic authors around the world in general and England in particular and this is one of the problems I propose to address in the present study.

As above discussion demonstrates, memories are made and reshaped within the frameworks of society and may tend to immune to the passing of time as they can be reproduced without alteration. According to Halbwachs, forgetting is not always an individual failure, but rather a limitation in recollections: "Depending on its circumstances and point in time, society presents the past to itself in different ways: it modifies its conventions" (172-73). An incident can only be recalled only if its mode of narrative fits within the framework of the contemporary needs and interests. The contextual specificities of society modify recollections to favour the presence. Social beliefs are, therefore, collective recollections and collective memory adjusts itself and shapes the present-day belief system. Halbwachs provides a distinction between memory and history. Collective memory, according to him, rarely relies on writing, in contrast to historical representation which only sets in when collective memory seems to disappear. While memory seeks to emphasise similarities, history recognises discontinuities and fragmentation.

Tradition then is "nothing but deformed memory, more organized perhaps, and seemingly more 'objective'" (Halbwachs

15). Halbwachs' insistence on the constructedness of memory or recollection, and his stress on the role of language rather than event in the process of memorialisation, echo the concept of discursivity developed by Foucault and other cultural theorists that takes a poststructuralist turn. Halbwachs' conceptualisation of collective memory, however, is apt to translate itself into a cultural one, with the shift of focus from the social communities to their modes of production. Pierre Nora, on the other hand, expresses his regrets over the erosion of the proper ambience whereby experiences and its recollection take place. Nora even rules out the possibility of any such larger or collective narratives that seek to unite the people in a 'nation-state'. In this sense, we do not have a living memory of our own but the dilapidated monuments of our old and authentic recollections and its odd residue. The real ambience of memories are all lost but what remains is the 'lieux de mémoire' (site of memory) through which contemporary memory "crystallizes and secrets itself" (Nora 7). Such memory spaces signify cultural landmarks, practices and expressions, and locations stemming from a collectively shared past, material or otherwise (language or traditions). In the threshold of such memory sites Nora offers a connection between the 'collective' and its 'cultural framework,' positing memory as something which is not at the control of the mind, but an entity the society is infused with:

> If we were able to live within memory, we would not have needed to consecrate lieux de mémoire in its name. Each gesture, down to the most everyday, would be experienced as the ritual repetition of a timeless practice in a primordial identification of act and meaning with the appearance of the trace, of mediation, of distance, we are not in the realm of true memory but of history. (8)

Resituating Bergson's contemplation of memory as a subjective discourse in which time takes the centre-stage, Nora emphasises the living quality of memory which is only meaningful in the present context, existing as "a perpetually actual phenomenon" (8), claiming spaces, objects and images for itself, eternally negotiating the tensions between the individual and the collective. Memory's place, thus, is at the intersection of a range of cultural phenomena: between individual and collective experience, between cultural selves and other selves, between empowered and marginalised histories and identities and between a number of semiotic and political domains.

It is vital, at this point, to reconsider whether a diasporic individual has any ethical responsibility to preserve and perpetuate this cultural memory and whether there is a moral duty on the part of the diasporic author to claim his/her cultural heritage which constitutes one's diasporic identification. Although it is prevalent among the diasporic individuals through the practice of story-telling, in the process of identity formation, it seems to be a burden more keenly felt by the diasporans owing to a marginalised belonging or being a traditionally dispersed community. Yet, any such disposition serves to suggest the homogeneity of the narrative voice that overshadows any recognition of hybridised construction in diasporic experience or identification. For example, Edward Said reflects on the sense of loss which plagues the diasporans who have been uprooted from their originary homelands, within the framework of a homologous term "exile" as aptly epitomising the common fragmented condition of these displaced:

> Exile is the unhealable rift forced between a human being and a native place, between self and its true home. The essential sadness of the break can never be surmounted. It is true that there are stories portraying exile as a condition that produces heroic, romantic, glorious, even triumphant episodes in a person's life. But these are no more than stories, efforts to overcome the crippling sorrow of estrangement. The achievements of any exile are permanently undermined by his or her sense of loss. (Said, "The Mind of Winter" 49)

This insurmountable sense of loss, as Said observes, however, is "transformed into a potent even enriching motif of modern culture" (Said, "The Mind of Winter" 49) and the diasporic, liminal space between cultures, as occupied by the members of the diaspora, turns out to be an empowering space of creativity. As Paul Larson posits, "most ethnic minorities anchor their collective identities in the remembrance of past and present victimization. Victims of social trauma and their descendants often engage in purposeful and explicit remembering as a form of empowerment and identity formation" (335).

The act of remembering itself, evidently, is not a homogenous process. Jeannette Mageo notes:

> Variation in shade, from light to twilight memories suggest the possibility that some memories are liminal... social universes are also replete with clouded narratives—obscured memories of unacceptable histories and half-discarded life ways...in as much as the differential privileging of certain memory changes when people recount or re-enact past times, remembering may also shift relations between cultural schemas. (3)

Salman Rushdie in *Imaginary Homelands* asserts that his narrator in *Midnight Children* commits a natural mistake through this "fallible memory" and thus provides a "fragmentary vision" of India (10). Rushdie, however, rejects the idea that such a "broken mirror" is wholly flawed or systematically unprivileged. Instead, he argues that the discontinuity of dislocation from an ancestral homeland intensifies and thus heightens the experience of recollection: "The shards of memory acquired greater status, greater resonance, because they were remains; fragmentation made trivial things seem like symbols, and the mundane acquired numinous qualities" (*Imaginary Homelands* 12). The image of the "broken mirror" is particularly important, in this context as symbolising the migrant's displaced position which is informed by fragmentations, fissures, ruptures and breaches. The transformations wrought into the lives of the diasporans through these movements empower their vision to replicate a multiple sense of home in the present context. McLeod notes that the "reflections of home seize it in pieces only; a sense of displacement always remains" (211). The migrants find themselves in a better position to view and review the world of immense possibilities which is never complete, pure or monolithic, subverting the conventional notions of rootedness and fixity: "Meaning is a shaky edifice we built of scraps, dogmas, childhood injuries, newspaper articles, chance remarks, old films, small victories, people hated, people loved; perhaps it is because our sense of what is the case is constructed from such inadequate materials that we defend it so fiercely, even to death" (Rushdie, *Imaginary Homelands* 12).

The awareness that this memory of the homeland is partial and incomplete is beautifully captured by the metaphor of the "broken mirror" (Rushdie, *Imaginary Homelands* 11) which seeks to heighten the emotional significance of these fragments of memory and urges the individuals to complete the fragments by imagining a world of possibilities around them. It is precisely the incompleteness of memory which assigns them a higher emotional status for recreation through fantasy. According to Vijay Mishra:

> The fantasy of homeland is then linked, in the case of the diaspora, to a recollected moment when diasporic subjects feel they are wrenched from their mother (father) land. This may be the traumatized 'middle passage' of slave trade or the sailing ships (later steamships) of Indian indenture, but what the 'real' nature of disruption is not an issue here; what is clear is the moment of 'rupture' is transformed into a trauma around an absence that because it cannot be fully symbolized becomes a part of the fantasy itself. (423)

This disjunction between here and there, past and present serves to suspend 'home' from the domain of time and space which is only available for a return of reclamation through the creative acts of imagination and fantasy. This cultural displacement can be equated in turn with the perspective of a diasporic author engaged in his creative process:

> It may be that writers in my position, exiles or emigrants or expatriates, are hunted by some sense of loss, some urge to reclaim, to look back, even at the risk of being mutated into pillars of salt. But if we do look back, we must also do so in the knowledge—which gives rise to profound uncertainties—that our physical alienation from India almost inevitably means that we will not be

> capable of reclaiming precisely the thing that was lost; that we will create fictions, not actual cities or villages, but invisible one, imaginary homelands, India's of the minds. (Rushdie, *Imaginary Homelands* 10)

The diasporic subjects thus juxtapose the fantastic memories of the past with the physical and temporal realities of the present to reconfigure their ideas of home, identity and belonging.

For Brah "'home' is a mythic place of desire in the diasporic imagination" which cannot be returned to but can be reconstituted "with the lived experience of a locality" (192) in all its physical and emotional manifestations. In his construction of 'imaginary homelands', Rushdie refers to the concept of 'translation' to describe this diasporic process: "The word 'translation' comes, etymologically from the Latin for 'bearing across'. Having been borne across the world, we are translated men. It is normally supposed that something always lost in translation...that something can also be gained" (Rushdie, *Imaginary Homelands* 17). The meaning of home then lies in the process of translation, the way diasporic subjects continually reconfigure the informing elements of their identity in the transactive confrontations with new realities they are now part of. Rushdie's idea of being 'borne across' resonates with Clifford's conceptualisation of 'routes' which entails a fluid notion of home, signifying "multi-locationality across geographical, cultural and psychic boundaries" (Brah 194). The concept of 'routes' or 'translation' allows the diasporic subjectivities to carve out an "ambiguous and shifting ground" (Rushdie, *Imaginary Homelands* 15) or a "liminal space" (Bhabha, *The Location* 5) for themselves which admits plurality and heterogeneity with an increasing emphasis on multiple places and journeys where cultural hybridity is the norm rather than exception:

> I am speaking now of all of us who emigrated...and I suspect that there are times when the move seems wrong to us all, when we seem, to ourselves, post-lapsarian men and women. We are Hindus who have crossed the black water; we are Muslims who eat pork. And as a result—as my use of the Christian notion of the fall

> indicates—we are now partly of the West. Our identity is at once plural and partial. Sometimes we feel that we straddle two cultures; at other times, that we fall between two stools. (Rushdie, *Imaginary Homelands* 15)

The diasporic individuals/authors are thus endowed with "a kind of double perspective: because they, we, are at one and the same time insiders and outsiders in this society. This stereoscopic vision is perhaps what we can offer in place of 'whole sight'" (Rushdie, *Imaginary Homelands* 19).

Rushdie, in his observation of the fallible memory's "fragmentary vision" (*Imaginary Homelands* 10), interestingly establishes a parallel between remembering and archeology which replaces the responsibility of the cultural preservation with an emphasis on universality, a re-articulation of "fractured perception" (*Imaginary Homelands* 12) or partial exposure as representative of the diasporic identity which is by its very nature incomplete and fractured. Rushdie attends to the problematics of the diasporic role as preserving cultural memory which itself is not a homogeneous entity emphasising the fractured plurality of experience and wonders: "...how can culture be preserved without becoming ossified?" (*Imaginary Homelands* 17). Rushdie is up against "the adaptation of a ghetto mentality...to continue ourselves within narrowly defined cultural frontiers" (*Imaginary Homelands* 19) through the rhetoric of claiming authenticity through perpetuation of historical narrative for it corresponds to the replicative act of erecting exclusionary boundaries of identity or belonging.

According to Jan Assman, cultural memory involves an inexhaustible source of reusable texts which are not static but a dynamic stock of productive and re-enacted artifacts. Assman observes that the archive of cultural memory includes two overlapping concepts, namely *Erinnerungskultur* or 'memory culture' and *Vergangenheitsbezug* or 'reference to the past' (124). 'Memory culture' refers to the preservation of generational elements through the continuity and maintenance of collective memory and 'reference to the past' pertains to the formation of a commonly shared past through a historical, collective consciousness. The emphasis on both collectivity and transience in this interpretation of cultural memory points out to the fact that cultural memory is to be reconstructed with a focus, not in the preservation of a monological narrative of the past but on the process of identity formation in the present. This shift highlights a wider ideological move from understanding history, which also includes cultural transformation to evaluating the various representations of history that informs the disparate cultural discourses in the twentieth century and beyond.

From the above discussion, it is understood that memory is one of the prime determiners of identity which can be reconfigured according to the pluralistic process of remembering in the contemporary socio-political contexts of diasporic connections. The migrants' position in this utter fluidity of belonging seems to incorporate a realisation that all meanings, all system of knowledge are untotalising, never absolute or pure, but incompletely muddled in a hybrid configuration. The rhetoric of diaspora, thus, involves forging new narratives of belonging which seek to accommodate the migrant's position more appropriately than the older totalising or holistic model of representations. The diasporic subjects do not have to secure their 'roots' in a fixed place, a nation or an ethnic group, rather they must ceaselessly devise for themselves itinerant cultural 'routes' which take them emotionally to multiple places and into contact with different groups of the populace forging a connection between past, present and future, without presuming a linear, continuous movement through time. Diaspora, then, is keen to construct new modes of existence whereby "the grounded certainties of *roots* are replaced with the transnational contingencies of *routes*" (McLeod 215). These dynamic ways of thinking about identity and belonging transcend the older fixated model of cultural and nationalist representations and tend to merge the contextualities of diasporisation with the theoretical formulations of post-structuralism. Homi Bhabha, in a similar vein, advocates the formation of a new space to accommodate these 'new ethnicities' which offers intriguing points of reference about the discourses of identity created from "the great history of the languages and landscapes of migration and diaspora" (*The Location* 235).

According to Bhabha, migrants who live a "border live" on the margins of nations need a new "art of the present" that depends upon accepting the contrary logic of the borders which are vital thresholds of belonging, full of contradiction and ambivalent relationships (McLeod 217). Borders are important because these include disparate points of joining and separation from which one seeks to move beyond the barrier. Bhabha infuses the term "beyond" with an in-between dialectics of transition: "the 'beyond' is neither a new horizon, nor a leaving behind of the past...we find ourselves in the moment of transit where space and time cross to produce complex figures of difference and identity, past and present, inside and outside, inclusion and exclusion" (*The Location* 1). This in-between space of transit is variously described as being 'liminal', 'interstitial' or 'hybrid' where the binaries do not exist as opposites, but commingle and coalesce. Bhabha urges to "think beyond narratives of originary and initial subjectivities," because the in-between space of cultural translation provides "the terrain of elaborating strategies of selfhood—singular or communal—that initiate new signs of identity" (*The Location* 1).

Bhabha's formulation here emphasises the discursivity of identity as a product which is processed through 'articulation' and 'elaboration' of cultural differences. The migrant, living at the border, becomes an important agent of change, mobilising the existing ideas and refashioning them with the contrary logic of transformation.

Bhabha writes that cultures do not exist in isolation and any contact between them is not a passive exchange or encounter but a dynamic process of mixing which effectuates the production of something new. This newness, in turn, is not an end product, but continually replicates, composed from disparate sources, materials and locations—always in a state of flux—subverting the fixed conceptualisation of cultural identity as stable, pure and monolithic. Bhabha considers the term "part culture" to elaborate his idea of the "connective tissue between cultures"

(Hall, "Reinventing Britain" 54). This "connective tissue" is instrumental in forming dynamic borders which questions the idea of cultural, racial or national rootedness, evolving an inclusionary logic of hybridity which entails "overdetermination of communal and group differences and an articulation of baffling alikeness and banal divergence" (Bhabha, "Culture's In-between" 54).

In *The Location of Culture*, explaining cultural hybridization, Bhabha uses the example of Renée Green's figurative description of her exhibition namely *Sites of Genealogy* in which she remarks:

> I used architecture literally as a reference, using the attic, the boiler room, and the stairwell to make associations between certain binary divisions such as higher and lower and heaven and hell. The stairwell became a liminal space, a pathway between the upper and lower areas, each of which was annotated with plaques referring to blackness and whiteness. (qtd. in Bhabha, *The Location* 5)

For Bhabha the liminal space of the stairwell stands for the concept of hybridity which moves away from the fixed exclusionary, binary notions of identity to a framework that is continually in motion "pursuing errant and unpredictable routes, open to change and reinscription" (McLeod 219). This hybrid entity exists as an in-between space of cultural constructs from which these new identities emerge:

> [It] becomes the process of symbolic interaction, the connective tissue that constructs the difference between upper and lower, black and white. The hither and thither of the stairwell, the temporal movement and passage that it allows, prevents identities at either end of it from settling into primordial polarities. This interstitial passage between fixed identifications opens up the possibility of a cultural hybridity that entertains difference without an assumed or imposed hierarchy. (Bhabha, *The Location* 5)

Benjamin Graves thus points out that Bhabha, with the help of a complex range of Lacanian psychoanalysis, Derridian deconstruction and the postmodern concept of mimicry and performance, favours a thorough re-evaluation of cultural and nationalistic representation which emphasise 'ambivalence' or 'hybridity' that informs the ambience of colonial discourse—"a 'liminal' space in which cultural differences articulate" and as Bhabha argues, actually "produce imagined 'construction' of cultural and national identity" (Introduction 4, *Nation and Narration*). Dominic Head pertinently observes that the term 'liminal' is important because it carries two meanings in one: "... 'inhabiting a borderland', as well as 'incipient' or 'just emerging'—are simultaneously implied" (183). Bhabha suggests that identity is never fixed and it does not cohere into a complete entity because it is always embedded in a partial culture. In his essay "Culture's In-Between", Bhabha explains that "It is indeed something like culture's in-between, baffling both alike and different" (54). In *The Location of Culture,* Bhabha writes that "the question of identity is never an affirmation of a pre-given identity, never a self-fulfilling prophecy—it is always a production of an image of identity and the transformation of the subject in assuming that image" (64). Bhabha's diasporic logic of 'transformation' resonates with Hall's conceptualisation of the process of "suturing" which seeks to expose the partial autonomy of the subject position in the construction of identity. Identities, according to Hall, are constructed positions which the subject must take up "while always 'knowing' (the language of consciousness here betrays us) that they are representations," and that "representation is always constructed across a 'lack' across a division, from the place of the Other, and thus can never be adequate—identical—to the subject processes invested in them" ("Who Needs Identity" 6). Hall's explication of the process of identity is thus marked by terminology such as constructions, representations, gaps, incongruities, etc., ensuring a radical divergence of reality. Bhabha, similarly, posits the partial but ambivalent dialectic of a hybrid culture which is described as "the contaminated yet connective tissue between cultures" ("Culture's In-between" 56), undermining the claims to totalisation and proclaiming "the heterogeneous array of signs in modern life and the various ways of living with difference" (Papastergiadis 192). The partial culture of hybridity, thus, is keen to reconstruct the notion of community and historic memory that provide the minority positions with a narrative form to interact across cultural supremacy and sovereignty. Papastergiadis attempts to cartograph Bhabha's perception of the notion of hybridity in the following words:

> Like Bakhtin, he notes the sense of separateness and unity in a single semantic field. Hybrid identity is thus not formed in an accretive way in which the essence of one identity is combined with another and hybridity is simply a process of accumulation. 'Hybrid hyphenations emphasize the incommensurable elements—the stubborn chunks—as the basis of cultural identifications'. The hybrid is formed out of the dual process of displacement and correspondence in the act of translation.... The hybrid, therefore, is not formed out of an excavation and transferal of foreignness into the familiar, but out of this awareness of the untranslatable bits that linger on in translation. (194)

Stuart Hall, like Bhabha, argues that cultural identity is a relational and interactive concept existing as unstable points of belonging or identification which reveals "the constant process of differentiation and exchange between the centre and the periphery and between different peripheries, as well as serving as the metaphor for the form of identity that is being produced from these conjunctions" (Papastergiadis 190). Hall suggests that identities are constituted within, not outside the representations and thus is a matter of "becoming rather than being: not 'who we are' or 'where we came from'", but "what we might become" ("New Ethnicities" 4). Hall, in "New Ethnicities," claims that identities with an increased focus on 'becoming' and 'representation' "relate to the invention of tradition as much as to tradition itself, which they oblige us to read not as an endless reiteration but as the 'changing same'...: not the so-called return to roots but a coming to terms with our 'routes'" (4). Cultural identity, for Hall, is relational which is constructed through, and not outside the differential equations. It is constructed and reconstituted "through the relation to the Other, the relation to what it is not, to precisely what it lacks" (Hall, "New Ethnicities" 4). This relational evolvement of cultural identity as discussed by Hall, according to Grossberg, reveals the impracticality of "fully constituted, separate and distinct identities" which ruled out the "existence of authentic and originary identities based on a universally shared origin or experience" (89). Grossberg describes the ways in which Hall deliberates the evolvement of a relational model of identity, defying the essentialist propensities of identities that embraces purity and singularies rather than heterogeneity and plurality:

> Identities are always relational and incomplete, in process. Any identity depends upon its difference from, its negation of, some other term, even as the identity of the latter term depends upon its difference from, its negation of, the former.... Identity is always a temporary and unstable effect of relations which define identities by marking differences. Thus the emphasis here is on the multiplicity of identities and differences rather than on a singular identity and on the connections or articulations between the fragments of differences. (89)

****

Having discussed the notion of home in diasporic consciousness and the relationship of memory with identity with its informing features, it is now imperative to focus on England itself as a diasporic location where a number of diasporas, both Asian and non-Asian, meet, intersecting with one another in a range of developing relationships, reshaping the cultural space of the multi-ethnic Britain.

When we refer to the English literary heritage, most of us tend to bring into our minds imagery of Wordsworth, Dickens, Eliot and others, whose works have most often been regarded as the classics of English literature. These canonical authors, born and brought up in Britain and well-grounded in a history of imperial configuration, seem to hold the monopoly of a quintessential Britishness. Britain, however, ironically connotes a diverse and cosmopolitan nation in which diasporic themes and experiences turn out to be the most informing element to an understanding of contemporary English Literature. England has been the 'home' of many diasporic authors and individuals whose narrative voices are vital in moulding the British cultural space and identity, adding to its complexity and negotiative rhetoric of diasporisation. Authors such as Sam Sevlon, Kazuo Ishiguro, Hanif Kureishi, Ambavalner Shivanandan, Romesh Gunesekera, Monica Ali, Meera Syal, Sunetra Gupta and others form a rich galaxy of diasporic writers in the literary scenario of Britain migrating from various parts of the world. These writers, albeit, nourish a connection with their respective homelands, feel themselves utterly at home in England, searching and forging new modes of belonging to be identified with.

There are various reasons for these migrations into Britain but the white majority was unwilling to accept a huge number of coloured immigrants into their nation. The influx of these migrants had its effect on the diminishing popularity of diasporic population in Britain. Discrimination in housing and employment led to the ghettoisation of many Black and Asian British communities. Racial tensions erupted in various parts of the country, resulting in successive riots, such as the Liverpool riots in 1948, White riots in Camden in 1954 and those carried out in Nottingham and North Kensington Hill in the mid-twentieth century. Gradually a shared 'Black' consciousness was formed among these coloured immigrants which formed the crux of these movements against racism. As Malik observes, it was "a strong sense of determination to make their lives in Britain as comfortable and successful as quickly as possible, to work hard and invest in education" (*Representing Black Britain* 14). The 1960's witnessed a number of incidents that left an enduring impact on mass migration and the ensuing race relations in Britain. Bills such as Commonwealth Immigration Act were passed in 1962 to discourage people from migrating to Britain. Enoch Powell, the leading post-war racist politician of Britain, in April 1968, declared that the coloured immigrants could never become 'truly' English, despite their obtaining British citizenship, pointing out to the impossibility of racial integration. Powell's declaration in favour of race and nation sadly sanctioned political respectability to racism and instantly attracted popular support. In the 1970s, racial attitudes began to animate the discussion on nation, citizenship, law and order of the Englander. The Immigration Act of 1971, for example, "limited domicile to those born in Britain, or whose parents or grandparents were of British Origin" (Head 164). These initial turbulences of race relations in Britain also set the stage for Thatcherism in 1980. Margaret Thatcher, the then Prime Minister of Britain, sought to redefine British nationality with the conservative party policy of 1980 which declared: "Future immigration policies if they are to be sensible, realistic and fair, must be founded on a separate citizenship of the UK and it is therefore essential that a reformed law of nationality should, for the first time, make clear who are the citizens of UK" (qtd. in Layton-Henry 191). Thus, the preservation of the "English way of life" was emphasised as against the fear of the "alien culture" which began to saturate the general life of Britain (Brah 37).

Another momentous redefinition of British nationality "was enshrined in the 1981 British Nationality Act which abolished the automatic right to British citizenship for children born in Britain" (Head 164). The frequent shifting of policy statements of the British Government, according to Head, is indicative of the fact that identity that is founded on nationalist affiliation is a political representation which is mutable and unstable (164). Head claims that the state policies on migrancy "colluded with public misperceptions of nationality, and has helped to foster a denial of postcolonial obligations and a rejection of the postcolonial heritage" (164). Furthermore, towards the end of the twentieth century, a large number of people across the world have migrated to Britain, making it a densely diasporising land whereby a varied range of cultural and ethnic groups have diversely stimulated the image of Britain as a multicultural and cosmopolitan nation.

In contemporary England, therefore, an uncomplicated conceptualisation of Englishness or English national identity is hard to form owing to the intensity and frequency of migration which have become an unbreakable reality of the evolving

Englishness. Britain, in its new cultural configuration at present, as Nyman remarks, develops a porous, permeable model of representative culturation which replaces the old system of Englishness as an exclusive notion by an all-inclusive pattern of mutual adjustment and collaboration:

> The belief in the British race and nation as embodiment of the national character has been called into question, and different constructions of British identities have emerged—terms such as Black British and British Asian now challenge the traditional division into the four traditional ethnicities. Similarly, the increased migration from the Commonwealth and former Dominions since the 1950s and contemporary immigration from various part of Europe has called into question migration policies and notions of citizenship that can no longer be based on racial basis. (47)

Reflecting upon the narrowness of the previous versions of Englishness, Nyman argues for the "need to revise the once exclusive notion of Englishness into a more inclusive direction" (47) which involves hyphenated, hybrid identity construction that challenges and subverts the traditional concept of ethnicity and becomes an emphatic claim for a multicultural Britain.

Bhabha, in his "Manifesto," published in the journal of *Wasafiri*, Spring 1999, refers to this idea of a hybrid culture by attending to the existing condition of the world that there are about more than 100 million people in the world who live as immigrants in countries and cultures which are not their own and that these people continue to live in a kind of "in-between state, where they are not fully accepted as nationals" (40). Although, they are accepted as belonging to England in legal terms, indeed they are regarded by others as "not fully integrated" as "a group apart" from the general English life of the country and the originary discourses of Englishness (Bhabha, "The Manifesto" 40). Bhabha, however, is attentive to the creative participation of those immigrants in the national life of England in a range of productive possibilities: "...these people are not always talking about their own victimage or their own declaration, they are producing very positive images. They are actually producing creatively a whole range of cultural and social acts, meaningful acts" (Bhabha, "The Manifesto" 40).

Understanding the existence of the disparate diasporas in contemporary England then is not limited to their actions and expressions of victimage or marginalisation, but rather their ability to productively engage a whole gamut of multiple perspectives in the socio-cultural ambiance of the host land. Susheila Nasta emphasises the in-between positionality of these diasporans who find themselves torn between two world views, straddling two cultures simultaneously, often in a conflictual relationship:

> The position of the migrant and immigrant I would add is enabling in this way for it allows a doubling of perspective, a view of the inside from the outside—though in reality the two perspectives are always linked. But this vantage point has both the precision of distance and intimacy and is essentially an ambidextrous one. (42)

One of the important aspects of the Parekh Report titled *The Future of Multi-Ethnic Britain*, published in October 2000, was ethnic diversity in Britain. The report champions the vision of a pluralistic culture in Britain. Vikhu Parekh in The Report attacked the essentialised conceptualisation of the community and the self and aims at evolving a new national narrative, claiming that Britain is not only "Community of Citizens," but also a "Community of Communities" (Preface ix). The report is an onslaught against the prevailing British model of representing "integration" as "a one way process in which 'minorities' are to be absorbed into the non-existent homogeneous cultural structure of the 'majority'" (Preface x). The Report is sweeping in its pronouncement as it aims at developing a balance between cohesion, equality and difference, eliminating all form of racism to rethink notional identity and culture. As part of the goal, it seeks to subvert the myth of Englishness as homogenising the cultural constants and proposes an anti-essentialist model of all-inclusive Britishness which nourishes an understanding that all identities are in a process of transition and pursuing a pluralistic vision of human culture.

Steven Vertovec, in his paper "Transnational Challenges to the 'New' Multiculturalism," traces an undercurrent of anti-essentialist tendency in the Parekh Report which deliberately distances itself from all forms of essentialist exclusivities and advocating a flexible form of plurality and hybridity: "Rather than reified 'cultures', references to 'interacting and overlapping communities'...and individuals' multiple identities run throughout The Report" (6). The emphasis on realising a broader perspective creates new terrains of cultural belonging, ironing out the narrowness and differences of the mind in a range of overlapping, intersecting relationships:

> People have compelling attachment to nation, group, subculture, region and city, town, neighborhood and the wider world. They belong to a range of different but over-lapping communities, real and symbolic, divided on cultural issues of the day...identities, in consequence, are more situational. This makes Britain, contrary to stereotype, more open. (Parekh, *The Future* 25)

To feel at home in England, thus, warrants a systematic disruption of the container model of the nation-state, underscoring the need of core values pertaining to Britishness or Whiteness which proposes a common belonging with "shared cultural meaning" (Parekh, *The Future* 16) and stature, emphasising social cohesivity and cultural pluralism. The globalising interconnectedness of human belonging demands a permeable pattern of heterogeneity in which England can no longer afford to pursue an oppressively defensive nationalism and must opt for an all-inclusive Englishness which should ever contextualising itself in "an open framework, continually in the making" seeking to "accommodate other worlds, other vocabularies, other memory" to make it truly cosmopolitan (Chambers, *Border Dialogues* 47-50).

****

Kazuo Ishiguro was born of Japanese parents in Nagasaki on 8 November 1954. In a tender age when he was five year old, he moved with his family to Britain in 1960. His father, an oceanographer, started a one-year research project under the British Government. But what was formerly supposed to be a temporary visit gradually turned out to be a permanent one. After spending his childhood in Surrey where his father worked, he studied at the University of Kent and became a graduate in English and Philosophy in 1979. He then spent some years in literary pursuits and resumed his study at the University of East Anglia and obtained a Master's degree in creative writing. Even after his long stay in England, Ishiguro, however, admits that his homeland Japan had registered in him a sense of "emotional bereavement or emotional deprivation" (Vorda and Herzinger 77). The proclivities to compensate for physical and emotional losses stem deeply from his autobiographical past and his novels clearly substantiate that the memory of the past enables the immigrant subjectivities to come to terms with their own identities. Memory, thus, becomes a means to reconfigure one's own identity and to find solace in the land of the unconsoled.

Ishiguro has authored many novels till date, most of which have won awards and accolades for their emotional depth and technical craftsmanship such as *A Pale View of the Hills* (1982) which was awarded the Winifred Holtby Memorial Prize, *An Artist of the Floating World* (1986) which won the Whitbread Book of the year award and was shortlisted for the Booker Prize, *The Remains of the Day* (1989) was awarded the Booker Prize for fiction and was later made into an award-winning movie, starring Anthony Hopkins and Emma Thompson, *The Unconsoled* (1995) was awarded the Cheltenham Prize in 1995, *When We Were Orphans* (2000) was shortlisted for both the Booker Prize in Fiction and the Whitbread Novel award, *Never Let Me Go* was published in 2005 and *The Buried Giant* was his latest novel published recently in 2015. Ishiguro was recently awarded the most coveted Nobel Prize in literature, 2017 for his lifetime achievement in writing world-class novels having great emotional virtuosity, probing the underside of our illusory sense experience of the world around. Ishiguro's fictions are explicitly preoccupied with memories—their fragile potentials to digress and distort which blend the private reminiscence with the collective memory of a disillusioned past. Ishiguro is often grouped with V.S. Naipaul, Rushdie, Timothy Mo, Hanif Kureishi et al. as his novels are ceaseless experimentations, dramatising the inward alienation and isolative bereavement within the framework of the decolonising polemics of reorientation.

Hanif Kureishi was born of bicultural parentage on 5 December 1954 in Bromley, England. His parents allowed him to adopt a cosmopolitan lifestyle which is augmented further by his studying philosophy at King's College in London when he aspired to be a writer. Along with other literary pursuits, he started writing plays to be performed in theatre. Early in 1981 he won the George Devine Award for his plays *Outskirts* and *Borderline* followed by his screenplay for the film *My Beautiful Launderette* in 1984 which was nominated for the Oscar award. His first novel *The Buddha of Suburbia* (1990) won him the Whitbread Prize and was reproduced as a drama for the BBC in 1993. In 1995, he published his second novel *The Black Album* which seems to complement Rushdie's *The Satanic Verses* in its fundamentalist undercuts and presentment of a cultural struggle for self-actualisation. The next novel *Intimacy* was published in 1998 and was later adopted as a film in 2001 which won the Golden Bear Award at the Berlin Film Festival. His latest novels, such as *Gabriel's Gift* was published in 2001, *Something to Tell You* in 2008 and the *Last Word* in 2014. He also published a number of short story collections and non-fictional works, including the essay collections *Dreaming and Scheming* and *The Word and The Bomb* which are immensely popular since its publication and have received with great critical acclaims. Kureishi, in his novels, seeks to delineate the hybridised positionalities of the immigrant subjectivities who inevitably experience an in-between perception of fragmented culturality as belonging to more than one culture simultaneously. He is particularly attentive to the factors that effectuate a fast transformation of the conventional notion of identity as fixed, essential and strictly homogenised to a recognition of the migrant's experience of belonging and identification as shifting, fragmented and non-monolithic.

Romesh Gunesekera was born to a Sinhalese Christian family in Sri Lanka in 1954 where he spent his early childhood before migrating to Philippines at the age of twelve. He moved to England in 1972 where he continued to live and work since. Gunesekera starts his literary career with the publication of the book *Monkfish Moon* (1972), a collection of short stories dealing with the ethnic and political tensions that had unsettled Sri Lanka since independence in 1948. Since then he has published many novels and short story collections such as *Reef* (1994), *The Sandglass* (1998), *Heaven's Edge* (2002), *The Match* (2006), *The Prisoner of Paradise* (2012) and *Noon Tide Toll* (2013) and has received a lot of awards and prizes for his literary pursuits.

His *Monkfish Moon* fetched him the Commonwealth Writer's Regional Prize in 1993. *Reef* is the most acclaimed novel, which was shortlisted for the Guardian fiction prize and the Man Booker Prize in 1994. His works primarily draw upon the ever-confounding issues of home, immigrant experiences, the unbroken and continued connection between the time past and the time present, and the problematics of nostalgia and loss.

Ishiguro, in his novels, addresses a deep-rooted sense of cultural estrangement that haunts the lacerated memories of the protagonists which are the outcome of a more temporally incarcerated disruption than a spatially dispersed catastrophe they dread reminiscing. Ishiguro is remarkably dexterous in blending personal dislocation and a sense of cultural bifurcation into his characters in a numerous transmutative, psychological trajectories. As Norman Page astutely remarks, Ishiguro, with his discursive style, is particularly successful in "transferring to an English context a mode of communication and behavior that resembles the Japanese in its use of highly formal surface to cover tensions, concealments and self-deception" (167). Sheng-mei Ma, therefore, describes Ishiguro as a "child of Asian Diaspora" who strives to delineate the representative, fragmented sensibilities in an occluding narrativisation suggestive of the writer's "split personality" and "buried self" (41).

Analogously, Ishiguro, in his novel *The Remains of the Day* explores the confrontational problematics of writing personal memory within the historical context of a multi-ethnic globalised world, linking expatriate experiences to a psychological sense of exile in his representations of the formation of personal, cultural or national identities and the formulation of 'home' that offer intriguing points of reference to cultural, personal and generic hybridity. The novelist does not directly reflect upon the debilitating sediments of immigrant experiences like Kureishi, Rushdie and others, but pertinently construes a capricious site for retrospective interrogation which enables the individual to link his/her personal losses and nostalgia with the post-war bewilderment which drastically reshuffled their personal and professional lives, to expose the inherent frivolity and nuances of stable categories and phenomena like self/ other, master/servant, coloniser/colonised, etc. The novel *The Remains of the Day*, thus, offers a negotiation of the nature of national consciousness and individual identity. Stevens, the protagonist, must reconcile to the decisions of the past with that of the ever uncertain present in a revisionary poetics of unreliable narration, meditating past selves in the realm of cultural hybridity and multicultural belonging. Ishiguro, thus, is keen to depict "diaspora as a tragedy more communal than individual, a disjunction more historical than geographical and most noticeably a phenomenon more global than regional" (Cheng). Ishiguro's ambivalent position in this "stuck on the margins" (Vorda 68) dialectics renders the protagonist Stevens' homeless mind as Barry Lewis suggests a "perfect representative of the century's displacement" (7) and locates the novel "in the transnational moments of history, when one set of values is replaced by another" (144).

The novel *The Remains of the Day* serves as a saga of self-resurrection which identifies the subtle mechanism at work in the reconfiguration of diasporic identity through the comforting process of redefining the past. Stevens, the narrator-protagonist, recognises the fragile power of memory to reconstitute and subsequently evaluates all his past engagements in/with Darlington Hall with the belief that "when with the benefit of hindsight one begins to search one's past for...'turning points', one is apt to start seeing them everywhere" (*The Remains* 175) which reveals the multifarious elusiveness of truth fragmentarily integrated from the realities of the past.

Ishiguro uses *The Remains of the Day* as a tool to explore the "imperial pretensions of a fading British empire" (Lewis 14). Indeed, Britain finds in Stevens a parallel to its rationalising proclivities towards the errors of the past, rewriting the histories of its dismantled Englishness. Stevens realises that he has wasted all his powers in services to Darlington Hall in the pursuit of an eluding, mythopoetic Englishness which leads him to maintain a polished, imperial version of the language he seeks to uphold. The novel seeks to deconstruct the dominant metaphors of the legacy of Englishness, questioning its purity and essentiality which becomes an emphatic claim for a cosmopolitan inclusivity of fragmented loyalties and multiple attachments. As Barry Lewis argues: "If *The Remains of the Day* is seen as an allegory of the decline of British Empire, then it can be interpreted both pessimistically and optimistically. Stevens' failure is a fable in the passing of a certain conception of Englishness; but it is a death many would not wish to mourn" (100).

The reconstitution of the personal past, of origins and identity are central to *When We Were Orphan* which deconstructs its own detective plot by filtering the narrator/protagonist's delusions, rewriting history as spaces of personal nostalgia emerging in revolutionary ways as constructive and creative impulses. The novel tends to oscillate between two localities—England and Shanghai—and presents the protagonist as "stuck on the margins" (Vorda 68), ceaselessly moving between the centre and the periphery in the quest of his lost identity. The novel, like *The Remains*, brings out the historical and political significance of national events in the formation of individual identities. Christopher Banks' circuitous memory, like that of Stevens' meandering journey, unfolds by degrees the various decisive dealings in the past, including the mysterious disappearance of his parents, linking them with the disparate forbearing of the present. Memory here takes a nostalgic turn as Ishiguro reflects upon the recollective inclinations of his protagonist by saying that most people consider this nostalgia in terms of its negativities, treating it to be an obsessive enunciation of the past, but for him "it can be quite a valuable force in our lives" which can serve to become an "emotional equivalent to idealism" (Shaffer "An Interview" 7).

In addition to Banks', there are in the novel, two more orphans in the form of Sarah Hemmings and Jennifer which seem to universalise the condition of 'orphanhood', metaphorically multiplying Banks' own sense of homelessness into a collective experience of encompassing rootlessness of the whole human race. As Pascal Zinck contends, "orphanhood becomes a central metaphor for universal trauma" and the individuals across the globe in the present cultural configuration "must face the world as orphans" (147). The novel, with its multiple, replicative evocation of homelessness, thus, presents several tentative locations and places of identifications. When, after his parents' disappearance, Banks is transported to England, he feels himself to be "an odd bird" (5) and suffers the anxiety and trauma of being different from other schoolboys in the group. Later in the novel, when he meets his friend Akira again as a Japanese soldier on the war-torn field, he admits, "all these years I've lived in England, I've never really felt at home there and that the international settlement...will always be my home" (301). Being marginalised for the lack of English ways, the boy Christopher asks Uncle Philip: "How do you suppose one might become more English" (76) to which the later admits the utter untranslatability of the human self into any unified mode of life because the world has become increasingly multicultural in which every human being is bound to be "a bit of mongrel" (76), presenting a perpetual hybridisation of cultural consciousness. Uncle Philips adds that "It's healthy...people need to feel they belong" (77).

Banks' orphanhood, then, is figuratively encompassed to represent a collectively experienced orphanhood as a result of colonisation, mass migration and stereotypical exclusion. Banks' liminal position in the novel places him in an in-between condition of hybridity and at the same time seeks to subvert the ways in which history is (mis)interpreted and (mis)presented. Banks' anxiety of rootlessness leads him appropriating his sense of identification to a particular culture he feels inwardness with, reconfiguring his identity according to the present contextualities. Thus, to be himself, he must alter a part in himself; to feel at home he must search for himself in a foreign land as Tim Christensen incisively posits: "Banks' home is always already—definitively—also a state of exile—it is a home that is not a home, or a home that is defined by its own absence, its meaning lying elsewhere—for Banks is English, despite being physically located in China and England is elsewhere" (214).

Hanif Kureishi, in his novels, celebrates the fluidity of boundaries and the free-floating idea of identity as imagined constructions. Kureishi's novels such as *The Buddha of Suburbia* and *The Black Album* are set in England which depict the individual's perception of cultural identity as diasporic, heterogeneous and always in the process of making, informed by different cross-cultural connections. In Kureishi's novels, hybridity is glorified as a "radically deconstructive presence in a world obsessed with clear-cut definitions of cultural or ethnic identity" (Schoene, "Herald of Hybridity" 117). Kureishi presents the struggles of the immigrant subjects living in an alien ambience who strive to resolve their crisis of otherness that is the result of being suspended between two positions—the native culture and the host culture. Kureishi strongly reacts against the fundamentalist proclivities of the Western culture that seek to reduce identities and ethnicities to equivocal constants with changeless properties, in terms of cultural normativity, and emphasises the fluidity of the subject positions in relations to the cultural configuration that is never authentic or pure, subverting its apparent essentialist exclusivity.

The Buddha of Suburbia by Kureishi is an exercise in this differential diasporic sensibilities which demonstrates both the impact of race and class relations on individual and how the colonial subjects are caught up in the ambivalence of colonial discourse and pushed into a new space, expressing themselves to be hybrid, ambivalent and in-between souls in the Bhabhasque dialectics of relocation of culture. The moral dilemma the protagonist faces in the novel reflects a deconstructive presence of two critical voices in the systematic consumption of the centre as pure and essential. Karim, the narrator/protagonist, must thrive on an acting career that manifests itself on his engagements in a multiplicity of fluid, shifting and imaginary selves to augment his process of self-actualisation. He must disguise and sell the essentialising stereotypes of cultural and ethnic identities which he believes to be a colonialist construct and which can be reconfigured by non-essentialist performative projections. As Bhabha cogently contends in *The Location of Culture*:

> The subject of the discourse of cultural difference is dialogical or transferential in the style of psychoanalysis. It is constituted through the locus of the Other which suggests both that the object of identification is ambivalent, and, more significantly, that the agency of identification is never pure or holistic but always constituted in a process of substitution, displacement and projection. (162)

This temporal dislocation and double consciousness are representative of a postcolonial representation which seeks to bridge the gap between 'margin' and 'frontline' are central to Kureishi's migrant position that assumes symbolic reflection of a professional mutator, the "Everyman of the...century" (*The Buddha* 141) who carries with himself immense possibilities of transcultural formations as he does not accurately fit into any of the given cultural configurations.

Karim, in the novel, is thus placed in a borderline culture whereby "cultural differences are not synthesized into a new 'third term,' but continue to exist in a hybrid 'third space'" (Thomas 63) as he introduces himself in the very outset of the novel as "an Englishman born and bred, almost...a funny kind of Englishman, a new breed as it were, having emerged from two old histories...it is the odd mixture of continents and blood, of here and there, of belonging and not that makes me restless and easily bored" (3). Mark Stein argues that it is the impulse of being an "odd mixture", divided between "here and there" that allows him to be "an Englishman with qualification" (116). Karim is aware of his propensities towards Englishness despite his being of mixed origins which "emphasizes the condition of an ambivalent cultural attachment" that brings out the real significance of "the insider who simultaneously knows the perspective of an outsider" (Stein xiii).

Similarly, Kureishi's *The Black Album* presents the cultural struggle of the protagonist Shahid, a university student who is torn between contradictory forces of liberal and conservative values. He falls into a hopeless love affair with his teacher Deedee Osgood, develops a flexible form of liberalism and religious tolerance, but at the end unwittingly forces himself to a fundamentalist group headed by Riaz, in the course of helping his fanatic friends. Shahid finds himself perpetually suspended between these two positions—the Muslim friends of his college such as Riaz, Chad and Hat who resist the white supremacy and strongly react against racism and Deedee Osgood who is a freedom-loving individual strongly grounded in the expressive culture of the West. Like Karim of *The Buddha*, Shahid is portrayed as a restless youth in the novel in search of his lost identity who "wants a new start with new people in a new place" (16), but unlike Karim, he is presented as intellectually more sound and responsible than the former and likes "to be challenged intellectually and in every other way" (5) which should liberate him from the constraints of culture and the fetters of fundamentalism.

Shahid's conflictual evolvement of the dualistic dichotomy between Islam and the liberal outlook of the Western culture finds a parallel in Kureishi's own struggle of a similar pattern of in-between positionality which makes Ruvani Ranasinha to remark: "Kureishi avers that notions of Asian and British that cannot be defined separately. His protagonists live the potentials and experience, the pitfalls of mixing and mestigge, emphasizing the precarious ambivalent nature of all cultural translation. His work parodies the idea of homogeneous, distinct, racially distinct communities" (13).

Deedee's presence in Shahid's life relieves his pressure of this conflictual configuration of identity when he is surrounded with contradictions and uncertainties. Shahid and Deedee together cross every limit of restrictive frameworks prescribed by the society and culture, breaking the boundaries and barriers of racial and religious institutions. Deedee seems to be an adaptation of Haroon's character of *The Buddha*, preaching all "limitations are prisons" (25). Shahid chooses to enjoy the present life with Deedee "until it stops being fun" (276), neglecting the call of the Riaz group of friends which will again put him into dreadful uncertainties. It is this influence of the sexual self which makes him alter the content of Riaz's manuscript which he is asked to type, according to his own sexual fancies. To Shahid, poetry infuses beauty into life and makes it worth living. It is this ideal which leads Shahid to transmute the political content of Riaz's writing into wonderful poetry. Kaleta observes: "When Shahid transforms Riaz's writing into poetry rather than transcribing his political tract, he turns the fundamental political observations into poems so lush that he gets erection" (139).

Shahid and Riaz represent the age-old conflict between art and morality. For Shahid art is a liberating impulse—boundless and unrestricted, but for Riaz morality is fixed and unquestionable, otherwise chaos will let loose in the world. Shahid in his search for identity, discovers that there is no morality underneath to make life meaningful. Ironically, it is this morale of life that leads him to the realisation of his identity "as fluid, uncontained, always in the process of becoming" (Weber 125). Shahid takes to the pop culture of the 1980's England "where fragmentation, change, undecidability are the norm" and with his firm assertion—"I can't be limited" (272)—embarks on a riveting journey with Deedee Osgood, keeping his options open with his liberalism and individualism. Shahid's artistic ambition eventually clears his vision and dawn in him a new reality that "there was no fixed self surely our several selves melted and mutated daily" (274).

Romesh Gunesekera, through his fictional manoeuvres, allows us to re-evaluate the dynamics of cultural representation enacted by the influx of diasporic movements across the world that collapse the spatial and temporal boundaries of identification. His novels are explicitly focused on the idea of self-refashioning in which memory plays a pivotal role in reconfiguring one's belongingness, connecting the fragmented diasporic past with a yet unsettled presence. Gunesekera, as a diasporic author, seeks to recreate and reshape the inner landscape of belonging "for it is through a journey into the incommensurable spaces within memory itself that these writers enact individual passages which can no longer be sustained by the recognition of any easily identifiable or firm boundary lines whether of tradition, language, place or time" (Nasta 212). Susheila Nasta describes writers like Gunesekera as "birds of passage" whose locations are always in a state of flux—refigured and reconfigurated by the confluence of individual and collective memories and desires-projected into the obsequious phenomenon of time.

Gunesekera's novels, such as *Reef* and *The Sandglass*, prefigure a diasporic situation which mingles immigrant experience with nostalgia and loss, pointing out to the disjunctures, compressions and conflations of the past with the present to reconfigure the inner landscapes of the protagonists as liberating ways for subverting cultural marginalisation. *Reef* itself becomes a suggestive symbol not only of an irreparable human loss, but a constitutive impulse of self-refashioning in the transformative poetics of a fragmented diasporic past:

> You see this polyp is really very delicate. It has survived aeons, but even a small change in the immediate environment...could kill it. Then the whole thing will go. And if the structure is destroyed, the sea will rush in. The sand will go. The beach will disappear...you see, it is only the skin of the reef that is alive. It is real flesh: immortal. Self-renewing. (54)

The lyrical novel *Reef* tells the story of a young and efficient chef named Triton who is steered into the service of Mister Salgado, a marine biologist experimenting with the movement of the sea and the disappearing reef which poses a threat to the equilibrium of the island. The narrative unfolds in flashbacks as Triton, from his current stay in England where he has immigrated to establish himself as a restaurateur, reflects upon his past engagements with Mr. Salgado in Sri Lanka. Triton, in his self-refashioning, like the coral reef, raises himself from ordeal to glory and instantly becomes a favourite of his master Salgado. Although Triton becomes Salgado's alter-ego, in the new land, to which they migrate, while the master is attentive to his exiled existence, the servant learns to adjust himself to the new environment and carves out a new identity and home of his own. Whereas Salgado has to return to the island defeated, "summoned by a desire to hold on to a lost dream and memory of a lost love" (Nasta 214), Triton, the orphaned figure, successfully integrates himself to the new society: "It was the only way I could succeed: without a past, without a name, without Ranjan Salgado standing by my side" (180).

Inaugurating the role of memory in the refurbishment of individuality, Ranjan Salgado, at one point, in the novel, warns Triton of its omnipotence: "You know Triton...we are only what we remember, nothing more...all we have is our memory of what we have done or not done" (180). While Salgado is forced to return to his promised homeland, trapped by his memory, Triton uses his memory as a survival strategy to reconfigure his inner self as a step towards erecting his 'imaginary homeland,' because "in the end, belonging has to do with people you're with—not with places", says Gunesekera in one of his interviews and alienation..."has nothing to do with being in a different country" (Hussein). Melanie A. Murray, in her book *Island Paradise*, contends that "the erosion of the reef by the sea can be read as a warning against the erosion of cultural identity... the meaning of home becomes a fictional creation" (98). Triton and his mentor Salgado, in the novel, then can be considered as orchestrating the author's cultural hybridity—a diasporic sensibility which reflects the tensions between homeland and host land, settlement and dispersal. Avtar Brah claims that "diasporic journeys are essentially about settling down, putting roots 'elsewhere'" (182) and thus register a 'homing desire' in the migrant individual, perpetually critiquing the discourses of fixed origins. This kind of migrant, as Sonia Floriani believes "aims to double the here and now of his life, and reassess the elsewhere and then" (80). As in one of the poignant epiphonic moments Triton summarily realises: "I was learning that human history is always a story of somebody's diaspora" (174).

In his novel, *The Sandglass*, Gunesekera in a Rushdian fashion, portrays memory as fragmented, the mirror which is broken and mutilated beyond repair and flawed by an elliptical narrativisation, yet instantiating the ways to the recognition that "it is perhaps only memory that is left to define the migrant's true home" (Nasta 228). The narrative opens up when Prins Ducal, the eldest son of Pearl Ducal, returns to London for his mother's funeral. In an attempt to decipher the truth behind the mysterious death of his father Jason Ducal, Prins reflects on his fragmented past with the company of Chip, the narrator who aids to bridge up the gaps with bits and pieces from the history of the three generations of the Ducal with the rivalling Vatunases.

The novel focuses on a retrospective reconstitution of the various exploits of the two families—The Ducals and the Vatunases—recollected through the conversations between Chip and Pearl which are telescoped in a span of twenty-four hours, leading to a thickening sensation of the distant past, running parallel with the immediate past of the characters, experienced as British immigrants with the structural framework of Pearl's funeral. The novel, with its careful maneuvering of juxtapositions, intricately complex actions and meditations liberate "the historical narration from spatial and temporal mooring" (Salgado 153). Minoli Salgado pertinently remarks: "History is spatialized, leveled into simultaneity and space temporalized, marked by the vicissitudes of an emergent time, so that both are rendered inherently provisional and unstable. It is a context in which dwelling is permanently displaced, making settlement permanently temporary" (153). Analogously, Chip, the narrator, is constantly on the move, unsettled in his linear narrativisation of the events. His momentary residence with his adopted mother Pearl is repeatedly destabilised by Prins' episodic visits and re-visits and excludes him from his so-called settled lodging. Moreover, the manner in which Chip emphasises the channelization of his substances through the narrow passage of the sandglass helps "assuaging his longing to capture the realities of a world forever remade in 'the capricious acts' of disappearance which occur every day, we gain an insight into the complexity of Gunesekera's own task as a writer and his attempts in this novel to celebrate the 'resilience of all stories, even ones of disappearance to make new'" (Nasta 232). As suggested by Pearl in the chapter 'Darkness': "You see clearly only when it is empty, no? You can't look back until it is, but by then it's over. Empty. Gone. You have to turn yourself upside down and start all over again" (159).

The novel thus seeks to address the complexities informing the notion of home and belonging that is viewed as a transformative negotiation of identity in relation to the experiences and emotions encountered in Sri Lanka and England. The fractured memories of a diasporic past and a desire to reinvent colour the displaced lives of the individuals in their restless quest for self-re-actuation. Memory and desire, therefore, play an important role in the process of individuation and are intricately interlinked with one another as Uma Parameswaran argues: "...both occupy the same space to evolve to the centre; but the centre is located in a sense of exile, in a place that never was and hence the perpetual interplay, and endless torment" (*Writing the Diaspora* 321). Each and every character in the novel is thus endlessly tormented by an innate urge to belong—to feel at home in their respective dreamlands of identification. As Prins simply put it: "you have to escape and go where you can find yourself, or you stay and transform what is around you until it becomes your own" (37). Transforming the surrounding, however, is contingent upon reconfiguring the inner landscape of the mind as home is ceased to be a place and becomes an emotional entity circumscribed by the provisional premises of memory and desire.

****

As mentioned earlier, the thrust area of this research has been foregrounding the significance of 'home' and belonging in diasporic consciousness and their representation in fictions by the Asian diasporic authors such as Kazuo Ishiguro, Hanif Kureishi and Romesh Gunesekera, focusing on the multifarious dynamism of individual and collective memory in the reconfigurement of identities from the existing conditionalities of a contemporary multi-ethnic Britain where these writers permanently settled. These writers are particularly attentive to the instability and disparity that are registered in the social life of contemporary England, arising out of various cultural contacts and confluences due to the increasing influx of migratory activities transacted across cultures in the recent years. The writers considered in this research are widely different from one another in their thematic concerns and technical craftsmanship, but can be scrupulously compared and contrasted in terms of their fluid poetics of negotiative mediation between cultures in the differential discursivity of diasporic self-identification. The protagonists and characters, as depicted by these writers, in the framework of the novels, recognise the play of difference, ambivalence and heterogeneity that come with such diasporic dislocations, movements and replantations in a foreign land as it inevitably involves interrogating the all-encompassing nature of the binaries and challenging their fixated and stabilised connotations.

Considering the technical aspects of the study, it was indeed a complicated task to structure the research into chapter divisions following the consultation of a large number of resources—primary and secondary. Out of the different options at disposal, I find it highly appropriate to my purpose to divide the work into eight basic chapters including introduction and conclusion; the first few chapters are being deliberately attentive to build a wholesome theoretical framework for the research at hand. The last four chapters are entirely devoted to the authors and their works where I propose to engage an in-depth study of the texts, resituating my arguments in the contextualities of the critical ambience developed in the methodologies of the previous chapters. At the end, a conclusion is provided which summarises in brief the main points and premises of the study. It will review my entire discussion and reflect on how my findings relate to my study including the scope and limitation of the research.

The first chapter of this book titled "Introduction: Theoretical Background and Scope of the Study" introduces the topic under discussion including the authors and their works that are vital and form the crux of the study. It intends to build a complete theoretical framework for the study which supports my thesis statement highlighting the scope of the research, with special focus on important keywords such as home, identity, memory, Englishness, belonging, etc. and their interplay in the lives of diasporic individuals. It states the main objectives of the research at hand and involves a literature review of the authors whose works are essential to the meaningful understanding of the research problems. It closes with a brief introduction of the chapter divisions of the study.

The second chapter titled "Relocating Home in Diasporic Imagination: Translating Diasporic Desire" seeks to address the notion of home and belonging in diasporic consciousness, outlining the theoretical approaches to such entities from the perspective of postcolonial, diasporic and cultural studies. The idea of home, in diaspora studies, is a question of identity and belonging which involves extending solidarity with the local and the transnational with a strong 'homing desire' to recreate a lyrical space which transcends the territorial and temporal frameworks of homeland identification, challenging the holistic and essentialist notion of home as static and firmly located in a community or a place. It deliberates a systematic inversion of these grounded certainties of *roots* which are replaced with the transnational contingencies of *routes* or 'translation' as the conceptualisation of home allows for heterogeneity and plurality because of its emphasis on multiple locations and journeys. The entire chapter thus is an attempt to investigate how diasporic experiences and shifting transnational connections impact and shape the notion of home in diaspora with its multiple, plurilocal and constructed representations, radically distancing itself from the ideas of fixity, rootedness and nostalgic exclusivity.

The third chapter entitled "(De)constructing Diaspora: A Study in Composite Identities" attempts a detailed study of the concept of diaspora and composite identity formation, narrowing down the discussion to the specificities of Asian immigrants diasporised in England through the complexities of interaction, interrogation and transactive negotiations with the adopted land of diasporisation. The chapter seeks to locate issues like ethnicity, race relations and cultural difference which need to be addressed within specific contexts in relation to particular histories of migration and/or settlement in order to chart the complex realities underlying individual historical moments only to de-historicise these variables between and across diasporic formations. Diasporas, in this sense, are composite configuration made up of many journeys, each with its own history, effectuating a confluence of narratives, reproduced through individual as well as collective memory and re-memory which subvert the fixed and stable notion of diasporic community. The chapter thus seeks to deconstruct the dominant forms of fixity and boundedness within diasporic formations in the framework of trans-historical representations, generating a plethora of discursive narrativisations perpetuated through composite configuration of individuality which exists as an essential condition for cultural translation and negotiation to conjure up ambivalent images of homeland as the need for reimaging the diverse possibilities of belonging.

In the fourth chapter titled "Rethinking Englishness: Multiculturalism and the Politics of Belonging", I propose to demonstrate the ways whereby England, with its cosmopolitan inclusivity, manages to reinvent itself, nourishing a common culture of interracial relations and discursive formations created out of the multiple movements and cross-connectivities of migration and multicultural realities. Cultural theorists have claimed that the idea of homogeneity attached to the idea of Britain as a nation was both a result of the imperial agenda and the evolution of a Eurocentric modernity that was unable to catch the true spirit of an inevitable immigrant past. However, to invoke the notion of national belonging, terms like 'England' or 'Englishness' is deliberately worked out into play in the cultural and literary cartographies of representation to inaugurate and illustrate a specific spirit of Englishness. The essential myth of Englishness associated with this particular ethnicity is long endured, but exists with an intercultural divergency and racial mixture that heterologically informed the British life. The idea of a multicultural society challenges its homogenising premises of essentialist identification with its diversified, heterogeneous accommodations, pointing out a summative erosion of the legacy of Empire and its exclusively nationalistic connotations. The fixity of boundaries is to be reconfigured in a progressive model of transcultural representation as the 'invented tradition' of Englishness is viewed as a necessary development of an organic integration of these diasporic black and Asian communities to a central phenomenon of belongingness. This chapter thus suggests a notion of Englishness that defies any fixed framework of cultural representations which, in the course of time, has enlarged itself to include a medley of disparate culturalities and discursive possibilities that warrants an important step towards merging a global open society with the diverse, localised forms of attachment and belonging.

The main focus of chapter five titled "Identity, Memory and the Shifting Contour of Home: Kazuo Ishiguro's *The Remains of the Day* and *When We Were Orphans*" includes an exhaustive textual analysis of Kazuo Ishiguro's novels, particularly *The Remains of the Day* and *When We Were Orphans*, in which the novelist is constructively involved to confer migrancy a privileged sensibility and emphatic omnipotence to carve out a cultural space for the displaced diasporans from the very fragmentation of cultural rootedness, subverting the critical forces that downplay and reject paradigms of monolithic territoriality and nationalistic belonging in contemporary literary discourse. The chapter draws attention to the subtle mechanism of exilic self-fashioning in Kazuo Ishiguro's fiction which is metacritical in its trajectories, suggesting an increased emphasis on the elucidation of cosmopolitan cultural production through the negotiated specificities of diverse diasporic encounters. Ishiguro is particularly successful in inverting the conventional status of diasporic bewilderment which challenges the established notion of alien locality and ethnic identity as his protagonists, instead of being marginalised figures, are duly balanced cultural forces on the adopted localities, inevitably moulded by the waves of a negotiative historicity which is linked up with their own version of reality. This chapter, therefore, is an attempt to resituate Ishiguro's conceptualisation of 'home' with its varying degrees of deterritorialisation and belongingness in which the reconstitutive memory of the undeciphered past is viewed as having metamorphic levels of transcultural dehomogenisation of homing enterprises to productively exacerbate the splitting sense of identification in the process of self-actualisation.

The sixth chapter of this book is titled "Featuring the Self: Hybrid Identities and the Idea of In-betweenness in Hanif Kureishi". In this chapter, I am inclined to argue that the second generation immigrants in England, as portrayed in Kureishi's novels, exemplify the postcolonial rhetoric of cultural fragmentation whose identities are perceived as hybrid and relational rather than pure and essentialist; thus always in the process of becoming, admitting uncertainties and ambivalent relationships to its existing configuration. Citing a wide range of critical concepts from the works of the cultural theorists such as Bhabha, Hall, Gilroy and others, it seeks to evolve a mutable conceptualisation of identity that is keen to disrupt the narrative of a dominant culture, introducing a fluid hybridisation of the discourses of cultural purity and rootedness to creatively reconfigure the dialectics of dominance and resistance in the framework of transactive cultural encounters. Kureishi, in his novels, evidences this hybrid potentiality of the protagonists, perpetuating multiple conceptions of Britishness, scrupulously distancing themselves from the static and holistic notion of national belonging. This chapter, thus, highlights the manners in which Kureishi, in his novels, subverts and dismantles the preconceived notion of cultural identity which is viewed as plural, partial and hybrid to foreground the overlapping constructs of race, ethnicity, religion and sexuality, precipitating a profound process of redefinition whereby origins and self-refiguring subsist in an uneven and unstable interactions as forms of liminal and in-between spaces.

In chapter seven of this study titled "Reconfiguring the Inner Landscape: Self-refashioning and Belongingness in Romesh Gunesekera's Novels" a detailed, in-depth analysis is attempted to recapture the process whereby immigrants in the adopted land of diasporisation learn to cope and construct self-images of survival in their vast psychic terrains of personal and collective memory, interrogating the temporality and territoriality of belonging which is indelibly marked by emotional determinants. His novels such as *Reef* and *The Sandglass* prefigure a diasporic situation which mingle immigrant experience with nostalgia and loss, pointing out to the disjunctures, compressions and conflations of the past with the present to refashion the inner landscape of the protagonists as liberating ways to resist transcultural marginalisation. Both the 'reef' and the 'sandglass,' at different points and levels of association, become suggestive symbols, not only of an irretrievable human loss, but also of a reconstitutive, recurring impulse of self-refashioning in the transformative dialectics of cultural confrontations. The chapter, thus, proposes to outline the significance of the interplay of memory and desire that exist constantly on a narratological reformative poetics of representation while exposing the intrinsic insubstantiality of identity, belonging and the idea of homesickness in the narrative of the sequestered self.

Chapter eight of this research concludes the study with a summative re-evaluation of the already discussed issues about home and belonging and their cartographies in the diasporic imagination of the migrant subjects. Here, I would like to sum up with the findings of the research by stating that spatial parameters of home, both as fixed and liminal, problematise the rhetoric of identity formation and the supposed land of identification. Home tends more towards a range of fluid locationalities as the diasporans seek to embrace multiple possibilities, complex and innumerable ways of being, and a permanent process of movement, change and unsettling.

Chapter 2

Relocating Home in Diasporic Imagination: Translating Diasporic Desire

> "Perhaps home is not a place but simply an irrevocable condition."
>
> —James Baldwin, *Giovanni's Room*

> "Home is no longer one place, it is locations."
>
> —Bell Hooks,
> *Yearning: Race, Gender and Cultural Politics*

> "A place does not merely exist, it has to be invented in one's imagination."
>
> —Ernest Gellner qtd. in Benedict Anderson,
> *Imagined Communities*

The idea of 'home' is an eluding concept in the history of human civilisation which is imbued with meaning in the subjective imagination of the individual. It is intrinsically and inevitably associated with the practices of exclusion and inclusion, operating in an individualistic space of psychic investment under given circumstances. The homeless dialectics of the postmodern diasporic world triggers a sense of 'homing desire' in the people displaced from their native land of identification in a range of differential and discursive possibilities. The diasporic subjects thus feel a constant urge to reconstruct their own image of homeland, creating an imaginative space for themselves, reconfiguring the inner landscapes of their mind.

The chapter thus aims at exploring and relocating 'home' in diasporic imagination, translating diasporic desire with its multiple and conflicting cultural identities that defies strict premise and connotation in the problematic dialectics of permeable patterns of cultural representations.

The notion of 'home' involves a complex configuration of relationships which moves beyond the simplified rhetoric of nostalgia attached to diasporic displacements and relates to the whole range of personal and political struggles over the societal constraints of belonging. We live in a complex world of belonging and deprivation where millions of people do not live in their original places, where many others live a homeless life within their native lands and there are many who have homes or homelands, but are abandoned in the quest for better opportunities elsewhere across the world. The ease of movement and the promise of fulfilment thrust their lives over a constant flux in which the human subject rejects the static dialectic of a traditional mode of life. These pluralities of dwelling resulting from an eternal shifting of locations add new intricacies to the idea of home and belonging.

To conceptualise the ethos of 'home' one has to attend to the social, economic and historical factors behind the creation and construction of these dwelling places, regardless of where one relates one's homely feeling to and what does it really mean 'to feel at home' in a world where location and belonging fluctuate amidst an ever changing perspective of integration and rupture. Thus, the new shifting phenomena of location, dislocation and relocation proliferate into the oversimplified understanding of these dimensions and subjectivities, in the emotional and imaginative construction of home in an all-inclusive cosmopolity.

A question we often encounter in our daily walks of life in relation to our places of identification is 'Where are you from?' which relates to the whole networks of our belonging and evokes in us a sense of urgency to belong. Thus, home becomes a site where one negotiates belonging and unbelonging in relation to the cultural identity which is firmly grounded in one's homeland. We, in the postmodern world, live a semi-nomadic life where the term 'home' is no more reducible to a thing in itself, but becomes an important emotional determinant in the construction of identity. People, now in a globalised world, tend to move ceaselessly between borders, creating new temporal homes involving a growing mixture of cultures with which they identify themselves. Of course, the difference between a home and a house is readily obvious that can be properly complimented by the 'thing theory' of Bill Brown which suggests that house is an objectification of the thingness of the home ("Thing Theory" 4). By thingness he seems to refer to an array of human sensibilities like meaning, memory, emotion, etc. which are attached to the 'homing desire' of the individuals—its home qualities, energies and the inherent will to possess and belong. The present condition of the world is unmistakably one of connections and movements and the "experience of space is always socially constructed" (Gupta and Ferguson 7). Anthropologists have accepted the view that the land which is being divided into nations is tied to culture, and people are being 'rooted' into these nations. The ways people construct their notions of home is as much influenced by this concept of 'rootedness' as by the individual and collective imagination of the past, present and future (Pink 40). The idea of home, both in its real shape as a place or homeland and in its imaginary semblance, provides the various emotional determinants of identity. Thus, home is both a real and symbolic place that becomes synonymous with intimacy, security, familiarity, identity against the vast anonymity of unfamiliar categories and relations. Roger Silverstone argues in this connection:

> Home, of course needs to be understood in both literal and metaphorical senses. The defense of home is a defense of both the private spaces and intimate social relations and domestic security—the household; as well as of the larger symbolic spaces of neighbourhood and nation—the collective and the community. (442)

Home is therefore considered as several sites occupied by a person over the course of his/her life—some concurrently occupied and others connected through travel, time, memory, relation, and transition. The notion may involve "an actual place of lived experiences and a metaphorical space of personal attachment and identification" (Armbruster 20). It can cogently be defined in terms of identity, memory, a sense of involvement and inclusion and above all, a "mythic place of desire" (Brah 192). Avtar Brah in *Cartographies of Diaspora: Contesting Identities* describes this homing desire in a different perspective of trans-geographical representation:

> ... 'home' is a mythic place of desire in the diasporic imagination. In this sense it is a place of no return, even if it is possible to visit the geographical territory that is seen as the place of 'origin'. On the other hand, home is also the lived experience of a locality. Its sounds, smells, its heat and dust, balmy summer evenings, or the excitement of the snowball, shivering winter evenings, sombre grey skies in the middle of the day...all this, as meditated by the historically specific everyday of social relations. (192)

For Brah, the shifting memory of home juxtaposes the fantastic memory of the past when individuals of diaspora are confronted with the present in both its physical and temporal manifestations. As powerfully put by Sara Ahmed in her paper "Home and Away: Narratives of Migration and Estrangement": "home is implicitly constructed as a purified space of belonging in which the subject is too comfortable to question the limits or borders of her or his experience" (339).

Home is a key concept in the diasporic signifying practices and the process of transnationality. An immense critical analysis has been devoted to analyse how diasporic transnational migration unsettles the notion of home in all its modalities and multiple attachments in the different level of mobility, location and dislocation. As Blunt and Dowling believe, "transnational homes are...shaped by ideas and experiences of location and dislocation, place and displacement, as people migrate for a variety of reasons and feel both at home and not at home in a wide range of circumstances" (154). Further, Brah highlights the ways wherein not all kinds of dislocation and displacement share the sense of return or reclamation, precisely noting the difference between 'homing desire' and nostalgia for native land (180). Thus, the chapter seeks to critically explore the relation between home, identity and memory in three ways. First, it analyses home as an emotional construct characterised by a 'homing desire' in the diasporic imagination which transcends the physicality of homeland and subverts the essentialist notion of home. Secondly, it attempts to demonstrate the connection between 'home' and memory and how reminiscence can be a virtual site for the recreation of a lyrical self to obliterate the distinction between 'home' and 'not home'. Lastly, the research would draw upon reflections on diasporic identity formation and the notion of belongingness in translating the diasporic desire for home in the dislocated individuals' subjective consciousness.

In diasporic engagements, extended cultural boundaries enable the formation of new, pluralistic, domestic and collective homes. As cultural boundaries expand, the idea of home admits instability into its assumed notion of purity and homogeneity. Home, in any case of diasporic representation is always ambiguous and fluid. It is never fixed and permanent as the ideal notion of home is assumed to be in its essentialist position, having the quintessential quality of privacy, security, a habitual shelter to return to. This ideation of home is not similar to any kind of home anywhere in the late modernity, where the boundaries of space and privacy between the real and the symbolic are infinitely blurred (Silverstone 442). Since 'home' ceases to be a real place, feeling at home is essentially a subjective and culturally determined link to the imaginary. We attach great importance and cherish the memory of home when we are away from it. It becomes more emphatic and intense when there is a fear to lose it. The memory of home is recreative of the inner poetry of the private self which is evoked by emotion and not by factual recapitulation:

> Memories of the outside world will never have the same tonality as those of home and, by recalling these memories, we add to our store of dreams; we are never real historians, but always near poets, and our emotion is perhaps nothing but an expression of a poetry that was lost. (Bachelard 87)

Doreen Massey argues against the stable and introverted nature of home and opines that a sense of place does not concern its stability and purity, rather it is dependent on the unique position it holds as a site for intersection in the wider contextual relations ("A Global Sense" 3). Nostalgia, strangeness, incompatibility and a sense of loss and disruption intensify the endeavour to belong—to make a house home. When individuals are uprooted from their houses, they experience a strong sense of loss and long for the thingness of the home, its qualified ability to be a home. To be detached from one's home and belonging is a detachment from anything that is familiar and stable. This separation from home and homeland is one of the important parameters of diaspora and is clearly reflected in the diasporic consciousness of the diasporan living in the West as diaspora cannot exist without the loss of home or displacement from the homeland. As rightly pointed out by Anat Hecht, "... to lose a home is to lose a private museum of memory, identity and creative appropriation" (123).

Thus, the individual's connection to an ancestral homeland is an inherent feature of diaspora. As Avtar Brah, in *Cartographies of Diaspora: Contesting Identities*, insightfully notes, the term diaspora "embodies a notion of centre, a locus, a 'home' from where dispersion occurs" (181). It evolves images and metaphors of multiple journeys and displacements. The idea of home is central to the notion of diaspora. Far from being just the point from where the scattering initiates, it becomes an idea which establishes an unbreakable link between the diasporic population and the point of scattering. It refers to a new place of abode, a virtual space to settle down or putting roots everywhere away from the homeland. Thinking through diaspora, one can address and attend to the essential link between the place of origin and the new place one is relocated to and develops a sense to belong. Thus, the position of the diasporic representation is an ambivalent one and the members of the diaspora find themselves to be suspended in a space where they are torn between two contradictory forces—allegiance to the native land and affiliation with the new land of settlement:

> A fundamental ambivalence is embedded...a dual ontology in which the diasporic subject is seen to look in two directions—towards a historical cultural identity on one hand, and the society of relocation on the other. In a diasporic subject, then, we see in stark relief the hybrid and the dual characteristics that one most often associated with postcolonial discourse. (Ashcroft, Griffith and Tiffin, *The Post-Colonial* 425)

Diasporic displacements in these ways controvert the supposedly mythical stature of a nation with its concept of nation, nationalism and national identity. This tendency of disruption is implicit in all diasporas—the establishment of a continued link to the homeland, the features which distinguish diaspora from other immigrant positions cannot fully be expressed by the homological concept of nation-state as essentialist and pure:

> The nation-state, as a common territory is questioned, time is traversed and to a varying degrees subverted by diasporic attachments. Diasporic populations do not come from elsewhere in the same way that 'immigrants' do. In assimilationist nationalist ideologies such as those of United States, immigrants may experience loss and nostalgia but only en route to a whole new home in a new place. Such ideologies are designed to integrate immigrants, not people in the diasporas. Whether the national narrative is one of common origins or of gathered populations, it cannot assimilate groups that maintain important allegiance and practical connections to a homeland or a dispersed community located elsewhere. People whose sense of identity is centrally defined by collective histories of displacement and violent loss cannot be "cured" by merging into a new national community. (Clifford, "Diasporas" 307)

This connection between two or more locations or more nation-states simultaneously does not allow the possibility of a singular structure or fixed sense of belonging. It moves beyond the firmly demarcated borders and boundaries which is long held to be an important quotient of national identity and formation of a nation-state as the diasporic individuals seek to maintain identifications outside his/her homeland in order to be incorporated with the foreign land and to live inside with a difference. Ashcroft, Griffith and Tiffin write in this connection that the transactive encounters across national boundaries, dispersion and diffusion through the space of many different national groups disrupt this process of homogenisation, "of establishing metaphysical links with a particular geographic location with a particular community that lives within these border" (*The Post-Colonial* 426) which is so important a phenomenon of nationalism. Uma Parameswaran in her paper "Contexualizing Diasporic Location" says "home is where your feet are, and may your heart too, and I would hope that we write about the world around us and not about the world we have left behind" (291).

Since the 1970s, the globalising world experiences the fragmentary phenomenon of diasporic overlapping and intertwined identity formation mixed with a trauma of being uprooted, loss of home and the resulting identity crises have informed many writers of Asian diaspora in Britain who are haunted by a sense of loss and an urge to reclaim the displaced past with an afflicted wisdom of the incapability of reclaiming specifically the thing that was misplaced. This is the reason why they filled their world with a fragmented vision of rebirth and lost memory where the individuals have to reinvent a lost home in their fictive consciousness of diasporic sensibility and reconfigure their recollected identity.

As said earlier, the connection to an ancestral homeland is an implicit but inevitable characteristic of diaspora. Edward Said in his paper "The Mind of Winter: Reflections on Life in Exile" seeks to define this position with the connotation of an insurmountable sense of loss which he claims to be "transformed into a potent even enriching motif of modern culture" (49) and the diasporic 'liminal space' between cultures which conditions the displaced individual becomes a site of creativity which would ink them into eternity.

Salman Rushdie in *Imaginary Homelands*, describes this diasporic self-refashioning from a fragmented past with the image of "broken mirrors" (suggestive of fragmentation) which rules out the possibility of a complete and real return to the lost world and suggests the course of substitution and replacement in the process of self-actuation, aligning the mutated memory of the past with that of the present (11). The image of the broken mirrors projects a form of a disintegrated reality which symbolises distorted memory and falsification of history in the negotiative experiences of diasporic subjects. The diasporic writers are thus faced with the problem of recollecting and reworking an irretrievable past in their psychological journey into the collusive caves of memory and re-memory, highlighting the importance of the diversity of diasporic desire as creative as well as subversive impulses in the imaginative reconstruction of identity and home. Elucidating what he means by 'imaginary homelands' he contends that the incompleteness and ruptured memory serves as a dynamic urge to bridge the fragmented schemata of identification by imagining and restructuring the world around them. With reference to his seminal epic venture in the form of *Midnight Children* he reflects on this evocative motif of reinvention:

> ... but the point I want to make is that of course I'm not gifted with total recall, it is precisely the partial nature of these memories, their fragmentation, that made them so evocative for me. The shards of memory acquired greater status, greater resonance, because they were remains; fragmentation made trivial things seem like symbols, and the mundane acquired numinous qualities. (*Imaginary Homelands* 12)

Rushdie aptly quoted the first line of Hartley's novel *The Go-Between*, "the past is a foreign country" when he refers to the ancient photograph as an evocation of the memories of the past only to invert the idea in a diasporic turn of impulse to say that "it's my present that is foreign, and that the past is home, albeit a lost home in a lost city in the mists of lost time" (*Imaginary Homelands* 9).

Fragmentation and dislocation, then is a strength in disguise, allowing the writer to present their fiction as transaction with past in a permeable poetics of transhistorical reformulation. This condition opens up an immense world of novel possibilities "with the realisation that new knowledge and ways of seeing can be constructed out of the myriad combinations of the 'scraps' which Rushdie describes—knowledge which challenge the authority of older ideas of rootedness and fixity" (McLeod 215). Thus, cultural displacement becomes a claim for a multi-perspective creative process. He extends his discussion on the complexity of diasporic reterritorialisation in relation to the retrospective imaginary notion of an ancestral home:

> It may be that writers in my position, exiles or emigrants or expatriates, are haunted by some sense of loss, some urge to reclaim, to look back, even at the risk of being mutated into pillars of salt. But, if we do look back, we must also do so in the knowledge—which gives rise to profound uncertainties—that our physical alienation from India almost inevitably means that we will not be capable of reclaiming precisely the thing that was lost; that we will create fictions, not actual cities and villages, but invisible ones, imaginary homelands, Indias of the minds. (Rushdie, *Imaginary Homelands* 10)

The meaning of home for him lies in the interactive process of cultural translation—the multiple ways in which the displaced individual strives to relocate 'home' in diasporic imagination. Rushdie's idea of cultural negotiation is similar to the concept of 'routes' rather than 'roots' that James Clifford emphasises in his work *Routes: Travel and Translation* which proclaims the fluid notion of home (78) signalising the "multi-locationality across geographical, cultural and psychic boundaries" (Brah 194). The notion of 'routes' or 'translation' as home or homing desire allows for a plurality of perception and heterogeneity of identification because of its emphasis on multiple locations and journeys. It involves a fluctuating contextualisation that Rushdie calls "ambiguous and shifting ground" (*Imaginary Homelands* 15) or Homi Bhabha's "liminal space" (*The Location* 5) which point out to the inevitable non-essentialist conceptualisation of diasporic space where cultural hybridity becomes the defining principle.

Apparently, and quite naturally, the diasporic texts strive to uphold individual psychic accounts, imaginative projections of memories and weave a fictional enchantment around private and collective histories and therefore suggest alternative ideas of documenting incidents and experiences of the past in the diasporic consciousness. Memories and experiences which are the prime indicators of identity serve as the raw materials of literary representation and the diasporic writers try to retrieve them imaginatively and stitch them coherently into a meaningful narrativised totality. It is the sense of separation which makes him write and empowers his world of imagination. Abdulrazak Gurnah's words translate this diasporic desire, combining the metaphor of journeys with that of a recollective imagination: "Travelling away from home provides a distance and perspective, and a degree of amplitude and liberation. It intensifies recollection, which is the writer's hinterland. Distance allows the writer uncluttered communication with this inner self and the result is a freer play of the imagination" (59).

Equally, with memory which is faulty and incomplete and subject to distortion and falsification of history, the diasporic writer faces the challenges of restructuring and reinventing a lost consciousness of the past that is left behind. What the diasporic writers in their present land of stay do then is to recreate histories and restage an incommensurable presence in the spatial dialectics of fragmented fictionality which questions the authenticity of these images created by memory when the "imaginative truth is simultaneously honourable and suspect" (Rushdie, *Imaginary Homelands* 10). Wondrously enough, this corresponds well with the essential intrinsic fictionality of all homes. A place does not exist somewhere in the geographical location or relocation, it has to be invented and reconfigured in the emotional reconstitutive terrains of mind. As there is no map to measure the mystical memory, so there is not a singular notion of home which is only a symbolic phase of articulation of identity. Home, then, becomes an emotional construct and the present study seeks to demonstrate this significance of diasporic representations which subvert the essentialising properties of all home-making projects in general.

It could be said that writers like Rushdie who experience this sort of diasporic fragmentation in Britain and many others who follow the suit feel evocatively empowered, precisely by these transactive traditions. Rushdie puts it gracefully, reclaiming his own identity as a literary artist who takes to a similar conglomerated tradition that Britain has so prudently nourished throughout its cultural history which critically echoes the Eliotisian philosophy of an all-encompassing literary tradition inclusive of not only the "pastness of the past but of its presence" (Eliot 68)—a temporal cosmopolitical perception:

> Let me suggest that Indian writers in England have access to a second tradition, quite apart from their own racial history. It is the culture and political history of the phenomenon of migration, displacement, life in a minority group. We can quite legitimately claim as our ancestors the Huguenots, the Iris, the Jews: the past to which we belong is an English past, the history of immigrants in Britain. Swift, Conrad, Marx are as much our literary forebears as Tagore or Ram Mohan Roy. (Rushdie, *Imaginary Homelands* 20)

We cannot forget in this connection writers like Hanif Kureishi, Ramesh Gunesekera, Vikram Seth, Monica Ali, et al., just to mention some of those who have lived in England and already secured literary fames and names in the rich galaxy of diasporic writers in Britain. It is interesting to note that Rushdie's alluded literary history of performative tradition forebears in the Indian and British traditions alike which is reverberated in the diasporic intellection of another writer belonging to a different diaspora—Caryl Phillips—who published his anthology entitled *Extravagent Strangers*: *A Literature of Belonging* which addresses the inherent tension of diasporic reformulation in a widely varied authors like Olaudan Equiano, Linton Kwesi Johnson, Romesh Gunesekera, Kazuo Ishiguro, Thackeray, Conrad, Kipling, Whyndham Lewis, Orwell, etc. all of whom were born outside Britain and contributed the metamorphic reconstruction of their 'imaginary homelands' to English literature. Phillips wants to suggest that Britain has always been the home of numerous immigrant souls where different diasporas have combined happily into shaping its peculiar diversified identity which defies all forms of homogeneity in diasporic disposition:

> Readers will come to accept that as soon as one defines oneself as "British" one is participating in a centuries-old tradition or cultural exchange, of ethnic and linguistic plurality, as one might expect from a proud nation that could once boast she ruled most of the known world. The evidence collected here confirms that one of the fortuitous by-products of this heterogeneous history has been a vigorous and dynamic literature. (Phillips, *Extravagent Strangers* xii)

The authors, in such positions, are conditioned by experiences of an ever-encompassing, evolving system of knowledge which is discursively formed in a pluralistic culture, challenging every effort at claiming fixed rootedness of diasporic perception which is considered essentially a "variable and complex function of discourse" (Foucault, "What is an Author?" 221).

The deconstructive theorist Jacques Derrida points out that it is the ceaseless process of deferral and difference in texts that makes the production of meaning dynamic. According to him, words as signifiers can never completely represent their original signified which only projects a gap to be filled in by other words in an infinite regress of meaning. So, there is no unit, no wholesomeness, no fixed structure that authorises, guides, and sustains this free play of meaning. This process of differential reconfiguration corresponds to the diasporic desires of self-refashioning and home-making practices of the displaced individuals in the quest for meaningfulness of their lost home and identity.

Thus, the idea of difference highlights the aspect of fluidity and fragmentation, the non-fixedness and ambiguous nature of identity which precisely unveils the immense dynamicity of diverse possibilities:

> The sign represents the presence in its absence. It takes the place of the present. When we cannot grasp or show the thing, state the present, the being present, where the present cannot be presented, we signify, we go

> through the detour of the sign. We take or give signs we signal. The sign, in this sense, is deferred presence. The circulation of sign defers the movement in which we can encounter the thing itself, make it ours, consume or expend it, touch it, see it, intuit its presence. (Derrida 9)

Stuart Hall, in his paper "Who Needs Identity," questions the cultural identity of the indisposed diasporas, combining the post-structuralist critical approaches with a philoshophy of discursive identity formation, which not only addresses the autonomy of the diasporic individual, but also recognises the possibility of a multicultural negotiative atmosphere where identity becomes a construct in relation to the temporal as well as timeless attachment of the subjective positions to a particular social discourse:

> I use 'identity' to refer to the meeting point, the point of suture, between on the one hand the discourses and practices which attempt to 'interpellate', speak to us or hail us into place as subjects of social discourses and on the other hand, the process which produces subjectivities, which construct us as subjects which can be 'spoken': Identities are thus points of temporary attachment to subject positions that discursive practices construct for us. (5-6)

The idea to 'feel at home' refers to the place where one is familiar with, comforted with protected boundaries, but 'not being home' dawns a realisation of the self that home is an illusory reference to safety and firmly grounded on the marginalisation of specific moments of oppression and resistance in the national histories and is reflective of a conflictual, differential repression within oneself—an unending internal battle that unsettles conventional notions of identities, boundaries and positionalities. Bell hooks seeks to clarify these complexities of home in his book *Art on My Mind: Visual Politics* when she contends that "home is no longer just one place. It is locations. Home is that place where one discovers new ways of seeing reality, frontiers of difference. One confronts and accepts dispersal and fragmentation as part of the construction of a new world order that reveal more fully where we are, who can become... " (148). When the 'homing desire' of the individual is allied with a deep feeling of loss and sadness and the idea of home is entangled with a sense of irrevocable displacement, home ceases to be a place anymore and becomes an emotion. Home, in this sense, transcends the physical limits of fixed boundaries and nationalities and is metamorphosed into a non-spatial entity spawned by the silenced memories and unspeakable desires of the past.

Different modalities and complexities related to the idea of 'home' are explored in the Asian and South-Asian writers settled in England. The different generations of diasporic writers in Britain elicit diverse diasporic experiences and shifting transnational connections which impact and shape the notion of home in diaspora that is formed in the mind of the diasporic subjects and their representation in fiction, focussing on the concept of identity as hybrid, fluid and fragmentary in the differential problematics of trans-generational intersections. The categorisation process in the diasporic generational difference also plays a significant role in the representation of diasporic homes:

> Clearly the relationship of the first generation to the place of migration is different from that of subsequent generations, mediated as it is by the experiences of disruption and displacement as one tries to reorientate, to form new social networks, and learns to negotiate new economic, political and cultural realities. (Brah 194)

For example, the first generation of South-Asian immigrants who had moved to Britain found it problematic in adjusting themselves to their new homes than their second generation counterparts. Obsessed and anguished with a sense of nostalgia and trauma, they wish to get back to their land of origin. This experience of the first generation people again differs from one another relating to the temporality of their dislocation. For instance, since the writer Nadeem Aslam from Pakistan, whose novels are ceaseless experimentation in cultural hybridity, had migrated to Britain at a much earlier age than Ambalavaner Sivanandan of Sri Lankan origin, their experiences are surely coloured by widely different perceptions even if both are labelled as first generation diasporic writers in British cultural set up. However, these generational differences are not absolute and are subject to transgressive infiltration. The immigrants share both commonalities and difference with their descendents and hosts in a complex, overlapping and intersecting condition of diasporic self-actualisation. Ironically, however, amidst all diasporic longings and nostalgia, there is an urge to resist the fascination for the homeland as they feel a sense of unbelonging to both their past and present location. This impulse diminishes with the second and third generation migrants and reduces their perception of cultural and ethnic identity which Mary Waters in *Ethnic Options: Choosing Identities in America* defines as "plasticity of ethnic identities among the third generation and beyond" (qtd. in Kivisto 32). Thus, the sense of disruption and unbelongingness propel them to recreate an imaginative space for themselves to perpetuate and renew their lost sense of 'homeliness' in an unreceptive ambience of incompatibility, effectuating a reintroduction of cultural permeability.

In the introduction to an impressive collection of essays analysing the multiple modality of diasporic identity formation, Vijay Agnew attempts to retrieve the metaphors of shifting identities and diasporisation where experiences of happiness and miseries are all fraught with a tremendous tension between "living here and remembering there, between memories of places of origin and engagements with places of residence, and between the metaphorical and the physical home" (4). Later in her second essay, in the collection, "A Diasporic Bounty: Cultural History and Heritage," Agnew reflects on the cosmopolitan significance of India's gems and jewels that were forcefully looted and disposed by the imperialist powers as their righteous possessions, now finding places in different museums of the world. Instead of viewing them as symbols of loss and colonial oppression, she sees them as humanity's common possession, reflecting a collective assimilationist heritage as she believes homes and heritage obviate to "coincide with national and geographical boundaries" (181). So, the notion of ownership is fraught with cosmopolitan properties of pluralistic appropriation, of cultural domain which has to be transgressed through a sense of collective re-territorialisation and the artefacts are to be seen as "the markers of history and the bounty of diaspora" (186) in the permeable dialectics of general consciousness. Rishma Dunlop maintains, in this regard, that in this negotiative philosophy, the diasporic individual experiences a medley of conflicting socio-historical forces that have dethroned him/her from the place of origination which evolves a "historiographic poesis" (117) of unselved experiences.

The individual is encountered with the issues of "fractured identities, discarded languages, and the will to bond oneself to a new community against the ever present fear of failure and betrayal" (Dunlop 116). Dunlop develops her points drawing largely from the concept of hybridity and double consciousness because it "moves the mind beyond the dualism into a multiple consciousness cognizant of multilocalities" (117). It is interesting to note that the idea of home is located in a cosmopolitical textuality wherein artistic venture becomes "shelter of words" not delimited by the boundaries of "national, political, ethnic, or other allegiances and categorizations" (Dunlop 115). Hence, she maintains that like writers, immigrants "imagine and re-imagine history, memory, the material reality of their lives, testifying to the fact that boundaries of nation, culture and gender are slippery inventions requiring continuous interrogation" (149).

The study thus attempts to explore and highlight the multidimensional contours and contents of diasporisation in the process of restoring the unselved souls in their respective reconstituted homes. Formation of homes, therefore, entails a haunting spectrality of reminiscences which is allied with a hope of reconfiguring the psycho-geographical boundaries of the inner landscape through the ways of negotiation and reinvention. The location of the diasporic individuals is presented as a phantasmal condition "where the political unreality of one's present home is to be surpassed only by the ontological unreality of one's place of origin" (Agnew, "Introduction" 13).

Analogously, Anh Hua in "Diaspora and Cultural Memory" develops a multicultural model of diasporic counter memorialisation to examine the diverse patterns of remembrance in migrant communities. Hua argues that the displaced diasporas are endowed with a dual perspective of interactive existence between locations and find "the politics of diasporic spaces" as "contradictory and multi-accented" (195) which are thoroughly "heterogeneous and contested sites differentiated by gender, class, sexual orientation, generation differences, language access, historical experiences and geographical locations" (204).

The urge to construct new set of norms to live in a new home then acts "as a catalyst for self-recovery and community building" (Hua 203). In such a diasporic contemplation, memory can serve as a survival strategy to sustain social justice, by recalling the forgotten or suppressed to bear witness; yet, it is a strategy that needs seeing "the past as conflictual, evidence as problematic, all questions as suspect" (Matsuda 15). The diasporic subjects are thus caught between ambivalent dynamic desires for an unseen paradise with its own firmly grounded cultural paradigms which is lost or powerless to be reborn and an urge to be assimilated completely with the newly evolved cultural norms of an alternative home.

The notion of home is not a fixed entity and depends on the struggling individual's shifting definition of new inner or outer barriers and the kind of location that has crept into his/her life. The main focus of this study is to explore these discursive dispositions in the presentment of home and homeland which becomes a transcendental code to be invented and reinvented over and over again by a subjective reconfiguration and refurbishment of identity. Similarly, Mohamad Hafezi develops and distinguishes two types of categories for the notion of home: the first, dislocation which he labels as geographical is based on rigidly demarcated physical boundaries, evocative of mystified and glorifying accounts of the past that he safely terms as exilic and the second, he rightly calls 'diasporic' which is rather transnational in dismantling the shadowed lines of estrangement and becomes "a constructed space in the present through contacts, memories and activities" (8). Home, in this sense, maybe re-assembled through transactive interaction of past, present and future. For the exilic writers, memorialisation of home "create a ground of creativity and reinvention exactly because of its remoteness, intangibility and inaccessibility" (Hafezi 135) for they are haunted by an enamoured hope of return to the homeland till they find it disappointing to discover that their remotely imagined portrait of homeland is far gloomier than their present home in a new location they ever dreamt of. Exilic home or identity in this case is mimetic, reproducing and re-enacting a modified version of reality that is elemental to the detached homeland which results in a distorted and fantasised presentation traced in the exilic authors.

Conversely, diasporic sensibility is characterised by a "weakening of memory and a dispersion and rupture of identity, twilight of oblivion. Therefore, an ethics of exile is conservative, while an ethics of diaspora is progressive, i.e. open to the possibility of change and non-mimetic" (Hafezi 147). Hence the exilic subjects of diasporas nourish a solidified image of the homeland, evolving a stigmatised presentation of precedent, ancestral home, unlike the diasporic subjectivity which is languorously liberated from the shades of absolutist prejudices, resorting to the formulation of fluxing, disintegrated sets of images of the fluctuating past that encompasses and involves a universal, humane, deconstructed sense of belonging.

These wistful trans-historical projections conjure up an array of refabricated homing possibilities. Since memory has a crucial role to play in ensuring access to the remote past in restoring the lost identity, diaspora memory texts are replete with socially constructed images and metaphors of the past, imaginary homes and diasporic desires. The term diaspora traditionally evokes imagery of rupture, the relentless ways by which immigrants construct, reconstruct and deconstruct the self-images of their homes and identities in the new cultural set-up they inhabit. It is the process by which they abandon with anxiety the old ways of life and adapt themselves to change, painfully learning and internalising a new way of life and culture. Immigrants, having uprooted themselves from their older societies, thus, absorbingly endeavour to reinvent new homes recalling other homes miles away.

The earlier discussion of diaspora was heavily oriented towards the conceptual homeland, be it the Jewish dispersion from their homeland or any other form of mobilised displacement, sustaining a strong sense of nostalgia resulting from their silenced, victimised voices. But after 1980, diaspora was extended to proffer a metaphorical connotation which includes different categories of displacement—"expatriates, expellees, political refugees, alien residents, immigrants and ethnic and radical minorities" (Cohen, *Global Diasporas* 21). The rich extension of the meaning of diaspora in the present context is what is called by Brubaker "let-a-thousand-diaspora bloom" approach that has taken the diaspora to such an all-inclusive proportion that it has lost its significance to be distinguished with its primal properties—the universalisation of diaspora—paradoxically dissolves the divide of diasporas (Brubaker 3). The recent discourses of diaspora, however, have some strong connections with the Jewish experiences of dislocation and the resultant recollection of homely properties in the spatial dialectics of the mind. The individuals of diaspora carry with them some unalterable qualities of their homelands wherever they go and the collective memory forces them to idealise it in multiple ways. In this way, the symbolism associated with the sense of belonging produces strong nostalgic tendencies and is continued to be involved in home and homeland politicisation of textual meaning.

Defining diaspora, in this global context, recently has been made increasingly complicated because of the mass mobilisation and dispersion in large scale and multiple dislocations and displacements worldwide. However, all notions of diaspora involve the idea of identity and belonging which are constructed in disparate ways flexibly in relation to the space the displaced individuals wish to reconstruct. As James Clifford writes in *Routes: Travel and Translation in the Late Twentieth Century*: "...multi-locale diasporas are not necessarily defined by a specific geopolitical boundary" as they tend to consciously misconstrue a "principled ambivalence about physical return and attachment to land" (246-48). This points out to the fact that such diasporic formulations include shared feeling of alienation and homogenising identification with a spatial collectivity. The first-generation diasporic sensibility comprises a strong nostalgic re-enactment of home which Steven Vertovec, in "Conceiving and Researching Transnationalism," defines as "diaspora consciousness" that is "marked by dual or multiple identifications" (450). Hence, there is a presentment of the diasporic individuals as experiencing "decentred attachments, of being simultaneously 'home away from home', 'here and there'" where majority of people live the life of multiple identities "that link them simultaneously to more than one nation" (Vertovec, "Conceiving" 450-51). The second generation shares a 'transnational consciousness,' rather than diasporic, because they are not rigidly fixated in a singular space of identification or experience major traumatic dispersion and help effect an inclined movement towards a transnational identity formation. Hence, the second-generation challenges the essentialising properties of home and identity and maintains little or no attachment to any place, choosing to be global nomads, transcending the constricted nationalist space. As forcefully put by Arif Dirlik in *Global Modernity: Modernity in the Age of Global Capitalism*:

> The new diasporas have relocated their self there and other here, and consequently borders and boundaries have been confounded. And the flow has become at once homogenizing; some groups share in common global culture regardless of location while others take refuge in cultural legacies that are far apart from one another as they were at the origin of modernity. (352)

The diverse forms of displacement over the globe have projected different transactive interactions which permeate the experiences of diasporic individuals in the transgressive dialectics of border-crossing. Bhabha, in his *The Location of Culture*, revisits the concept of identity which is viewed as a productive condition for negotiation and articulation—an in-between space of cultural translation (2). Thus, diasporic transpositions endure a sense of cultural impurity and resort to a fluxing shift of cultural representations. Bhabha in *The Location of Culture*, develops the model of the "third space" (56) as an act of pure enunciation of cultural fragmentation. He focuses on the spatio-temporal dimension of cultural analysis which defies the logic of synchronicity assumed by the traditional method of cultural evaluation. The evolution of the 'third space', therefore, destroys the symmetrical representation of cultural formation as fixed and static. It deconstructs the historicity of cultural identification as homogenising, unifying and absolute force. For this reason, Bhabha contends that the in-between third space occupied by the diasporic individual is stuffed with creative possibilities: "It is the space of intervention emerging in the cultural interstices that introduces creative invention into existence" (*The Location* 12). Thus, diasporisation challenges the territorial form of nation-state and questions the rubrics of nation, nationalism and cultural homogenisation:

> The marginal or 'minority' is not the space of a celebratory, or utopian, self-marginalization. It is a much more substantial intervention into those justifications of modernity—progress, homogeneity, cultural organicism, the deep nation, the long past—that rationalize the authoritarian 'normalizing' tendencies within culture in the name of the national interest or the ethnic prerogative. (Bhabha, *Nation and Narration* 4)

In a similar vein, Patchett's paper "'Corpus Cartography': Diasporic Identity as Flesh and Blood" evolves a dualistic concept of diasporic identity as based on the dichotomy of homeland/host land dialectics which recognises the persistence of dislocated composite identity which can be the site of multiple fragmented possibilities (51). Patchett devises the definition of a 'Corpus Cartography' as a discursive structure of the body's situatedness which poses a rhizomatic challange to post-modernity, "thus contemplating the potential for a new way of thinking about diasporic identity" (65). Patchett uses the concept of rhizomatic cartography to demonstrate the degree of diasporic conditionality by which the body as corpus can be measured by the mind. Negotiated permeability of diasporic identity is, therefore, defined by the principles of connection that comprises only lines, but not points or positions: "I am taking corpus to mean both performative body acting out the discursive conditions of diaspora, as well as the body in circuitry within which subjects in a diasporic group must perform and embody multiple and connective lines of flight" (Patchett 52).

Diasporisation has long been a part of human civilisation and entailed the creation of multiple identities and affiliations. The intermingled condition of cultures opens up new routes and modes of speculation for the diasporic individual and collective identities which subvert the stereotyped experiences of uprootedness, displacement and dislocation. Diasporic situations inhabit liminal, interstitial spaces with an inter-subjective approach and outlook which reconstitute the dislocated diasporan as hyphenated, hybrid individuals. As different from the organic hybridity which is natural, it affects a self-reflective reshuffling of existing properties which is the result of negotiative contestation among its informing elements. The fluidity of identity is thus reaffirmed as a contingent upon the refigurement and reconfiguration of the displaced identity. As remarked by Stuart Hall, in "Cultural Identity and Diaspora", the diasporic sensibility is defined, not by essence or purity, but by the recognition of an evolving heterogeneity and diversity; hybrid and diaspora identities "are constantly producing and reproducing themselves anew, through transformation and difference" (58). Displaced and uprooted from a familiar engagement, the diasporans are suspended between a mutilated memory of the past and a desire to recreate new memories for the future by a discursive encounter with an incommensurable presence. They give an open outlet to these simmering fragmentations by a constant movement from reality to fiction to invent new realities of life. The Jewish philosopher Theodor Adorno astutely observes: "Every intellectual in emigration is, without exception, mutilated, and does well to acknowledge it to himself. His language is expropriated, and the historical dimension sapped. The isolation is made worse by the formation of closed and politically controlled groups, mistrustful of their members, hostile to these branded different" (33).

Paul Gilroy, in his discussion in *The Black Atlantic*, assumed epistemic centralities of diasporic theory and is convinced of the ceaseless process of transcultural becoming that is evolved as a result of enforced migration or otherwise (1-2). Gilroy conceived the position of the black Atlantic as a theoretical vehicle for an exclusively transnational and intercultural approach which thrives on the constitutive fluidity of being and becoming while emphasising the significance of 'routes' or dynamism of movement rather than one of 'roots' or originary establishment in a remote land of identification (Gilroy, *The Black* 87). The displacements, multiple dislocations and relocations challenge the traditional essentialist notion of cultural configurations as being fixed and unified, rooted in a specific cultural condition. By crossing the shadowed lines of delimiting borders, the diasporic individuals carry their transnationality to translate themselves into fresh cultural terrains of multiple possibilities in which identity is viewed as an evolving process of becoming. Through the metaphors of journey they conjure up new meanings for these cultural complexities, recasting the sensory realities in the fragmented universe of disparate histories, nationalities and cultures. Paul Gilroy's model of a ship is used as presenting this dynamic transitivity of evolving diasporic existence. Gilroy observes "the image of the ship—a living, micro cultural, micro political system in motion effectively captures the transnationality and intercultural relations, the exchange of ideas and activism" (*The Black* 24). This amalgamated sense of identification lands the diasporas in absolute placelessness which is amply reflected in their fictional projections that bear witness to this 'inbetweenness' or 'nowhereness'. The immigrant positions in this homeless conditionality struggle for a place in the new location which Uma Parameswaran describes in her paper "Contexualizing Diasporic Location" as a Trishanku-like existence in the liminality of space. Her allusion to the mythical king Trishanku, who stays suspended between heaven and earth for his ambivalent desires, invokes the image of a bifurcated locality as a symbol of diasporic disposition (195) as the individuals of diaspora want to locate a space that exists in ceaseless continuity as well as in "selected discontinuities" (Mishra 441).

Gilroy's description of the diaspora as a space "marked out by flows" ("Diaspora and the Detours of Identity" 328) implies the global dynamism of disparate 'flows' of peoples, cultures, ideals, and institution which is developed into an all-inclusive notion of cultural citizenship in the dramatic politicisation of transformative identity formation. As Gilroy puts it in "Diaspora and the Detours of Identity", diasporic consciousness "stands opposed to the distinctively modern structures and modes of power orchestrated by the institutional complexity of nation-states. Diaspora identification exists outside of and sometimes in opposition to the political norms and codes of modern citizenship" (328-29). The spatial configuration of the displaced thus rules out the possibility of a real returning desire in the diaspora studies and argues against the ethics of return to the homeland, seeking to promote the recreation of diverse cultural localities which requires a less stringent structure of relationship between dispersed communities and homelands. Dismissing the lure of the land from diasporisation, Stuart Hall opines that it does not have to invoke "those scattered tribes whose identity can only be secured in relation to some sacred homeland to which they must at all costs return" ("Cultural Identity" 57). Home is conceived not in terms of where one is from but rather where one's feet are. The diasporic dialectics thus rejects the notion of excessive emphasis on connection to the homeland and seeks to detach this idea from diaspora in favour of a non-essentialist narrativisation of longing, belonging and origination.

The older diasporas seek to sustain a remote relationship with the homeland even with the knowledge that such a return is near impossible which "remained frozen in the diasporic imagination as a sort of sacred site or symbol, almost like an idol of memory and imagination" (Paranjape, "Writing Across Boundaries" 243). The new diasporas, on the other hand, have least access to the homeland and develop a displaced anxiety of belongingness which is beautifully reflected in the works of the diasporic authors. They celebrate not only an imaginative recreation of the motherland, but also the justification of that diasporic displacement (Paranjape "Displaced Relation" 10).

According to Hall, diasporic identity formation constantly relies upon the acts of reproduction and transformation through difference and instead of being a site for relocation of an essentialised past, it opens up an immense possibility of cultural signification ("Cultural Identity" 55). Similarly, Samir Dayal in "Diaspora and Double Consciousness," traces the ambivalent allegiance of the individuals in the endless transformation and translation of the self; the assumed solidarity with the ancestral home on the one hand, and the summative sensibility of the desire for a new home on the other (54):

> There is a strategic value in cultivating a diasporic double consciousness. First, it affords an interstitial perspective on what it means to be, say, "British" or "American"—a perspective that allows for the emergence of excessive and differential meanings of "belonging" as well as "a parasitic" location (to use Rey Chow's term) ...entails an emancipation from a merely nationalistic or infranational pedagogical. Yet, it is not directed or "oriented" just towards the expressivity of the diasporic in the metropole. (47)

Focusing on the indeterminacy of the fluid positions held by the diasporic identities which disrupts the stable homology between racial, cultural and national identity, Bhabha contends that this self-reflexive hybridity is an "insurgent act of cultural translation" (*The Location* 7) which exists as subversive potential to unsettle the hegemony of power relations as it explores the multiple possibilities of cultural negotiations and contestations. Hybridity, thus, offers "an alternative organizing category for a new politics of representation which is informed by an awareness of diaspora and its contradictory, ambivalent and generative potential" (Bhabha, *The Location* 10). Avtar Brah highlights the overlapping commonality of diasporic negotiations:

> Diaspora space is the intersectionality of diaspora, border, and dislocation as a point of confluence of economic, political, cultural and psychic processes. It is where multiple subject positions are juxtaposed, contested, proclaimed and dissolved. (208)

Bhabha and Brah, in multiple ways, seek to expose the non-essentiality of the political content and historical specificity of diasporic positions and tend to equate this with a postmodern pastiche culture, pointing out to the 'diaspora space' as a highly contested site of cultural production which is relational and strictly anti-hierarchical:

> ... the point at which boundaries of inclusion and exclusion, of belonging and otherness, of 'us' and 'them' are contested ... diaspora space as a conceptual category is 'inhabited', not only by those who have migrated, but equally by those who are constructed and represented as indigenous ... the concept of diaspora space (as opposed to that of diaspora) includes the entanglement, the intertwining of the genealogies of dispersion with those of 'staying put'. (Brah 205)

Vertovec regards this kind of transgressed localisation as "multiple ties and interactions linking people or institutions across borders of nation states" ("Conceiving" 447). He explores the five areas through which transnational connections could be achieved: social morphology, kind of consciousness, mode of cultural reproduction, avenue of capital, site of political transaction and reformulation of home or locality (Vertovec, "Conceiving" 447). Crang, Dwyer, and Jackson describe about this conglomerated space which they elucidate as "constitutive of transnationality" (1) in which "different diasporas are characterised by different geographies that go beyond simple oppositions between the national and transnational, the rooted and routed, the territorial and the deterritorialised" (2).

Deluze and Guattari in *A Thousand Plateaus* recast this multiplicity of cultural representation with the rhizomatic theory of difference, turning away from the concept of conceptualisation in which the world is no longer viewed as being comprised of distinct entities—aggregative and integrative. Rather, the notion of difference becomes a condition for the possibility of phenomena: "Every phenomenon refers to an inequality by which it is conditioned. Every diversity and every change refers to a difference which is its sufficient reason. Everything which happens and everything which appears is correlated with orders of difference: differences of level, temperature, pressure, tension, potential, differences of intensity" (Deluze, *A Thousand* 222).

This possibility of reconceptualization takes us away from a signifying register to a signifying system where multiplicity becomes an essential condition for inverting the traditional representational paradigms and fixative enunciation. There is, therefore, no essence, no facts, but only interpretation—a fundamental insubstantiality, impermanence and reinterpretations of all phenomena. Simon O' Sullivan represents this multiple trajectivities inherent in cultural studies as rhizome, "a dynamic open system ... that changes its nature as the number of its dimensions increase" (88).

Diasporisation in this cultural praxis, far from being ossified, exists as possibilities of destratification. The cosmopolitan nomads have multiple locations, consolidations and affiliations, where "multiplicities are defined by the outside: by the abstract line, the flight or deterritorialization according to which they change in nature and connect with other multiplicities" (Deluze and Guattari, *A Thousand* 9). Deluze and Guattari do not present the rhizome and the root as incompatible dualities, rather it is the natural quality of rhizome to be broken and it is the nature of the root to ceaselessly produce rhizome: "A new rhizome may form in the heart of a tree, the hollow of a root, the crook of a branch or else it is a microscopic element of the root tree, a radical, that gets rhizome production going" (*A Thousand* 15). Diaspora, as a form of cultural studies, then involves exploring potentiality of becoming—the realisation of an existing entity of self-overcoming. As Sullivan argues: "as such the molecular—the rhizome—is a kind of guerrilla war against representation. A war with no winner and in which the taking of sides is always strategic and pragmatic" (92).

Diaspora, like rhizome, defies the dimensions of oversimplification—on one hand, it focuses on the lines of articulation of sedimentarity, strata and territories; on the other, it attends to the lines of flight, movements of deterritorialisation and destratification. Thus, it is the territorialisation which constantly replicates the possibilities for deterritorialisation.

Deluze and Guattari analyse this "principle of a signifying rupture" as set "against the oversignifying breaks separating structures or cutting across a single structure. A rhizome may be broken, shattered at a given spot, but it will start up again on one of its old lines, or on new lines" (Deluze and Guattari 9). Every rhizome, in this non-representational disruption, "contains lines of sedimentarity according to which it is stratified, territorialized, signified, attributed, etc. as well as lines of deterritorialization down which it constantly flees" (Deluze and Guattari 9). Arjun Appadurai further problematises the spread of culture across the globe by small groups and communities in an attempt to 'reproduce' themselves afresh and their cultural forms—"it is in this atmosphere that the invention of tradition (and of ethnicity, kinship and other identity markers) can become slippery" (44), where both points of departure and arrival are always in a constant flux. Rosemary Marangoly George's *The Politics of Home: Post Colonial Relocations and Twentieth Century* explores these multiple dimensions of home which transcend the stable physicality of belonging and becomes "an imagined location that can be more fixed in a mental landscape than in actual geography" (11). Davies, like George, analyses the representational politics of homemaking which is argued as a contested space for re-writing of the self in which the significance of writing 'home' is viewed as a critical connection in the articulation of identity:

> Migration creates the desire for home, which in turn produces the rewriting of home. Homesickness or homelessness, the rejection of home, become motivating factors in this rewriting. Home can only have meaning once one experiences a level of displacement from it. Still, home is contradictory, contested space, a locus for misrecognition and alienation. (84)

In reconfiguring the familiar dichotomy between 'roots' and 'routes,' Avtar Brah, in *Cartographies of Diaspora*, dissociates diaspora from the conceptualisation of homeland foundationalism arguing that it promotes "a critique of the discourse of fixed origins" (180) and dynamic intercultural relations. The reconceptualisation of 'home' and 'homing desire,' thus within this 'deterritorialised' framework, sees diasporic space as enabling the production and extension of new identities, subjectivities and affiliations that subvert the stability of nationalistic discourse. The second generation immigrant characters, as portrayed by Kazuo Ishiguro, Hanif Kureishi and Ramesh Gunesekera, for whom the homeland exists as a myth in the collective memory, is displaced by an assimilative acceptance of hybridity and multilocationality. Since the diasporic perceptions flow across the national and transnational boundaries, the people of diaspora develop an ontological episteme of existence that enable them to move beyond 'all home-making-projects' that claim essentialist configurations. The diasporic subjects are endowed with a double perspective of performative negotiation in translating the symbiosis between two mode of experiences which is reflected in their literary works as a "device to decode the epistemology of diaspora"—a diasporic imagination that appropriates 'reality' not in the mode of absolutist positions, but an ever-fluxing process of becoming coloured by heteroglosic and polyphonic overtones (Dalai 8).

Chapter 3

(De)constructing Diaspora: A Study in Composite Identities

> "Diaspora involves a radical ... redefinition of place. Simultaneously nowadays diaspora increasingly transcends place."
>
> —S.M. Stewart, "Citizenship and Belonging"

> "What we are never solve the problem of our conditions because we are always changing and becoming different."
>
> —Charles Taylor, *Sources of the Self*

> "One think of identity every time one is no longer sure where one feels at home.... 'Identity' is the name given to the search for an exit out of this uncertainty."
>
> —Zygmunt Bauman, *Life in Fragments*

Diaspora studies warrant a review of the notions of identity and belonging in the process of individuation which seeks to reformulate the attributes of 'home', relating it with the lived experience of the immigrant's consciousness. Composite identity formation, in this context, which is evolved as a result of diverse diasporisations, is a ceaseless process in which the diasporic individuals fail to streamline themselves in any of the cultures they have experienced before, triggering the emergence of a disconcerted space of multilocational belonging. The present chapter, in its essence, is an attempt to recapture these shifting cultural and transnational connections which impact and shape the framework of identity formation, subverting the fixed and stable notion of diasporic community that dramatically challenges the reductionist dialectics of methodical homogenisation.

The study seeks to deconstruct the dominant forms of fixity and boundedness within diasporic formations in the framework of transhistorical representations, generating a confluence of narratives reproduced through composite configuration of individuality which exists as a conducive condition for cultural translation and negotiation to conjure up ambivalent images of homeland as the need for reimagining the possibilities of belonging.

The term 'diaspora' carries multiple shades of meaning in the academic discourse today. In its most inclusive connotation it involves the displacement of numerous communities across the world from their original geographical location to another land elsewhere in the globe. The resulting spatial movements emphasise the centrality of the commitment to the homeland as a prime informing feature in the identity formation of the diasporic individual. The recent discussion on diaspora has strong affinity with the Jewish experience of collective dispersal from their homeland. The retentive collective consciousness of the community that results from such dislocation and displacement leads to the augmentation of a sense of homelessness which is a key concern in diaspora studies. The homeland/host land dichotomy developed in the classical model of diaspora by Safran in his article, "Diasporas in Modern Societies: Myths of Homeland and Return" revolves around the notion of ethnicity as a cementing factor in the reestablishment of commonality and solidarity among its members who tend to nourish a strong restorative memory of their ancestral homeland which is idealised in different ways as a connective link between their homing locations. Human history is thus replete with the horrors of displacement and endless quests for home in a new cosmo-cultural configuration. The dislocations and displacements with a keen 'homing desire' help develop in the diasporic subjects an urge to reproduce the way of life in a new setting that is elemental to their homeland which inaugurates in the diasporic consciousness a sense of utter rootlessness in the nostalgic recapitulation of a remote past.

The term diaspora juxtaposes two Greek words—'dia' meaning 'through' and 'speirein' meaning 'to scatter'—which evolves the sense of dispersion, historically applying it to the mass scattering of Jewish population around the world which is permeated with a messianic ideology of 'return'. Outlining the main characteristics of diaspora, Safran discusses a medley of collective sensibilities experienced by the diasporic subjects:

> (1) ... they, or their ancestors, have been dispersed from a specific original "center" to two or more "peripheral," or foreign, regions; (2) they retain a collective memory, vision, or myth about their original homeland—its physical location, history, and achievements; (3) they believe that they are not—and perhaps cannot be—fully accepted by their host society and therefore feel partly alienated and insulated from it; (4) they regard their ancestral homeland as their true, ideal home and as the place to which they or their descendants would (or should) eventually return—when conditions are appropriate; (5) they believe that they should, collectively, be committed to the maintenance or restoration of their original homeland and to its safety and prosperity; and (6) they continue to relate, personally or vicariously, to that homeland in one way or another, and their ethno-communal consciousness and solidarity are importantly defined by the existence of such a relationship. (83-84)

Pointing out to the ambiguity and lack of comprehensiveness in Safran's model of diaspora, Robin Cohen apparently adds three more characteristics into it when he suggests that diaspora in its basic disposition must involve, "a troubled relationship with host societies, suggesting a lack of acceptance at the least or the possibility that another calamity might befall the group" with a "sense of empathy and solidarity with co-ethnic members in other countries of settlement" and the "possibility of a distinctive yet creative and enriching life in host countries with a tolerance for pluralism (Cohen, "Diaspora and the Nation-State" 515).

Understanding diasporisation may, however, vary with different contextualisations within and between diasporas. The diasporic subjects tend to get assimilated into their new cultural ambience, but often associate to their dispersion a unique significance that registers an enduring allegiance to the dislocated past in their attempt to remain distinct from the 'institutionalised other'. The networks of relationships they try to evolve affect the adaptation of the usual patterns of identification of a particular ethnic community which are sternly grounded in a common awareness of primordial specificity such as religion, language, origination, etc. However, even with a strong assimilative process of adjustment and acculturation, it does not altogether entail a complete breaking free from the ideology of homeland orientation.

Diasporisation is not a homogeneous process and fluctuates from one community to another, depending upon their territorial, temporal and emotional orientations and diversifications. Robin Cohen distinguishes between the 'solid diaspora' which is indelibly marked by the myth of common origin and belonging, territorialised collectively in an ancestral homeland, and 'liquid diaspora' which is reconstructed through new cultural connections and mode of substitution in an endless process of representation (Cohen, "Solid, Ductile and Liquid" 125-27). Paul Gilroy, in this context, rightly observes:

> Diaspora identifies a relational network, characteristically produced by forced dispersal and reluctant scattering. It is not just a word of movement, though purposive, urgent movement is integral to it. Under this sign, push factors are a dominant influence. They make diaspora more than a vogueish synonym for peregrination or nomadism. ("Diaspora" 318)

The "current meaning of 'diaspora,'" according to Vertovec, concerns its manifestations in three dimensions namely—diaspora "as social form", as "type of consciousness" and as "mode of cultural production" ("Three Meanings of 'Diaspora'" 2). Diaspora, experienced as social form, involves a negative situation closely associated with "forced displacement, victimisation, alienation, loss" with an archetypal dream of return (Vertovec, "Three Meanings of 'Diaspora'" 2). These traits are connected with Armenian and African dislocations and other large-scale dispersions. Other common traits attributed to the social category of diasporisation which transcends the

Jewish model of diaspora include voluntary or forced migration, consciously maintaining a collective identity, institutionalising networks of transactive encounters, effectuating new communal organizations, sustaining ties with the homelands, evolving solidarity with members of same ethnicity and the "inability or unwillingness to be fully accepted by 'host society'—thereby fostering feelings of alienation, or exclusion, or superiority, or other kind of 'difference'" (Vertovec, "Three Meanings of 'Diaspora'" 3-4). The South Asian diasporic writers living in Britain often focus these traits in disparate ways to nourish this triadic social relationship between the ethnic groups, the location or conceptualisation of their residence and their ancestral homeland. Secondly, diaspora, as a type of consciousness, demonstrates "a variety of experience, a state of mind and a sense of identity" which create the awareness of multi-locality ... is comprised of ever-changing representations which provide an 'imaginary coherence' for a set of malleable identities" (Vertovec, "Three Meanings of 'Diaspora'" 8). Diaspora, in this form, leaves behind a trail of indelible memory collectively consolidated about another place that serves as creative impulses creating new cartographies of desire and attachment. Effectuated by a multi-spatial awareness, "the 'fractured memories' of diaspora consciousness produce(s) a multiplicities of histories, 'communities' and selves" which, instead of being a "schizophrenic deficit," redefines the identities of the diasporic individuals "as a source of adaptive strength" (Vertovec, "Three Meanings of 'Diaspora'" 9). Thus, both doubling and modification shape the minds of the diasporic individuals who seek to revive their identities from the mutilated memories of a cultural past that must be redefined with reference to a new culture they recently inhabit. This sensibility is grounded with a heightened awareness that the individual's own life and also the lives of others, are cumulatively shaped by culture as a represented heritage with "an awareness that whatever one, or anyone, does and thinks is intrinsically and distinctively culture-bound, and defined both in relation to one's own culture and the cultures of others" (Baumann, *Contesting Culture* 107). This mode of diasporisation as a type of consciousness, as rightly observed by Vertovec, is "variously described as being marked by a dual or paradoxical nature. It is constituted negatively by experiences of discrimination and exclusion; and positively by identification with a historical heritage" ("Three Meanings of 'Diaspora'" 8). Thirdly, diaspora as a mode of cultural production is reinstated in terms of an all-inclusive global cosmopolity that moves beyond the anthropological approach of dislocation in which diaspora is viewed as a global phenomenon of cross-cultural transformations:

> Also with reference to the questions of globalization, an interest in 'diaspora' has been equated with anthropology's now commonplace anti-essentialist, constructivist, and proccesual approach to ethnicity ... in this approach, the fluidity of constructed styles and identities among diasporic people is emphasized. These are evident in the production and reproduction of forms (increasingly the focus of interests in cultural studies) which are sometimes called syncretic, creolized, 'translated', 'cross over', 'cut 'n' mix' hybrid or 'alternate'. (Vertovec, "Three Meanings of 'Diaspora'" 9)

This diverse heterogeneity of diasporic discourse is remarkably demonstrated in the discursive writing of the Asian authors diasporised in Britain. The Asian immigrants come from different cultural backgrounds and have different religious affiliations and emotional orientations. They, in the process, however, are vigorously influenced by the Western mode of life and socio-linguistic institutions, constantly renovating their conception of identity through a transformative transaction with the lived reality as experienced by them. As Stuart Hall aptly remarks:

> The diaspora experience as I intend it here is defined not by essence or purity, but by the recognition of a necessary heterogeneity and diversing; by a conception of 'identity' which lives with and through, not despite, difference; by hybridity. Diaspora identities are those which are constantly producing and reproducing

> themselves anew, through transformation and difference. ("Cultural Identity" 52-53)

To map the diverse modalities and specificities of diaspora identity, one must attend to the different factors that determine the construction of identities in the specific contextualisation of its defining characteristics. Identity, as it is viewed is endlessly suspended between the desire for autonomy and the impulse for contextualising the mode of cultural production through a differential politics of assimilation. The meaning of 'home' for the diasporic individuals, which is the most informing principle of identification, then is a process and not a stable entity territorialised by place. Identity formation is an eternal process of translation or 'bearing across' that signals the "multi-locationality across geographical, cultural and psychic boundaries" (Brah 194) which exists ever-fluxingly in the diasporic consciousness as the "ambiguous and shifting ground" (Rushdie, *Imaginary Homelands* 15) on which new norms of cultural identifications can be erected:

> I suspect that there are times when the move seems wrong to us all, when we seem, to ourselves post-lapsarian men and women. We are Hindus who have crossed the black water, we are Muslims who eat pork and as a result—as my use of the Christian notion of the Fall indicates—we are now partly of the west. Our identity is at once plural and partial. Sometimes we feel that we straddle two cultures; at other times that we fall between two stools. (Rushdie, *Imaginary Homelands* 15)

Historicising identity formation, we may confront the essentialist philosophy of Rene Descartes which is expostulated in one of his most quoted pronouncements, "I think therefore I am" (qtd. in Ashcroft, Griffiths and Tiffin, *The Post-Colonial* 220) which attempts to stabilise the autonomy of the thinking individual. Individuality is quintessentially situated in the conscious mind as a unified being. This has been the most secure premise of the philosophy of Enlightenment which focuses upon fixed hierarchies and stable categorisation of the object—subject dichotomy. However, in the recent times, this concept is powerfully challenged by the seminal doctrines of Karl Marx, Sigmund Freud, Jacques Lacan and others. Marx is convinced of the importance of the economic structure which is at the base of all socio-cultural formations. Freud reveals the functions of the unconscious as determining factor in the conceptualisation of the self. Analogously, Lacan poses a dramatic challenge to the essentialist proposition of Descartes when he says, "I am where I think not" (qtd. in Lodge and Wood 200)—that is in the unconscious, Lacan reinforces the fluidity of the subjective position when he remarks that the "unconscious is structured like a language. The human mind, the chief agent, which interacts with the outer world in the process of identity formation, is thus claimed analogous with that of the discursivity of the language system. Similarly, Althusser notes that the individual is surrounded by a set of ideologies from the very beginning which is based on an imagined relationship evolved from the interaction of the individual with the real conditions of existence. Familiarity with the environment influences the ideologies of the individual in the integration of identity: "All ideology hails or interpolates concrete individuals as concrete objects" (47). Lacan, in his psychoanalytical model of 'Recognition' and 'Misrecognition', observes that the construction of identity involves a process in which identity is deliberately formed by recognising the self as different from other (Lacan 80). Derrida, in the most post-structuralist vein, emphasises the variable aspects of dynamicity in all modes of textuality, non-fixedness and the ambiguous nature of identity by pointing at the non-absolutist properties of these entities which posit the instability of the system of binaries and that the meaning is infinitely deferred in a web of indeterminacy (Brah 245). Assimilating the assumptions of the poststructuralists, discursive theory and ideological intellection on the notion of identity, Stuart Hall identifies the autonomy of the subjectivities as well as the set of discourses that surround the individual's life which define Identity theorem as:

> the meeting point ... between on the one hand, the discourses, and practices which attempt to 'interpellate', speak to us or hail us into place as subjects of social discourses, and on the other hand, the processes which

> produce subjectivities, which construct us as subjects which can be 'spoken'. Identities are thus points of temporary attachment to subject positions that discursive practices construct for us. ("Who Needs Identity" 5-6)

The notion of identity is ever contaminated with a tinge of non-essentiality which can never be affirmed as pre-determined and stable: "it is always a production of an image of identity and the transformation of the subject in assuming that image" (Bhabha, *The Location* 64). Stuart Hall seeks to subvert these essentialised constructions of identities in his essay, "New Ethnicities" and explains in terms of Black Britons—a term he derived to designate, British African, British Afro-Caribbean and British South Asian:

> ... the recognition that 'black' is essentially a politically and culturally constructed category, which can't be grounded in a set of fixed transcultural or transcendental racial categories and which therefore has no guarantees in nature. What this brings into play is the recognition of the immense diversity and differentiation of the historical and cultural experience of black subjects. ("New Ethnicities" 166)

The composite identities which are evolved as a result of diverse diasporisation is a ceaseless process in which the diasporic individual fails to streamline himself in any of the culture he has before experienced which effectuates the emergence of a 'third space': "the importance of hybridity is not to be able to trace two original moments from which the third emerges, rather hybridity to me is the 'third space' which enables other positions to emerge" (Bhabha, *The Location* 211). All Asian group identities in Britain are thus permeated with multiple journeys and meeting points which help them to recreate themselves in a range of diverse possibilities which interrogate the essentialised conceptualisation of group identities. As Brah contends, "...in their need to create new political identities, dominated groups will often appeal to bonds of common cultural experience in order to mobilize their constituency.... This will remain problematic if a challenge to one form of oppression leads to the reinforcement of another" (127).

Diasporic experience involves a heterogeneous identity formation which exists as a contested space of contextualised implications that develops among its members a sense of recognition of the shared commonalities which is lived and re-lived in multiple modalities in diasporic consciousness: "Diasporic journeys are embarked upon, lived and re-lived through multiple modalities, for example of gender, 'race', class, religion, language and generation. As such all diasporas are differentiated, heterogeneous, contested spaces, even as they are implicated in the construction of a common 'we'" (Brah 184).

Diaspora, then, is a stateless power functioning in transnational moments of fragmentation (Tololyan 18), comprising of communities of hybrid, 'in-between' identities positioned between host culture and culture of organisation, with a shifting conceptualisation of 'home' (Bhabha, *The Location* 148)—an open structure to be quested and re-quested beyond ethnic differences and through multi-dimensional relationships such as gender, class, race, power-relations, etc. Dalai, in *Poetics of Polyglossia in the Island Diaspora*, traces this composite identity formation which exists as an inherent tendency of reconstitutive perception from the time of colonisation to the recent phenomenon of globalised diasporisation that is described as "one among several enigmatic epistemologies of our times of diaspora. It is a complex, constant and constitutive aspect of human life (more so in our time) since the conception of modernity through colonization till the recent phenomenon of globalization" (8). Diaspora, with its labyrinthine model of discursivity, forms mobilised identities—manifest, multifaceted narrativisation and dialogic engagements that are located in a shared in-between space as a corrective direction to ethnocentric cultural practices. It questions the stabilised monolith of modernist certainties and absolutist construction of essentialised knowledge:

> In this manner they diffuse our critical demeanours through their hybrid and fragmented identities, which renders the multiplicity, mobility, and dynamicity of epistemologies not only conceivable but also inevitable.

> The creation of diasporic spaces allows creative improvisation as non-finite and dynamic locales for negotiating with difference, the 'self' and 'otherness'. The notion of Diaspora needs to be complicated as it entails an amalgamation of dispersion, memories, myths, alienation, nomadism, ongoing and hybrid identities, complex histories of dwelling and travelling, or in Clifford's words (1997), 'dwelling-in-travel'—all of which force us to rethink the rubric of our old concepts, monolithic discourse and epistemologies. (Abu-Shomar 3)

As dynamic spaces of contestation and nomadised dispersion, the notion of diaspora thus entails a textual and narrativitised confluence of diverse ideas and belief systems to subvert the traditional rubrics of fixity which proffers myriad, displaced sites of contestation to the hegemony and homogenising perception (Brazial and Mannur 2003).

The creation of these multiple diasporic possibilities proliferates into the general condition of human life which is not territorialised in a single place. This lure of revisionary deconstructivism also reflects the eluding and enigmatic conceptualisation of the term as a constitutive aspect of human life and belongingness. For this reason, Fernandez sees diaspora as a concept that works as a catalyst for interdisciplinary research pursuits which has the power to demonstrate and bridge the gap between theory and practice (6). Diaspora, in this epistemological dialectics, interrogates the very nexus between conceptualisation and condition, breaking free from the bounds of a closed system (Fernandez 6):

> ... diaspora can be managed meaningfully if we understand that it is in itself an open-source and that any attempt to limit its scope or its definition transgress the boundaries of both its conceptual and epistemological framing. Diaspora is derived from the idea of scattering of seeds. As such the concept must be allowed to take root, transplant, cross-fertilize, rather than fossilize. (Fernandez 7)

The concept of Diaspora, therefore, revolves round a duality, split or fragmented identities between multiple cultural references the diasporic subjectivities are exposed to, a "dual reference which affords immigrant subjects some individuality, the unique experience of immigration to individuals, created by the intersection of both structural and cultural conditions specific to a particular diaspora" (Collymore 11). Epistemological diasporisation, in this sense, evolves dual points of references between the homeland and the host land where all knowledge becomes constructs, effectuating a 'split-epistemology'. Thus, the multi-cultural domain of Asian diaspora in Britain works through a 'diasporic epistemology' of cultural contestation which Mishra believes to have exposed the redundancy of the cultural knowledge and other forms of hegimonising and ethnocentric modalities (Mishra 427). Clifford refers to this spatial virtuality as "contact zones of nations, cultures and regions" ("Diasporas" 303) that views diasporic perception as transitional connection between belonging and unbelonging, disrupting the fixity and fetishism imposed by ethnic systematisation of human objects.

As argued before, diasporic identities are diversely ambiguous and heterogeneous in its manifestation. The South-Asian subjectivities, even if having a shared ethnicity, differ remarkably in terms of their class, gender, profession, nationalistic and religious affiliations. The differences, even, are blown out of proportion resulting in the ambivalent diasporic identity formations. Ambivalence rules out the possibility of determinate meaningfulness because of simultaneous co-existence of similarity as well as differences. Discovery of the ambivalent representation effectuates the multifaceted heterogeneity of the diasporic positions for the coloniser's similarity to the colonised undermines the colonial authoritative discourse. Bhabha uses the term 'mimicry' to describe the complex relationship between the coloniser and the colonised in a range of cultural reproductions which are traceable as the "desire for a reformed recognizable other, *as a subject of a difference that is almost the same, but not quite*" (*The Location* 122). Bhabha observes that the coloniser wants the colonised to be very similar, yet different in multiple ways. Bhabha uses the term 'slippage' to elucidate the condition of difference which defer the colonised individual to completely merge in the host culture of the coloniser. The authoritative discourse of the colonial power-relations depends upon this partial recreation of the colonised subjects through the assemblage of contradictory forces and stances that stand in opposition to one another resulting in "mockery, where the reforming, civilizing mission is threatened by the displacing gaze of its disciplinary double" (Bhabha, *The Location* 123). The strong undercurrent of humanism generated by the post-enlightenment European discourse favours the colonised individual positively, crowning him with impulses to be like the native that is well-informed by the western ways of life. However, the colonial desire of the colonised to be like the coloniser is fraught with the ambit of ambivalence which undermines the essentialities of colonial authority:

> The discourse of mimicry is constructed around ambivalence; in order to be effective, mimicry must continually produce its slippage, its excess, its difference. The authority of that mode of colonial discourse that I have called mimicry is therefore stricken by indeterminacy: mimicry emerges as the representation of a difference that is itself a process of disavowal. (Bhabha, *The Location* 122)

The interplay of similarity and difference is then crucial in the transactive interactions of composite identities in which each identity with its diverse dimensions is both similar and different from other identities in the same diasporic group. The effect of 'slippage' or split between individual identities thus ambivalently leads to a 'mockery' of the unified, absolute notion of identity. Analogously enough, this slippage creates rooms for a hegemonic inversion of the unifiedly evolved diasporic culture and interrogates the subjective singularity of the British-Asian diasporic culture.

The multiple facts of differences are thus pivotal in the creation of meaning. Although differences are quite obvious in the field of political, social, religious and cultural domain, the most significant one is the race which is reflected in the eurocentric discourse of the so-called civilised world (Chatarji

20). The determined dichotomy and split between nature and culture is consequent upon this relational assumption of difference which empowers culture over nature as civilised forces controlling an unruly, savage and barbaric other which is encapsulated in the primary binary opposition of white/black:

> There is a powerful opposition between 'civilization' (white) and 'savagery' (black). There is an opposition between biological or bodily characteristics of the 'black' and 'white' races, polarized into their extreme opposites—each signifiers of an absolute difference between human 'types' or species. There are rich distinctions that are clustered around this supposed link, on the one hand, between the white 'races' and intellectual development—refinement, learning and knowledge, a belief in reason, the presence of developed institutions, formal government and law, and a 'civilized' restraint in their emotional, sexual and civic life, all of which are associated with 'culture'; and on the other hand, the link between the black 'races' and whatever is instinctual—the open expression of emotion and feeling rather than intellect, a lack of 'civilized refinement in sexual and social life, a reliance on custom and ritual and the lack of developed civil institutions, all of which are linked to Nature. (Hall, "The Spectacle" 243)

Socio-cultural differences are the prime markers of identity formation, and the radicalised other would always be different in this signifying differential philosophy of reproduction which is amply reflected in the literacy representation of the Asian diasporic writers in Britain:

> Sociocultural differences among human populations became subsumed with the identity of the individual human body. In the attempt to trace the line of determination between the biological and the social, the body became the totemic object, and its very visibility the evident articulation of nature and culture. (qtd. in Hall, "The Spectacle" 244)

Skin colour as the chief signifier, thus, results in the connotative fixation of traits and features in the reductionist process of differential signification. Bhabha, in a similar vein, cites the title of Frantz Fanon's seminal work *Black Skin, White Masks* as capturing this tension of differential signification in which skin color functions as having diverse implication in the formation of this fetish: "Skin, as the key signifier of cultural and racial difference in the stereotype is the most visible of fetishes, recognized as 'common knowledge' in a range of cultural, political and historical discourses" (*The Location* 112). Bhabha connects the stereotype of the colonised to the Lacanian imaginary phase of identification in which a child at the minor stage identities itself in terms of an alienating process based upon a perceived lack that "simultaneously alienating and hence potentially confrontational" (*The Location* 110), yet bridging the gap resulting from the lack to recreate a composite subjectivity through the methods of recognition, metaphorisation and substitution (*The Location* 110).

Hall questions this method of representation which is fundamentally driven by race/skin signification and attempts to evolve the "counter-strategies" ("The Spectacle" 269) to disrupt this preponderant representational praxis. Hall emphasises the non-fixedness of meaning and exposes the reductionist essentialism of stereotypical representations which are also subject to an ever changing transnational redefinition. Derrida's theory of différance and the dialogism of Bakhtin review the ways meanings are constructed through a range of non-absolutist possibilities which Stuart Hall referred to as "trans-coding"—a practice that offers a refurbishment of referentiality resorting to an infinite process of signification ("The Spectacle" 270). Diasporic identity, which is analogous to this tension, involves foregrounding the diverse or heterogeneous properties of individual identity as multifaceted, contextual and fluxingly dynamic. It demonstrates the discursivity of identity formations, exposing them to be mere 'constructs' composed of differential 'non-meanings'.

Stuart Hall thus seeks to reconstruct the approach to cultural identity and the conceptualisation of race and ethnicity which filters out the pitfalls of essentialism and stereotypical reductionism. The notion of diaspora appears as a way of rethinking and redefining the issue of black identity and extending its domain away from the concept of essential black subjects (Hall, "New Ethnicities" 190). The focus is on conditional positioning as "histories have their real, material and symbolic effects" (Hall, "Cultural Identity" 53).

The postmodernist model of diaspora connotes a condition rather than being definitive of a community. Not only this condition displays a strong proclivity towards multiple journeys and localisation, but also exhibits a subversive impulse of disrupting the boundaries of the binaries. It effectuates a differential redefinition of cultural accommodation and syncretism. The diasporic space is thus created by the transgressive border-crossing in this cultural amalgamation which points out to the danger of fixity and fetishism since "the intermediate spaces in-between subject-positions are loaded as the locale of the disruption and displacement of hegemonic colonial narratives of cultural structures and practices" (Meredith 2) which posits hybridity as the condition of an in-between third space which exists as the "cutting edge of translation and negotiation" (Bhabha, *The Location* 56). The third space in the cultural hybridisation evolves out a condition that combines cultural differences into recreative connections in a process of "amalgamation where the mind, conditioned by cross cultural contacts, can no longer acquires cultural authenticity or return to the pure past" (Sadiq 33). The substantiality of hybridity is thus re-asserted by the recreative third space which is presented as a mode of articulation in the performative politics of engendering reflective possibilities and exists as an "interruptive, interrogative and enunciative space of new forms of cultural meaning and production blurring the limitations of existing boundaries and calling into questions established categorizations of culture and identity" (qtd. in Meredith 3).

Diasporisation and hybridity then share the commonalities, the denial of the essentialist positions of home and belonging, purity and inherent authenticity of cultural formations. The metaphoric 'homelessness' becomes a questing urge for identity, to relocate the self in the essential 'I'. Diasporic hybridisation thus takes up the virtual 'third space' as an incontrovertible 'in-between' position that challenges fixity, authenticity and fetishism of cultural configuration.

The actualisation of 'self' as well as 'other' is believed to be constructs on the same ground and allows an unprecedented cosmopolitical nomadism which eternally dynamicises the idea of belonging and fixity:

> People belonging to such *culture of hybridity* have had to renounce the dream or ambition of rediscovering any kind of 'lost' cultural, purity or ethnic absolutism ... are not and will never be unified in the old sense, because they are irrecoverably the product of several interlocking histories and cultures, belong at one and the same time to several 'homes' (and to no one particular 'home') ... they must learn to inhabit at least two identities, to speak two cultural languages, to translate and negotiate between them. Cultures of hybridity are one of the distinctly novel types of identity produced in the era of late modernity, and there are more and more examples of them to be discovered. (Hall, "Fundamentalism, Diaspora" 630)

Diasporic consciousness thus recognises the significance of hybridity that seeks to bridge the gap between 'sameness' and 'difference', 'us' and 'them', 'here' and 'there', 'Asian' and 'Western' in a globalising world of complicated entanglements which cumulatively evolves "a gradual spectrum of mixed-up differences" (Geertz 148). The discourse of diaspora gradually gains currency in a postmodern globalised world which reshapes the economic and political tension and cultural erosion in the postmodern nation-state. In this "transnational moment" the growing assertiveness of the Asian diasporas in Britain reconfigure themselves as transnational subjectivities which makes the nation-states to "confront the extent to which their boundaries are porous and their ostensible homogeneity a multi-cultural heterogeneity" (Toloyan 5). Diaspora is viewed as having potentiality to subvert the constraints of national borders and boundaries and takes up transnational spatiality of diasporic imaginary as liberating impulse of deconstructing the essentiality of difference. "The nation-state is cast as the limiting, homogenizing, assimilating power structure, which is now, finally, being deconstructed from within by those groups who used to be marginalized within its borders but are now bursting out of them through their diasporic transnational connection" (Ang, "Together-in-difference" 3). The hybridised contextualisation of diasporic specificity confronts and further problematises the stable boundaries of a coherent community which signals the unsetting of stable identity formation. As such, the meeting point of the 'West' and the 'rest' is constantly frazzled with the inevitability of mistranslation, and misrepresentation and hence, the resulting intercultural tensions. "Hybridity is not the solution, but alert us to the difficulty of living with differences, their ultimately irreducible resistance to complete dissolution. In other words, hybridity is a heuristic device for analyzing complicated entanglement" (Ang, "Together-in-difference" 3). Contextualising Asian Diaspora in Britain, thus, involves a suspended in-between space which is neither essentially Asian nor authentically Western-embedded in a Western culturality, yet, exhibiting tendency of disengagement, disengaged from Asia, and yet emotionally connected to it. This hybrid, in-between positioning is an ambivalent ambit which re-inaugurates the multiple possibilities of cultural permeability. As Robert Young rightly observes, hybridity "is a key term in that whatever it emerges it suggests the impossibility of essentialism" (Young, *Colonial Desire* 27). Cultural theorists like Hall, Gilroy and Bhabha view this hybridity as inherent in each cultural formation as subversive tendency to bridge the gap between the 'self' and the 'other', the 'privileged' and the 'marginalised' the 'orient' and the 'occident' which critically develops the concept of 'Black British'—a position reflective of a hybridised enunciation, re-enacting a formula of self-actualisation and cultural representation which questions the essential whiteness of the British national identity by a general inversion of the idea of blackness. The hybrid dialectics of representation, then, is a strategic intervention "involving both a disarticulation of exclusionary conceptions of Britishness as essentially 'white' and its articulation as a necessary impure and plural formation that can no longer suppress the black other within" (Ang, "Together-in-difference" 9). The diasporan, therefore, learns to celebrate this spatial dynamics of hybridity as fusion which can be demonstrated as partial, incomplete and improbable as the relative ideological closure makes it near impossible to destabilise the difference which is hard to absorb or assimilate: it destabilises established cultural power relations between white and black, coloniser and colonised, centre and periphery, the "west" and the "rest", not through a mere inversion of these hierarchical dualisms, but by throwing into question these very binaries through a process of boundary-blurring transculturation (Ang, *On Not Speaking* 198).

This plurality of approach is favorable to the diasporic positions who are keen to evolve the potentiality to absorb differences into a new spatiality of cultural fusion and synthesis that carves out new meaning for diaspora and displacement which becomes an emphatic claim for transcultural reconfiguration breaking free from the clutch of reductionist normalisation (Lo 152) of the 'self' and the 'other'. The 'happy hybridity' that is created by this pluralistic hybridisation "has now to be seen not as a final destination, a distant horizon, but as one moment in a larger relation, permanently open to contestation, open to the moment when difference contests sites of normalized identity and demands a rearrangement of the terms, and perhaps ever the very *idiom*, of consensus" (Scott 298).

The idea of hybridity problematises further the contours of 'ethnicity' that is so important a notion in the diasporic discourses which is referred to as "the idea of naturalized group identity" (13) by Appadurai is not a combinatory culmination of the primordial concept of kinship but is contingent on the process of cultural displacement based on the dynamic process of differential mobilisation infused into articulating a group identity. Multiple ethnicities diasporised into Britain thus exert their impact either in the forms of official engagement and multiculturalism or in the imaginative process of reconstructive strategy as a means of overcoming the differences by a co-existential fluidity with many heterogeneous others. Diasporans are then "the globalized embodiments of such ethnicized imagined communities. The very ubiquity of ethnic claims today points to the apparent paradox of ethnicity's mobilising power in a thoroughly hybridized world" (Ang, "Together-in-difference" 10). It focuses on the differential sets of interests these communities have nourished in sustaining their 'real' or 'imagined' boundaries. However, this multicultural poetics of ethnicity is not always to be viewed as benign or emancipatory as Werbner has astutely observed: "Policy decisions, state fund allocations, racial murders, ethnic cleansing, anti-racist struggles, nationalist conflicts or revivals even genocide, follow on essentialist constructions of unitary, organic cultural collectivities" (Werbner 229).

In this socio-cultural innovative ambience, the fundamentalist tendencies of fatalism dwindle deep into nothingness and new rooms are created for a negotiative intercultural confrontation. The encounters are not always harmoniously constitutive and smoothly transacted across cultures, resulting in hybridised exchanges, journeys and mutual entanglements and disentanglements. What has been emphasised is the counter-balancing forces of diaspora against the absolutising properties of essentialist reductionism, generating the construction of porous, permeable and softened borders of interconnectivity in the vast spatial dialectics of intersectionality. The effect of diaspora is thus re-asserted in the hybridised metaphorisation of the displaced self in intersecting, overlapping positionalities. As Rita Felski cogently contends:

> Metaphors of hybridity and the like not only recognize differences within the subject, fracturing and complicating holistic notions of identity, but also address connections between subjects by recognizing affiliations, Cross-pollination, echoes and repetitions, thereby unseating difference from a position of absolute privilege. Instead of endorsing a drift towards ever greater atomization of identity, such metaphors allow us to conceive of multiple, interconnecting axes of affiliation and differentiation. (12)

Human history has long been a repetitive record of control, dominion and conquest. Eurocentrism, for instance, is a conscious practice of placing emphasis on European or

Western discourse at the expense of other which is fraught with endless distortion and misrepresentation of the oriental ways of life. Reality has been blown out of proportion and truth is produced and reproduced to circulate this occidental discourse for the benefit of the colonial power. From the very beginning of imperialism and colonialism, the native has been repainted with an indelible negativity by the settler or imperialists, condemning them to a curse of inferiority or immobility. The colonised people are made to survive in these utter constraints and confinement, reducing them to be homeless entities in their own land. Fanon laments this beatific negation of man, curtailing their liberty in the vicious anomalies of civilisation: "When I search for man I see only a succession of negations of man, and an avalanche of murder" (Fanon 252). Similarly Edward Said details the subtle mechanism of imperialism at work in British colonial systems to which literature and culture in general largely contributed. He lays bare the discursive and textualised construction of colonial meaning and the creation of structures of attitudes and impulses that normalise the monstrously depraved vision of the hegemonic colonialism (Said, *Culture and Imperialism* 42). Said attempts to explore the multiple modalities of cultural formations, postulating the dominant features of colonialism and imperialism as informing the practice of ruling remote territories from a distant centre:

> Neither imperialism nor colonialism is a simple act of accumulation and acquisition. Both are supported and perhaps even impelled by impressive ideological formations that includes notions that certain territories and people recognize and beseech domination, as well as forms of dominion...the vocabulary of classic nineteenth century imperial culture is plentiful with such words and concepts as 'interior' or 'subject races', 'subordinate peoples', 'dependency', 'expansion', and 'authority'. (*Culture and Imperialism* 8)

Europes's imperial ventures in the oriental, hypothetical East are then a disciplined project, "a Western style of dominating, restructuring and having authority over the orient" (Said, *Orientalism* 3) which is manifest in multiple proclivities towards exhibiting a lasting normalcy in these discourses of dominion to resist a class of civilisation. The notion of 'orient' is thus a mindless arbitration of Western civilisation as a cultural construct. The image of western culture or occidental identity is developed from this exclusive identification of itself as a super-culture which stands in opposition to the subordinated image of the oriental by identifying it to the immediate other. The imputed 'otherness' creates and confirms to the Western image. *The Empire Writes Back* by Ashcroft, Griffith and Tiffin is an intense metaphorisation of the oriental anxiety of reclamation to revive the sense of belonging and identification of the 'self' which has so far been obliterated by the colonial discourse of opposition and displacement. The poetics of place and the dialectics of displacement thus take a central position in the postcolonial and diaspora studies in a postmodern world. The new generation of diasporic writers such as Hanif Kureishi, Romesh Gunesekera, Salman Rushdie, Timothy Mo, Arundhati Roy, Kazuo Ishiguro, et al. are successful in integrating these diasporic tensions of transactive territoriality in their literary works to reinvent this colonial position in constructivist presentments. Such progressive inversion of ideological framing resituates the marginalised indisposed into a centrally operated ambience of equality which is regarded by Achebe as "the process of 're-storying' peoples who had been knocked silent by the trauma of all kinds of disposition" (79). Said moves a step further to identify these prejudiced propensities as resulting not only from a falsely implicated hegemonic influences, but the very discursivity of their positionality in the Western discourses as to how meaning is produced and reproduced through the distorting web of texuality itself.

Said here quotes Nietzsche's words about the multifarious properties of truth as being "a mobile army of metaphors, metonyms and anthropomorphisms ... which after long use seem firm, canonical and obligatory to a people: truths are illusions about which one has forgotten that this is what they are" (qtd. in Said, *Orientalism* 203).

Bakhtin, through his dialogic model of hybridisation, views this metalinguistic narrativisation as a process of textual unmasking of meaning through a 'double-styled' differential conceptualisation:

> ... there is no formal—compositional and syntactic—boundary between these utterances, styles, languages, belief systems; the division of voices and languages takes place within the limits of a single syntactic whole, often within the limits of a single sentence. It frequently happens that even one and the same word will belong simultaneously to two languages, two belief systems that interest in a hybrid construction—and consequently, the word has two contradictory meanings, two accents. (*The Dialogic Imagination* 304-05)

Bhaktin stresses the ways in which hybridised language carries profoundly new world views with new 'internal forms' in which they are not mixed, rather set dialogically against each other, effectuating a hybrid space of enunciative negotiation, resulting in a new speech act indicative of this discursive tension of doubleness:

> ... The hybrid is not only double voiced and double accented ... but is also double-languaged; for in it there are not only (and not even so much) two individual consciousnesses, two voices, two accents, as there are [doublings of] socio-linguistic consciousnesses, two epochs ... that come together and consciously fight it out on the territory of the utterance.... (*The Dialogic Imagination* 360)

Bakhtin's discursive doubleness thus provides a ground for cultural negotiation in the spatial dialectics of confliction and fusion. The idea of hybridity is evolved into a racial and cultural model of condition and intervention involving "an antithetical movement of coalescence and antagonism" (Young, *Colonial Desire* 22) which unites and fuses and also maintains a separatist displacement undermining the authoritative discourses of authenticity or singularity. In this differential politics of heterology the focus is shifted to the subversion of essentiality through the hybridisation of the post-colonial conditionality which reveals a strong undercurrent of ambivalent positionality in the traditional discourses on 'authority'. Bhabha seeks to recast these post-colonial tendencies with a hybridised model of interstitial in-betweenness which creates ground for the evolution of a liminal space that annihilates the temporality of representation and rewrite histories from an ever-fluxing mode of cultural and spatial plurality (*The Location* 5). Salman Rushdie commenting on his *The Satanic Verses* summarises this intermingled, mongrelised tension which in a similar vein cogently echoes the Bhabhasque dialectics of cross-cultural formations:

> *The Satanic Verses* celebrates hybridity, impurity, intermingling, the transformation that comes of new and unexpected combinations of human beings, cultures, ideas, politics, movies, songs. It rejoices in marginalization and tears the absolutism of the Pure. Melange, hotchpotch, a bit of this and a bit of that is how newness enters the world. It is great possibility that mass migration gives the world, and I have tried to embrace it. *The Satanic Verses* is for change-by-fusion, change-by-conjuring. It is a love-song to our mongrel selves. (*Imaginary Homelands* 394)

Thus, postcolonial diasporisation carries with it a critique of the centre, transmuting the lost time into an imputed space of cross-culturality and recognizes the mythic delusion attached to the idea of purity or essence. It challenges the Eurocentric model of reductionist stereotyping and demonstrates its power by replacing the syncretic presentation of the world with a hybridised space of multiple possibilities. The postmodern negotiative ambience does not, however, proceed through assimilation or collaboration but by an "interstitial" (*The Location* 3) entity as Bhabha argues which questions the very duality between these positions. It ruled out any form of binary presentment of the seemingly opposite categories and does not seek to register supremacy or sovereignty in cultural transactions. The position of hybridity thus reverses the structures of colonial dominion and promotes the emergence of a ground of intervention to reclaim its own identity and to revive the displaced moment of silence and suppression. This hybrid moment of cultural signification exhausts any differences between the binaries in which "the transformational value of change lies in the re-articulation, or translation, of elements that are neither the one (unitary working class) nor the other (the politics of gender) but something else besides which contests the terms and territories of both" (Bhabha 41).

A new hybridised cultural dynamics is thus evolved in contextualising the Asian diaspora in England which is suggestive of a transmutative cross-cultural ambit of transformation, necessitating not only a fusion, but also a dialectical articulation of that cultural or ethnic difference (Young, *Colonial Desire* 23). In this most subtle representation, it occupies a stance in which the minority cultures devise a language that is basically disruptive to the colonial dialectics and interrogative of the authority of dominance. Stuart Hall traces this discursive quality of these consciously sublayered meanings in the black literary tradition in Britain which points out to the revolutionary effects of hybridisation on contemporary culture. Hall in "New Ethnicities" records this shift in diasporic positions in the differential dialectics of black cultural formation in Britain when he claims that the term "Black" at the outset was applied to mean a range of shared experiences and marginalised positions and "Provide the organizing category of a new politics of resistance" (163) among the various displaced groups and communities having even disparate histories, traditions and ethnicities. It was a moment of evolving group identities based on homological commonalities which is constructed to counter the hegemonic discourses of imperiality. It facilitates "an organic hybridization" (Young, *Colonial Desire* 24) which can be set against as a strategy to contest the positional representation of black subjects by the literary and cultural practices of the Whites. This, however, according to Hall, effectuates the inauguration of a new mode of representation which involves an understanding of their experience as necessarily "a diaspora experience" which carries with it a condition "for the process of unsettling recombination, hybridization and 'cut and mix'—in short, the process of cultural diaspora-ization" to which it thrives upon (Hall, "New Ethnicities" 165). Analogously, Kobena Mercer in

"Diaspora culture and Dialogic Imagination" points out to the inherent tension of dialogic tendency traceable in black visual mode of representation. There is a dynamic virtuality at work which "critically *appropriates* elements from the master-codes of the dominant culture and 'creolizes' them, disarticulating given signs and re-articulating their symbolic meaning otherwise" (Mercer, "Diaspora Culture" 57). Hybridity in this spatial domain of culturation simultaneously functions in two ways: it works 'originally' as a hegemonising impulse creating new spaces, scenes and structures and 'intentionality' as a diasporising discursivity which introduces the metaphors of intervention as forms of subversion, translation and transformation (Young, *Colonial Desire* 25). This new evolving position which Bhabha calls a hybrid space, a third space of communication and translation is closely associated with the dialectics of 'home' and 'belonging' and relates to the homeless positionality of the diasporic existence. Certainly, Bhabha is not speaking of an independent syncretised third space, already existent as enticing entity, but a medium of negotiating cultural differences which has to be acknowledged in each and every kind of exclusivist dialectics: "Culture does imply difference, but the differences now are no longer, if you wish, taxonomical; they are interactive and refractive" (qtd. in Bhabha, "The Third Space" 221).

The doubleness of representation is thus pivotal in the hybridised positions which diasporic individuals assume to themselves. Its multiple movements and moments of disjunctive ruptures reveal the redundancy of those cultural theorists who seek to define race, ethnicity and culture as pure, fixed and essential. Its dialectical positions indicate the replicative repetition which they resort to, with an incipient "raceless Chaos" (Young, *Colonial Desire* 25) loosed upon these displaced positionalities. Hybridisation as such "produces no stable new form but rather something closer to Bhabha's restless, uneasy, interstitial hybridity: a radical heterogeneity, discontinuity, the permanent revolution of forms" (Young, *Colonial Desire* 25). This position itself, in turn, is never absolute and exists in a temporal virtuality mostly on the liminal borders and in the border crossing between cultures. In this differential conditionality which is utterly anti-reductionist and anti-essentialist, meaning and values are not codified in absolutist entities but is replicated, misrepresented and illusively adopted through the discontinuous process of translation and negotiation (Bhabha, *The Location* 38). Thus, in this ambit of negotiative translation, former ethnic communities translate their traditional identities and value systems into western mode of multiple cultural representations and new hybrid identities emerge through the cultural reorientation and reconfiguration of former colonial communities.

Hybridity, thus creates a 'third space' "which enables other positions to emerge" (Bhabha, "The Third Space" 211). Hybridity then becomes a key structural device to annihilate the essentiality of all structural representations which favour multiple cultures to merge and cohere yet celebrating the differences exacerbated by its incipient liminality:

> 'We' all require "culture", but let us cultivate (colere) a culture of self-differentiation, of differing with itself, where 'identity' is an effect of difference, rather than cultivating 'colonies' (also from colere) of the same in a culture of identity which gathers itself to itself in common defense against the other. (Caputo 115)

Homi Bhabha contends that all cultural juxtapositions and transactions are constructed in a space that he refers to as "the third space of the enunciation" (*The Location* 38) and that cultural identity emerges in this ambivalent spatiality and the recognition of it creates opportunities for multiple cross-culturations. Bhabha argues against the essentialising tendency of the third world countries and claims that all sense of nationhood as a fixed entity is narrativised. Bhabha traces an undercurrent of the effect of colonialism manifested in the nation's history and culture which intrudes upon the transformative dialectics of the displaced individuals. Instead of viewing colonisation as a ground for dominance and opposition he sees it as a site of complex cross-cultural relations and intersections. He highlights the ways in which the West is perturbed by its inevitable double, the East. The emergence of this double creates an anxiety in the West to redefine its identity and to relocate its rational self-image in an age of cosmopolitical nomadism and widespread globalisation. To be precise, the Western civilisation is not unique and superior to any other civilisation in the globe, and that cultural meanings are always open to re-interpretation and re-definition. The individual position in this ambit of territoriality is subject to transformation and reconfiguration of the inner landscape. The incongruity between the delusion of difference and the reality of sameness, between the coloniser and the colonised lead to the creation of a gap in colonial discourse which can be used as a counterbalance to resist colonial oppression and marginalisation. Bhabha in *The Location of Culture* evolves many concepts like hybridity, mimicry, interstice, liminality, etc. to undermine the dichotomy between the self and the other and between the homeland and the host land. Sailing away from the Western metaphysics of polarised reductionism, he advocates a dialectical realignment of the basic systems of cultural analysis through a "performative" (*The Location* 148) and enunciatory (177) re-evolution of their fundamental categories. Bhabha seeks to destabilise the implementation of binary oppositions, to liberate these basics from the strangleholds of tradition in which cultures can be seen as interacting, transgressing and transforming in complex ways with one another in an ever-fluxing mode of permeable spatiality (*The Location* 51). Bhabha claims that 'hybridity' and 'linguistic multi-vocality has the power to disrupt the conditions of coloniality which has so far been interpreted in terms of political discourses. He, therefore, uses terms like mimicry, liminality, interstice and hybridity to say that "cultural production is always most productive where it is most ambivalent" (qtd. in Al-Taee 10). Bhabha believes that the colonial positionality arises as a result of the transactive encounter between the coloniser's white conditionality and the colonised's apparent black differentiality. In this dialectics of difference and semblance, the colonial subject is excepted to confirm to an objectification of an image that is reductively created by the coloniser which produced neither compete identities nor well-defined differences. Thus, the postcolonial individual is torn between mimicking and mockery to occupy a hybridised space in the liminal interstitiality which is "but the effect of a flawed colonial mimesis in which to be anglicized is emphatically not to be English" (Bhabha, *The Location* 125). Whereas in Bakhtinian system of hybridisation, it subverts the strict homology and univocality of authorial discourse, in Bhabha, hybridity not only projects the enunciative conditionality of coloniality but also creates rooms for counteracting colonial resistance. It stresses the "transformational value of change" (*The Location* 125) which is reflected in the re-articulation and translation of properties that are situated in an in-between intersectionality defying fixed denominatives, but always exist in suspended proximities, contesting the ideas and ideals of both. Ania Loomba in *Colonialism/Post Colonialism* insightfully narrates Bhabha's conceptualisation of the hybrid:

> It is Homi Bhabha's usage of the concept of hybridity that has been the most influential and controversial within recent Postcolonial studies. Bhabha goes back to Fanon to suggest that liminality and hybridity are necessary attributes of 'the' colonial condition. For Fanon, you will recall, psychic trauma results when the colonial subject realizes that he can never attain the whiteness, he has been taught to desire, to shed the blackness that he has learnt to devalue. Bhabha amplifies this to suggest that colonial identities are always a matter of flux and agony. 'It is always', writes Bhabha in an essay about Fanon's importance in our time, 'in relation to the place of the Other that colonial desire is articulated'. (148)

Bhabha's model of ambivalent positionality is suggestive of the West's inability to replicate its own image perfectly among the eastern subjects. The black skin/white mask imagism modelled upon the oppressive ideology of the occident, therefore, elicits multiple interrogations about the suggestive conceptualisation of the mask/skin dicotomy as to whether it indicates hybridity or a violated authenticity. The incommensurable presence of the colonial identity is then ambivalent, a contested space of rupture and subversion which effectuates a permanent split between appearance and reality and its enunciation as repetition and difference.

Bhabha's concept of hybridity questions the very purity and essence of culture that has no discreet phenomena of representation and in which culture itself becomes an attempt towards fixity. The borderline cultures of in-between spaces are forever contested as claiming diversity in a supposedly singular culturality. Bhabha's conceptualisation of hybridity can thus be cited as answering Spivak's question "can the subaltern speak" in affirmative. The 'marginal' have spoken and reasserted their identity in the mode of cultural hybridity which can be served as a powerful instrument to undercut the age-old disparity between the 'West' and the 'rest'. This concept of hybridisation is further extended to include diasporic displacements and other forms of translocations over the globe. Christopher Bracken thus cogently summarises the hybrid project of Bhabha:

> For Bhabha, the human subject is not grounded in a fixed identity but rather is a discursive effect generated in the act of enunciation. When migrants, refugees and the decolonized take up positions in Western discourse, they divide it from itself by repeating it and creating a clear space within it for new, hybrid subjectivities. The hybrid post-colonial subject negotiates the interstices of Western discursive systems, operating in between the dichotomies of colonizer and colonized, self-other, East and West. Once a mode of Western discourse is altered through repetition, moreover, it loses its "westness" and exposes itself to difference. Iteration is therefore a way of translating between cultures. It opens the possibility of an international culture of hybridity generated through discursive activity. (506)

Stuart Hall, like Bhabha, analyses cultural identity as a relational and interactive entity: "... fluid, contigent, multiple and shifting" (McLeod 225) which can be contrasted with the 'border lives' of Bhabha in which concepts are continuously overlapping, hybridized in shifting subjectivities that promotes the "possibility and necessity of creating a new culture" (Mercer, *Welcome to the Jungle* 4). Hall's idea of 'new ethnicities' facilitates a shifting, fluid position which can overthrow the myth of essentialist representation. However, it is crucial to recognize as McLeod argues that these new spaces should not be mistaken with the kind of "postmodern playground of 'anything goes', where all kinds of identities are equally valuable and available as if in a 'multicultural supermarket'" (McLeod 225). It is important not to overlook the troublesome politics of diaspora identities when promoting their possibilites (McLeod 225-26).

In these diasporic moments of post-coloniality, displacement and exilic movements become emblematic of the fissured, fragmented identities and hybrid subjectivities generated by colonial translocations. In diasporic and postcolonial studies, therefore, concepts such as hybridity, mimicry, ambivalence have become debatable issues. The celebration of hybridity and its assimilating tendencies negate the imbalance and disparity of the power relations and hierarchical systematicity of culturation. As Leela Gandhi contends, "the West remains the privileged meeting ground for all ostensible cross-cultural conversations" (136). Robert Young regards this hybrid space as an influential weapon of discursivity to de-historicise temporal and territorial essentiality of colonial discourse. But Bhabha like Fanon argues that hybridity is a necessary condition of coloniality. Cultural identity reconfigures itself in this ambivalent space of enunciation in which there is no hierarchical systematisation, and the colonial presence registers a permanent split between reality as authentic and authoritative and textuality as repetition and difference. Bhabha remarks that this colonial presence doesn't perpetuate a distinction between 'self' and 'other', the home culture and the host culture but the 'self' and its 'doubles', "a mother culture and its bastards" (*The Location* 150) which downplays the politics of polarisation because whatever is disavowed must be re-enacted in the hybrid space of ambivalence.

Similarly, mimicry or the repetitive mode of enunciation is an active weapon of hybridity that is keen on subverting the colonial discourse of dominion. It is a tactical perpetuation of colonial power and intellection by the coloniser. It is taken as a desire for a reformed and recognisable other as "a subject of difference that is almost the same but not quite" (Bhabha, *The Location* 86). This anxiety of ambivalence is a repetition with difference which is permanently tainted with a desire for the double and to be more effective: "mimicry must continually produce its slippage, its excess, its differences" (Bhabha, *The Location* 86). The civilising mission of the English people doesn't effectuate slavish imitation of the essential Westernities, but an "ambivalent mixture of deference and disobedience" (Gandhi 145-50) which involves a deliberate blurring of the gap between apparent authenticity and mis-translation. Christopher Bracken cites a bright example of these ambivalent structures operating upon the colonial discourses of the evolving relationship between Britain and India:

> Their discourse foresaw a colonized mimic who would be almost the same as the colonist but not quite. However, since India's mimicry of the English blurred the boundary between the rulers and ruled, the dream of anglicizing Indians threatened to Indianite Englishness—a reversal the colonists found intolerable. Mimicry is therefore a state of ambivalence to isolate the racialized essence of either the colonized or the colonizer. (506)

When the coloniser's desire enacts an encouragement for mimicking the values, assumptions and ideologies of the colonist by the colonised, the reproduction is never a linear one but is infested with a menacing tendency of disruption inadvertently suspended between analogy and disparity. Mimicry, therefore, explains the fluctuating intersectionality between two cultures undermining the sustained pretensions of colonialism and imperialism. We can perceive the irrelevance of the collusive commitment of Macaulay's reductionist educational project in India in his famous pronouncement in 1835: "We must at present do our best to form a class who may be interpreters between us and the millions whom we govern; a class of person, Indian in blood and colour but English in taste, in opinions, in morals, in intellect" (qtd. in McLeod 141). Mimicry unsettles this authoritarian discourse of replicative narrativity and proffers a double vision—a multi-layered notion of recognition in the process of self-actualisation. As Bhabha argues "hybridity is the introduction of cultural relativism or synthesized position resolving the dialectic of two cultures but a return of the content and form of colonial authority that 'terrorizes' authority with the ruse of recognition, its mimicry, its mockery" (*The Location* 115). Mimicry then is an exaggerated version of realistic presentation subverting the ideologies of ideation effectuated by the act of re-writing, replication and mimicked representation of reality in which the identity of the subjectivities are constantly slipping away, reproducing and re-inventing themselves in an eternal enterprise of substitution and metonymic representation:

> The native subject often appears to observe the political and semantic imperatives of colonial discourse. But at the same time, she systematically mispresents the foundational assumptions of this discourse by articulating it. In effect, mimicry inheres in the necessary and multiple acts of translation which oversee the passage from colonial vocabulary to its anti-colonial usage. In other words, 'mimicry' inaugurates the process of anti-colonial self-differentiation through the logic of in-appropriate appropriation. (Gandhi 149-50)

Neutralising thus the claim of culture, Benhabib develops a complex model of dialogic culturality, subverting the strict internal homology of culture. She pleads for a "radical hybridity and polyvocality of all culture" and considers them as "multilayered, decentred and fractured system of action and significations" (26) re-enacting a permeable pattern of cultural representation where hybridity turns into a non-instrumental ground for inverting the exclusionary politics of essentialism:

> ... hybridity turns into a difference-erasing concept, negating the foreignness of the foreigner, the otherness of the other. Indeed, this capacity to 'normalize' cultural difference, and thereby to neutralize the political claims of culture, explains its appeal: it subverts any normatively compelling non-instrumental grounds for preserving cultural differences and rescuing endangered cultural resources. Thus for those political theorists whose skepticism towards the political claims of culture inclines them to frame those claims as requiring

> citizens of multicultural democracies to choice between their 'rights' and their culture ... hybridity is the ideal conceptual tool for neutralizing those claims. (Kompridis 322)

Bhabha's model of postcolonial hybridity doesn't move towards a criticism of the influence of modernity of traditionality, rather it stands as a resistance for the inbound disarticulation and exposes identity as ambiguous. Bhabha seems to be in line with Lee who argues that the substantiality of transformation "lies in the intersections and interstices of process beyond the nation-state that have their own global infrastructure. Hybrid spaces created by diasporic migrations are inhabited by bilingual and bicultural resident nomads who move between one public sphere and another" (Lee 174).

Home, for these diasporic individuals becomes narrativised with a sense of loss, and which can be reinvented imaginatively but incompletely in the intensified imagism of the homeland that helps to "control the terror and the chaos of liminality" (Naficy 128). Hybridity thus creates a critique of the status quo in which ambivalence can be viewed both as strength and a weakness. The function of boundaries then is to promote differences and the recognition of hybridism dissipates differences. Hybridity can be used as a weapon to dissolute boundaries which is found to be a precondition of developing difference (Lamont and Molnar 187). Similarly, Newman remarks that hybrid identities are formed when boundaries get converted into frontiers when diverse cultural communities interact with one another. The hybrid consciousness thus proceeds with an ambiguous structure and challenges the "hegemonic definitions of belonging which still privilege identification, recognition and exclusion of the other" (Rosello 6) that re-conceptualises the process of ideation and identification involving a critique of all forms of exclusionary totality and rejects the boundary logic of hyphenated and pure identities (Eriksen 234).

Bhabha was convinced of the discursivity of the nationhood as a mode of belonging. He, therefore, introduces into the ideation of the nationhood the pulses of a performative 'in-betweenness'—a boundary-blurring phenomenon—that redefine nation as 'pure' narration:

> The linear equivalence of event and idea that historicism proposes, most commonly signifies a people, a nation, or a national culture as an empirical sociological category or a holistic cultural entity. However, the narrative and psychological force that nationness brings to bear on cultural production and political projection is the effects of the ambivalence of the 'nation' as a narrative strategy. As an apparatus of symbolic power, it produces a continual slippage of categories, like sexuality, class affiliation, territorial paranoia, or 'cultural difference' in the act of writing the nation. What is displaced in this displacement and repetition of terms is the nation as the measures of the liminality of cultural modernity. (*The Location* 140)

Bhabha thus encourages a rigorous revolution of these trans-national discursivities, recasting them in an ambivalent spatiality of colonial contestation—a "'liminal space' in which cultural differences articulate ... actually produce imagined 'constructions'" of cultural and national identity (qtd. in Phan 45).

In exciting ways, he attempts to revolutionise the concept of hybridity and liminal spatiality problematising it further with the complicated collusivity of psychoanalysis and the postmodernist notion of mimicry. In this differential mutability, identity is reborn from "the great history of the languages and landscapes of migration and diaspora" (Bhabha, *The Location* 235). Bhabha envisions the border as a site eternally infested with a duality of disproportionate combinations, creating in-between contrary homelands. In this intermediate positionality, new complex forms of narrativisation reappear, disrupted by the possibility of cross-culturation:

> ... living at the border, at the edge, requires a new 'art of the present'. This depends upon embracing the contrary logic of the border and using it to rethink the dominant ways we represent things like history, identity

> and community. Borders are important thresholds, full of contradictions and ambivalence. They both separate and join different places. They are immediate locations where one contemplates moving beyond the barrier. (McLeod 217)

Bhabha thus engages the enunciation of a negotiative philosophy which attacks the assumptions that cultures are holistic and disconnected entities of essentialist representations. Hence, identities cannot be "ascribed to pre-given, irreducible, scripted, ahistorical cultural traits that define the conventions of ethnicity" (Graves, "Homi K. Bhabha: The Liminal"). Instead, one must recognise the porous permeability of cultural borders which addresses the "heterogeneous array of signs in modern life and the various ways of living with difference" (Papastergiadis 192) transcending the boundaries of cultural and historical tradition.

Chapter 4

Rethinking Englishness: Multiculturalism and the Politics of Belonging

> "Englishness paradoxically became most itself when it was far off ... best performed far from home, a global identity into which others could always translate themselves."
>
> —Robert J.C. Young, *The Idea of English Ethnicity*

> "... if national identity is understood as an effect of discourse, national identity in a national culture can never achieve the unified homogeneity it wishes for itself."
>
> —Anthony Easthope,
> *Englishness and National Culture*

> "... all cultures are involved in one another; none is single and pure, all are hybrid, heterogeneous, extraordinarily differentiated and unmonolithic."
>
> —Edward Said, *Culture and Imperialism*

The notion of Englishness defies any fixed framework of cultural representation which in the course of time has enlarged itself to include a medley of disparate culturalities and discursive possibilities. The idea of a multicultural society challenges the homogenising premise of essentialist identification with its diversified heterogeneous accommodations, pointing out to a summative erosion of the legacy of the Empire and its exclusively nationalistic connotations. As a post-imperialist nation, England is fast losing its hold on the faltering myth of Englishness and its sense of coherent national identity, making rooms for a large number of non-English populace at different levels of identification and belonging. The chapter thus seeks to demonstrate the ways in which England with its cosmopolitan inclusivity, manages to reinvent itself, nourishing a common culture of fragmented loyalties and affiliations, created out of the multiple movements and cross-connectivities of migration and multicultural realities.

What is Englishness? There is no familiar response to this specific culturality as Englishness has become an eluding concept in the discourse of nationality and belonging. It is because the English have always been reluctant to provide a well-defined definition of Englishness. The quest for a quintessential elementality of Englishness has thus become a common question in the cultural and literary discourses of the diasporic world which has continually informed and influenced the national life of England with multiple journeys and homing practices. Affected by the disparate consequences of decolonisation, diasporic migrations and an increasingly multicultural cosmopolity, the social life of England is fast changing resulting in the development of a more inclusive and diversified Englishness that acknowledges the identities of all its people living in a post-imperialist multicultural Britain.

In the contemporary world, no nation can exclusively be designated as a specific point of origin, transit and destination as almost all nation are affected by the multiple and varied experience of globalising diasporisation. The migrants crossing the borders from a familiar territory and settling in some alien ambience register a sense of unbelonging, and nourish an urge to redefine their inner selves and to reinvent their respective 'homes' in an estranged territoriality. Though displacement and dislocations are performed for varied reasons, they have historically strengthened and reshaped the social cohesion as well as enriched the cultural lives of the people living in this amalgamated totality. England in this context has become one of the diasporic centers of migration to which people from erstwhile colonies migrate for better prospects of their lives.

England with its geographical and cultural spaces seeks to evolve a "new world order" (Farrior 403) in which there is scope for the immigrants to reconfigure their identities, resisting the power structures and dominant ideologies of race and ethnicity and explore possibilities for a happy multicultural existence and relationships. This opens up an undeterred discourse about the irrelevance of the old Eurocentric model of representations, reorienting it towards a new world of multicultural belonging that is ordered around multiple movements and negotiations. This discursive turn effectuates a globalising space which is found to be productively in a constant flux.

Englishness then becomes a constructed concept that lingers in the ritualistic grammar of England as a post-imperialist nation in its multicultural presentment which needs to be redefined in transnational and intercultural perspectives. To be specific, England has had Black and Asian population for over four hundred years which is as old as the history of the Empire abroad. It is worth mentioning says Susheila Nasta in *Home Truths: Fictions of the South Asian Diaspora in Britain* that "Britain was as much the home of the colonial encounter as the colonies themselves normally situated abroad in the so-called peripheries" (2). She astutely remarks that the historians like Burton, Fryer and Visram have successfully argued that the Black and Asian immigrants' arrival in Britain for generations in the moments of decolonisation and after independence was not simply the residue of the end of the empire but was the culmination of a long but often hidden relationship, a relationship that has persistently been written out of the nation's politico-cultural and literary histories (2). The substantial presence of the Black and Asian population in Britain during the years following the Second World War thus challenged the "embedded conceptions of Englishness" which is viewed as an "imagined homeland" grounded on the "ideas of purity, rootedness and cultural dominance" and exposes "the less palatable realities underlying the ancient myth of England as a green and pleasant land" (Nasta 2).

Many cultural critics have pointed out that the myth of homogeneity attached to the idea of Britain as a nation was both a result of the imperialist agenda and the evolution of a Eurocentric modernity that was unable to catch the true spirit of an inevitable immigrant past. At this critical juncture, the essentialist myth of Englishness is long endured but exists with an intercultural divergency and racial mixture that heterologically informed the British life. For the last few centuries, "Englishness has often been constructed as a heterogeneous, conflictual composite of contrary elements, an identity which is not identical with itself" that focalises the inner dissonance of the ruptured self of England divided within itself for it cannot be represented and characterised by "an essential core identity from which the other is excluded" and it is this non-fixedness that "enabled it to be variously and counteractively constructed" (Young, *Colonial Desire* 3). As Susheila Nasta has rightfully observes:

> Britain will inevitably become a polarized cultural territory, an embattled space where difference signified by race, colour or ethnicity is forced into makeshift 'ghettos' on the edges of the nation. Moreover, the 'homes' of those living in such spaces necessarily become temporal and temporary in the xenophobic imaginary of the white population, no-go areas on derelict estates, which contrast with the supposedly 'fixed' landscapes of Anglo-English settlement in the suburban Home Countries. (3)

Nasta quotes Caryl Philips who sarcastically laments the dissolution of a once great colonial power Britain who "always sought to define its people.... By identifying those who don't belong" (qtd. in Nasta 3). Thus, the Asian migrants in Britain have to face the inherent problematics of belonging and challenge the existing cartographies of Englishness by creating rooms for an all-inclusive spatiality which embraces the logic of coherent cultural acceptability and representation:

> For in a post-imperial nation that, by the end of 20th century, was fast losing its grip on any sense of a coherent national identity, the presence of these others within exposed the underside not only the faltering myth of Empire and its waning fantasy of an invented

> 'Englishness', but also complicated the apparently seamless history of western modernity itself. (Nasta 6)

Thus, the diasporic presence in Britain needs to be redefined in relation to the shifting notions and contours of Englishness in the elusive terrain of belonging and multicultural existence. The fixity of the boundaries is to be reconfigured in a progressive model of inclusivity which is contingent on the frequent and deliberate erosion of the nation by the diasporic communities in Britain. The "invented tradition" (Nasta 3) of Englishness then can be seen as necessary development of an organic integration of these diasporic Black and Asian communities to a central phenomenon of belongingness:

> For the walls of Britain as 'island nation' have consistently been eroded and reconfigured by the uncovering of a more permeable and diasporic geography, a geography which both contradicts and complicates the comfortable nationalist binaries of home and abroad, and provides an alternative reading of ways in which the bases of modernity have most frequently been conceptualised. Moreover the voyages in of Britain's post-colonial subjects ... have consistently drawn the attention of cultural critics to the liberatory, transgressive and shape-shifting elements of being 'unhoused', redefining the terms and opening up the reductive prescriptions of essentialist ideologies, whatever their racial or cultural derivations. As a result, the narrow agenda of Britain's domestic policy of cultural containment has been progressively deconstructed. (Nasta 3-4)

Anderson in *Imagined Communities* describes nationality as a "cultural artifact" that is indelibly influenced by specific historical and cultural contexts and is "capable of being transplanted" in a variety of cultural contexts derived from a range of nostalgic cross connections to an idealised temporality and territoriality (4). The notion of Englishness is rooted in the

19th century imperialist ideology which attempts to define its spirit in the form of a common belief in a national identity that depends upon a "unity of identity and purpose" (Brooker and Widdowson 141). To invoke the notion of national belonging, terms like 'England' or 'Englishness' is deliberately worked out into play in the cultural and literary cartographies of representation to inaugurate and illustrate a specific spirit of Englishness. One of the stock representations in the period is built on the image of the 'gentleman' which is said to represent the quintessential characteristics of Englishness: "... it is impossible to think of the character of England without thinking also of the character of a 'gentleman' who is modeled on a bunch of refined civic qualities—"a code of conduct—good from the not doing of things which are not done: reverse: a habit of understatement" (Giles and Middleton 59) which is well-exploited by Kazuo Ishiguro in his novel, *The Remains of the Day* in the form of a dignified butler affecting a concentrated form of exclusionist Englishness:

> It is sometimes said that butlers only truly exist in England. Other countries, whatever title is actually used, have only manservants.... Continentals are unable to be butlers because they are as a breed incapable of the emotional restraint which only the English race are capable of.... In a word, 'dignity' is beyond such persons. We English have an important advantage over foreigners in this respect and it is for this reason that when you think of a great butler, he is bound, almost by definition, to be an Englishman. (43)

The Victorian youngsters were strongly guided and educated to feel themselves "as exemplars of a civilized society—perhaps the only civilized society" (West 8). This involves a sense of culture and civilisation around which the concept of Englishness is constructed. Similarly, Silvia Mergenthal defines Englishness as a construct which "does not reflect a preestablished 'reality'", but a "discursive field, in which various groups of individuals are identified as 'English' on the basis of (historically variable) attributions" (Mergenthal 24).

Examining the issue of national identity in the historic temporality, Paul Langford argues that the coinage of the term is of relatively recent origin which but doesn't entail that the idea of nationality has not existed before (1). The "great foundational moment of Englishness" can however be traced back to a period between 1650 and 1700 (Easthope 28). Before identifying as having a distinct national awareness which is held in contradiction to an overall British identity at the outset of 20th century, the English rather identified themselves in term of regional localities and "thought of themselves as either locals or cosmopolitans" (Kumar, *The Making* 120). Perception of Englishness thus differs within the specific culture and locality, their lived experience of the physicality of the land as evolving into the national character as Kumar states:

> Englishness embodied the aspiration and self-images of a particular section of society for much of the time, those of the dominant upper and upper-middle classes. It was their politics, their church, their sports, their manners and ways of speaking ... their view of history that provided much of the content of the 'national character.' ("Englishness" 53)

Englishness then is not a well-defined term having clear-cut premises of conceptualisation but rather was linked to the civilising project of imperialism as the English would take pride in their inevitable role as empire-builders (Kumar, *The Making* 11). Featherstone chalked out the ways in which Englishness became to be associated with the images and metaphors of the traditional, rural and Idyllic England, happily permeated with its vigorous landscapes. Literature and other visual modes of representation tried to catch this spirit of Englishness, creating and disseminating their exclusive images of English landscapes connected to this original idea of national identity in the construction and rebranding of Englishness in the late 1990 (Featherstone 17). Englishness can be felt more vigorously in the signifying images of the rural background, an "idealized rural landscape in which England is figured as a pastoral Eden" (Giles and Middleton 34). This rural experience of England's elementalities in 20th century was increasingly restricted to an English elitist minority occupying country houses and estates which exist as symbolising the demeaning magnificence of England as an Empire. Ishiguro's *The Remains of the Day* for instance, exemplify this nostalgic reconfiguration of Englishness, in the words of the narrator-protagonist Mr. Stevens: "a good accent and command of language, general knowledge on wide-ranging topics such as falconing or newt-mating" (35) are essential features of a distinguished person professing Englishness.

After the end of Second World War and the dissolution of British Empire, a new world order emerges in Britain which seeks to reconstitute the rigid socio-cultural systems, inverting the traditional conception of Englishness by introducing to it a permeable pattern of re-discovering the self and national identification. Caryl Philips summarises these new ideals as belonging to 'a new world order' in which everyone is viewed as equal, a part and parcel of the globalising territory they inhabit:

> The New World. A twenty-first century world. A world in which it is impossible to resist the claims of the migrant, the asylum seeker or the refugee.... The old static order, in which one people speaks down to another, lesser, people is dead. The colonial, or postcolonial, model has collapsed. In its place we have a new world order in which there will soon be one global conversation with limited participation open to all, and full participation available to none. In this new world nobody will feel fully at home.... In this new world order of the twenty-first century we are all being dealt with an ambiguous hand, one which may eventually help us to accept the dignity which informs the limited participation of the migrant, the asylum speaker, on the refugee. (*A New World* 5-6)

Caryl Philips feels that the multiple migrations from different corners of the world to Britain has not only enhanced the nation but also effectuated a transformational poetics of heterogeneous belonging in which social, political and cultural landscapes are eroded and inverted by other groups of people, staging a multicultural model of identification. In the contemporary world, nations are in search of ways to forge new discourses of belonging to address and include these 'foreign elements' in the core culturality. Philips is attentive to his own diasporic condition of displacement as having experienced the trauma of racial discrimination and ethnic prejudices ever since his transportation from Caribbean: "I still felt like a transplanted tree that had failed to take root in foreign soil" (*A New World* 9). Arjun Appadurai thus focuses on the creation of an "ethnoscape" which he described as "the landscape of people who constitute the shifting world in which we live: tourists, immigrants, refugees, exiles, guestworkers and other moving groups and persons constitute an essential feature of the world and appear to affect the politics of (and between) nations to a hitherto unprecedented degree" (33). Appadurai, however, doesn't fail to recognise the inherent relative stability of the communities and groups, but he is particularly interested in the multiple movements and journeys there diasporas make which point out to an anxiety which they feel in their mind desiring to twist these stabilised connections and constructions. Europe's imperialist ventures and the history of colonisation rather act as one of the disruptive forces which destabilise such group cohesion and communal proximities. Gayatri Spivak, in her paper "Diasporas Old and New" distinguishes between two kinds of historical displacements—the old diaspora and the new diaspora (Spivak 246). The old diaspora can be seen as a result of slavery and indentured labour, trade, conquest and economic migration within Europe itself and the new diaspora, which however, is the representative of Eurocentric movement across the world transformed the ways in which individuals form their sense of identification, regenerating a new lifestyle, a new reality infused with ceaseless mobility, cross-border movements, creating new terrains of cultural representations (Spivak, "Diasporas Old and New" 246-47). Hence, all claims for a stable, homogeneous national belongingness are rejected as a result of the multiple transnational dispersion and diffusive reconstruction. The migrated communities to England rather strengthen the economy of the state and contribute to the nation-building yet they are significantly excluded from the centre merely for the racial and ethnic variation. Caryl Phillips thus observes in *The European Tribe* that "Europe is blinded by her past, does not understand the high price of her churches, art galleries and architecture" (128). Paul Gilroy, analogously, undermines the role of England in colonialism and attacks the iconic Englishness of an imperial reality:

> We are all, no doubt, fond things which appear unique to our national culture—queuing perhaps or, the sound of leather on willow. What must be sacrificed is the language of British nationalism which is stained with the memory of imperial greatness. What must be challenged is the way that these apparently unique customs and practices are understood as expressions of a pure and homogeneous nationality. (*There Ain't No Black* 69)

The fact that British nation has always emphasised the civic rather than an ethnic framework also explains the ways in which many Black and Asian British individuals who were born and bred in England have been absorbed into the centrality of Englishness and think themselves to be hyphenated British; i.e. 'Black British' or 'British Asian' and sometimes Britons.

In the latter half of the 20th century, the population of England underwent many significant changes as a result of the growing number of immigrants. Migration from the former British colonies and other nationalities makes the English world emergently diversified and challenges the ethnic make-up of the nation that has formerly for most part been white (Weedon 27). The postcolonial displacements and dislocations create a new space for cultural diversity and cross-cultural negotiation that makes the nation of fixed national identity seem unstable and problematic (Head 199). England in this fertile ambience of multiculturality is subject to a series of changes in the reproduction of its quintessential Englishness. Because the narrative of national unity is open to the diverse forms of representation and cultural diversity, each modern nation becomes a cultural hybrid. Cultural intermixing further is intensified due to mass mobilisation of electronics and informatics worldwide and the process of globalisation (Barker 255). Bhabha in *Nation and Narration* argues that nation as an idea is culturally compulsive to the "impossible unity of the nation as a symbolic force" (Introduction 5). The foundational functions of a nation in this differential discursivity are unable to define its explicit premises where "the origins of national traditions turn out to be as much acts of affiliation and establishment as they are moments of disavowal, displacement, exclusion and cultural contestation" (Bhabha, Introduction 5).

Critics have argued that English national identity has been shaped and continually transformed by the history of British imperiality, and English culture has been developed as a cumulative cultural encounter between the British and the non-British as a result of the imperial pursuits of Britain. The cultural encounters between and with the colonial 'other' promote a dialectic framework in which the same cultural condition is being replayed in the British home ground which used to be a reality in the former colonies. As Gilroy has convincingly argued: "... the immigrants is now here because Britain, Europe, was once out there, that basic fact of global history is not usually deniable" (*Postcolonial Melancholia* 100). Gilroy further identifies the presence of an undercurrent of Eurocentric discourse in the exclusionary practices of Britain which tends to resist the cohesivity of ethnic transactions. Gilroy's anxiety can be represented as an urge to reconceptualise the multiethnic, multicultural and postcolonial relations of Britain to its signified 'others': "Today, any open stance towards otherness appears old-fashioned, new-agey, and quaintly ethnocentric. We have been made acutely aware of the limitations placed upon the twentieth century's cosmopolitan hopes by the inability to conceptualize multicultural and postcolonial relations as anything other than risk and jeopardy" (Gilroy, *Postcolonial Melancholia* 4).

Kumar, reinforcing an inversion of the imperial attitude of the West, argues that it is worthwhile to "see English national identity as a kind of residue; the response to and the result of England's engagement with its imperial venture, and of its perception of its mission in the world" ("'Englishness'" 44). Stuart Hall in "Conclusion: The Multicultural Question" explains how Britishness is historically formed and can be seen as an "empty signifier, the norm, against which 'difference' (ethnicity) is measured" (221). As Hall observes, "the continuous intercourse with 'difference', which was at the heart of colonization has framed the 'other' as a constitutive element of British identity" ("Conclusion" 218). Hall believes that English identity is based on the concept of nation(al) and racial others and Englishness is the projection of that quality of being different from other as a racially dominant entity ("Conclusion" 218). Therefore, 'race' is only applied to those who are not white as whiteness is regarded and privileged as a prime signifier which is said to function as the "human form" (Dyer 1). Analogously, Brah posits that while the effects of class, gender, race, sexuality is experienced alike both by the white and black communities, "racialization of white subjectivity is often not manifestly apparent to white groups because 'white' is a signifier of dominance" (105).

In his seminal book *There Ain't No Black in the Union Jack,* Paul Gilroy discovers the inherent waves of incompatibility between the black and the white people living in Britain and the manner it marks the evolution of the image of the black which is formed historically as a source of all negativities (Pines 58). Jim Pines reflects upon the title of the book which symbolises the white dominance over black in England and points out to the apparent irreconcilability of both categories as the flag is closely associated with the political far-sight (58).

The flag as an emblem of the nation's invented tradition helps the formation of a national cohesivity in term of racial similarity (McLeod 70). The diasporans to England brought with them their various cultural practices and introduce to the life of England a new form of representation which necessarily clash with the kind of life the white were living. They embrace an anti-normative life and thus posed a threat to the once homogeneous, traditional English way of life and thus, "the process of national decline was presented as coinciding with the dilution of once homogeneous and continuous national stock by alien strains" (Gilroy, *There Ain't No Black* 45-46). The traditional English social order is disrupted by the inflow of diverse migrants into Britain which generates a new reality by reshaping the old values of English society with novel progressive form. The cultural 'others' represented by Black community acts as a "real presence and cultural threat to the personal image of England" (Gikandi 70). The developing complicacy of antithetical politicisation between blackness and Englishness is clearly reflected in the racist discourses and the ideologies of the political history of Britain which is aptly summarised by Gilroy in *The Black Atlantic*: "Nationalism and racism become so clearly identified that to speak of the nation is to speak automatically in racially exclusive terms. Blackness and Englishness are constructed as incompatible, mutually exclusive identities. To speak of the British or English people is to speak of the *white* people" (27-28).

Tilley and Heath outline the ways in which the modern age is especially vulnerable to a diminishing sense of the value of nationalism in Western countries. The effects of globalisation and economic transactions around the world have greatly influenced the formation of traditional national identities and demonstrate a marked decline of interest in national pride (Tilley and Heath 662). Tilley and Heath, however, are attentive to the past image of Britain and attempt to recollect the spirit of cultural diversity in Britain which has always been an inseparable feature of Englishness:

> Britain's constructed national identity was built in the course of the eighteenth and the early nineteenth centuries on conflict with the 'other' of Catholic France, on the common project of the British Empire with its economic and military successes and opportunities and on shared protestant religious and cultural traditions.... More recently the foundation of the welfare state has been a major sense of pride and perhaps in a literal as well as metaphorical sense of social cohesion. (662)

In contemporary England, an uncomplicated conceptualisation of Englishness is hard to form owing to the intensity and frequency of migration which have become an unbreakable reality of the evolving Englishness. England which has been held in reverence as a "precious stone set in the silver sea" (Gervais xiii) has now become nostalgic of its hey days of imperial magnificence but despite its problematic proclivities, Englishness is asserted in the popular culture of the present-day England. Featherstone eloquently summarises this process as:

> ... partly explained by a historical willingness to subordinate national expression to broader domestic

> and global structures of colonial and imperial power. Such a process has also led to the absence of cultural imperatives that shaped the intellectual foundation of other national relatives in the United Kingdom. England has no threatened indigenous language such as Welsh or Gaelic; it has no urgent need to record and preserve residual social formations or traditional cultures that might encode national identities; and it acknowledges no tradition of resistance to an outside cultural hegemony that is represented in the United Kingdom itself. (3)

Britain, in its new cultural configuration at present, as Nyman remarks, develops a porous, permeable model of representative culturation which replaces the old system of Englishness as an exclusive notion by an all-inclusive pattern of mutual adjustment and collaboration:

> The belief in the British race and nation as embodiment of the national character has been called into question, and different constructions of British identities have emerged—terms such as Black British and British Asian now challenge the traditional division into the four traditional ethnicities. Similarly, the increased migration from the Commonwealth and former Dominions since the 1950s and contemporary immigration from various part of Europe has called into question migration policies and notions of citizenship that can no longer be based on racial basis. (Nyman 47)

Nyman's construction of Englishness comprises several layers of complication—one of them is the differential relationship between the notion of Englishness and that of Britishness. Krishan Kumar in this connection argues that the notional tension between the two terms is instrumental in the figurative constructions of Englishness. The non-white members of Britain are more apprehensive of the gap between these two concepts than the native people of the island because they are especially attentive to "the lordly English habit of subsuming British under English" (Kumar, "'Englishness'" 41) which provides a solid ground to perpetuate the hegemonic discourse of Englishness over the British Isles. Kumar argues against the exclusionary politics of Englishness which tend to view "all the major events and achievements of national life as English" in which other minority "ethnic groups are brought on in minor or supporting roles" ("'Englishness'" 41-42). Nyman argues that 'Englishness' is pregnant with a variety of meaning which can be contextualised corresponding to specific historical movements and moments of mass mobilisation. Literature in this moment of anxiety was used to reshape and re-integrate the values of Englishness "to function as the backbone of the nation and [became] a superior subject that promotes both moral development and reproduces imagining of nationhood" (Nyman 30). Literature then becomes an inevitable medium to facilitate an easy imagining of the idealised images of England as representing the green innocence of the rural and the pastoral which stand in opposition to the degenerated traditional images of Englishness as representing the urban, sophisticated spaces of the city (Nyman 30). Thus, the idealised images of England, perpetuated by the ethnic representative of the nation along with the narrativisation of Englishness amidst notable re-imagining of the English elementalities, cumulatively help evolve the image of England as the leader of the British Empire (Nyman 33).

The overlapping and intersectional tension between Blackness and Englishness can be clearly understood in the racist representative model of British political discourses of the 1950s. The new immigrant presence is seen as a possible threat to the homogeneity of ethnic Britishness and its essentialism which is quite evident in the views of the conservative party member Enoch Powell. Gikandi says that Powell's engagement aspires to brand black subjects as the largest potential threat to the English nationality without citing the consequences of the British imperiality which generates this black presence in Britain (Gikandi 71). Powell believes the British to be ethnically superior to its differential 'others' and Englishness is viewed as a space of "tradition and national excellence" that is to be preserved against the racially inferior 'others' whose cultural values are at odd with the authentic Englishness (Nyman 2). Powell thus prepares a ground for a permanent dichotomy between the English and the non-English, between the formal, political membership to a nation with reference to the legality of the law of migration and "the more substantive membership which derives from the historic ties of language, custom and Race" (Gilroy, *There Ain't No Black* 46). Similarly, Margaret Thatcher, the former Prime Minister of Britain who came to power in 1979 effectuated a reworking of the contours of Englishness in which the preservation of the "English way of life" was emphasised as against the fear of the "alien culture" which informed the general life of Britain (Brah 37). The declaration of the policy statement of the conservative party in 1980 clearly reveals the inherent contradiction that disrupts the definition of British nationality: "Future immigration policies if they are to be sensible, realistic and fair must be founded on a separate citizenship of the UK and it is therefore essential that a reformed law of nationality should, for the first time, make clear who are the citizens of the UK" (qtd. in Layton-Henry 191). Reflecting upon the narrowness of these contradictory versions of Englishness Nyman argues for the "need to revise the once exclusive notion of Englishness into a more inclusive direction" (47) which involves hyphenated, hybrid identity construction such as British Asian, Black British, etc. which challenge and subvert the traditional concept of ethnicity and becomes an emphatic claim for a multicultural Britain. Pines describes this complicated relationships as producing a new form of cultural identity that can be termed as Black Britishness or even Black Englishness in which "identity is coterminous with a reinvented idea of England which has been struggling to (re)define its own sense of national identity" (65) to realise its suspended authenticity in a fast-forming globalised world.

The supposedly homogeneous combination of a nation then is a myth which can never be translated into reality. As Robin points out, "the imagined unity of the [English] nation has always struggled to cope with actual diversity and difference" (486) that is suggestive of a movement from the nationalistic to an urban framework of representation, in this case, the city of London as the centre of global transactive interactions which replace the traditional model of cultural cohesiveness with a hybrid system of multiple projectivities (Robin 486-

87). The city of London then can interestingly be represented as having dual function and is viewed as a metaphor for the nation that incubates new cultural formations, disrupting the old forms of stabilised cultural formation. London as the home of many disparate ethnicities becomes multifarious and multi-dimensional in its referentiality and while 'nation' proffers "stability and continuity the city offers important possibilities for cultural unsettling and transformation" (Robin 491).

New forms of belonging are thus evolved from this multicultural reality represented by metropolitan city life in which new modes of identification and belonging are carried out and the reconstruction of this Englishness as Byrne argues "involved imagination of openness, as cosmopolitanism and vibrancy" which is the hallmark of an English society (152).

The ideal of the empire that takes Britain to new heights, the greatness that begins to be closely associated with this power and ideology and then following the dissolution of that magnificence during the colonisation, the major part of which is largely the result of the Britain's victory over the Nazis in Second World War, constitute significant markers of history in the formation of the traditional master narrative of British identity. In this crucial juncture, the lesser disruptive forces of the empire are totally overlooked at the expense of the most significant achievement of the nation as empire staging a victory over the evil Nazis which reasserts the greatness of the British. The contemporary Britain is now thus left with that historical greatness as empire builder—monumental and relicing a lost sense of Englishness. To what level, then, this discourse of Englishness can take precedence in the contemporary construction of British identity, therefore, is a burning question to respond to in the ambience of a multiethnic and multicultural demography.

What constitute Englishness then is overloaded highly with provocative and contested questions in a densely multicultural society like Britain where identities are overlapped and posed in intersectional referentialities in the 21st century world.

Trevor Philips, the Chairperson of the Equality and Human Rights commission believes that multiculturalism leads to a resulting segregation of the communities so far that monocultures co-exist together with minimal interactive engagements. He thus perpetuates a re-inculcation of British belief and values in the immigrant communities which he describes as being British. The civilising mission of Britain is thus translated in this enforced Englishness, "belief in democracy and the rule of law" as being the basic beauty of Britishness ("UK/Race Chief Wants Integration Push"). The commission thus summatively transforms the essential features of Englishness into ambiguous political projections, rejecting the heterogeneous notion of British identities. It fails to integrate the unifying, cultural elements of the ethnic 'others' which permeates the British national identification today. Trevor Philips, in an interview with the BBC, mentions Shakespeare whom the nation has lost as a literary icon which he interprets as a loss particularly "bad for immigrants" ("UK/Race Chief Wants Integration Push"). The mention of Shakespeare in this context points out to a literary canon which moves beyond the political realm and dialectically centers on the same ground of cultural representation. Said, in *Culture and Imperialism*, traces such a framework of cultural identification in which narratives of belonging are modelled on the views of these literary masters. They serve as the building blocks of British literary history and cultural identity and legitimise the normalcy of the imperialist pursuits. This, in turn, analogously sanctioned the British supremacy over other ethnicities. Colonialism and imperialism together laid the foundation of a strictly hierarchical society in which the skin colour can be viewed as an important marker of identification and which can be explained in term of a poetics of inclusion and exclusion. The relic of the empire is still evident in everyday British life as a commuter of the racist ideology of dominion. Catherine Hall attempts to explore these imperial images of England which is still obvious in the common life of contemporary Britain:

> The buildings which offer material reminders of imperial connections, the Banks of England and the Royal Exchange symbolizing the financial centre of the globe, the reliefs of Africans' heads with elephants

> on the facade of the Liverpool Exchange marking the significance of the slave trade to that city's wealth, the great museums of London, packed with imperial treasures, the Hyderabad Barracks of Colchester reminding us of the links between Britain and India, the West India Dock Company's elegant building just by Canary Wharf, once the meeting place of slave traders and sugar merchants, now the site of refurbished flats for city folks. The streets of every town mark historic battles and moments, from Trafalgar to Mafeking, profoundly shaped by imperial expansion and danger. The novels which form national literature, from Jane Austen's *Mansfield Park*, an English country home financed by sugar plantations of Antigua, to Charles Dickens's unfinished novel *The Mystery of Edwin Drood*, touched with racial fear engendered by the "Indian Mutiny" of 1857 when "natives" serving in the British Army rebelled against their colonial masters. The quintessential national beverage, tea imported from Ceylon and India, the demand for it changing the shape of whole regions as tea gardens were laid out, the sugar served with it which transformed the British Caribbean islands into gigantic sugar mill, and changed the economy and society of Africa and the Caribbean forever. (27-28)

Addressing to the Fabian society in January 2006, Prime Minister Gordon Brown defines his concept of Britishness which focuses on the shared values and collaborative togetherness for a common purpose:

> If we look to the future I want to argue that our success as Great Britain, our ability to meet and master not just the challenges of a global economy, but also the international, demographic, constitutional and social changes ahead and even the security challenges, require us to rediscover and build from our history and apply on our time the shared values that gird us together and give us common purpose. ("Speech to the Fabian" Para 10)

A sense of nostalgia for the Empire thus still remains to be of utmost significance for the British cultural life; where as many of the systems of belief have not yet been questioned and reconceptualised. Stuart Ward advocates a probing into the reactions to decolonisation as the first attempt to decipher the dialectics of imperial ideology. The various visions of the decolonising process promulgated by different historians and cultural theorists are each a "relatively benign issue in post-war culture" (1-2).

The decolonizing process which begins after Britain's victory over the Nazis in the Second World War results in the gradual diminishing of British power on the world stage. Britain's former supremacy as the mightiest empire is overshadowed by the growing importance of America and Soviet Union who rise to become super power controlling the most dominant power structures of the world. In his *Anatomy of Britain,* Antony Samson argues in favour of this idea of a disintegrated Britishness which informs the life of the Britons after World War II which crumbles the cultural fabric of Britain:

> A loss of dynamic and purpose and a general bewilderment, are felt by many people, both at the top and the bottom in Britain today.... It is hardly surprising that, in the twenty years since the war, Britain should have felt confused about her purpose—with those acres of red on the map dwindling, the mission of the war dissolving, and the whole imperial mythology of battleships, governors and generals gone forever. (qtd. in Ward 8)

This persistence and obsessive reiteration of the glorious past with a deliberate allusive referentially of the British victory over the Nazis is beautifully summarised by Paul Gilroy in the context of a British multicultural reality:

> I think there is something neurotic about Britain's continued citation of the anti-Nazi war. Making in a privileged point of entry into national identity and self-understanding reveals a desire to find a way back to the point where national culture—operating on a more

> manageable scale of community and social life—was, irrespective of the suffering involved in the conflict, both comprehensible and habitable. The memory of the country at war against foes who are simply, tidily, and uncomplicatedly evil, has recently acquired the status of an ethnic myth. It explains not only how the nation remade it-self through war and victory but can also be understood as a rejection of deferral of its present problems. That process is driven by the need to get back to the place or moment before the country lost its moral and cultural bearing. Neither the appeal of homogeneity nor the antipathy towards immigrants and strangers who represent the involution of national culture can be separated from the underlying hunger for reorientation. Turning back in this direction is also a turning away from the perceived dangers of pluralism and from the irreversible fact of multiculture. (*Postcolonial Melancholia* 89-90)

The breakdown of the British Empire is a major event in both the national and personal lives of the Britishers. The Government of Ireland by 1920 proceeds on the idea of Republic of Ireland and seeks to govern itself (Leese 18) which is a major blow to the national politics of Britain. To make the matter worse, after the World War II, scarcity of food and coal makes people go cold and hungry, with natural disaster like flood, etc. threatens the general life of the people to a large extent (Leese 25). Precisely the War left the empire wounded and fragmented and the encroachment of the other empires pose a great threat to the British Empire downplaying the endeavours of "nationalist movements within the colonies" (Ferguson). The empire with its important parts has to move though an internal storm of purposive dissolutions by the mid-1960s which makes the government to review and revise its laws and policy statements owing to a inspired influx of immigration in Britain and the revolution in Scotland, Wales and Northern Ireland. It is worthwhile to notice that the collective identity of English have inevitably been tied with the British imperialism from the very beginning of the colonial enterprise. Britishness seems to be a more incisive term than the English which can absorb multiple, diversified identities into its land. Englishness, on the other hand, has aligned itself to one single identification with an exclusionary politics of English essentialities which continuously strives to manage the conflation of English and British by perpetuating an Anglocentric discourse in Britain which is described by Kumar as "the lordly habit of subsuming British under English" ("'Englishness'" 41) . By consenting to an aggregative confluence, the non-English "reinforce them in their bad habit" which benefits the English and the England (Kumar, *The Making of English* 1). Englishness has thus long been "the hegemonic component in the supposedly broader term of Britishness" (Morley and Robin 4). This summative arrangement with mutual consents has assumed the superiority of the English as a larger imperial power over its allies Wales, Ireland and Scotland. England is forever haunted by the glory and magnificence of its imperial past and is apprehensive of its disintegrating twilighted existence as losing a pervasive sense of power in the wake of other superpowers across the Globe. Tom Nairn traces these simmering waves of Englishness which is intrinsically tied with the desire for the creation of an empire:

> Too internally differentiated for the vulgar measurements of nationalism, the English then spread themselves too far externally. Empire diluted the imponderable essence even farther, to the point where the recapture has become impossible. That is why there is no national dress, an obscure and unresurrected folklore, and a faltering iconography. (280)

Paul Gilroy observes that the multiple ways in which the image of the empire is recreated in the British national consciousness point out to the lack of the reworking of a colonial history and its effects and a resistance which is registered to exclude the multi-ethnic reality of the contemporary Britain. Gilroy elucidates this lack of engagement of national history not only as a result of the casualties of colonialism but also this nostalgic re-vivification of the imperial past that seek to preserve its absolute essentialities, blocking the possibilities of a non-racialised society. Gilroy describes this inability and unwillingness of accepting this precarious condition as "Postcolonial Melancholia". This psychological condition of British depravity can be explained as a "melancholic reaction", (*Postcolonial Melancholia* 99) to a "loss of a fantasy of omnipotence" (qtd. in Gilroy, *Postcolonial Melancholia* 99) engendered by a gradual loss of esteem and potentialities once associated with this supposedly 'great' empire:

> ... before the British people can adjust to the horrors of their own modern history and start to build new national identity from the debris of their broken narcissism, they will have to learn to appreciate the brutalities of colonial rule enacted in their name and to their benefit, to understand the damage it did to the political culture at home and abroad, to consider the extent of their country's complex investments in ethnic absolutism that has sustained it. The multilayered trauma—economic and cultural as well as political and psychological—involved in accepting the loss of the empire would therefore be compounded by a number of additional shocks. Among them are the painful obligations to work through the grim details of imperial and colonial history and to transform the paralyzing guilt into a more productive shame that would be conducive to the building of a multicultural nationality that is no longer phobic about the prospect of exposure to strangers and otherness. (Gilroy, *Postcolonial Melancholia* 99)

Reworking of the history thus involves a reconfiguration of the national identity and its imagined borders in a more inclusive and permeable patterns of acculturation by letting go the melancholic nostalgia for a lost empire.

Benedict Anderson in his influential book *Imagined Communities* observed that the evolution of national identity in an imaginary one: "... it is imagined because the members of even the smallest nation will never know most of their fellow-members, meet them, or even hear of them, yet in the minds of each lives the image of their communion" (6). Anderson argues that nationality and national identification can never be translated into concrete terms as they are "cultural artefacts of a particular kind" (48) which can be reconceptualised in respective historical moments. Analogously, Raymond Williams posits that the masses are faceless, a communal conglomeration of differential properties and recognising them is a step towards identifying an inner affinity with them which explains the anticipation and formation of the imagined community: "The masses are always the other, we see these others regularly, in their myriad variations; stand physically beside them.... To other people, we are also masses. Masses are other people" (299-300). This imaginary realm of identification is a central metaphor in ideological formations which is argued by Terry Eagleton as "a sphere of abstract, disconnected ideas" (*Ideology: An Introduction* 70) which subverts the stable homology of the idea of border and borderlands. Problematising further the "stabilizing myth of nationalism," Nairn contends that it is not so much the abstract but the "concrete emotive notion anchored in popular experience of the lone" that contributes to the generation of that imagined community (283). It is then both the concrete and abstract features of commonality that go to make a negotiative assimilation of differences which Bhabha argues as "contradictory and antagonistic instances that open up hybrid states and objectives of struggle, and destroy these negative polarities between knowledge and its objects, and between theory and practical-political reason" (*The Location* 37-38).

The intersection of Englishness and whiteness, for instance, is grounded up on this conflation of concrete and abstract mode of representing and propagating the national and imperial identity. Similarly, Renan in his paper "What is a Nation" argues that the idea of nation is a summative alignment of two modes of reality—the past and the present: "... one is the possession in common of a rich legacy of memories; the other is present day consent, the desire to live together, the will to perpetuate the value of the heritage that one has received in an individual from" (19). Reinventing the past in the present, with a sense of cultural inwardness is what helps to create the abstract mode of identification and by staying with people together, living a common reality is what forms a concrete mode of national identity. Renan posits that often "race is confused with nation ... it is a population's race which remains firm and fixed. This is what constitutes a right, a legitimacy" (8-13). It is this assertion of legitimacy with which race is often equated with nation in its historical positionalities, a supposedly unbreakable lineage that can be traced back to its origination. On the other hand, Kumar's observation on cultural nationalism (synonymous with ethnic nationalism) as "a community of fate" rather than a "community of choice" exposes the manner in which the multiple layers of the legitimisation of nationhood is masked ("'Englishness'" 48). Kumar further critically puts it in his essay "'Englishness' and English National Identity" that "the hallmarks of this ethnicity were held to be language, religion, history and blood or 'race'. These expressed the 'soul' of the nation and every nation, it was felt, must have a soul" (48).

Legitimacy has thus become a keyword in the definition of national belonging which tends to standardise categories such as race and nation which are constructed on the exclusionary recognition of a negative presence. As Hall powerfully puts in: "... identity is always, in that sense, a structured representation that achieves its positive only through the narrow eye of the negative" ("The Local and the Global" 174). Anderson, therefore, views nationalism as a development of this negativity—"the pathology of modern developmental history" (qtd. in Anderson 5) which is most often ideologically perpetuated. Eagleton argues that to claim something as ideological is to "claim that it is powered by a ulterior motive bound up with the legitimation of certain interests in a power struggle" (16). Eagleton astutely remarks that ideology musters its force by circulating a normalising discourse in the society ironing out the differences among communities which seems to assume a universal positionality: "An important device by which an ideology achieves legitimacy is by universalizing and 'eternalizing' itself. Values and interests which are in fact specific to a certain place and time are projected as the values and interests of all humanity" (56). The artifice of Englishness which is formed as a result of this ideological normality applies the polarities of boundaries to create a specific sense of the 'self' and the 'other' in the construction of national identity. Replying to Orwell's version of Englishness which is to be found in certain fragmented images such as the "Clatter of clogs in the Lancashire Mill towns" (qtd. in Bragg 201), Peter Mandler says that the image of the national character has been replaced by an image of the national identity. Identity as different from character thus becomes "the consciousness of belonging to a group, though not sharing with it all one's innermost qualities" (196). While describing the features of the Victorian notions of Englishness, Anglia Poon observes that Englishness is "resistant to language and representation, more easily felt than described" (1-2). This concept of Englishness seems to resituate the spirit of Englishness in the lived experience of its inhabitants rather than stereotyping certain interests, values and concretised proclivities. Describing Englishness as a feeling, furthermore, problematises the concept of English identity as it leads to the naturalisation of some of the general assumptions about the essentiality of English identity as Stuart Hall explains is a common motivation: "... one sees what one always sees when one examines or opens up on an ethnicity. It represents itself as perfectly natural: born an Englishman, always be, condensed, homogeneous, unitary" ("The Local" 175).

Any attempt at a cohesive evaluation of identity, therefore, is a myth. As Hall argues in "The Local and the Global," "English never was and never could be that still, unitary point" (175), rather it is an empty spatiality in which Englishness is lived and re-lived with a continuous re-configurement of its primal properties. Therefore, the imaginary notion of Englishness is not to be overlooked in the reshaping of a national identity. Brocklehurst and Phillips thus consider this idea of unified representation as "collective forgetfulness" that echoes Jung's notion of the 'collective unconscious'—the accumulation and sustenance of communal memories and shared ethos at experiences—which involves "the reconstruction or deconstruction of the past for the sake of the nation" (xxiii). This collective forgetfulness is at the root of the developing discontent among the Britishers for the influx of migrants that trespass and subvert the cultural boundaries of Britain and reproduce explicit forms of global Englishness. Anthony Glyn in *The British: A Portrait of the*

People identities this tendency of transnational border-crossing when large-scale migrations and controversial displacements inform and intervene the national life of England (23). The migrants such as West Indian, Pakistani, Asian migrants and others who flooded Britain after the Second World War, Glyn argues, results in "the greatest change in the image of the British man since the Norman Conquest" (23) which exposes and reveals irrelevance of the tacit analogy of Brocklehurst and Phillips's idea of 'collective forgetfulness'. All these point out to the hard fact that identity or knowing the self is a partial attempt, never finished or authentic: "... it is always constructed and stitched together imperfectly, and therefore able to join with another to see together without claiming to be another" (Haraway 193). Belonging in a multicultural society like Britain then is a question of complex involvement and shifting positionality in which identity is shaped and reshaped in a potentially indefinite number of modalities:

> Identity is about belonging, about what you have in common with some people and what differentiates you from others. At its most basic it gives you a sense of personal location, the stable core to your individuality. But it is also about your relationships, your complex involvement with others and in the modern world these have become ever more complex and confusing. Each of us live with variety of potentially contradictory identities, which battle within us for allegiance: as men or women, black or white, straight or gay, able-bodied or disabled, 'British' or European.... The list is potentially infinite, and so therefore are our possible belonging. Which of them we focus on, bring to the fore, 'identify' with, depends on a host of factors. At the centre, however, are the values we share or wish to share with others. (Weeks 88)

Englishness then can be reasonably theorised in Foucauldian terms as working through a discursive field in which different key institutions play significant roles in its perpetuation.

Let us now reflect at this point on the relation of multicultural belonging in Britain to the globalising inclusive patterns of Britishness which is fast replacing a monocultural presentment of Englishness. To think in a more general framework of intellection, human nature has an innate tendency towards diversity and each culture has a singular, inexplicable, ineradicable identification which embodies a distinct vision of life. The influence of culture colours the individual's way of thinking and it is a human need to belong to some familiar culture. All cultures are equal and they nourish and sustain certain human capacities, cultivating different virtues and temperaments. Stuart Mill was very sensitive to the spirit of diversity. He believes that, "the absolute and essential importance of human development is in its diversity" (qtd. in Parekh 41). Diversity adds richness and variety making the world aesthetically more livable as well as stimulates creativity, curiosity and differential imagination. Each culture in this world of diversity is equally important because they mean much to their fellow members and is conducive to their needs. Cultural diversity is an inseparable phenomenon of human life which suggests that cultures were not the results of geographical contextualisation reducible to temporal progressive entities in a linear historicity but the products of imagination in the playful curiousness of inventing new relationships.

The meaning of culture as Turner believes is undergoing historic transformation due to globalisation, information systems, consumerism, etc. in which multiculturalism has problematised itself with its conscious creation of cultural identities within multicultural models that acknowledge the new elements connected with its emergence:

> ... culture has come to serve as the basis both of imagined communities and individual identities deemed to be 'authentic' in contrast to repressive, alien, or otherwise 'inauthentic' normative codes, social institutions and political structures. This historical unwedging of culture and society as political-economic structures has converged with and greatly reinforced, the idealistic culturalism ... of the disciplines and thinkers primarily involved with multiculturalism. (qtd. in Deb 180-81)

Multiculturalism although initially viewed as a progressive discourse have recently attracted the attention of many cultural theorists and academic commentators who tend to see it as conservative and following a reactionary dialectics. Political multiculturalism is often directed to subvert the monistic essentialities of nationality, for instance, the notion of Britishness which persists through strict cultural homology of shared experiences. Multiculturalists, in this context, emphasised internal differentiation and shifting positionalities, evolving new definition of national belonging, deconstructing their constructivist ideologies.

The idea of the preservation of immigrant minorities is based on the opinion that cultures are discrete, stable, homogenous and impervious to external forces and that there is no conflictual pattern to be found within cultures and thus they are to be given opportunities to define themselves which seem to be behaviourally shaped by them. Multiculturalism in its most innocent and non-reflective form is said to underlie the following assumptions identified by Feuchtwang on his essay "Racism: Territoriality and Ethnocentricity":

> The premise of sorting populations by ethnic origins according to presumed cultural essence is that a culture is a community of deep-seated values. For values one may also read social rules and meanings, or customs and traditions. But what makes cultural origin a category of population is the additional assumption that a culture is a community of original identity, to which individuals belong by birth. By the common sense of being and belonging which sets the tone of this cultural recognition, all those born into a community absorb and ineradicably sediment within themselves its customary ways of thinking, feeling and being. Even if they do not so identify themselves, they are nevertheless properly identified with that community, whatever subsequent layers of other cultures they may have absorbed to cover over the original sediment. (4)

Multiculturalism as a concept both at personal and national level has received considerable critique since it was applied in the public sphere in the 1970s. In this political context, the new immigrants and ethnic mobility have further problematised the ambit of multiculturalism. Multiculturalism in its philosophical enterprise can be safely summarised as "abandoning the myths of homogenous and monocultural nation states" and "recognizing rights to cultural maintenance and community formation, and linking these to social equality and protection from discrimination" (Castles, "Migrant Settlement" 12). In every institutional field it seeks to introduce the multicultural model of representation. It is a demographic description of diverse kinds of population inhabiting a particular locality, a set of specific public policies advocating a reconstruction of institutional specificities, a mode of streamlining cultural expression. Multicultural societies are subject to the increasingly complex process of economic and cultural globalisation. It is impossible, therefore, to maintain a self-contained and isolated form of society. Contemporary societies tending multicultural configuration have emerged against the backdrop of the traditional ideal of homogenising nation states. In the pre-modern societies, cultural communities were viewed as the representative of collective rights and left free to inaugurate their customs and practices. The modern state, however, is grounded on a very different idea of social unity. "It generally recognized only the individuals and the bearers of rights and sought to create a homogeneous legal space made up of uniform political units subject to the same body of laws and institutions" (Parekh 8-9).

Multiculturalism at this critical juncture has been passionately defended, defined, redefined and criticised. Those who subscribe to the views of multiculturalism support equality in civil rights, emphasise its positive value which becomes a claim for a tolerant society based on social harmony. However, criticism has been showered on those multicultural advocates who with some political and societal practices seek to eroticise 'otherness' in principle (Grillo 44).

Such policies are identified derogatively as 'tokenism'. Turner at this point distinguishes between two kinds of multiculturalism—difference multiculturalism and critical multiculturalism.

According to Turner, difference multiculturalism with its political policy making is a reductionist celebration of diversity (Grillo 45) whereas the challenges evolved out of critical multiculturalism can serve as a vigorous claim for a vital and "democratic common culture" (408). Other critics opine that multiculturalism is based on a divisive concept of creating factions among the inhabitants, intimately favouring one community over another which promotes conflictual patterns of competition. They observe that it creates ethnic differences essentialising their defining qualities and limits the individual's right for self-expression. Multiculturalism, therefore, is identified as a form of political correctness that stands in opposition to the earlier liberal model of cultural representation. W. Kymlicka terms multiculturalism as confusing because it proceeds on to drawing on the ambiguity between 'multinationalism' and 'polyethnicity' which relates to the fact of coexistent self-governing societies as political units and the issues of migration (107). It needs a re-evaluation since the claims of minority rights of indigenous people are necessarily be different from those of the immigrants.

Anthropology has already responded to such stable interpretation of cultures challenging the associative tendency of the theoretical and methodological framework which relates to the distinctive properties of each culture with cultural closure. Cultural boundaries are not reducible to fixated form of structural barrier, rather they are permeable pattern of non-exclusive systems which promote a subjective shifting of the idea of identification as Edmund Leach has rightly observed, the individual choices are crucial in this shifting sense of identification because they promote changes to the smooth continuity of social structure, rather than subversive enforced structural changes (34). Furthermore, the closed systems of culture and its distinctive uniqueness may stand in opposition to the individual choice and their sense of freedom which is basically a subjective entity which may even involve a rejection of one's own inherited culturality (Gutmann 2). Democracies in this modern context ought to strike a balance between the individual and the collective spheres, and ethnic identity can be grounded with a positive value if it doesn't clash with the universal identity and society's common norms and values.

Ralph Grillo in this context identifies and distinguishes between two forms of multiculturalism—weak multiculturalism and strong multiculturalism. Weak multiculturalism is based on a diverse patterns of culturality in which private sphere is recognised with a condition of high level cultural assimilation that is expected from the immigrants and ethnic minorities in the public institutions—governmental, educational, legal, etc. Strong multiculturalism, on the other hand recognises cultural difference in both public and private sphere including political presentment (Grillo 19).

Steven Vertovec in his paper "Transnational Challenges to the 'New' Multiculturalism" quotes Ralph Grillo who outlines six commonly identified problems in multicultural theory and practice in its present manifestation: "(1) Multiculturalism's implicit essentialism; (2) The system of categorization which underpins it; (3) The form that multicultural politics takes; (4) The ritualization of ethnicity often associated with it; (5) The elision of race (and class) that it appears to entail; and (6) The attack on the 'common core' which it represents" (Vertovec 4). The new culturalism which multicultural engagements seek to represent in the present political context is reductionist and minimalist in its approach which is called by Yasmin Alibhai-Brown as "boutique multiculturalism" which tends to "keep diversity in a box" (42). All these misconception are rooted in a faulty presentation of culture in terms of fixed categorisation and systematic reification of cultural constants:

> In this set of understandings, 'culture' is: a kind of package (often talked of as migrants' 'cultural baggage') of collective behavioural-moral-aesthetic traits and 'customs', rather mysteriously transmitted between generations, best suited to particular geographical locations yet largely unaffected by history of a change of context, which instils a discrete quality into the feelings, values, practices, social relationships, predilections and intrinsic nature of all who 'belong to' (a particular) it. (Vertovec, "Multiculturalism, Culturalism" 41)

Alibhai-Brown thus attacks the essentialist model of multiculturalism by observing that it has created a sense of white exclusion which entails only the elites entrenching inequalities and fostering stability which erects group barrier. It is posed as a strong antithesis to the idea of globalization. Favell, on the other hand, develops a nation-building model of strong multicultural relationship within the state which becomes a claim for a re-imagined, balanced cultural diversity based on a formal equality in terms of status and belonging:

> ... ethnic minorities are offered cultural tolerance, even, multicultural rights and institutions, in exchange for acceptance of basic principles and the rule of law; they are imagined as culturally-laden social groups, who need to be integrated and individualized by a public sphere which offers voice and participation, transforming them from 'immigrants', into full and free citizens; they are to become full, assimilated nationals, in a nation-state re-imagined to balance cultural diversity, with a formal quality of status and membership. (213-14)

Factors such as globalisation, mass migrations, displacements and information revolutions, etc. have disrupted the stable collective entities and identities which are organised territorially by the politics of the nation state. Subverting the exclusionary essentialities of cultural presentation, it entails that it is not only the politically motivated multiculturalism that seems problematic but the notion of a unified self turns out to be an utterly unrealistic theme:

> If we feel we have a unified identity ... it is only because we construct a comforting story or 'narrative of the self' about ourselves.... The fully unified, completed, secure and coherent identity is a fantasy. Instead, as the systems of meaning and cultural representation multiply, we are confronted by a bewildering, fleeting multiplicity of possible identities, any one of which we could identify with—at least temporarily. (qtd. in Modood 380)

Identity being continuously exposed to shifting positionalities, the individual consequently feels the need to protect it from transformative involvements which results in transactive negotiations between cultures. When identity is used to be socially grounded, it appears "predetermined and non-negotiable" (Bauman, *Identity* 24). As a response to the external changes and upheavals, selfhood changes accordingly and is continually transformed by the fast evolving, challenging social conditions and cultural configurations. The present form of multicultural model established in Britain in particular and Europe in general rather seem to ignore this fact of fragmented affiliations and sanction a "container model" (Vertovec, "Transnational Challenges" 5) of the nation state in which identity is shaped by static territorialities:

> The European nation has, at least in principle, grown up around an 'ideal' of cultural homogeneity, established and reinforced through the state controlled transmission of literate culture ... alongside state control over entry and acquisition of citizenship; thus the nation represents territorialized cultural belonging, while the state formalizes and controls legal membership. (Morris 194)

The essentialising model of multiculturalism based on cultural homogeneity, which expects the immigrants to develop a sense of belonging, is thus reconceptualised in this context. The broad objective is to reject the cultural assimilationist vision that aims simply to dissolve cultural difference to form an integrated cultural identity. As it amounts to an illogical imposition of the culture of the majority on its unprivileged minorities, one of the recent commentators of multiculturalism, Jonathan Sacks summarises this desperate tensions of the cultural theorists and commentators in his book *The Home We Build Together* which cogently captures this mood:

> Multiculturalism has run its course, and it is time to move on. It was fine, even noble idea in its time. It was desired to make ethnic and religious minorities feel more at home in society.... It affirmed their culture. It gave dignity to difference. And in many ways it achieved its aims.... But there has been a price to pay, and it grows year by year. [It] has led not to integration but to segregation.... It was intended to promote tolerance.

> Instead, the result has been ... societies more abrasive, fractured and intolerant than they once were. (3)

Sacks warns us of the negative tendencies of multiculturalism in a public realm which is about to break apart. Multiculturalism, he says, creates for us not a 'home' where to belong but a 'hotel' in which inhabitants co-exist but without having common purposes (3). This results from the progressive rejection of the shared public values rooted in universal principles and the movement into a relativistic celebration of unique 'differences'. Charles Taylor proposes, in this regard what he calls a "presumption of equal worth" by which he means the ways in which we begin transaction with a different culture with the assumption that it is at least worthy of respect if not proven to be fruitful in a given context:

> It is reasonable to suppose that cultures that have provided the horizon of meaning for large numbers of human beings, of diverse characters and temperaments, over a long period of time—that have, in other words, articulated their sense of the good, thc holy, the admirable—are almost certain to have something that deserves our admiration and respect even if it is accompanied by much that we have to abhor and reject. (256)

Taylor traces the manner in which multicultural theorists then take a fatal step further. They seek an openness to be projected in cultural negotiations affirming the value of cultural diversity as well as they begin to claim that disparate cultural configurations should be assumed as having equal moral worth. Taylor therefore insists that every culture must be prepared to pass adverse moral judgements on the facets of other cultures including their own. Empathising thus across the cultures doesn't entail an abandonment of the vigorous intercultural transaction through critiques and arguments:

> A favourable judgement on demand is nonsense ... the giving of such a judgment demands an act of breathtaking condescension. No one can really mean it as an act of respect.... A favourable judgment made prematurely [by passing any critical exploration of a

> culture] would not be only condescending but also ethnocentric. It would praise the other for being like us.... By implicitly invoking our standards to judge all civilizations and cultures, the politics of difference can end up making everyone the same. (254-55)

According to Boas, as they are of equal importance, cultures should be viewed from a neutral framework and the evolutionary categorisations of culture and the ethnocentric value judgements are to be rejected (130). Even if well-intentioned, cultural relativism is faced with heavy challenges although quite popular especially after the Second World War on account of its association of 'cultural' relativism to 'moral' relativism. Resonating the political criticism of cultural relativism, Mathew Parris, while discussing the potential dangers of multiculturalism in a paper published in *Times Online*, writes that multiculturalism may lead to a disguised form of apartheid (Prato 5). He questions the very idea of particularistic multiculturalism which believes in recognising the role and contribution of each culture and subculture integrating them to a unified culture of a country (Prato 5). This approach, however, is different from that of pluralistic multiculturalism which aims at preserving the cultural diversity within the framework of overarching values in which diverse cultures can thus transact peacefully across other cultural configurations while sustaining their cultural diversities in a smooth "cultural mosaic" (qtd. in Prato 6). Parris thinks that particularistic multiculturalism could end in radicalisation of cultural differences and the formation of cultural ghettoes which mask the regular authenticities of political recognition (Prato 6). Similarly, Trevor Phillips, the chairman of the commission for Racial Equality warns against the reified overtones of multiculturalism which he wants to be scrapped altogether and argues that the most talked-about idea of tolerance for cultural diversity has led to the summative isolation of many communities and that multiculturalism is the reason behind the lack of integration of some minority cultural groups in Britain (Prato 6).

Pluralism in cultural representation thus is an inevitable reality, an inescapable feature of cultural communities that "can neither be washed out of existence nor suppressed without an unacceptable degree of coercion, and often not even then" (Parekh, *Rethinking Multiculturalism* 196). Isaiah Berlin makes a distinction between the pluralistic and relativist ideals of cultural presentations by saying that relativism delimits out mental faculty to make value judgment while a pluralistic approach stirs this capacity and enables an imaginative empathy for the supposed 'other':

> Members of one culture can, by the force of imaginative insight, understand ... the value, the ideals, the forms of life of another culture or society, even those remote in time or space. They may find these value unacceptable, but if they open their minds sufficiently they can grasp how one might be a full human being, with whom one could communicate, at the same time live in the light of values widely different from one's own, but which nevertheless one can see to be values, ends of life, by the realization of which men could be fulfilled. (10)

Similarly, Bentley's notion of 'organized groups' established a connection between the group and the imagined nation-state: "... when the groups are adequately stated, everything is stated" (208). According to Parekh, the value of cultural pluralism lies in acknowledging the enriching quality of other cultures that the individuals of the minority cultures need to be encouraged to nourish and cultivate their insights in a complementary dialectics of relocation for the common humanity as a whole:

> Since human capacities and values conflict, every culture realizes a limited range of them and neglects, marginalizes and suppresses others. However rich it may be, no culture embodies all that is valuable to human life and develops the full range of human possibilities. Different cultures thus correct and complement each other, expand each other's horizon of thought and alert each other to new forms of fulfilment. The value of other cultures is independent of whether or not they are options for us ... inassimilable otherness challenges us intellectually and morally, stretches our imagination,

> and compels us to recognize the limits of our categories of thought. (*Rethinking Multiculturalism* 176)

One of the important aspects of the Parekh Report titled *The Future of Multi-Ethnic Britain* published in October 2000 was ethnic diversity in Britain. *The Report* champions the vision of multiculturalism in Britain. *The Report* was ground breaking in its approach and recommendation which seek "to analyse the current state of multi-ethnic Britain, and to propose ways of countering racial discrimination and disadvantage and making Britain a confident and vibrant multi-cultural society at ease with its rich diversity" (Preface viii). Parekh, in *The Report*, attacks the essentialised conceptualisation of the community and the self and aims at evolving a new national narrative claiming that Britain is not only a "community of citizens" but also a "community of communities" (Preface ix). *The Report* is an onslaught against the prevailing British model of representing "integration" as "a one way process in which 'minorities' are to be absorbed into the non-existent homogeneous cultural structure of the 'majority'" (Preface x). *The Report* is sweeping in its pronouncement as it aims at developing a balance between cohesion, equality and difference, eliminating all form of racism to rethink national identity and culture. As part of the goal, it promotes a sophisticated understanding of the national history and the discussion of the cultural questions such as "how to reimagine English, Scottish and Wales history so that it includes everyone; how to understand identities in transition; how to balance cohesion, difference and justice; how to deal with racism" (Parekh, *The Future* 6). *The Report* seeks to subvert the myth of Englishness as homogenising the cultural constants and proposes an anti-essentialist model of all-inclusive Britishness which nourishes an understanding that all identities are in a process of transition, and pursing a pluralistic vision of human culture. Steven Vertovec in his paper "Transnational Challenges to the 'New' Multiculturalism" traces an undercurrent of anti-essentialist tendency in the *Parekh Report* which deliberately distances itself from all forms of essentialist exclusivities and advocating a flexible form of plurality and hybridity:

> As part of this goal, the commission quite consciously seeks to distance itself from the bounded, essentialized notions of 'community' conveyed in earlier approaches to multiculturalism. [Such distancing stems, not least, like from the Commission's composition that includes people like Stuart Hall, one of the foremost intellectuals associated with critiquing essentialism and conceptualizing 'hybridity'. Through its seminars and invited statements, the Commission also obviously listened to a number of academics who were highly critical of essentialized notions of 'culture' and community.] Rather than reified 'cultures', references to 'interacting and overlapping communities' ... and individuals' multiple identities run throughout *The Report*. (6)

The Report includes reflections on culture, social institutions and aims to chalk out the ways for change questioning the role and significance of national identities and history:

> A sense of national identity is based on generalizations and involves a selective and simplified account of a complex history. Much that is important is ignored, disavowed or simply forgotten. Many complicated strands are reduced to a simple task of essential and enduring national unity, with everything in past history leading inexorably up to a triumphal conclusion. (Parekh, *The Future* 16)

The Report markedly shows an inclination towards a renewed reconfiguration of 'community' and cultural belonging. It challenges the stable coherent-looking concept of 'communities' and 'historic groups' inaugurating an overlapping format of cultural representation. It seeks to resituate cultural belonging in a more inclusive framework of multiculturalism:

> Britain is a land of many different groups, interests and identities, from Home Countries English to Gaels, Geordies and Mancunians to Liverpudlians, Irish to Pakistanis, African-Caribbeans to Indians. Some of these identity groups are large, powerful and long-

> settled. Others are small, new and comparatively powerless. Some are limited to Britain but others have international links; some of the boundaries are clear, some are fuzzy. Many communities overlap; all affect and are affected by others. More and more people have multiple identities—they are Welsh Europeans, Pakistani Yorkshire women, Glaswegian Muslims, English Jews and Black British. Most enjoy this complexity but also experience conflicting loyalties. The term 'communities' can give the impression of stable, coherent, historic groups with tidy boundaries. But situations and relationships are changing. It is simply wrong to think that there are easily measured groups of people—working class Scots, black Londoners, Jews, Irish, 'middle' England—who all think alike and are not changed by those around them. For everyone life is more interesting than that. (Parekh, *The Future* 10)

Parekh report is a unique claim for the conception of a broader perspective of interdependence which focuses on the group dynamics in the past and emphasises the process of selection and simplification in the formation of a dominant narrative history of the past. *The Report* is apprehensive of the ideological role of these apparatuses in the construction of a shared national identity which empowers the minorities to join hands in the nation building enterprise:

> Of course its effectiveness in binding society together is less real because much of it is invented or distorted. Its purpose is not to give an accurate historical account but to enable individuals to position their personal life-stories within the larger, more significant national story. Identification, not knowledge is its raison d'être. It allows individuals to identify with something outside, and greater than, personal experience. It binds individuals into a broader interdependence with others in the nation-building project. (Parekh, *The Future* 16-17)

The emphasis on realizing a broader perspective creates new terrains of cultural belonging, ironing out the narrowness and differences of the mind in a range of overlapping relationships. It aims at exposing the stereotyping attitude of the people in cultural identification and belonging:

> People have compelling attachment to nation, group, subculture, region, and city, town, neighbourhood and the wider world. They belong to a range of different but over-lapping communities, real and symbolic, divided on cultural issues of the day ... identities, in consequence, are more situational. This makes Britain, contrary to stereotype, more open. (Parekh, *The Future* 25)

The Parekh Report seeks to simplify the complex multicultural reality in Britain by pointing out to the fact that identity is increasingly relational, complex and exists not as a unified whole but as an overlapping entity in intersectional positionality with other individuals living in a particular society. It is an attempt to publicly emphasise a non-essentialised understanding of identity, community and culture that takes multiculturalism to new heights unrealized in its conversational form in the last two or three decades:

> To speak of 'the black community', 'the Irish community' 'the Bangladesh community' and so forth, is to refer accurately to a strong sense of group solidarity. But it may also imply a homogeneous set, with fixed internal ties and strongly defined sense of group solidarity and strongly defined boundaries, and this is a hopelessly misleading picture of a complex, shifting multicultural reality.... These communities are not, and have never aspired to be, separate enclaves. They are not permanently locked into unchanging traditions, but interact at every level with mainstream social life, constantly adapting and diversifying their inherited beliefs and values in the light of the migration experience. (Parekh, *The Future* 27)

Identifying the key features of cultural formation, *The Report* stresses the informality of cross-cultural connections at work beneath the polished exterior of formal rules and legalities. It tries to evolve an imaginative framework of cultural relations by fostering the idea that England has always been the home of many immigrant communities from the different corners of the world and that England would best prosper with a realisation of its identity as an imagined community:

> Cultural meanings appeal to people's imaginations but are difficult to pin down. They are embedded not in formal rules and laws but in all the informal aspects of cultural life that are taken for granted: Customs, habits, daily rituals, unwritten social codes, the way masculinity and femininity are expressed, speech idiom and body language, feelings for the landscape, and collective memories of national glories—especially those associated with war.... Image, metaphor and shared symbols play a crucial role in construction and maintaining the idea of England as an imagined community. They not only express solidarity but also construct a solidarity that was not there before. (Parekh, *The Future* 20)

Proportionately, with the changing face of Britain, *The Report* proposes a set of common values and recommends a new mode of multiculturalism, mitigating the race differences and discriminations by suggesting equality of treatment without overlooking "real differences of experience, background and perception" (Parekh, *The Future* 296). Emphasis is given to bridge the gap between individual identity and group identification, pointing out to the meaningless insufficiency of such entities without the existence of the other in a fluid, non-fixative, permeable pattern of cultural configuration:

> ... communities today are neither self-sufficient nor fixed and stable. They are open, porous formations. It is impossible to invest totally in communities as the sole bearers of the legal right to difference. Many individuals with a strong sense of belonging and loyalty towards their communities do not intend their personal freedom to be bound in perpetually by communal norms.... The boundaries round a community can be quite hard and fast making it difficult to join or leave voluntarily. But often they are fluid, unfixed. It is in any case entirely

> possible for someone to be a member—significant member—of several different communities at the same time; indeed, this is usual. (Parekh, *The Future* 37-51)

The commission on *The Future of Multi-Ethnic Britain* attempts in a systematic way to address various key factors of 'identity' and 'belonging' including, migration, globalisation and devolution, narrating people's variegated impressions of national and transnational notions of belongingness. It is, however, not silent about England's long standing but proud claim as an empire and its subsequent involution as a super power and attacks the normative stance of Britishness as a dominant narrative of British history and of racism, advocating an inclusive accounts of history, traditions, culture and belonging. It discusses the hegemonic narativisation of national history, condemning it as constructed around an exclusivity of racial superiority ties upon the traditional notions of Britishness. It seeks to rewrite history in more inclusive term inverting the ideal a of lost empire:

> The absence from the national curriculum, of a rewritten history of Britain as an imperial force, involving dominance in Ireland as well as in Africa, the Caribbean and Asia, is proving from this perspective to be an unmitigated disaster ... is often described as the shedding of a burden whose time has passed. However, expunging the traces of an imperial mentality from the national culture, particularly those that involved seeing the white British as a superior race, is a much more difficult task. This mentality penetrated everyday life, popular culture and consciousness. It remains active in projected fantasies and fears about difference and in racialized stereotypes of otherness. The unstated assumption remains that Britishness and whiteness go together, like roast beef and Yorkshire pudding. There has been no collective working through of this imperial experience. (Parekh, *The Future* 24-25)

The new vision of multiculturalism presented by the commission aims at disrupting the container model of the nation-state, underscoring the need of core values pertaining to Britishness or whiteness and proposed a common belonging with "shared cultural meaning" (Parekh, *The Future* 16) and stature which emphasises social cohesivity with an eternal disregard for "the oppressive uniformity based on single substantive culture" (Parekh, *The Future* 56).

The discursive position *The Report* encourages, however, is severely criticised by various News groups, cultural commentators and theorists. Various conservative presses reacted against the critical stance developed by the commission on Britishness and British history. M. Bentham, the social affairs correspondent of *Daily Telegraph*, unwittingly described the report as a celebration of the Britain's race relations and suggests that "race relations in Britain are the best in Europe and the notion that the country has severe racial problem is a 'skewed and partisan' lie" (qtd. in Weedon 33). *The Daily Telegraph* described the report as "cauldron of political correctives" (qtd. in Weedon 33) and the commission as a "crack-brained think tank" (qtd. in Weedon 33) motivated by self-serving individuals which alarms its conservative readership. Other political groups challenge the stance adopted by the commission, explicitly addressing white community as a homogeneous group whose interests are categorically threatened by the report; repeatedly retorting that "you can feel Britishness in your bones. That sense of history, fairness, justice and landscape that makes you proud just to be part of it" (qtd. in Weedon 34).

Lord Ali, Managing Director, Carlton Production focuses rather on the perception of diversity and shared properties:

> We are a diverse nation and we are richer for that. Our heritage is drawn from many traditions but at its heart is a Britishness with values which I share of tolerance, individualism and inclusiveness. To say that is not to deny my roots. But I was born here and I am part of this country. Being British should not be a political statement. It should, for all of us, just be what we are. (qtd. in Weedon 34)

The progressively conservative recognition of the role of history as forming dominant narratives of the nationality that questions the legitimacy of the status quo is met with vehement responses, one of which is registered by Boris Johnson in "Thursday column" of *Daily Telegraph* on 12 October 2000 who describes *The Report* as a propagandist part of "a war over culture" in which the government is in complicity with the outsiders:

> The reason we oppose Ouseley ... and the rest of the Runnymede rhubarb, is that we can sense that people want to demolish things that are valuable in our culture.... This is a war over culture, which our side could lose. Why should children be taught that the British Empire was an unadulterated evil, when it plainly wasn't? You won't encourage Britain's minorities—the vast majority of whom think of themselves as British—to achieve more or feel more at home, by deprecating the achievements of dead white men. And it is not just British triumphs that this Government would like to erase, but the British character. (qtd. in Weedon 35-36)

Similarly, the widely circulated tabloid *The Sun* carried a headline on the day of the publication of *The Report* on 11 Oct. 2000 which reads "Course of the Britain Basher" with a sub headline "Ministers Welcome Report" which says "British" is racist and all our history must be rewritten (qtd. in Weedon 38). Daley rejects the idea as ludicrous saying that it is impossible to rewrite history and asserts that Britain "is still the best country in the world" valued by immigrants for "freedom and tolerance, the right to a free health service and respect for the law" (qtd. in Weedon 38). Daley, similarly, emphasised the progressive outlook of Britain and rejects the idea that "minorities associate Britishness with colonization and empire" (qtd. in Weedon 38) any more. Analogously, Thomson highlights the progress in race relation, although perhaps, he is little distasteful in his pronouncement: "But not so long ago, most people assumed that a black man in possession of a nice car must have stolen it and I believe it is an achievement that most people in Britain don't think that way any more" (qtd. in Weedon 38). The conservative *Daily Mail* subsequently, cogently quoted some of the much discussed statements about Britishness and national history and brings to the fore a non-white Briton named Raj Chandran, one of the serving members of the commission for Racial Equality, who claims that Britain is "an increasingly tolerant multicultural society" (qtd. in Weedon 39). Chandran inadvertently overlooks the economic factors motivating migration and questions: "If the UK is not hospitable and accepting, why would millions of people—black, brown and yellow—have struggled so hard, first to come here, and then to become, British citizens over the past half century" (qtd. in Weedon 39-40)?

In contrast to all the views expressed earlier by the conservative press, Johnson seems to be assimilative and purposeful when he says that "Britain has a long tradition of unbiased, objective and truthful historical writing, avoiding propaganda and hagiography, and not fearing to criticize the ruling elite when necessary" (qtd. in Weedon 43). Johnson in his essay, however, sustains a progressive vision of British history and the widely diverse population that informs the national life of Britain internally:

> British history is the story of freedom and respect for the law and Britain's relationship with the world beyond our shores is the story of benefaction, not exploitation, of course, not oppression, and the desire to enlighten, to improve, to reach and to help.... It is not a story of which any one of us need to be ashamed. Nor is it a story which needs to be rewritten. On the contrary: it can be rewritten only by inserting bias and dogma, propaganda and downright lies. (qtd. in Weedon 43)

Here the conservative response to the commission is simply reduced to an assertion that the problem really doesn't exist which the report so emphatically highlights for Britain has always been an enriched site of cross cultural transaction and negotiative benefaction, and that the undermining of national history and empire is but a biased recrimination of political correctness.

Belonging, in this problematics of contextualised transculturation, has become an increasingly complex term to define as "our contemporary condition is marked by the emergence of new forms of identity politics around the globe. The new forms complicate and increase centuries-old tensions between the universalistic principles ... and the particularities of nationality, ethnicity, gender, 'race', and language" (Benhabib vii). The contemporary nature of 'belonging' has thus unsettled the implicit assumptions in the conceptualisation of nation because self-identifications are the "products of social relations and that groups themselves are not discrete entities" (Young, "Polity and Group Difference" 226) and the distinctions in terms of class and ethnicities don't hold ground "but do entails social process of exclusion and incorporation whereby discrete categories are maintained despite changing participation and membership in the course of individual life histories" (Barth 10). Walzer opines that the idea of nation is evolved when "a single dominants group organizes the common life in a way that reflects its own authority and culture" (160) which is certainly a concern for those cultural theorists who believe that the minorities will crucially feel outsided when the majority take "the polity as an expression of their nation, on agreed purpose" (Taylor 272). The notion of belonging in these critical cross-cultural connectivities thus critiques "the myth of homogeneous and monocultural nation states" when advocating the rights of minorities in an alienated foreign atmosphere (Castles, "Migrant Settlement" 5). There is therefore no strict relationality between the individual and the nation, the ethnicity and the nationality as created nations are "imagined political communities" and are both "limited and sovereign" (Anderson 6) because ideas can serve as powerful basis of social action and reaction. The notions of 'nation' and 'nationality', however, are modern constructions:

> The idea of man without a nation appears to impose strain on the modern imagination. A man must have a nationality as he must have a nose and two ears. All this seems obvious, though, also, it is not true. But that it should come to seem so very obviously true is indeed as aspect, perhaps the very core, of the problem of nationalism. Having a nation is not an inherent attribute to humanity, but it has come to appear as such. (Gellner 6)

Hence, identity is about belonging which gives you a sense of location in shifting relationships in a complex involvement with the outer world. It is, therefore, "never complete, always in process" (Hall, "Cultural Identity" 51) "partial in all its guises, never finished ... always constructed and stitched together imperfectly" (Haraway 193) which is capable of joining with others to recognise a shared belonging without claiming to be another:

> The growing complexity of the modern world and the awareness that this inner core of the subject was not autonomous and self-sufficient, but was formed in relations to 'significant others', who mediated the subject values, meanings and symbols—the culture—of the world he/she inhabited.... Identity in this sociological conception, bridges the gap between the 'inside' and the 'outside'—between the personal and the public worlds. The fact that we project 'ourselves' into these cultural identities, at the same time internalizing their meanings and values, making them 'part of us', helps to align our subjective feelings with the objective places we occupy in the social and cultural world. (Hall, "The Question" 275-76)

The in-between ambivalent position of the Asian and non-Asian immigrants in Britain, in this context, warrants an important step towards the goal of refashioning a global open society with diverse localised forms of attachment and belonging. Cultural affiliation, then, is possible outside the stabilising border of the nation state in a range of multicultural possibilities. With this regard, James Clifford writes in "Mixed Feelings" that "identity is never only about location, about shoring up a safe "home", crucial as that task may be in certain circumstances. Identity is also inescapably, about displacement and relocation, the experience of sustaining and mediating complex affiliations, multiple attachments" (369). Englishness, in this sense, is ever admitting new features of multicultural belonging into its framework, filling its "curious emptiness" of "cultural essence" (Young, *The Idea* 236) which points out that "Englishness Paradoxically became most itself when it was far off ... best performed far from home, a global identity into which others could always translate themselves" (Young, *The Idea* 3). The globalising interconnectedness of human belonging demands an outward stance in which English historical tradition and social inclusivity are well positioned to exploit the situational spatiality and multicultural relations in an ever-constitutive cosmopolity. It would be drastically unfortunate if England loses this opportunity in pursuit of an oppressively reminiscent and defensive nationalism.

Chapter 5

Identity, Memory and the Shifting Contour of Home: Kazuo Ishiguro's *The Remains of the Day* and *When We Were Orphans*

> "All of Ishiguro's novels to date, narration is, at least partly, a therapeutic process. The novels are not attempts to render the past convincingly, but rather to pursue how individuals interpret and construct that past."
>
> —James Procter, "Kazuo Ishiguro"
>
> "Great literature is written in a sort of foreign tongue. To each sentence we attach a meaning, or at any rate a mental image, which is often a mistranslation. But in great literature all our mistranslations result in beauty."
>
> —Marcel Proust, *Contre Sainte-Beuve*
>
> "Memories, even your most precious ones, fade surprisingly quickly. But I don't go along with that. The memories I value most, I don't ever see them fading."
>
> —Kazuo Ishiguro, *Never Let Me Go*

Critics have praised over the decades the masterful control and proportion of Kazuo Ishiguro's fictional projections which are inextricably bound up with blending private reminiscence with the collective memory of a disillusioned past. The ambivalent position which Ishiguro holds in the history of world literature provides him a new perspective of reconfiguring identity through the transformative transaction with a fragmented past, that is retrospectively rendered by fragile memorialisation. The unimaginable largeness which Ishiguro projects into his novels becomes an emphatic claim for an all-inclusive cosmopolity that exquisitely rehearses a dispersed, deterritorialised experience of multi-locationality, permeated with a deeply seated existential estrangement, drastically altering the inner space of cultural permeability. Studying Ishiguro's works in the discourse of this diasporic dialectics evokes a deceptively extraordinary sense of post-imperial exoticising associations. Above all, Ishiguro is often grouped with Naipaul, Rushdie, Hanif Kureishi, Timothy Mo and others for his novels are ceaseless experimentations in delineating the inward alienation and isolative bereavement within the framework of the decolonising polemics of reorientation. The present chapter is an attempt to resituate Ishiguro's conceptualisation of 'home' with its varying degrees of individuation and belongingness in which the reconstitutive memory of the undeciphered past is viewed as having metamorphic levels of transcultural dehomogenisation to constructively exacerbate the faltering sense of identity in the process of self-actualisation.

Inverting the conservative status of diasporic bewilderment, Ishiguro challenges the established notion of alien locality and ethnic identity for Ishiguro's characters, instead of performing as peripheral figures in adopted localities, are duly balanced cultural forces on the home front, but are inevitably bent by the waves of a negotiative historicity which is linked up with their own version of reality. Each of Ishiguro's novels graphically focalises a poignant plot of wartime reverberation artfully contrived with incisive observations to expose the complacency of the complicitous and rivalling categories in the re-presentment of a glorious but disrupted past. Evolving his fictional characters, Ishiguro insightfully transmutes the challenging existence of the "cultural amphibians" into an impressionistic style of intricate assimilation in a particular discursive ambience "characterized by their ability to comply with divergent codes without losing their intellectual and moral integrity" (Buendia 27). This chameleon-like permeability as Buendia observes, "allows them to cross cultural borders unnoticed" and "put different contexts in dialogue and—in doing so—transform them" (Buendia 27).

Thus, at the crossroads of two or multiple cultural forces, he seems to suspend his narrators eternally into a self-reflexive dissection of the catastrophic historicity with an immediate association of some ideological contention of the disillusioned past. A deep-rooted sense of cultural estrangement haunts the lacerated memories of the protagonists which is viewed more as a result of temporal disruption rather than a spatially informed transposition. However, instead of presenting his autobiographical speculation as an immigrant writer, he blends personal dislocation and a sense of cultural bifurcation into his characters in a numerous transmutative psychological trajectories. For this reason Sheng-mei Ma in *Immigrant Subjectivities* describes Ishiguro as a "Child of Asian Diaspora" who strives to delineate the representative, fragmented sensibilities in an occluding narrativisation suggestive of the writer's "split personality" and "buried self" (41). Kazuo Ishiguro in his novel *The Remains of the Day* thus explores the problematics of writing personal memory within the historical framework of a multicultural globalising world, astutely linking expatriate experience to a psychological sense of displacement in his representation of personal, cultural and national identities and the spatial conceptualisation of 'home', precipitated by an inner urge for self-identification. Stevens, the narrator-protagonist of the novel must reconcile the decision of the past with an ever uncertain present in a revisionary poetics of unreliable narration mediating past selves in the realm of a displaced territoriality. The novel *The Remains of the Day* serves as a simplified saga of self-resurrection which identifies the subtle mechanism at work in the reconfiguration of diasporic identity through the comforting process of redefining the past and the self-conscious recollection of nostalgia as a survival strategy in an alien environment. Stevens subsequently, questions all his past engagements in/with Darlington Hall in which memory acts like a filter, through which individual episodes are evoked in the prismatic presence. The novel critically acknowledges the significance of memory with the belief that "when with the benefit of hindsight one begins to search one's past for ... 'turning points', one is apt to start seeing them everywhere" (Ishiguro, *The Remains* 175) which reveals the multifarious elusiveness of truth fragmentarily integrated from the realities of the past. The present privacy and solitude in Stevens' life precipitates in him the desire for a voyage to the dishevelled past through the distorting waves of a refractive memory.

Similarly, Ishiguro's novel *When We Were Orphans* revolves round a supposedly detective plot in which the protagonist-narrator Christopher Banks is engaged with an incessant search for his disappeared parents in Shanghai in which the historico-political background of the Shanghai Settlement resulting from Sino-Japanese war plays a significant role in shaping the sensibility of the main characters. The negotiative reconstitution of a remotely personal past, relocation of origins and identity are central to the novel which finally seeks to deconstruct its own detective plot by filtering the protagonist's delusion with multiple facets of reality. The novel is an imaginary experiment with the private memory—the undeciphered past of the protagonist, in search for a lost identity and 'home' in the actualisation of the self. Albeit it is understood that nostalgia may bring misery, "that nostalgia can be dangerous, Ishiguro also demonstrates that it can serve as a foundation for imagining a world better than one's present" (Weston 337). Christopher Banks thus dwells on his memories to unravel his true identity and the cause of his orphanhood which poison all his remaining life. Each of Ishiguro's protagonists suffers the cathartic effect of a re-constitutive memorialisation which leads them to a summative realisation of the reality as James Procter insightfully observes, "All of Ishiguro's novels to date, narration is, at least partly, a therapeutic process. The novels are not attempts to render the past convincingly, but rather to pursue how individuals interpret and construct that past" (qtd. in Abdulgawad 5). Ishiguro in *When We Were Orphans* explores this idea of fragmentation which struggles to arrive at a modest sense of identity and positionality in terms of psychic displacement in the global and domestic spheres.

Born of Japanese parents in Nagasaki on 8 November 1954, Kazuo Ishiguro, in a tender age, moved with his family to Britain. His father, an oceanographer joined his work in Surrey at the National institute of Oceanography. Spending his childhood in Surrey, he studied at the University of Kent and became a graduate in English and Philosophy in 1979. After spending some years in literary pursuits he resumed his study at the University of East Anglia and obtained a master's degree in creative writing. Thus, what was intended to be a short visit was prolonged beyond proportion and Ishiguro had to stay in England the rest of his life. As a child, however, Ishiguro found an unsevered tie that is linked to his homeland and Nagasaki in particular, and nourished an inherent ideology to return: "And so as a small child, I was taken away from people I knew, like my grandparents and my friends. And I was led to expect that I would return to Japan. But the family kept extending the stay. All the way through my childhood, I couldn't forget Japan, because I had to prepare myself for returning to it" (Ishiguro, "The Novelist" 110). The delayed return to this homeland creates an anxiety in him which challenges his inward vision of home which he seeks to recapture in his fictional representations:

> I wished to recreate this Japan—put together all these memories, and all these imaginary ideas I had about this landscape called Japan. I wanted to make it safe, preserve it in book, before it faded away from my memory altogether. (Ishiguro, "The Novelist" 110)

Having involved in social work for some years he published his first novel, *A Pale View of Hills* in 1982 which gained high critical acclaim fetching him the Winifred Holtby Memorial prize. Set in Japan and England the novel tells the story of Etsuko, the protagonist who seeks to decipher nostalgically the painful engagements of the past which portrays a sense of regret, cultural displacement and the trauma of the War which informed many of Ishiguro's later novels. In a similar fashion, Ono, the protagonist of Ishiguro's second novel *An Artist of the Floating World* (1986) reflects upon his past with the aid of his fragile memory to find a purpose for his life in a fast changing world that aims to replace the old ideals with new ones as a negotiative encounter with the remote past. Ishiguro's third novel *The Remains of the Day* (1989) which won the Man Booker Prize, one of the most prestigious literary awards, is considered as one of the most highly regarded post-war novels. It portrays the suppressed emotions of Stevens, the narrator-protagonist who must reconsider his past life in a revisionary poetics of reconfiguring his identity from the very shadow of the past, maintaining a high level of restraint throughout his life, in his denial of human warmth to upheld a 'dignity' which he is supposed to inherit from his father and his master Lord Darlington. In his later novels such as *When We Were Orphans* and *Never Let Me Go* the protagonists Banks and Kathy respectively hold on to their childhood memories to reinvent their lost selves by diving deep into their shards of memories to evaluate the very basis of their isolation. Their nostalgia resulting from a blurry confrontation with the simmering past lead them to significant discoveries which even become more intolerable for them to resist. Ishiguro thus explains his pre-occupation with memory in an interview:

> I like memory, at various levels. At a purely technical level, I like it as a method of telling story—it gives me plenty of freedom.... And I just like the texture of memory as well. I like that the scenes are necessarily foggy around the edges, because they are open to manipulation and they're open to self-deception and embroidery. And they're often tinged with nostalgia, some kind of strong emotion. I like all these layers that come with a scene. Thematically, I have been interested in memory itself. (Liquori)

This emphasis on manipulation, distortion and self-deception are the basic qualities with which Ishiguro deliberately invests his characters and foregrounds their memories in the narrativisation of their self-identification. Barry Lewis has powerfully remarked that, "the novels are all engaged with memory and memory, by its very nature, is uncertain, quivering, subject to erasures and displacement" (128).

Ishiguro thus engages his protagonists to relocate their private selves in a recontextualising dialectics of self-actualisation.

Memory, in this context serves as one of the building blocks of identity formation which is rather not a fixed entity but a process, always in the making, "as a 'production', which is never compete, always in process, and always constituted within, not outside, representation" (Hall, "Cultural Identity" 51). Analogously, Jerome Bruner believes that self is basically a construction, a result of replication and symbolisation in which different visions of the world is formed in the minds of the individuals created out of personal memories and the narrativisation of the world around the self (130). In this critical context, self can be equated with a text which is meaningful only with its relationships with the others' positionalities in the world:

> I think of Self as a text about how one is situated with respect to others and towards the world—a canonical text about powers and skills and disposition that change as one's situation changes from young to old, from one kind of setting to another. The interpretation of this text *in situ* by an individual is his sense of self in that situation. (Bruner 130)

For Ishiguro's characters, past is essentially meaningful in the construction of identity. The present sense of alienation can be understood through an evaluative journey into the collusive caves of memory and those who transport more of their past lives into their lived presence "both confirm their own identity and enrich the present with the past's amplified residues" (Lowenthal 198). Remembering, then is a complex sub-conscious process that problematises the idea of simplistic chronological relations, linking the events of the past with that of the present in the continuity of human experience in which the "subject is recognized by its inexplicable ties to what cannot be experienced or subjectified fully" (King, *Memory, Narrative and Identity* 12). Laplanche and Pontalis point out to this transcriptive tendencies of memory which indelibly involves the awareness of the past deprivation and denials in the recreation of the meaningful present (111). In this contextualisation of the fresh conditions, memory re-transcribes itself taking materials not only from the actual new circumstances of the real-life situations of the subject but also from the wish-fulfilling fantasies that has been denied in the past itself which challenges the homogeneity and fixity of self-identification. The traumatic experience of the self is a summative, unremitting process of revision emphatically tracing the deferred tendencies of memorialisation. Laplanche and Pontalis thus enumerate this unassimilated experience of recapitulation:

> Experiences, impressions and memory-traces may be revised at a later date to fit in with fresh circumstances or to fit in with a new stage of development. They may in that event be endowed not only with the new meaning but also with psychical effectiveness.... It is not lived experience in general which undergoes a deferred revision but, specifically, whatever it has been impossible in the first instance to incorporate fully into a meaningful context. The traumatic event is the epitome of all such unassimilated experience. (111-12)

Maintaining a uniform totality of sense experiences and a reflective awareness of the relationship between the experiences of the past and that of the present are central to the evolving sense of individuality. In the narrative act of rewriting the self, Ishiguro thus explores a transactive model of self-awareness, integrally weaving memory with a phenomenal narrative strategy which enables the characters to accumulate the fragments of their past lives to stitch the racks of the present with all of their flaws and failure. Formation of identity is a continuous result of presenting and representing one's individuality to oneself and to the world around. As Daniel Dennett insightfully observes:

> We are almost constantly engaged in presenting ourselves to others, and to ourselves, and hence representing ourselves—in language and gesture, external and internal ... our human environment contains not just food and shelter, enemies to fight or flee, and conspecifics with whom to mate but words, words, words. These words are potent elements of our environment that we readily incorporate, ingesting and extruding them, weaving them like spider webs into self-protective strings of narrative. Indeed...when we let in these words, these

> meme-vehicles, they tend to take over, creating us out of the raw materials they find in our brains. (417)

Ishiguro's *The Remains of the Day*, in this respect is an extended experimentation in the poetics of identification reconfigured by the fragile fragments of memorialisation. The entire novel is constructed around the motif of a journey—Stevens' real journey has a metaphorical parallel in the trip his mind takes to the narrative residues of the past in which his recollection is purposive of the prefigurement of his life as well, for the butler generates a new version of his past life that is more acceptable to him than his real-life story. To impart his existence a substantial novelty, he seeks to narrate his life in a manner that conceals the "terrible mistakes" (239) of his life. Ishiguro comments on this occluding inclination of his narrator-protagonist: "Stevens ends up saying the sorts of things he does because somewhere deep down he knows which things he has to avoid ... why he says certain things, why he brings up certain topics at certain moments, is not random. It's controlled by things he doesn't say. That's what motivates the narrative" (qtd. in Shaffer, *Understanding* 64).

Stevens' actualisation of his identity is a cumulative process which involves the combination of his disparate engagements with the various issues the novel seems to address and relocate that includes his unreliable narration, his conceptualisation of dignity, his repressive ideology of self-denial, his reconciled critique of the twilighted existence of the British Empire and the notion of Englishness which are explicitly related to the idea of home in the reformulative dialectics of identity and belonging. Let us discuss the issues in detail.

Ishiguro in *The Remains of the Day* presents an *autodiegetic* framework of narrativisation in which the narration in an unreliable pattern engages in long monologues about himself being obsessed with his disrupted past which reflects on a largely ego-centric accounts of events. Stevens' narration is unreliable in the sense that he doesn't undergo all experiences and the past events are described as imaginative projections into an exhausted temporality of his being.

Stevens also warns about the deceptive properties of memory: "it is possible this is a case of hindsight colouring my memory" (87). Bruno Zerweck describes this "unintentional self-incrimination" (156) of the narrator as part of the unreliable narration which provides frameworks for the reader to reason out the referentialities of these realities. The narrator with his prolonged monologue may focus on a positive side and conceal other implications in a naturalising mode of unintentionality. As Amit Marcus observes, the narrators in this mode of representations are "self-deceiver(s)" who seem to be "unaware of the strategies they employ to convince themselves of the veracity of the lie, and therefore their state of mind is not a consequence of an intentional act of deception, as opposed to the state of mind of the other deceivers" (188). Stevens' unreliable narration is in fact is an effective strategy to address these contradictions between the lines which question the traditional conceptualisation of the unreliable narrator:

> Ishiguro's most recent novel is as much about unreliability as it is about the conflict between the public and private personae, between professional and human duty, between the facade of dignity and the expression of emotion. Indeed, Stevens' narrative unreliability is a key means through which these conflicts, largely unresolved for him, are demonstrated. In turn, the novel challenges our usual definition of an unreliable narrator as one whose "norms and values" differ from those of the implied author, and questions the concept of an ironic distance between the mistaken, benighted, biased, or dishonest narrator and the implied author, who, in most models, is seen to communicate with the reader entirely behind the narrator's back. (18)

Chatman argues that the apparent conflict between story and discourse brings out the significance of the gap between appearance and reality in which the verbal tics gives explicit indications of these preoccupations that make their narration problematic. It, therefore, proposes an intuitively interactive process of reading "between the lines":

> In "unreliable narration" the narrator's account is at odds with the implied reader's surmises about the story's real intentions. The story undermines the discourse. We conclude, by "reading out," between the lines, that the events and existents could not have been "like that" and so we hold the narrator suspect. Unreliable narration is thus an ironic form.... The implied reader senses a discrepancy between a reasonable construction of the story and the account given by the narrator. Two sets of norms conflict, and the cover set, once recognized, must win. The implied author has established a secret communication with the implied reader. (Chatman 233)

Stevens' narrative unreliability is manifested in different patterns of verbal enunciations that maintained a highly elevated diction which according to Kathleen Wall "serves to establish a distance between him and a modern reader" (23). This is evident in the multiple ways in which the butler shifts markedly from the regular usage of the 'personal pronouns'. The formal gloss of articulation, however, masquerades this tendency of transposition:

> ... when Stevens feels as need to erase some part of himself, his shift from 'I' to 'one' is unfailing...such a distancing is evident in his comment on his father about whom his feelings are ambiguous at best.... Thus he continually avers that his trip to see miss Kenton has only professional motives, or that the impact of her departure from Darlington Hall would be felt only in the professional sphere, or that he inquires into her marriage only for professional reasons. (23-24)

The novel is replete with these kinds of modalising elocutions which reveal the defensive proclivities of the butler. In phrases like 'I should say', 'Let me make it immediately clear', 'I should point out', etc. are used as unconscious strategy of a defensive narrativisation "necessitated by the (unarticulated) questions of the narratee that, in the absence of any physical presence, seem to voice Stevens' own unexpressed and perhaps even repressed uncertainties about his values and his career" (Wall

24). Stevens, in using the words such as 'seem', 'as if', 'appears', 'undoubtedly', 'perhaps', etc. Allows him a hypothetical distance to assert things without stepping beyond the internal focalisation (Genette 203). The multiplicity of these hypothetical modalities "suggests much more the insolubility of the problem" (Genette 203) which creates space for a confidential evocation of a naive narratee as yet again a defensive gesture on the part of Stevens for there is an absence of the "physical presence in the novel to account for the 'you' he so frequently addresses" (Wall 24). Taking into account how Stevens "recalls" or "remember"; it can be inferred, states, Lilian Furst that although he sometimes seems to be able to remember his dislocated past he appears to be unsure of his memory and "these sporadic defects" in Stevens' memory do have the effect of "casting a shadow over what he claims to recall well" (535-36). As Genette pointed out, "narrative always says less than it knows, but it often makes known more than it says" (198), the character of Stevens is problematised with a dichotomy between what he 'knows' and what is buried in his unconscious, Kathleen Wall argues that the unreliable narrativisation concerns our "perceptions of a conflict between the scenes he narrates and the interpretation that he gives to those scenes" (25). One can note how Stevens is afflicted with the conflictual problematics of reconciling his behaviours with the feeling he reports and the way he is unable to notice emotions or reactions that others apparently notice. Also it is obvious that the motives he seems to ascribing on to others are not cognizant with the activities which results from those motives. By taking dignity as his primary values which he seems to inherit from his father, and by renouncing this facade only when he is alone to himself, Stevens has "attempted to avoid, in his life as well as in his narrative the voices and needs of the feeling self" (Wall 26). In this unreliable discursivity, "(w)hatever doesn't suit the values that he has given so much time and energy to construct must be ignored or avoided; the emotions or emotional turmoil of the private man must not be allowed to interfere with the duty and dignity of the public persona" (Wall 26). The conflict between the private and the public self has remained a recurrent theme in the novel which accounts for the oblique narrative strategy of Stevens. Cynthia Wong, in this context, contends that Stevens is able to project his insecurities onto others to reinvent the displaced memories, precisely because he can enunciate both *extradiegetic* and *homodiegetic* mode of narrativisation (*Kazuo Ishiguro* 14). An *extradiegetic* narrator is supposed to narrate the past events with a certain degree of aloofness, in contrast to the *homodiegetic* narrator who is grounded as a character himself within these waves of memories (Wong, *Kazuo Ishiguro* 14). The result is that Stevens is both inside and outside—"both central and peripheral to" (Wong, *Kazuo Ishiguro* 14) the events he narrates. This mode of representation is a process in which "the story and the narrating can become entangled in such a way that the latter has an effect on the former" (Genette 217). This anxiety between *extradiegetic* and *homodiegetic* modes of narration is a manifestation of Stevens' phantasised projection of maintaining authorial control over his feelings which seems to dominate him. He thus uses a form of negotiative rewriting of the past to "dissociate his present self from his past self" (Wong, *Kazuo Ishiguro* 6) and to relocate the strains of the past as a strategy to regulate his nostalgic regret. Stevens' words are deliberately deceptive in a circumlocutory constructedness which David James claims as "purposely arranged rather than spontaneous, more strategically organized than we might expect from a story composed from involuntary memories" (56). This mode of narration is cultivated to make things more palatable in the very act of telling (Wong, *Kazuo Ishiguro* 38). Despite Stevens' futile attempts to integrate the distorted memories, he rather attracts the readers to focus on the inconsistencies and disruptions.

Stevens, with his narrative unreliability seems to create a palatable version of reality for being unsuccessful in repressing his sense of loss and at times projecting it onto Miss Kenton.

The thought of Miss Kenton, weeping just behind her door doesn't entail an intuitive reflection on his past, but a projection of his grief at the idea of losing her to Mr. Benn. Yet, he transmutes this projection into a layer of defense by attaching this intuition to the demise of Miss Kenton's aunt rather than to her announcement of her engagement with the suitor. The warning of Miss Kenton's departure from Darlington hall is thus transformed into a less troubling sensibility, in the flow of Stevens' consciousness. Part of the unreliability involves in the ways one naturalises the text bridging its gaps on schemata (general directions) to evaluate the probable accuracy or motivation of the narrator's assertiveness. The dynamics of the relationship between Stevens and Miss Kenton and their feelings about each other's unexpressed emotions remain indeterminate to the end as neither character in the situation is presented as having adequate insight into others motives or behaviour. "In creating the text that is, at some points thoroughly indeterminate, Ishiguro foregrounds the problem of 'truth' perhaps challenging us never to figure out 'what really happened', and hence to take only an ironic pleasure in reaching what few conclusions come our way" (Wall 30).

The encompassing aspect of losing identity engenders Stevens with a self-idealising, acquisitively omnipotent notion of dignity and human greatness, in his service as a great butler to a distinguished lord in a great country house. This extended notion of greatness is an obsessive displacement of dignity on wrong things which is an outcome of his threatened sense of self-identification. As Stevens claims:

> The most deeply satisfying in the world...best summed up in the word, 'greatness'.... I distinctly felt that rare and unmistakable feeling ... that one is in the presence of 'greatness'.... We call our country Great Britain ... the landscape of our country alone would justify the use of this lofty adjective.... I would say that it is the very lack of obvious drama or spectacle that sets the beauty of our land apart ... the calmness of that beauty, its sense of restraint. (28-29)

Stevens' inauguration of the theme of dignity into what is "ostensibly a travel narrative" is argued by Kathleen Wall as "forced and bizarre enough to suggest quite clearly that Ishiguro is speaking to us over Stevens' voice, asking us to question the motives for the digression" (25). Stevens' obsessive linking of the 'calmness of that beauty' of the landscape, 'its sense of restraint' with that of the greatness of the butler is yet an example of misappropriated affiliation which reflects a hyperactive tendency towards achieving greatness by self-denial and negation:

> And let me now posit this: 'dignity' has to do crucially with a butler's ability not to abandon the professional being he inhabits. Lesser Butlers will abandon their professional being for the private one at least provocation. For such persons, being a butler like playing some pantomime role; a small push, a slight stumble, and the facade will drop off to reveal, the action underneath. The great butlers are great by virtue of their ability to inhabit their professional role and inhabit it to the utmost; they will not be shaken out by external events, however surprising, alarming and vexing. They wear their professionalism as a decent gentleman will wear his suit: he will not let ruffians or circumstances tear it off him in the public gaze; he will discard it when and only when, he wills to do so, and this will invariably be when he is entirely alone. It is, as I say a matter of 'dignity'. (43)

Stevens' hyper-dynamic sense of clothing is yet another version of unreliability projected into his characters. His sense of clothing is represented as both disguising and revealing the need for a veil of essentialist professionalism to mask the entirety of his emotional life. His consideration of his 'costume' on planning the trip as either a new travelling outfit or Lord Darlington's old-fashioned, formal suits reflects his professional inclination when he chooses the later as a part of a special kind of inheritance. Similarly, his frequent resorting to symbolisation, like his sense of clothing obscures his self-motivation and reveals his emotional dislocation. The maintaining of a formal, formulaic exterior is carefully designed to cover the actual self and to exclude emotions from professional life as evident in his self-betraying highly formal voice; at once pompous, assertive and contradictory. When Miss Kenton catches him reading a romance, one can notice how Stevens is very particular on covering up the real tension by explaining that it is only a language learning programme intended for the enrichment of vocabulary:

> The book was ... might be described as a 'sentimental romance'—one of a number kept in the library, and also in several of the guest bedrooms, for the entertainment of lady visitors. There was a simple reason for my having taken to perusing such works; it was an extremely efficient way to maintain and develop one's command of the English language.... It has never been my position that good accent and command of language are not attractive attributes, and I always considered it my duty to develop them as best I could ... such works tend to be written in good English, with plenty of elegant dialogue of much practical value to him. (167-68)

Stevens' sense of dignity, however, towards the end is challenged by his interaction with Harry Smith when he recognises that there is something less than being dignified in allowing one's affiliated loyalty to another as a means to build one's own life, yet he may never acknowledge the extent to which his professionalism has shaped his life. *Remains of the Day* thus challenges the approach to unreliable narration that emphasises "a fixation with an authoritative version of events that the implied reader cleverly constructs in spite of the narrator's purposeful or unconscious obfuscation" (Wall 37). It is problematised further in these ways to judge Stevens' own level of awareness of the contradictions that fill the narrative and the paradoxical values that inform his life along with the degree of self-knowledge he possesses to confirm to the poetics of a narrative reliability. As Kathleen Wall insightfully observes:

> An entirely reliable version is presented as impossible—a point that Ishiguro makes by leaving us with several insoluble aporia. Because "truth" is problematical and because, unless lying is highly motivated, narrators who are witnesses to events usually report them with a fair degree of accuracy, we need to re-think entirely our notion that unreliable narrators give an inaccurate version of events and that our task is to figure out "what really happened". (37)

Like Stevens, we also have to move to and fro about the circle of reason to figure out the full implications of what we have nourished all along but unlike him we must recognise the necessity and immutability of these duplicities.

This discrepancy between presentation and reality largely results from Stevens' misplaced conception of dignity. He considers having "dignity in keeping with his position" as the most important feature for becoming what he calls "a great butler" (33). Stevens elucidates that this dignity "has to do crucially with a butler's ability not to abandon the professional being he inhabits" which demands great "emotional restraints" on a butler's part (43). The professionalism of a butler, Stevens thinks, involves a repression of all wishes and projections that do not fit with that of the formal position of butlership. It is gradually evident that the ideals which he attaches to butlership are founded upon a blind loyalty to the employer Lord Darlington. As regards the dismissal of two Jewish servants from Darlington Hall, he suppresses his opinion and in contrast to Miss Kenton's obvious shock he asks her to "conduct herself in a manner befitting her position" (149) evading any further responsibility on the occasion. He believes that servants are not supposed to ponder over "judgements of such a high and mighty nature" and seeks to diffuse the protest against anti-semitism by calling them "foibles and sentiments" which need to be suppressed for the sake of a greater cause namely, serving the employer's wish unconditionally and unquestionably (149). Similarly, Stevens' sense of misplaced identification is revealed in his response to Miss Kenton's question about his ultimate contentment when he says, "the day his lordship's work is complete, the day he is able to rest on his laurels, content in the knowledge that he has done all anyone could ever reasonably ask of him, only on that day, Miss Kenton, will I be able to call myself, as you put it, a well-contented man" (173). Stevens in a transferential dialectics of identification transmutes the responsibilities of his own life into the life of his Lord, Mr. Darlington. Life, for him is only meaningful in the context of serving his Lord which comes into conflict with the commonsensical observation of a common villager whom Stevens meet in the country side: "there is no dignity to be had in being a slave" (186) which he cannot reconcile with: "There is, after all, a real limit to how much ordinary people can learn and know, and to demand that each and every one of them contribute 'strong opinions' to the great debates of the nation cannot, surely, be wise. It is in any case, absurd that anyone should define a person's 'dignity' in these terms" (194).

Ironically enough, Stevens' whole life can be seen as perpetuating this absurd notion of dignity which is clashed with that of many others in the course of the novel. This is the reason why Stevens feels loss of words when responding to the questions of the 'dignified gentlemen' assembled in Darlington Hall regarding the correctness of their views on democracy, as he has no self other than that of a servant which not only delimits his sense of identification but also restricts him to a position in the strict hierarchy of a totalitarian regime. The notion of dignity is thus reduced to a simple wish to fulfill the desire of a person who is placed higher in this hierarchy. Apart from this, Stevens is also misguided by a false sense of dignity in his belief that great butlers are meaningfully mobilised by great gentlemen worthy of national service as Lord Darlington himself through whom he can achieve the goal of "serving humanity" (117) by creating possibilities to "make our own small contribution to the creation of a better world" (116). In this differential negotiation of identities, Stevens, in order to sustain a strong sense of identification with a magnificent household, "struggles to reconcile his own private memories of Lord Darlington ... with the public vilification of Lord Darlington after the war" (Lang 145). He tries, at this level, to brush aside all his memories associated with Lord Darlington's ideal of Nazi appeasement "to avoid any possibility of hearing any further such nonsense concerning his Lordship" (126) which would make him revisit his suppressed emotions in the service of a wrong master. Stevens, again, is misguided by a false delight at contributing to organising the meeting between Lord Halifax and Herr Ribbentrop who seem to change "the course of the history" (134), although he is aware that he is contributing to an evil endeavor. He, therefore, finds himself in the crossroads of utter confusion, unable to judge as to whether he satisfies the qualities of a great butler which is consequent upon having a great employer. One can observe the instances when Stevens refuses having worked for Darlington Hall. He pretends to be a gentleman among the naive villagers, doesn't disclose his true identity responding to the chauffeur and also displaces his positionality while inquiring about by Mr. Farraday's guest. Such incongruities between appearance and reality fairly contribute to the evolvement of an unreliable narrative strategy. Ishiguro, as Mike Petry contends "often reveals his narrator's attempt to hide, by having them stumble over their own contradictions and inconsistencies" (6). Stevens has to encounter with his own mistaken realities because he attempts to tell the truth which in turn is negated by his views. There is a systematic underscoring of ideas that need to be discarded and which do not fit well to the picture of reality he wants to project. There is, therefore, immense ironic possibilities resulting from the split between "the narrator's view of the fictional world and the contrary states of affair which the reader can grasp" (qtd. in D'hoker 466). Ishiguro with the help of Stevens thus provides an alternate version of recreating realities which revolutionise the way in which reality is reconstructed in a narrativised totality in the mode of the narratorial dialectics of the fictionalised world.

In a similar fashion, Stevens idealises his father as inhabiting the noble qualities of a great butler having a 'dignity' of his own and rationalises his suppression of emotion even when his father is in his death-bed, on the pretext of attending to a more important work in Darlington Hall and claiming idealistically that his father "would have wished me to carry on just now" (106). Stevens' troubling concept of dignity even doesn't allow him to project his emotions of grief openly to which the readers are only hinted at from other sources. For instance, it is Lord Darlington himself who enquires: "... you look as though you were crying" (105). This is another occasion, Petry observes, when Stevens chooses to discuss one thing in order to hide another in which "what is not told turns out to be as, if not more, significant as what is told" (10). Molly Westerman, in this context, argues in favour of the 'constructed' nature of the father as an ideal butler which allows Stevens to maintain an imaginary distance between the idea of the father as an exemplary great butler and a real person: "Despite his warm relationship with the construct of his father as paradigmatic butler, Stevens' relationship with his father, the actual person is unhappy and contradictory" (162). Tamar Yacobi explains this narratological evasiveness as "exegetical deflection" which involves "the speaker's mis-focusing" rather than a "direct misjudgment on his part: the issue most central or relevant ... is passed over in silence throughout the mediator's discourse, while side issues receive literal commentary" (34).

Analogously, with regard to Miss Kenton's letter, he claims to have identified "distinct hints of her desire to return" (9) but again starts playing with his thought and begins to discover the contrary aspects of this thesis prevented by his "professional relationship" (169). Furthermore, having angered her, in another occasion, with his usual indifference to her quitting the job to get married, he thinks for a moment "persistently lodged" (226) in his memory, hesitating in confusion outside the door: "quite certain that if I were to knock and enter, I would discover her in tears" (226-27). He then begins to displace this desire of empathising with Miss Kenton with a false belief that she might be sad because of her aunt's death. Unable to negotiate between contradictions and the significance of his hesitations outside the door, he immediately recollects a sense of triumph as an aspect of his dignity in overcoming a difficult situation at the end of the day. Barry Lewis in this context remarks that Stevens "simply discounts his obligations as a son and a potential husband" and mistakes them instead "as interruptions to his public duty. Tries but fails" (84). On his meeting with Miss Kenton, however, he acknowledges his feeling towards her when she says "there's no turning back the clock" by admitting that "at the moment, my heart was breaking" (239). But it was too late and Miss Kenton's remarks deprived him of his "vain hope of undoing the past" (Lodge, *The Art of Fiction* 156) and made him negotiate with his feelings.

Stevens, in his recollection of his relationship with other characters, is both within and outside the framework of narration. He is also confined with a particular set of emotions and experiences from which he could draw, by disrupting the meaning of systematically selected past events which he is able to discover with great joy or pain. Stevens, in this context, expands his self to meet the occasion—either by extending his awareness or by categorically confirming to his narrow vision by further assertions which essentially contributes to his ambiguous narrativisation of individual details. Ishiguro relates this deliberate attempt of Stevens for a false expansion of the self which he himself at times does not understand:

> When Stevens says that the greatness of Britain paradoxically comes from 'the lack of obvious drama or spectacle that sets the beauty of our land apart', he is also saying of something about himself. He thinks beauty and greatness lie in being able to this kind of cold, frozen, butler which isn't demonstrative and who hides emotion in much the way he's saying that the Britain landscape does with its surface calm: the ability to actually keep down turmoil and emotion. He thinks this is what both butlers and the British landscape beauty and dignity. And of course that view-point is the one that actually crumbles during the course of Stevens' Journey. (Vorda and Herzinger 76)

Stevens thus replicates an intimate life with a falsely dignified sense of professional duty, with his ideology of self-negation and denial. Raising in his mind, the possibility of Miss Kenton's departure from Darlington Hall, Stevens muses, "This was indeed a disturbing notion, for it was not hard to see that Miss Kenton's departure would constitute a professional loss of some magnitude, a loss Darlington Hall would have some difficulty recovering them" (180). Stevens, at this expense, seeks to shroud his personal proclivities with densely cultivated professional metaphors in order to rationalise such self-negation in the name of professional duty. He constitutes a theory on the professionalism of the great butlers from a certain Hayes 'society' and its publication *A Quarterly for the Gentleman's Gentleman* as incorporating the most qualifying features of entering into a membership of it is what "possessed of a dignity in keeping with his position" (33). As dignity turns out to be equating restraint, Stevens then creates a positionality for himself not to bestow greatness on himself. For David James, "the pathos of the situation is that Stevens ends up rehearsing a discussion of esteem for which he refuses to become the ideal case study" (57).

It is interesting to note how Stevens struggles to reconfigure his affiliative identification in keeping with his values of dignity and well-cultured professionalism in a repressive ideology of unquestioning service to Lord Darlington which was not after all, "intelligently bestowed" (Jaggi 117) or dignified. As Ishiguro reflects, "I was interested in how people lie to themselves just to make things palatable ... we all dignify our failures a brute bit" (Jaggi 117).

Ishiguro's emphasis on this dignified version of humanity's failure which strives to make bitter things palatable can be viewed as having larger implications: "these errors may be trivial in themselves but you must yourself realize their larger significance," (63) not only points out Stevens' acknowledgement of his wasted life but also reflects Britain's failure to reinvent its magnificent imperialistic past fostered by the potentially misguided ideals. The nostalgic melancholia and the summative disillusionment which permeate the novel are reflections of Britain's failed attempt to reassess its self-image as a powerful colonial power. Ishiguro with his masterful control of tone and oblique narrative "noted that Stevens' self-abnegation in the service of his master reverberates with larger implications about British politics, culture and society" (Tamaya 45-46).

Ishiguro does not directly reflect upon the deliberating sediments of immigrant experiences like Kureishi, Rushdie and others but construes a capricious site for retrospective interrogation which enables the individual to link his/her personal losses and nostalgia with the post-war bewilderment which drastically reshuffled their personal and professional lives to expose the inherent frivolity and nuances of stable categories and phenomena like self/other, master/servant, coloniser/colonised, etc. As Norman Page observes, Stevens in Ishiguro's *The Remains of the Day* resembles Etsuko and Ono (Protagonists of *A Pale View of Hills* and *An Artist of the Floating World* respectively) in their discursive styles of relocation, for Ishiguro is skilful in "transferring to an English context a mode of communication and behavior that resembles the Japanese in its use of highly formal surface to cover tensions, concealments and self-deception" (167).

Ishiguro's ambivalent position allows him a diasporic perspective of transformative transaction with the historical past. His novel *The Remains of the Day* focuses on the retrospective interrogation of a mytho-poetic Britishness which exists in the minds of its people as disillusioned encounters with a melancholic memorialisation. By exposing the insignificance of the English tradition, it subverts the grounds in the politicisation of the spirit of Englishness in a multicultural society like England. The chapter attempts to address and explore the diverse modalities and contours of Englishness as reflected in *The Remains of the Day* which serves as a national allegory of post imperialistic reconfiguration illustrating the debilitating decadence of the glorious British Empire. It seeks to deconstruct the dominant metaphors of the legacy of Englishness which becomes an emphatic claim for a cosmopolitan inclusivity of fragmented loyalties and affiliations.

The Remains of the Day by Ishiguro presents a colonial dialectics of the permanent divide between the Eastern and the Western, the Conqueror and the Conquered, subtly extrapolated into the life of the narrator from the transcultural sensibilities of the author. The entire novel through a metaphor of journey seeks to deconstruct the dominant legacy of the myth of Englishness so ostentatiously imposed on the Empire. Stevens, the protagonist of the novel, is apprehensive of the twilight existence of its aggrandising Englishness though he constantly silhouettes the travesty of the English essentialism resulting from highly multicultural and non-nationalistic presentations. *The Remains of the Day,* in its elitist undercuts conditioned by Stevens' wavering loyalty for his master towards the end of the novel seems to be an advocacy for a wider notion of Englishness which proffers inclusion of many cultural and transcultural possibilities. Steven Connor, in this connection argues that:

> The purpose of the performance of national identity that is *The Remains of the Day* is therefore to let in what such a restricted imagining of identity relies on keeping out. It aims to enlarge the possibilities for narrating identity across and between cultures and their alleged essential characteristics and conditions by performing the impossibility of a more constrained, coherent imagination of Englishness. (112)

The study attempts to highlight Ishiguro's preoccupation with the theme of Englishness in which he deliberately seeks to set his protagonist in a globalising cosmopolitan space critiquing the exclusive model and the monocultural pattern of Englishness. The Asian diaspora living in Britain are stuck between two modes of culturalities which warrants an important step towards merging a global open society with the diverse localised forms of attachment and belonging. The present chapter thus aims to explore this post-imperialist anxiety in Ishiguro's characters to reconfigure their notion of Englishness, questioning its purity and essentiality which points out its proclivities toward multiple attachments and complex affiliations.

Ishiguro's assertion of himself as a writer of international novels brings out the significance of his involvement in the reformative poetics of post-colonial reclamations and engagements which seeks to stigmatise the opposition between absolutist notions and categories and challenges the Eurocentric essentialism of the colonial discourses. Dominic Head traces a similar impulse in "the retrospective colonial fiction of the post war era" which carries out the dialectics of immigration outwardly, but inwardly is quite attentive to "the disappearing empire being of particular significance to the ongoing domestic reconstruction of Englishness" (125). Rather than confining himself with a fixed locality and temporal specificity, Ishiguro traverses national boundaries and linguistic barriers to transmute the post-war trauma and the resulting sense of emotional alienation of cultural disjunction, skillfully into the lives of the protagonists, demonstrating the essential inward defamiliarisation of the supposed uniqueness of the idea of Englishness. As Sean Matthews and Sebastian Groes argue, "Ishiguro never plays the 'identity card' ... he acts increasingly as a contemporary everyman" (Matthews and Groes, Introduction 2-3). In Ishiguro's fictions "otherness is not a function of identity but rooted in a deeply moral imagination. *The Remains of the Day* deals with British appeasement of the Nazis, but it is also a subtle indictment of the failures of the international community during the interwar period" (Matthews and Groes, Introduction 2-3). Ishiguro deliberately strands his narrative into a subtle thread of historical reflexivity to map the complexities and modalities of the wider collective or national responsibilities for this course of events which is infallibly mixed up with private memories and individual involvement under the corrosive impact of a crumbling Empire. Such associative reading of *The Remains of the Day* helps the readers to recover some of the indeterminate elements of historical specificity which the author consciously conceals behind a formal, polished, unoppositional exterior to elucidate the degrees of the protagonist's self-deception, the extent of temporal displacement in the process of self-relocation and the ethical, emotional and political accountability as Ishiguro rightly points out "a novel isn't some sort of nonfiction, Novels are about emotional manipulation" (qtd. in Iyer 45).

Accordingly, Ishiguro's *The Remains of the Day* engages in a cogent explication of the deranged confluence of internal and external focalisation of voices, moods, vagaries of post war existence and challenges which is exquisitely balanced "between elegy and irony" (qtd. in Wang and Guo 6). So, working with these insider/outsider polemics of structural representment, the novelist proposes an immutable and sustained relationship of memory with identity which effectuate the protagonist's self-conscious effort to reconstitute and reconfigure his presence from a dislocated past bound up essentially with the political history of England as an Empire in the recollective process of cultural formations. This impulse of nostalgic reconsideration can be described as an attitude towards "the emotions what idealism is to intellect" and that "it is a way of longing for a better world" (Shaffer, "An Interview" 7) in the process of post imperial reconfiguration.

Ishiguro in *The Remains of the Day* seeks to represent the cultural travesty of a collapsing Empire with the tactical intricacy of inverting the migrants' position of threatened cultural existence by a native's summative contentment by shaping his stories outside the framework of diasporic deterritorialisation and resulting identity formation. Thus, we notice in the novel that the entire story as it is being told by an English butler, Stevens, "a genuine old fashioned old butler" (124) who constantly camouflages his sense of bewilderment by wearing the mask of an imperial Englishness and utmost professionalism which helps adjusting himself into a new cultural set up. Stevens' adjusting himself to his new master finds a parallel in England's accommodative strategy of imperial relocation which is grossly apprehensive of its flickering flame of colonial power. It is, therefore, highly suggestive that the grand Darlington Hall which is presented as a miniature version of England is consequently bought by an American which is symbolic of the latter's strengthening hegemony over a densely hierarchical empire. Before submitting himself to his new master, Mr. Farraday, Stevens has served Lord Darlington for a long thirty-five years. In these years he develops a strong domicile disposition with Darlington Hall—a genuinely grand old English house and when it is sold to a foreigner he finds his own identity threatened before a new domesticating front at once helps dawning in him a realisation of his inability of bantering skills. We can only imagine how much it hurts:

> I've tried and tried, but whatever I do I find I am far from reaching the standards I once set myself. More and more errors are appearing in my work. Quite trivial in themselves—at least so far. But they're of the sort I would never made before, and I know what they signify. Goodness knows, I've tried and tried, but it's no use. I've given what I had to give. I gave it all to Lord Darlington. (225)

This is also no coincidence that the novel begins with the summer of 1956, the time of Suez Crisis which witnesses the gradual declining of England as an Empire in the post imperialist imagination of Englishmen. Christine Berberich rightfully observes: "the British Empire had all but disappeared, and Britain was struggling for her place in the world hierarchy. Ishiguro's novel uses quintessentially English stereotypes, such as gentleman, the butler, and the trope of the country house, in order to reflect on national identity and crucially, a national consciousness" (135).

Stevens' obsessive preoccupation with maintaining professional dignity to the utmost in serving Darlington Hall effectuates a kind of self-erasure on his part, a commodification of the emotional propensities, in the face of a colossal hegemonising power to which he must contribute and work, in the process of his own subordination. His frequent references to the 'acting' and 'clothing' tropes bring out the inherent drama as Meera Tamaya remarks, "of rigorous submission of the private self to the demand of the public persona" (48). A similar situational irony can be attended upon the conversation of Mr. Stevens and Miss Kenton regarding the dislocated position of the Chinaman when Miss Kenton warns Stevens against these trivial errors which may have larger significance to the casual disregard of the minor neglection of the later. Certainly, the positioning and repositioning of the Chinaman has broader implications and ramifications in the differential politics of cultural dissection. Stevens, in a moment of celebratory exhibition of professional dignity, expresses his firm belief upon the inevitable Englishness of butlers faintly referring to a dialectics of permanent divide between the East and the West:

> It is sometimes said that butlers only truly exist in England. Other countries, whatever title is actually used, have only manservants.... Continentals are unable to be butlers because they are as a breed incapable of the emotional restraint which only the English race are capable of.... In a word, 'dignity' is beyond such persons. We English have an important advantage over foreigners in this respect and it is for this reason that

> when you think of a great butler, he is bound, almost by definition, to be an Englishman. (43)

Steven Connor in *The English Novel in History* identifies a similar Oriental/Occidental antithesis, subtly nourished throughout *The Remains of the Day* and is suspended obliquely to the private and public domain of an Empire: "The fact that the contrast between orderliness and disorderliness is posed in terms of the contrast between the English and the Oriental gently registers the link between domestic space and the global space of Empire" (110).

Ishiguro in *The Remains of the Day* subverts the stereotyping assumptions and attitude related to the idea of English butlership and English gentleman to demonstrate the hollowness of these fixed categories, and how they fall an easy prey to the misguided ideal of their respective lives which are indelibly coloured by their individual experience of the national history.

Stevens seems to inherit his conception of high dignity from his father whose sense of honour consists in affecting a sensibility of elemental Englishness in his butlership: "It is my firm conviction that at the peak of his career at Loughborough House, my father was indeed the embodiment of dignity" (34). The overarching theme of dignity with a tinge of quintessential Englishness, provides a solid ground for the narrator-protagonist to dismantle the hollowness of the disproportionate display of British essentiality. Stevens in his quest for identity must create a shadowed hedge before him behind which he can use the costume of indirectness, unreliability, obliquity and ambiguity to achieve internal dramatisation of external deterritorialisation and fragmentation. Ishiguro in *The Remains of the Day* provides a dislocated catalogue of historical events through the disfigured chain of personal memory and transforms those deformed items in a broken consciousness of post war nostalgic manipulation. Stevens' frequent repressions of his emotional engagement is symptomatic of the internal turbulence and suppressive reflexivity of cold war situation at one level, at other, it points out a similar configuration of the novelist's life in the globalising dialectics of summative acculturation: "There is something in my make up ... something in my past perhaps—there is some wound or something that's never going to heal, that I can just caress at least. And I can only get to that wound by writing" (qtd. in Shaffer, *Understanding* 112). This displaced transposition and the matrix of regressive deference supply him a stimulus to dismantle the myth of Englishness projected exquisitely into the catastrophic discomfiture of both the servant and the master who are extremely obsessive of their shallow exhibition of imperial Englishness.

Darlington Hall symbolises Englishness, tradition and aristocratic propensities. Stevens' nostalgic memorialisation of the lost grandeur can be compared with the present status of the estate which is handed over to some Mr. Farraday is suggestive of the growing American influence, much to the dissatisfaction of the protagonist and the diminishing magnificence of Darlington Hall which appears to be under renovation as a large part of the house is now "under wraps" (6). Later in the novel, Mr. Farraday refers to the mansion as a prison curtailing the freedom of the inmates and stifling their emotions: "You fellows, you're always locked up here in this house all the time I'm away. Why don't you take the car and drive off somewhere for a few days? You look like you could make good use of a break" (4).

Stevens is blessedly content delimiting his engagement within the confinement of Darlington Hall which he confidently identifies as the best model of the picturesque England upholding the bright examples of Englishness. He is boastful of acquainted with his own native country—its landscapes and its dignitaries, only through a displaced sense of realising Darlington Hall and its way of life. He seeks to substitute his sense of alienation and aloofness from the outer world with a feeling of self-conceived greatness which is strongly derived from his supposed contribution to the great affairs of the state: "... those of our profession, although we didn't see a great deal of the country in the sense of touring the countryside and visiting picturesque sites, did actually see more of England than most, placed as we were in the houses where the greater ladies and gentlemen of the land gathered" (5).

Stevens' cartographies of England primarily involve the aristocratic upper circle of life which represents the essentialist rigidity of English consciousness and the notion of 'dignity'. There are emphatic suggestions in the novel as to how the unruffled elements of the initial situations give way to a nightmarish messiness of centrifugal dispersion later in the narrative with the popping up of graver issues like anti-Semitism, crypto-fascism and a developing mistrust in the butler's loyal service to his master in the course of his mnemonic revival of a so-called glorious past.

Also Stevens' patronising inclination is manifested in his sudden realisation of the unique picturesqueness of the English landscape which draws its force primarily from a pertinent property of delicate restraint which he promptly connects with his sense of dignity eulogising on the exemplary but formal demonstrativeness of the English butlers:

> What is pertinent is the calmness of that beauty, its sense of restraint. It is as though the land knows of its own beauty, of its own greatness, and feels no need to shout it. In comparison, the sort of sights offered in such places as Africa and America, through undoubtedly very exciting, would, I am sure, strike the objective viewer as inferior on account of their unseemly demonstrativeness. (30)

Stevens in his impressionistic observation and engagement develops a paternalistic model of imperialist Englishness which reflects the post-war melancholia of a decadent nation in ruin. Throughout his motoring journey Stevens attempts to uphold and re-establish the older order of aristocratic paternalism in his representative enactment of the spirit of Englishness in all its forms and hierarchies howsoever much meager that contribution may be. A sense of utter transience of old essentialising values attached to the idea of Englishness emerges in the narrative of Stevens which he consciously masquerades beneath a subtle reintroduction of aristocratic values as is internalised in the person of Stevens from Lord Darlington's presupposition. However, the new England he chances to discover poses a great threat to these values and renders his naturalising task of defending Lord Darlington's affairs almost hollow within.

In subscribing to the views of Lord Darlington who is quite convinced of the complicity of the hierarchical systematisation and strong leadership in State affairs: "... if your house is on fire, you don't call the household to the drawing room and debate the various options for escape for an hour, do you? It may have all very well once, but the world's a complicated place now" (200), Stevens seems to legitimatise the patronising attitude of a bygone era and adds unscrupulously to the Empire's disintegration which is still proud of its demeaning dignity he has so circumspectly tried to uphold. Stevens' preoccupation with dignity indicates a wider diplomatic manoeuvring in the world politics in which Britain had to continuously struggle to re-actuate its lost magnificence and its chief claim to be the most civilised nation, entrusted with the responsibility to instill the spirit of democracy in others. The value system Stevens espouses finds a parallel in Lord Darlington's well-intentioned defense of the paternalistic model of aristocracy. The master and the servant purportedly merge into one as both are victimised by their false consciousness of re-enacting a form of Englishness which is grossly inappropriate to the occasion. They are equally misled into the servile reworking of the myth of Englishness in their emphatic restatement of the 'idea of dignity' which is conceptualised differently in different contexts of the novel. This version of aristocratic Englishness displayed by Stevens falls into sharp contrast with that of the Harry Smith's which appears to be more democratic in its classless representation of an all-inclusive Englishness:

> Dignity isn't just something gentlemen have. Dignity is something every man and woman in this country can strive for and get ... there is no dignity to be had in being a slave. That's what we fought the war for and that's what we won ... no matter if you're rich or poor, you're born free so that you can express your opinion freely, and vote in your member of parliament or vote him out. That's what dignity's really about, if you'll excuse me sir. (185-86)

Steven's reworking of the myth of Englishness drastically fails because the assumption he carries in defense of his master no longer holds ground in the politicisation of the spirit of Englishness in the post-war era. Stevens' deliberate fashioning and refashioning of himself as an English gentleman and the prototypes of English butler dramatically crumbles into insignificance at a crucial moment when the ownership of Darlington Hall is transferred to the American, Mr. Farraday which makes him question his own position in relation to the old certainties he seeks to re-establish rather than identifying himself as confirming to these views. Stevens' problem reflects a still deeper post-war disillusionment because of the lack of alternative models which should compensate the loss of initial appeal of the new form of life that emerges. With the change of ownership, Stevens' life too undergoes a similar transformation which is readily noticed in his reluctance to disclose to the guests his previous engagement with Lord Darlington and his grand estate to the much irritation of Mr. Farraday: "I mean to say, Stevens, this is a genuine grand old English home, isn't it? That's what I paid for. And you're a genuine old fashioned English butler, not just some waiter pretending to be one. You're the real thing, aren't you? That's what I paid for, Isn't that what I have" (124)? Farraday's insistence on 'the real thing' designates his desire to possess and exhibit a lost tradition relicing the glorious past. His words bring out the insignificance of the English tradition which has been commodified as an image of the past having market value in the process of its preservation.

The novel's open ended inconclusiveness points out to the incomplete, fragmented, traditional image of Englishness amongst which Stevens has to meditate the real meaning of his life, questioning his past services and loyalties, restructuring his old ideals and sensibilities when he discovers 'evening' as the best part of the day: "I should adopt a more positive outlook and try to make the best of what remains of my day" (257). In this epiphanic moment of self-realisation, Stevens reconnects his own 'remains'—the twilight years of his existence with that of the Empire which is in utter dissolution, fast replacing the old order and attitude with new and redemptive ones, yet nostalgic of its lost magnitude of imperial Englishness. Stevens' epiphany becomes an impeccable claim for the construction and reconstitution of a wider cultural perspective which can be built best upon the very remnant of the Empire's past, an all-inclusive Englishness which should ever contextualising itself in "an open framework, continually in the making" seeking to "accommodate other worlds, other vocabularies, other memory" (Chambers, *Border Dialogues* 47-50) in a densely globalising world. Stevens' entire life has thus been reduced to this few moment of truly personal meditation in which he is allowed a glimpse of the real meaning of human life when he asserts, "in bantering lies the key to human warmth" (259) which at once transforms him from an analyst to an enthusiast.

With regard to the cultural situatedness of the novel *The Remains of the Day,* Lawrence Graver writes: "... it is remarkable too, that as we read along in this strikingly original novel, we continue to think not only about the old butler, but about his country, its politics and culture." Ishiguro's ambivalent position in this "stuck on the margins" (Vorda 68) dialectics renders Stevens' homeless mind as Barry Lewis suggests, a "perfect representative of the century's displacement" (7) and locates the novel "in the transitional moments of history, when one set of values is replaced by another" (144). Ishiguro seems to work on more universal themes which may project a greater view of cultural inclusivity in contrast to the narrow reductionist view of an essentialist Englishness, because "all cultures are involved in one another; none is single and pure, all are hybrid, heterogeneous, extraordinarily differentiated and unmonolithic" (Said xxv).

Ishiguro uses *The Remains of the Day* as a tool to explore this "imperial pretensions of a fading British empire" (Lewis 14). Stevens discovers it problematic to find that the appearance of trivial errors in his work points out to a decline in his powers as irreversible as that of his father's. He realises that he has wasted all his energy in service to Darlington Hall in pursuit of an eluding, mythopoetic Englishness which leads him to maintain a polished imperial version of the language that he seeks to uphold. As Barry Lewis rightfully observes: "if *The Remains of the Day* is seen as an allegory of the decline of the British Empire, then it can be interpreted both pessimistically and optimistically. Stevens' failure is a fable in the passing of a certain conception of Englishness; but it is a death many would not wish to mourn" (Lewis 100). The novel attacks the pretensions of the twilighting British Empire as Ishiguro believes, "Britain is not the center of the universe" (Vorda 71); he seems to have evolved a universal model of cultural presentation transcending the general, exclusive notion of Englishness or Japaneseness.

Stevens' defense of the Lord Darlington's complicity with the Nazi is an attempt to revitalise a paternalistic model of Englishness in the disrupted moments of a post-war era. England, in this transferential displacement is equated with the wealthy visitors to Darlington Hall that Stevens has to attend to, before the war. His pre-conceived picture of England, however, is derived from a particular class of the English society described in the third volume of Mrs. Jane Symon's *The Wonder of England* which was written during the 1930s and who herself used to be a frequent visitor to the country house. He feels that Mrs. Symon's book will still be useful as "I don't imagine German bombs have altered our country side so significantly" (11). The prospective vision of his journey is thus mediated through the cartographies of England supplied by Mrs. Symons' version of a wonderful England:

> I had not looked through those volumes for many years, until these recent developments led me to get down from the Shelf the Devon and Cornwall volume once more. I studied all over again those marvelous descriptions and illustrations and you can perhaps understand my growing excitement at the notion that I might now actually undertake a motoring trip myself around that same part of the country. (12)

Moreover, Stevens' circuitous journey which reflects his circumlocutory pronouncements demonstrates his vain attempts to build up a particularly confined representation of England. His anticipated wonder of visiting the West Country is thus informed by an attempt to project a rehearsal of these values. The views of England and English landscape which he has envisioned in his mind do not exist in reality to which he must supplement to compensate the loss, with his usual, elaborative mannerism. The greatness which Stevens finds in the landscape is immediately transferred in his consciousness to a feeling of national pride that is coupled similarly with an unmistakable "restraint" which does confirm to a definite model of Englishness. Meera Tamaya argues that "this self-effacement is bred in the bone from generation to generation, even as the British class system has survived largely intact through the centuries" (48). The novel *The Remains of the Day* in this context represents a rigid world order which Ishiguro wants to subvert in the framework of Stevens' oblique narrative:

> Ishiguro is unique among post-colonial writers because unlike Rushdie, for example, who writes at such unwieldy length and with much obstructive polemics about the consequences of history, Ishiguro uses that consummately economical and British literary form—the novel of manners—to deconstruct British society and its imperial history ... thus heralding the end of Britain's long reign as the world's foremost colonial power. Not so coincidentally, on that particular day, the narrator/protagonist of the novel, Stevens, the quintessential English butler, sets out a journey across England and, in the process, recovers the tragic truth of his past, a truth inextricably bound up with the history of his country. (45)

In this sense, *The Remains of the Day* presents a "concern with place and displacement" which Ashcroft, Griffith and Tiffin describe as a "special postcolonial crisis of identity ... with the development or recovery of an effective relationship between self and place" (*The Empire* 8). Stevens, in this context, is not actually displaced geographically from a specific locality of culturation but indeed he experiences an uprooted sense of homelessness being alienated in his own cultural configuration at a moment of great socio-cultural transition. The novel also projects explicit "concern with the myths of identity and authenticity" which Stevens with his exquisite control over language so rigorously masquerades as critiquing an "imperial education system" which with its essentialist imposition "installs a 'standard' version of the metropolitan language as the norm, and marginalizes all variants as impurities" (Ashcroft, Griffiths and Tiffin, *The Empire* 7-9). In this metamorphic transposition, Ishiguro treats himself "as a kind of writer of exile" whose past immigrant experiences resulting from the cultural bifurcation indelibly colour "the emotional exile of his characters" (Wong, *Kazuo Ishiguro* 6). Ishiguro, "as a kind of homeless writer" assumes "no obvious social role" because he is not "a very English Englishman" and not "a very Japanese Japanese either" ("The Novelist" 115). Even without an oppressive colonial experience, Ishiguro feels an inward alienation of utter homelessness being diverged between two sets of cultural experiences "thereby aliening himself with the postcolonial emphasis on the marginal, that liminal, the excluded" (Lewis 13). Culturally, Ishiguro thus contributes to this model of liminal in-betweenness being straddled on two cultural 'homes' simultaneously. As Ishiguro clarifies:

> I grew of with a very strong image in my head of this other country. This very important other country to which I had a strong emotional tie.... Of course, I didn't know Japan, because I didn't come here. But in England I was all the time building up this picture in my head of an imaginary Japan.... I realized that this Japan, which was very precious to me, actually existed only in my own imagination, partly because the real Japan had changed greatly between 1960 and later on. I realized it was a place of my childhood and I could never return to that particular Japan. (Ishiguro, "Wave Patterns" 76)

Ishiguro's awareness as a homeless writer is evident in his assertion that he has no clear role to assume, not any particular country or society to write about and not even a specific history to be identified with ("Wave Patterns" 83). This emphasis on the disjunction from history points out to the very idea of a disintegrated identification being affiliated to no fixed locality which germinates possibilities for the construction of the 'imaginary homelands'. Salman Rushdie summarises this emotional emptiness that informs the mood of the immigrant writers seeking to create an all-inclusive universality from the very concretised, physical mode of discontinuity:

> It may be argued the past is a country from which we have all emigrated, that its loss is part of our common humanity which seems to me self-evidently true; but I suggest that the writer who is out-of-country and even out-of-language may experience this loss in an intensified form. It is made more concrete for him by the physical fact of discontinuity, of his being 'elsewhere'. This may enable him to speak properly and concretely on a subject of universal significance and appeal. (Rushdie, *Imaginary Homelands* 12)

Ishiguro, like Salman Rushdie seeks to relocate his 'home' built from the productive "shards of memory" which become all the more significant "because they were 'remains', fragmentation made trivial things seem like symbols and the mundane acquired numinous qualities" (*Imaginary Homelands* 12). Stevens of *The Remains of the Day* in his opulently oblique, and non-linear narrative methods revolutionises the concept of memory and identity by deftly concealing a world of realities about his moral negotiations and reconfigurement of his misguided ideals beneath the surface of a verbal mode that is elaborately inexpressive in rationalising neutrality in expressions. Ishiguro has demonstrated how historical events elliptically enunciated point out to the different facts of personal realities which in turn permeates the fabric and texture of interpersonal relationship. As Meera Tamaya contends:

> It is a measure of Ishiguro's novelistic genius while he presents the historical context of Stevens' tragedy with the dialectic economy ... the power of the novel resides in the precise and powerful articulation of human feeling, which is none the less painful for being oblivious of historical forces. For the majority of us who do not play leading roles on the world's stage, history is not experienced as "history", but as it affects the fabric and texture of personal relationships. What the critic Raymond Williams says about the great tradition

> of nineteenth-century fiction is applicable to *Remains of the Day*: "Neither element, neither the society nor the individual, is there as a priority. The society is not a background against which the personal relationships are studied, nor the individuals merely illustrations of aspects of the way of life." Every aspect of personal life is radically affected by the quality of the general life, yet the general life is seen at its most important in completely personal terms. (54)

The confluence of the historical and personal thus adds to the complexity of the discourse which reveals simultaneously a multi-layered pattern of acceptance and denial, manifestation and concealment which become the informing qualities of the butler's individuality and identity. It not only provides clues to the human motives and identities in the contextual negotiation of personality but also discovers the larger structures of historical relationship with a nation that is grossly nostalgic of its pretentious imperial power. Relocating the novel in its historicity, "the obsolescence of the myth of Britain as an imperial power is exposed ... through the collapse of the narrator's confident organization of the world" (Machinal 90).

Indeed Britain finds in Stevens a parallel of its rationalising proclivities towards the errors of the past in rewriting the histories of its dismantled Englishness. The disruption of Stevens' proud world of butlership and the magnificent Darlington Hall thus coincides with the final glow of Britain's supposedly glorious imperial enterprises. Stevens with his unreliable reminiscences presents the unreliable configuration of historical engagements in the catastrophic development of Britain's omnipotent imperiality. The historical allusions in the novel thus unfold a larger theme of negotiative encounter between the past and the present which happens to be a principal concern for the immigrant authors in Britain. Displacement, both in terms of temporal and spatial transpositions creates in them an anxiety to cartograph the modalities of 'home' where they can implant their lost sense of self-identification. These transcultural experiences involve not only the outward recognitions of changes and disruptions but also the underlying forces that colour such motivations. The writer's double-consciousness and situational in-betweenness activate a deeper insight enabling the writer to decipher a greater significance in the connection of these universal entities to its particular manifestations. The 'presence' of these writers, in this context, is recreated from the very past from which they are migrated into a new territoriality. Rushdie thus writes:

> Our identity is at once plural and partial. Sometimes we feel that we straddle two cultures; at other times we fall between two stools. But however ambiguous and shifting this ground may be, it is not an infertile territory for a writer to occupy. If literature is in part the business of finding new angles at which to enter reality, then once again our distance our long geographical perspective, may provide us with such angles. (*Imaginary Homelands* 15)

The Remains of the Day in its cultural commitment thus delineates this temporal and territorial transpositions of the individual with a discourse that eternally evokes the texture of memory as a negotiative transaction between past and present, the homeland and the host land, belongingness and dislocation—a claim in favour of an all-encompassing universality merging the local with the global which challenges the limitedness of cultural experience and essentialist identification.

Similarly, in *When We Were Orphans*, Ishiguro experiments with the reflective sensibility of a transcultural experience in which identity is viewed as being permeated with the fragmented strands of memory relating the past with the present. Potentially intended for an international readership, the novel oscillates between two localities—England and Shanghai and presents the protagonist as "stuck on the margins" (Vorda 68), moving between the centre and the periphery in the quest of his lost identity. The novel in a similar fashion like *The Remains* brings out the historical and political significance of national events in the formation of individual identities. Ishiguro here depicts how the fragmented memories of the past can be reviewed and re-examined to relocate one's 'home' or 'identity' in a globalising cosmopolity.

Christopher Banks, the protagonist-narrator of the novel is engaged in search of his lost parents in Shanghai who have mysteriously disappeared in his childhood. The first three parts of the novel are set in England when the protagonist is presented as a young adult, grooming himself to be a detective and establishing himself as pursuing a stable career in a well-settled place. In these three parts, Banks' childhood memories with his friend Akira in Shanghai are depicted at great length which reflects the nostalgic proclivities of Banks' psychological disposition.

Banks' circuitous memory like that of Stevens' meandering journey unfolds by degrees the various decisive dealings in the past, linking them with the disparate forbearing of the presence. Banks, in his childhood, has been taken to England and is raised by his aunt. Banks gets his admittance to Cambridge University and receives a good education before making himself a renowned detective in England. As informed later, Banks' mother is against the opium trade and eventually his parents, it seems, to have been kidnapped by the opium dealers who are supposed to pose a threat to the opium market in the territory. Banks with his fragmented memories attempts to evoke the scenes of the past to unravel the mysteries of his orphanhood. Often in the course of the novel, Banks' life is presented as essentially coloured by his engagement with the past events—his emotional attachment to his mother and Uncle Philip, and the faithfully shared moments with his friend Akira with whom he recreates the drama of his father's rescue, time and again, as a mock detective with his friends.

In England, working as an eminent detective, he develops a hopeless affair with Sarah Hemmings, an orphan and indeed he adopts a young orphan girl named Jennifer as his stepdaughter. Returning to China, he is, however, caught up in the ongoing war between China and Japan, but to his great relief is intimated about the whereabouts of his parents from Uncle Philip. Uncle Philip informs Banks that his father elopes with a woman in Shanghai and dies in Singapore pursuing his journey. His mother was kidnapped by a powerful drug mafia named Wang Ku and was kept by him as his concubine. Banks further traces the movement of his mother and finds her in a mental hospital in Hong Kong at the end of the novel.

Christopher Banks sustains these memories of the childhood, continuously examining them to make sense of the present. But gradually as the novel unfolds, we also get a clear view of the inner working of his mind when he seems to be deluding himself avoiding a direct confrontation with the traumatic past that has shaped his present life. Ishiguro, in this novel, uses memory as a thematic device to explore the dark spots of Banks' life unrecovered yet through the distorting web of the memory. In *The Remains,* Stevens has to visit the unscrutinised rooms of his memories to examine the mistakes of the past, but in *When We Were Orphans,* Banks must return to his childhood memories because he can't replicate them with anything whatever in the present conditionalities. Memory here, thus takes a nostalgic turn in an attempt to reinvent the past as a solution for the problematic present. Banks enjoyed his life at best when he was staying in Shanghai with his parents and playing with his friend Akira which has still a significant effect on his present life. Banks fails to accept the fact that the happiness of the past is no more a reality for him and that he has to nostalgically resort to it, constantly throughout his life to construct an integrated sense of his dilapidated memories. Ishiguro thus reflects upon these nostalgic inclinations of his protagonist by saying that most people consider this nostalgia in terms of its negativities, treating it to be an obsessive enunciation of the past but for him, "it can be quite a valuable force in our lives" which can serve to become an "emotional equivalent to idealism" (Shaffer, "An Interview" 7). Thus, for Ishiguro, nostalgia is to emotion what intellect is to idealism.

The childhood innocence of Banks is revisited time and again by him with a motive to snatch some graceful moments from this beautiful past and to resituate his lost sense of rootedness, in the process of his self-actualisation. The novel thus moves around a personal sense of nostalgia for one's own childhood days. Banks' nostalgia effectuates the strong sense of realising a better dream and a better place to belong. Nostalgia then becomes a positive influence which shapes the present condition of life ironing out the defects of the past. Indulging in nostalgia becomes an inherent claim for the quest of an identity in Banks' world of utter homelessness as Eber and Neal points out: "the search for identity in modern society stems from a sense of incompleteness" (169). The fragmented sense of homelessness inhabits the memory of Christopher Banks when he says towards the end of the novel: "there are those times when a sort of emptiness fills my hours" (368) that demonstrates the ways in which the fragmented experience of the world is subtly inculcated into the life of the modern man and it is difficult to evolve a central metaphor to represent this essential human condition:

> I think most people live in that kind of a world. Nothing is a perfect metaphor for the human condition. This is just one metaphor for one aspect of how people are. The strategy here is that we're looking at a very strange world, at a very strange group of people, and gradually, I wanted people to feel they're not looking at such a strange world, that this is every body's story. (Bates 216)

There are, in the novel, in fact, two more orphans in the form of Sarah Hemmings and Jennifer which seems to universalise the condition of 'orphanhood', that being orphaned is a common experience of the general humanity of "what happened when parents or guardians aren't really what they seem to be" (Bates 216) and there is a gradual losing of the sense of belonging. The individual sense of Banks' homelessness is thus metaphorically multiplied into a collective experience of transpired rootlessness which makes them to reconfigure their identities, resituating their lost sense of belonging through a productive transaction with their memories and fantasies for the creation of better world lives. To create a better world, however, is consequent upon solving the mysteries of the past, disentangling the devastating dues of the past. As Yugin Teo argues:

> For Ishiguro, nostalgia connects us to our childhood innocence when we believed the world to be 'a better, a nicer place' than it turned out to be when we grew up.... Nostalgia is intertwined with memory and

> fantasy, where we remember a time when the outlook on life was much simpler and more innocent, harking back to childhood and the days when we believed that everything that had gone wrong could be fully restored to the way it was before. The imperative behind Banks' quest to find his missing parents in Shanghai is a child's longing for things to be returned to the way they were. These poignant longings for a better world are often traced back to something that went wrong or had been left unresolved in the past, creating the imperative later on to set things right. (45)

Ishiguro, therefore, says that the trio "Banks, Sarah and Jennifer all feel that they have to repair something and only then that they can pick up where they left off" (Shaffer, "An Interview" 9). This is the motivation behind Banks' deliberate recollection of his family home and the way of life they were leading there, with a hope to recover them by imagining, even after years of their disappearance; that they might be held prisoner in some remote places in Shanghai and that they can still be traceable to a thorough search. Sarah Hemmings, however, who lost her parents in early childhood, has learnt to accept life as it is. Replying to Banks' question as to whether she has lost her parents long ago, she answers, "it seems like forever ... but in another way, they're always with me" which seems to serve as providing a solution to the universalizing problem of orphanhood of the whole human race. As Pascal Zinck contends, "orphanhood becomes a central metaphor for universal trauma" (147) and the individuals in the present cultural configuration of the world "must face the world as orphans" (168). The novel with its multiple evocation of homelessness thus presents several locations and places of identification. Christopher Banks, in his childhood days, identifies himself with Shanghai, the place where his parents live and where he establishes a happy friendship with Akira. When, after his parents' disappearance, he is transported to England, he cannot adapt to the life in England owing to his attachment to the former land and way of life there. Later in the novel, when he meets his friend Akira once again as a Japanese soldier on the war torn field he admits, "all these years

I've lived in England, I've never really felt at home there" and that "the international settlement ... will always be my home" (301). Shanghai holds Banks' past and becomes the centre of his longing and belonging. He has already developed an inwardness for the place lost in the mist of time.

Even after staying in England for years together, he can't forsake the desire of returning to this nostalgic 'home'. But returning home involves possibilities of a painful encounter with a disastrous past, an unfortunate moment in which he lost his parents and a familiar locality. Reflecting on the equation of nostalgia and home, Dennis Walder thus writes:

> Nostalgia begins in desire, and may well end in truth. It can, and often does, serve as a key to the multiple pasts that make us who and what we are, for better or worse. This is particularly the case in relation to the histories and experiences that fall under the rubrics of the post colonial.... Nostalgia is usually thought of in terms of longing and desire—for a lost home, place, and/or time. (*Postcolonial Nostalgias* 3-4)

Domestically, Banks' family suffers early displacement living in a settlement of transitory exile working in shanghai and living in a house owned by the company. It was his father who arranges for Banks the journey to England with a distant aunt, and a fairly good education with good 'connections' around. But Christopher Banks from his childhood has only nourished one idea in his mind—to be a detective, to return to Shanghai again and to rescue his lost parents. This desire to be a detective can be traced back to his early childhood days when they were living a happy life and suddenly his parents were kidnapped by a mysterious agency. Colonel Chamberlain arrives to pilot Christopher Banks to his new 'home' England when Banks, hopeful of a fateful turnout says: "the detectives are working extremely hard to find my mother and father. And they are the best detectives in Shanghai. I think they're bound to find them very soon" (27).

Banks, therefore, is very determined from his childhood days and later uses his nostalgia as a driving force behind his desire to become a detective and fight the evil out rescuing his father from the drug mafias. He learns that he cannot leave the world behind him which makes him reinvent the world of the past before him, in a still traumatic presence, transmuting his traumatic nostalgia into a narrative unreality that fits to hold these contradictory configurations. Dominique Vinet thus argues that it "corresponds to the slow emergence of the self which could never have been complete without a re-enactment of the game that the child had been playing with Akira" (141). Banks' nostalgia makes him quest for his identity and as he believes that Shanghai is the place where his identity is rooted. As Milan Kundera cogently sums up: "we are fatally rooted in the first half of life, even if life's second half is filled with intense and moving experiences" (qtd. in Elgrably) that raises questions about the formativity of individual experience, "of obsessions, of traumatisms which are inextricably tied to the first half of life which includes childhood, adolescence and adulthood" (qtd. in Mihailescu 212).

Not only his parents but also his friend Akira has an informing influence upon Banks' emotional make up. Akira and Banks have shared many intimate moments together and have become a familiar comfort and understanding to each other. It is by Akira's intimation that he learns his father has gone missing. The two friends together fantasise and dramatise many imagined and real events of the world even venturing to the mysterious place of the servants' room which they suppose to be infested with black magic turning hands into spiders, "we'll join arms again ... we do it together like that, then we'll be safe, nothing bad can happen to us. Nothing at all" (93).

Even in his childhood game the metaphor of 'return' is quite traceable. Although the boys want to replant the bottle of medication in its proper place, they don't find a chance to do so as on the day when they are supposed to return the bottle, it is found out that Banks' father is kidnapped (102-03). Banks thus recollects: "that was when Akira and I committed our little theft—an impulsive act whose wider repercussions in our excitement, we failed entirely to anticipate" (93). Banks appears to relate his parental loss to the question of a vain attempt to return the bottle. This may be the reason why upon finding the abandoned house towards the end of the novel, his language again becomes strongly nostalgic, recollective of the language that is used in his boyhood days. As they starts entering into the house Banks tells to Akira to join hand together, "just like that other time going into Ling Tien's room" (267). What Banks fails to achieve in his childhood days acts as an unsolved problem for him which he must attend to in an imaginative enactment of the unaccomplished. As Russell C. Jones powerfully suggests, the novel can be viewed as "one long metaphor for lost identity of Banks' and possibly that of the author" (qtd. in Sim 340). On close examination, Banks recollective engagement to recover the 'lost identity' can be understood as implying Ishiguro's in-between position between two places of culturation. Akira, both as a tangible and a figurative reality in the narrative, foregrounds the immanent need to re-imagine and theorise a process transcending the contemporary power relations. Shaffer while interviewing Ishiguro quotes Richards words that nostalgia is "an obsessive return" to a past which "freezes past existence, preventing rather than encouraging true investigation and dialectic" (Shaffer, "An Interview" 6). Ishiguro argues that nostalgia is a term invested with disapproval which is a focal theme in the novel and that "possessing it impedes people from doing things properly" (Shaffer, "An Interview" 6).

Even in his childhood days, Christopher longs for his father's closeness which is dramatically missing in his life. As his domesticities disintegrate, Banks, with his friend Akira, creates a world of fancy in which his father is viewed as being disappeared for some worthy cause and that he would return gloriously some day. They begin to play detective games in which he plays the role of a gifted detective in the course of rescuing his lost father. His mother's confidence in detectives, particularly inspector Kung and his positive assurance fuel Banks' desire to be a real detective later on in his life. As a Child, Banks has experienced the debilitating forces of fragmentation that have entered into their domestic life. Uncle Philip for whom he has utmost trust turns out not to be a friendly presence in his life and his manner changes. He knows exactly as he run to his home expectedly and alone, "that the thing had finished long ago" (123). Mother is no more there and as the front door is bolted. This is an immense shock for the young child to overcome, to have lost the parents one after another in quick succession.

Isolated from his beloved family, Banks suffers the trauma of orphanhood from an early age. Colonel Chamberlain comes to his aid to escort him to England. The desire for a return to Shanghai is also evident in their speech when Chamberlain says, "Think you'll be back again one day" to which Banks replies "Yes Sir, I expect I'll come back" (29). The Colonel's prospects of England, however, are in sharp contact with that of Banks. While the Colonel's focus is on the repressive tactics of erasing the memories of the past: "We all see once you are settled in England, I dare say you will forget all this quickly enough" (29), Banks' mind, on the other hand, is filled with the positive effect of his journey into a new land that he is "positively excited about life aboard the ship as well as by the prospect of the future that lay before" (32). Banks is particularly displeased with the Colonel for calling him "withdrawn and moody who is liable to burst into tears at the slightest thing" (32). Banks, however, has not forgotten the painful experiences of the past and uses that memory as a survival strategy for future engagements in all adverse situations in a new land, in the near future. The Colonel's words, "Look here, old fellow. You really ought to cheer up. After all, you're going to England. You are going home" at once activate a whole gamut of nostalgic reflection in Banks and he begins to map, albeit painfully, the shifting contours of 'home' which holds such a significance for him in his life. One can note the intense surge of his emotions being displaced from a familiar land and especially when he knows that his parents are still there somewhere, waiting to be reunited with him:

> It was this last remark, this notion that I was 'going home', which caused my emotions to get the better of me for—I am certain of this—the first and the last time on that voyage.... As I saw it, I was bound for a strange land where I did not know a soul, while the city steadily receding before me contained all I knew. Above all, my

> parents were still there, somewhere beyond that harbor, beyond that imposing skyline of the Bund, and wiping my eyes, I had cast my gaze towards the shore one last time, wondering if even now I might catch sight of my mother—or even my father—running onto the quay, waving and shouting for me to return.

This kind of repressive memory takes the form of a prolonged melancholia with which Banks obsessively tries to re-enact the same drama of suffering in his mind over and over again rather than working on a real process of return to speed up his search. This explains Banks' extended stay in England even after referring frequently to a desire for return to carry out the search for his lost parents. It takes him a long thirty years for a real return to Shanghai which shows the melancholic turn of his memory mostly occasioned by a regret for undoing a thing in the past that is realised as near impossible in the present. Banks has huge "regrets for what could have been and not for what could be" which makes him "to visit his mother after more than thirty years to check that dream is the imperfect of dreams" (Vinet 143). Banks' mother who lives in a 'diminished' world fails to recognise him, unable to recall her memories of the past. Although she is little stirred in her memory hearing the familiar name 'Puffin', she can only recollect her past in relation to the happy life spent with her family long years back and cannot ever expect his son to come back to him. She even seems to have forgotten all her painful experiences with the villain Wang Ku being kidnapped and used by him as a prostitute. Her memory, therefore, is unlike that of Banks who seems to nourish the trauma of the past for long three decades. Banks' suffering and trauma unlike that of his mother is, therefore, more intensified being always in proximity with that loss. Pascal Zinck remarks that the impairment of memory and its inhabiting tendency of belonging witness to are what comprise "two common scars of trauma" (149). Banks' attitude and behavior coincide with this assertion when we note the discrepancy in Banks' fragmented memory which can't be resuscitated according to the actual state of the past. Banks himself, in the course of the novel, refers several times to the unreliable nature of his memory which exists as fragments in the mind and which can only be evoked under associated circumstances, re-configuring itself to the present need. In his manipulative, narratological unreliability he tends to leave out many important events of his life, projecting a medium which seeks to bridge the gap between appearance and reality. Banks in his narration constantly seeks to hold some information in abeyance that seems to be more painful than other less painful moments of his life. With his manipulative association, he, therefore, drops the topic of his father's disappearance in the middle and resorts to a less painful topic of his misadventure with Akira to steal the 'magic lotion' of the Chinese servant. Dominique Vinet thus argues that in the novel "Some memories seem to stand in the way of reminiscence, screening the hidden object of true horror, veiling the heart of darkness of the narrative" (135): "My sullenness stayed with me well into the night, but of course this was interpreted as my reaction to the situation regarding my father.... I don't remember much about the days immediately following my father's disappearance, other than that I was often so concerned about Akira" (124-25).

Isolated and uprooted from his family and friends Christopher is replanted in a new environment with the prospect of realising new possibilities. To avoid being side-lined and discriminated among school children, he deliberately affects a narcissistic habit of imitating the elaborate mannerism of English children. It is intolerable for Banks that Osbourne has once referred to him as "an odd bird at school" which is regarded by Banks as a "casual judgment" on his part (7). This highlights Banks' desire to relocate himself in an alien ambiance reconfiguring his identity according to the socially accepted models evolved by a particular exclusivist society:

> In fact, it has always been a puzzle to me that Osbourne should have said such a thing of me that morning, since my own memory is that I blended perfectly into English school life. During even my earliest weeks at St. Dunstan's, I do not believe I did anything to cause myself embarrassment. On my very first day, for instance, I recall observing a mannerism many of the

> boys adopted when standing and talking—of tucking the right hand into a waist-coat pocket and moving the left shoulder up and down in a kind of shrug to underline certain of their remarks. I distinctly remember reproducing this mannerism on that same first day with sufficient expertise that not a single of my fellows noticed anything odd or thought to make fun. (7)

In Shropshire, living with his aunt, he begins to re-dramatise the game he used to play with Akira, this time, however with himself, playing both the roles which is branded to the much displeasure of the elders as too much of 'introspection' on the child's part. In the school, he can still feel his isolation as we learn from Morgan of Banks being called a "miserable loner" along with his friend Anthony Morgan, "one with whom he might have made a matching pair" which, however, he seems to displace with his manipulative memory rejecting as "simply a piece of self-delusion on Morgan's part—in all likelihood something he had invented years ago to make more palatable memories of an unhappy period" (184). One cannot afford to overlook here the occluding tendencies of Banks' narrative unreliability in which he ironically hides significant unpleasant things, attempting a more palatable version of reality.

At the beginning of the novel, Ishiguro depicts Banks as developed into an English gentleman adrift and expecting to meet the great detectives of the day as was his desire from his very childhood. He emulates the manner of a detective and nourishes the ambition "to be the great detective of the day ... to root out single-handedly all the evil in the world" (16-17). The 'father-rescuing game' of boyhood and the engendering desire to be a detective can be viewed as a prefigurement of a future project which Banks must attend to recover his identity from the very past that has created his fragmented memories. Pursuing a career as a detective thus is a strategy to link the present with the past. As Silvia Bizzini suggests, "... memories do not only belong to and recount a past time, but they are also instrumental in connecting past and present. The need to explore one's past life experiences is a way of dealing with one's life" (70).

In quest for his identity, Banks seeks to social connections and attaches himself to Lady Beaton's charity. However, he is naturally attached towards Jennifer who herself is an orphan and plans to take her responsibility for the lifetime adopting her as stepdaughter. But here also he becomes as grossly unreliable as his narration and re-enacts the same drama of separation by leaving the child in England for years together. The circuitous route of his fate places him in the same position where he has once found his parents to be. To prevent the sense of this troubling thought of separation from diluting his prospect of the project he regenerates further hope of his success in Shanghai which may serve as being 'triumphant memory' for Jennifer on his return to England.

On returning to Shanghai, he finds the city inherently miserable. The old city which he knew before has vanished in the waves of time and much to his displeasure, everywhere he is confronted with change and strangeness:

> The communists have refrained from physically tearing the place down, so that much of what was once the international settlement remains intact. The streets, though renamed, are perfectly recognizable and it is said that anyone familiar with the Shanghai of old would know his way about there. But the foreigners, of course, have all been banished, and what were once lavish hotels and night-clubs are now the bureaucratic offices of Chairman Mao's government. In other words, the Shanghai of today is likely to prove no less painful a parody of the old city than did Hong Kong. (300)

Also on reaching Shanghai Banks is troubled by the contemptuous habits and behaviours of the community living in Shanghai particularly "the way people here seem determined at every opportunity to block one's view" (181) unaware of his own inability to see the truth which does not meet his exception:

> ... the heart of the maelstrom threatening to suck in the whole of the civilized world, is a pathetic conspiracy of denial ... turned in upon itself and gone sour, manifesting itself in the sort of pompous defensiveness

> I have encountered so often. And here they were, the so-called elite of Shanghai, treating with such contempt the suffering of their Chinese neighbours across the canal. (162)

In Shanghai, Christopher is informed that his parents might be held in some unknown house opposite the house of a certain blind actor that he supposes to know. He decides to reach the place as quickly as possible but the driver takes a circuitous route to avoid the war zone. Christopher, as a detective knows exactly the significance of place and identity and how it contributes to solving of a case. As in another occasion he happens to see a photograph of a Chinese man on the back of a newspaper which he at once claims to have identified Wang Ku, the warlord who has kidnapped his mother and the main reason behind his family's disintegration:

> I will have to admit, incidentally, that I cannot say with complete certainty that the plump Chinese man I saw that day was one and the same man in the newspaper photograph—thc man now identified as the warlord Wang Ku. All I can say is that from the moment I first set eyes on the photograph, the face and it was the face not the gown, cap and pigtail, which of course could have been that of any Chinese gentleman—struck me unmistakeable as one I had seen during the days of my father's disappearance. And the more I have turned that particular incident over in my mind, the more convinced I have become that the man in the photograph was thc one who visited our house that day. (117)

The appearance of persons as aspects of identification is what permeates the work of a detective in the detection of crime. A single mistake in recalling the appearance of the accused may misguide the case to irrevocable limit. But Banks here seems to be quite sure of his detection of the criminal and therefore asserts to the reader that this is the face he had earlier noticed in his boyhood days on his father's disappearance. The readers, however, can only wonders at his assertive conviction as several times before he has acknowledged that his conviction generally grows stronger after some strong reflection. It is evident that where recollecting unpleasant events of the past Banks is highly apprehensive of the effect of his fragile memory that his memory fails in the memorialisation of the past. As he recalls the evening when Osbourne brought him to the Charingworth Club, he notes that the impressions he recollects are "exaggerated or unnatural" (14). The discrepancy between 'memory' and 'forgetfulness', distortion and reality are thus central to the texture of the novel and the protagonist-narrator resorts to a paradoxical distortion of reality in the narrativisation of memories as words. His language, therefore, is highly distortive and recreative of imaginary homes and belonging:

> For according to my own, quite clear memory, I adopted very ably to the changed realities of my circumstances. I remember very well that, far from being miserable on that voyage, I was positively excited about life abroad the ship as well as by the prospect of the future that lay before me. Of course, I did miss my parents at times, but I can remember telling myself there would always be other adults I would come to love and trust. (27)

Later when he meets Akira in Shanghai, he asks his friend to complete the game they have left unfinished. They have got an opportunity to translate their childhood concerns into a real presence. The rescuing game indeed is converted into a reality in the quest of his own identity through his father:

> 'I suppose we were like that too But it's not all downhill, I suppose'. I was trying hard now to combat the dangerous despondency setting over my friend. 'After all, when we were children, when things went wrong, there wasn't much we could do to help put it right. But now we're adults, now we can. That's the thing, you see? Look at us, Akira. After all this time we can finally set things right. Remember, old chap how we used to play those games? Over and over? How we used to pretend we were detectives searching for my father? Now we're grown, we can at last put things right. (263)

Like Stevens of *The Remains of the Day* Banks relies upon a narrative strategy of distorting reality while presenting the past selves to the readers and it is because the narrator's unreliable presentation is closely connected with the self-deception on their part (Veldeman 36) in which they deliberately mispresent facts to project a palatable version of reality which they can confront to reconfigure. Banks in the same process reconfigures its past realities which should fit to his own conscious pre-fixation of his self. One can notice, therefore, the foggy nature of his memory and his language which is densely drafted with an exclusive figurative language, replete with irony and paradox. Although he frequently refers to his memory as being reliable in the beginning, he also claims their fragmented qualities and a haziness that dilute his sense of memorialisation. His memory even helps him to restructure the limits of his past experience in which he sub-consciously lengthens the time period of his past pleasant moments when he says: "And that was how it began, what today in my memory feels like an entire era—though in truth it could only have been a period of two months or less—when day after day we invented and played out endless variations on the theme of my father's rescue" (107). At another place, he again acknowledges the haziness of vision which his memory has developed in appropriating vague recollections to the real ones:

> I allowed my words to fade in my mouth. For puzzled as I was, while the young man had been translating his grandmother's words, I had started to locate some vague recollection concerning some such arrangement regarding the old house and my essential return to it. But as I say, my memory of it was only a very hazy one, and I sense that by opening a discussion on the mater I would only embarrass myself. (189)

Ishiguro in *When We Were Orphans* attempts to subvert the standard expectation of readers to realist fiction. The fragmented non-linear movement of memory in organising the details detaches the readers from their conventional response to the reality presented by the narrator. Banks' carrier as a detective introduces into the novel the detective theme but Ishiguro here use this motif to present Banks' displaced desire to heal the wound of the past which he cannot tolerate in the stable present. The past then is viewed as an island of discovery to which the protagonist most returns to read his realities in his own eyes. The entire novel can be reduced some ten pages of real reflection on the recognition of his true identity and past entanglements as is found out in the conversation with uncle Philip towards the climax of the novel. Uncle Philip finally makes these shattering revelations dawn upon Christopher Banks. His revelation of the mother's sacrifice for the well-being of his son and that Banks real benefactor throughout the year is no other than the warlord Wang Ku shatter the world of Banks that he has so far projected onto himself. Banks finally has to pay the price for his curiosity, and the blind retention of memories of the past life and his innate desire to recreate his lost world of fantasy:

> But now do you see how the world really is? You see what made possible your comfortable life in England? How you were able to become a celebrated detective? ... your mother, she wanted you to live in your enchanted world for ever. But it is impossible. In the end it has to shatter. It's a miracle it survived so long for you. Now Puffin, here. I'll give you this chance here. (294)

Banks also confronts with the hard fact of his father's disappearance which he has nourished so far this age. All his imaginative desire to rescue his father from the kidnapper has whacked into pieces, that his father has not been kidnapped after all, and that he has eloped with a lady named Elizabeth Cornwallis:

> The truth, I'm afraid, Puffin was much more prosaic. Your father ran off one day with his mistress. He lived with her in Hong Kong for a year.... But Hong Kong is awfully stuffy and British, you know. They were a scandal, and in the end they had to rush off to Malacca or some such place. Then he got typhoid and died, in Singapore. That was two years after he left you. I'm sorry, old fellow, it's hard to hear all this, I know. But brace yourself. Because I've a lot more to tell you before the evening's out. (286)

Uncle Philip acts as a catalyst to speed up the process of Banks' discovery. In this climatic chapter, Banks' doubts are put to bay and real implications of all muted events of the past are revealed before him. He is informed how his mother was up against the opium trade in China and wanted to put to an end to it thereby inviting the antagonism of Wang Ku: "Your mother discovered that Wang Ku's motives were far from pure. Put simply, he planned to seize the opium shipments himself" (289-90). Uncle Philip, then, was apprehensive of the imminent danger which the encounter between his mother and Wang Ku portended:

> I did what I could to try and stop the calamity I knew would come. But it was no use. What he told me that afternoon was that far from being angered by your mother, he'd found her spirit—that's what he called it, her "spirit"—highly attractive. So much so that he wished to take her back with him as a concubine back to Hunan. He proposed to "tame" your mother as he would to a wild mare.... I didn't want him to take you too. Your mother, that was an inevitability. But for you, there was something to plead for and that's what I did. (289)

Banks is fatally grieved by the new discovery that for all the years he is under an impression that his "parents were being held captive in Chapei" (288). Moreover, Uncle Philip leads him to another graver fact that his childhood life along with the marital life of his parents was not a happy one which for a long time Banks seems to overlook and repress, for the sake of a new and better life, full of expectations. Uncle Philip also informs Banks that after his mother was held captive, he had had a chance to meet her after seven years when she said that the only desire she had now is to see her son well-settled and living a happy life unlike his parents:

> You see, until I saw her that time, she'd been utterly cut off from the outside world. For seven years she'd only heard what Wang choose to have her hear. What I mean is, she didn't know for certain that the financial arrangement was working. So when I saw her, that's

> what she wanted to know, and I was able to reassure her that it was. After seven years of torturous doubt, her mind was put to rest. I can't tell you, how relived she was. "That's all I wanted to know," she kept saying. "That's all I wanted to know". (292)

Uncle Philip's words make Banks revisit the seamy side of his traumatic underworld. Dissecting the fragments of the past, it is beyond his expectation that he should meet with such hard facts about his life. The curiosity of Banks finally leads him to see the discrepancy between reality and representation, between actuality and appearance, when Uncle Philip reveals before him yet another hard fact of the prismatic past which he calls his "darkest confession"—his own undercover desire for Banks' mother:

> I'll confess you the truth. About why I allowed Wang Ku to kidnap your mother that day ... something I wasn't able to confess even to myself for many years. I helped Wang take your mother because a part of me wanted her to become his slave. To be used like that, night after night. Because you see, I always lusted after her, right from the days when I came to be a lodger in your house. Oh, yes, I desired her and when your father went off like that, I believed it was my chance, that I was his natural successor.... I was as though I'd conquered her too. (295)

The above speech reveals the contradictory character of Uncle Philip who was not after all benevolent to Banks as a small child, and that the benign exterior which he maintained throughout was but to mask the rottenness inside. His character strikes a parallel to the unreliable subtlety of Banks' memory albeit in a positive way. It seems that Uncle Philip is the physical objectification of Banks' paradoxicality. His life, like that of Banks' memory, is modelled upon an apparent contradiction—an incongruity between what we want to see and what is presented before our eyes. Even while revealing the dark secrets of Banks' life to him, which holds so much significance to him, he is not altogether reliable, and like Banks, resorts to paradox and concealment in his language. After disclosing all the darker facts of life he says, "What I said before, yet, it's true enough. I had to safeguard you. Yes, yes, everything I said earlier more or less stands" which points out the antithetical properties of his language (295). Philip's character therefore is a focal point in the narrative which not only externalises the unreliable potentiality of Banks' memory but literally serves as a touchstone to differentiate facts from fiction.

With his usual narcissistic disposition, Banks restrains himself from 'obliging' Uncle Philip by not shooting him as the later requests, "'Now, now, kill me!' Why spare me? 'You've heard it! Here shoot me like a rat!'" (296). Philip adds that there are many other who can do this: "'Don't worry, no shortage of people willing to oblige the Yellow Snake'. He gave a quick laugh. Then he said in a weary voice: 'Goodbye Puffin, I hope you find her'" (296). Banks finally is able to crack the core of the mystery but not without painful reconciliation with the past and then braces himself up setting out to find her mother at any cost.

The novel, therefore, is an emotional extension, in which the protagonist has to determine the course of his memory that leads him to a "terribly treacherous terrain", because "the very ambiguities of memory go to feed self-deception" (Swift 39). As Ishiguro observes, in this kind of book, one can witness as "someone playing a kind of hide and seek with himself, his memories, and his conscience":

> I am really interested in unreliable narrators in so far as they have very interesting reasons for being unreliable, the deep reasons why we all have to be unreliable narrators. Because most of us when we look at ourselves, we have to be rather unreliable in order to face ourselves. So it's these serious reasons for being unreliable that interest me. How to hold onto your dignity when you think your life has been a failure. How you wrestle with things that you regret having done. The unreliability that comes up to those things interests me. (Gallix 139)

The novel is thus replete with metaphors of eternal, distortive confrontation with reality in which the protagonist deliberately mispresents himself to evolve a new model of reality. In these transferential projectivities, Christopher Banks consciously creates a room for himself for imaginative miscreation. At a literal level, he even hides the identity of his friend Akira to his mother:

> I can't remember ever attempting to challenge Akira on any of these claims. Once I mentioned casually to my mother something about my friend's adventures and I remember her smiling and saying something to cast doubt on the matter. I was furious at her, and thereafter I believe I carefully avoided recalling to her anything at all intimate concerning Akira. (101)

At a metaphorical level, Akira, whom he meets amidst the war towards the end of the novel, seems to be his own creation. The Japanese soldier whom he believes to be Akira never admits that he is his lost childhood friend. Christopher Banks later begins to doubt his own memory and says to the Colonel, "I thought he was a friend of mine from my childhood. But now I'm not so certain" (277). The unreliable nature of Banks memory is thus subject to transformative distortion in which he seeks to manipulate his standards and stances according to the present necessity. Silvia Bizzini writes, "Akira's unlikely presence provides both a guide to the past and a door to the present. Through him, Banks discovers that the past he remembers is a lie that has only ever been real in his mind" (73). Banks' narrative projects an occlusive framework in which the past is being controlled by him by transposing unpleasant images of the past by the palatable version of realities in his narrative presence. Ishiguro thus describes the vulnerable diachrony of Christopher Banks' memory which makes him to explore new subtleties of his life through a transactive encounter with the methodically muddled past:

> Christopher Banks is perhaps not quite that sort of conventional unreliable narrator in the sense that it's not very clear what's going on out there.... I wanted to actually have the world of the book distorted, adopting

> the logic of the narrator. In paintings, you often see that Expressionist art ... sometimes distorted to reflect the emotion of the artist who is looking at the world.... I'm then able to explore people's inner world much more thoroughly and with much more subtlety. (Wong, *Kazuo Ishiguro* 87)

Akira, the childhood friend of Banks has been a real influence for him till the end of the novel. Akira's immutable presence in the novel seems to have a bathetic effect upon the cumulative misery of Banks' life. Akira seems to be an alter ego of Banks whose creation in a way compensates Banks' loss of his parents. He even attempts to imaginatively heighten the distress of his friend Akira by giving false report about him when he is heartlessly ostracised for his migrated foreignness:

> From his very first day in Japan Akira had been thoroughly miserable. Although he never admitted this explicitly. I surmised that he had been mercilessly ostracised for his 'foreignness', his manners, his attitudes, his speech, a hundred other things had marked him out as different, and he had been taunted not just by his fellow pupils, but by his teachers and even—he hinted at this more than once—by the relatives in whose house he was staying. (89)

The repeated emphasis on Akira's misfortune is a projection of his own misery which can be viewed as an attempt to conceal his own distress by highlighting the distress of others. Akira's transposition is similar to that of Banks, when he is sent to England and is so keen to imitate the English manners and mannerism to be looked like English. Akira's situation in Japan thus prefigures Banks' condition in England, and this explains his desire to merge completely into an English culture by being a great English detective in a great land. The imaginative enchantment that is woven around the image of Akira is thus to emphasise that Banks' childhood has been essentially a happy one which can be compared to his present status. The past cannot be altered but can be presented as instrumental in shaping the presence of the protagonist. It is the trauma of his childhood that shatters his sense of a reliable memorialisation.

He must again confront and revisit the ever-haunting shadows of the past to be able to explain the cause of his orphanhood and apparent homelessness. Ishiguro argues that:

> There was a metaphorical direction in this condition of being orphaned. What I was interested in exploring here was the journey that we all must have made out a protective childhood bubble where we didn't know about the harsher world.... When I say 'orphan' it's in that very broader sense of having left the protective world of childhood that I am referring to. (Wong, "Like Idealism" 183)

In order to reconfigure his identity he must solve the mysteries of the past that has created his present condition. To be nostalgic then is a claim to "build good world" in the present recollecting "good memories" of the dead past (262) as Akira says to Christopher amidst the war. Together they discuss the importance of being nostalgic:

> 'One mustn't get too nostalgic for childhood'
> ' 'Nos-tal-gic' Akira said as though it was a word he had been struggling to find. Then he said a word in Japanese, perhaps the Japanese for 'nostalgic'. Nos-tal-gic. It is good to be nos-tal-gic. 'Very important.'
>
> 'Really, old fellow?'
>
> 'Important. Very important. Nostalgic. When we nostalgic, we remember. A world better than this world we discover when we remember. A world better than this world we discover when we grow. We remember and wish good world come back again. So very important. Just Now, I had dream. I was boy. Mother, Father, close to me. In our house.' (263)

For Banks, Shanghai hold his past to which he must return as a 'homecoming' acknowledging the therapeutic effect of his recollection and reflection. Amidst the war-torn atmosphere, it is this belief—to be reunited with the home that continually heals the physical wounds of Akira providing him sustenance to keep himself alive. Memory, in this nostalgic recollection is subject to the transformative manipulations of belief which reveals the substantial unpresentability of actual events. Ishiguro thus clarifies:

> I am trying to capture the texture of memory. I need to keep reminding people that the flashbacks aren't just a clinical, technical means of conveying things that happened in the past. This is somebody turning over certain memories, in the light of his current emotional condition. I like blurred edges around the events, so you're not quite certain if they really happened and you're not quite certain to what extent the narrator is deliberately colouring them. (Kelman 48)

The vulnerable fragility of Banks' memory is revealed in his blind pursuit of rescuing his parents from the kidnappers in the middle of a terrible Sino-Japanese battle. He is sure that his parents are being detained in some house in between and rushes there to hunt for the object of his desire but the truth is quite different. In the devastating battlefield, he rather discovers his childhood friend Akira, fatally wounded and waiting to be rescued instead, by someone. Banks' obsessive search for his parents points out his inherent desire to invert the condition of his orphanhood. A childlike inclination for home and a protective feeling of childhood haunt him always in his imagination, which make him redefine his domesticities until a point when reality is dawned upon him with all its vigour and violence. Silvia Bizzini insightfully observes:

> It is just this psychological attitude that forms the backbone of the story and lies at the origin of Banks's need to redefine his family romance. He tells (writes) his story to compensate for the feeling of loss and death that haunt him. In the reconstitution of the events that Banks describes in his notebook, his childhood and his childhood home are associated with security and protection. The feeling of orphanhood that will be with Christopher Banks throughout his (late childhood and) adult life originates at this point. That is to say, when his parents disappear from his life and his sense of protection and safety is shattered. He will be on a childlike quest almost up until the point when the

> truth about his life hits him with all its violence and cruelty. (73)

Individual memories which contribute to the emotional make up of the protagonist may be "highly elusive in some situations and dead wrong in others" but it is the foundation upon which the sense of identification can be resurrected because "memory's many limitations on the one hand and its pervasive influence on the other ... is central to understanding how the past shapes the present" (Schacter 7).

The novel supplies various instances in which Banks is presented as acknowledging the hazy texture of his memory only to demonstrate that the factual reality itself is dismantled and can't be represented through the absolutist framework of realistic signification. The following speeches of Christopher Banks are just a few examples of how he is "interested in the way words hide meaning" (Vorda 71):

> To take for instance, this episode I have just recounted concerning my mother and the health inspector: while I am fairly sure I have remembered its essence accurately enough, turning it over in my mind again, I find myself less certain about some of the details. (80-81)

> For according to my own, quite clear memory, I adopted very ably to the changed realities of my circumstances I remember very well.... (32)

> Consequently, I cannot be sure today how much of my memory of that morning derives from what I actually witnessed from the landing, and what extent it has merged over time with my mother's accounts of the episode. (64)

> I have been obliged to accept ... that with each passing year, my life in Shanghai will grow less distinct, until one day all that will remain will be a few muddled images. Even tonight, when I sat down here and tried to gather in some sort of order these things I still remember I have been struck anew by how hazy so much has grown. (67-68)

One can notice how ably Banks can blend facts with fiction in his circuitous flow of memory. Ishiguro reveals the psychological subtleties of Banks' subjective vision by deliberately presenting a narrative structure that seeks to dismantle itself mirroring the disruption in Banks' unconscious. Banks' evolution of his consciousness is strongly influenced by the informing models and urges he has nourished from his childhood days and thus his narrative voice reflects such tensions in approximating the lost object of his desire. Ishiguro himself manipulates the narrator's memories as an emancipatory impulse on the part of the protagonist in the reinterpretation of his reflective nostalgia:

> But I'm wondering if it's time to try to construct a voice, a way of writing, that somehow takes on board some of the Post-Freudian tensions of life, that comes not from buckling up, not from being unable to express yourself, but from just being pulled left, right and centre by possible role models and urges, by a sense that you are missing out. That would involve a different kind of voice, would imply a different kind of writing and would lead to a very different-looking novel. (Shaffer, "An Interview" 10)

In quest for a 'different kind of voice' for his narrator-protagonist, Ishiguro recognises "[p]eople's potential to change their lives or to change themselves somewhere in the middle of their lives, that has been under-estimated" (Matthews, "I'm Sorry" 120) in the narrative history of mankind. The novels such as *The Remains of the Day* and *When We Were Orphans* thus connect the private memories of the individual to the collective history of a nation, and expose the parallel between personal subjugation and political subjection, between personal disintegration and political disruption. Collective history like memory is examined in its multiple configurations subverting the colonial discourse of collective experience. Banks' orphanhood then is figuratively encompassed to represent a collectively experienced orphanhood as a result of colonisation and stereotypical essentialisation. Banks' liminal position in the novel places him in an in-between condition of multiculturality and at the same time, it also seeks to subvert the ways in which history is (mis)interpreted and (mis)represented. As Ishiguro observes:

> I am not interested in writing about storytelling, but I'm interested in storytelling in the sense of what a community or a nation tells itself about its past and by implication therefore where it's at the moment and what it should be doing next. If you want to draw a parallel between how individuals come to terms with their past and decide what to do next, and how a nation or a community approaches such things, then the issue of storytelling is an important one. (Matthews, "I'm Sorry" 117)

The novel is thus open to interpretation both at personal and collective level. The history of the international settlement in Shanghai is used as background to unravel the mysteries of Banks' family romance and the way the family gets entangled in the 'opium trade' in Shanghai. The novel presents Britain's dominance over Shanghai in opium trading in which Banks' father was actively involved. Banks' mother severely criticises the British traders supplying opium to Shanghai and China describing it terribly "un-Christian and un-British" (61):

> ... that the British in general, and the company of Morgan-Brook and Byatt especially, by importing Indian opium into China in such massive quantities had brought untold misery and degradation to a whole nation.... 'Are you not ashamed, sir? As a Christian, as an Englishman, as a man with scruples? Are you not ashamed to be in the service of such a company? Tell me, how is your conscience able to rest while you owe your existence to such ungodly wealth?' (60)

Ishiguro focuses on the vicious circuitry of historical connections which deliberate individuals to false hopes and frustration. Ishiguro attempts to focalise this connection between history and memory to discover the anxiety in the subjective mind which is viewed as a result of the overlap between historical and personal relationships. There is continuous transformative transactions between the individual and the collective which inform the human mind, placed with the external reality and every single fragments of experience in the past is imprinted in the human mind to return again later, refashioning itself in a new configuration which is described by I.A. Richards as an "apparent revival of past experience to which its richness is due" (94). The protagonists in such novels must question the distorting web of history refracted as disruptions in the individual conscience. Ishiguro thus reflects upon these historical changes which affect the private lives of his protagonists:

> I have always been interested in what happens to peoples' values when they have invested all their energies and their lives in the prevalent set of social values, only to see them change ... and to see what happens to people when, at the end of their lives, they find the world has changed its mind about what is good and what is bad. But for this particular individual, it's too late. They had the best intentions but history has proved them to be either foolish or perhaps even someone who contributed to evil. (Mason 7)

History's contributory power to evil is thus signalised and represented by the mysterious and powerful forces "lurking around the corner of us" that conspire to "put civilization to the torch" and which must be checked by Banks in his individual effort of "rooting out evil in its most devious forms" (*When We Were Orphans* 43). The dense metaphorisation of evil and 'devil' in the novel inaugurates the theme of the detective fiction in which Banks must fight the evil out of all kinds—"insidious, furtive" (43) or "devious" (52). Banks, like Stevens of *The Remains*, who represents the melancholic memorialisation of a twilighting Englishness, symbolises similarly a paternalistic model of colonial dominion as the master detective of a mythopoetic England. Chu-Chueh Cheng, in this context, observes:

> The construction of Stevens and Banks, likewise, capitalize on the popular belief that the English disposition is best illustrated in the butler's self-effacement and the detective's emotional restraint. It is from an insider-outsider's double vision that Ishiguro

> detects the fictionalization of national/racial myths, challenges the validity of metonymic presumptions, and exposes the emptiness of cultural signifiers. He prompts the reader to ponder how one's limited imagination dictates the monotony one detects in the other. (33-34)

As Brian Finney argues, the condition that Banks suffers from is "transformed by metaphorical multiplication into a collective experience. In fact, Banks occupies a liminal location in the novel, as he fills the child's role as an individual, and yet is a representative of the parental colonial power as the master detective from England" ("Figuring the Real" 15). Ishiguro in this novel depicts the general trauma of the whole humanity and their estrangement in a world structuralised by a colonial discourse. Ishiguro demonstrates the fact that individual moments are necessarily related to the traumatic history of a nation in which the construction of the self and the other is addressed through the same cultural and psychological processes. Accordingly, Banks in his detective quest for the truth, in his narrative uncertainty, reveals the misleading proclivities of memory as a device for deconstructing the traditional rationalistic closure of the detective plot, in a disruptive temporality. Banks, with his detective unreliability exposes the porous, narrativised heterogeneity of personal and national boundaries. Cheng thus reflects on the subversive properties of Ishiguro's detective fiction which cut across genre, identities and nationalities:

> ... each narrative, inherently heterogeneous, retains divergent potentials for plot and character development. The polygeneric nature of each text mirrors the indeterminacy of a nation that defies easy reduction. Writing against generic conventions, societal practices, and gender expectations, the Japanese-British novelist turns myths into cultural mockery, clichés into chic idea and stereotypes into captivating personalities. (35)

Banks' mother's protest against the colonial excess of the Britishers in Shanghai invites the displeasure of one of the warlords, at that time, and by searching for his mother, Banks denies his orphanhood as an attempt to combat evil in the war-torn Shanghai against the evils of British colonialism. His belief that by returning to Shanghai and rescuing his parents, he can save the British Empire seems delusive. This conviction of setting the civilisation right is later repeated by Sarah Hemmings and Sir Cecil Medhurst as they set off for China to mitigate the political tension in the parts of Asia in the 1930s. Ishiguro is thus successful in portraying one fragments of the colonial/imperial desire of retaining a belief that they are doing good even representing an exploitive system of oppressive coloniality.

It is this interconnectedness between familiar and national identity that Ishiguro emphasises on the arrival of Banks in Shanghai. Banks' peculiar in-between condition serves as a metaphor to represent the complexity of personal and national identification. The novel presents a disillusioned, decayed, self-centred picture of empires for whom Shanghai becomes the most cherished dream for colonial trade and imperial extension. Not only Britain and other Western countries but also Japan follows the suit. The time when the narrative starts, Shanghai finds itself at the crossroads of subversive and ungovernable forces that doesn't confirm to any particular administrative order. According to the historian Meng Yue:

> Shanghai carried within its birth a peripheral element, a subversive, rebellious spirit that was ungovernable by either the Qing Empire or the imperialist regime. It turned the city into haven for outlaws, as well as a cradle of anarchists, anti-Qing revolutionaries, early Chinese Communists, radical Journalists and strikers and demonstrators against imperialism. (qtd. in Perez 232)

This nightmarish vision of Shanghai serves as a background for the novel in which different world orders strike a confluence which encouraged stereotypical, symbolic reading of both the coloniser and the colonised. The unique positionality of Shanghai in world politics implies both a national and international status, developed by its relationship with Western countries including Britain. Mr. McDonald the officer in the British embassy says to Banks that Shanghai "isn't a British colony. We can't go ordering the Chinese about" (199). But Britain gain control of a region in China through the Treaty of Nanking along with others including Japan. In this struggle for dominance and economic exploitation, Japan takes the British Empire as it model (Perez 233). Banks' friend Akira believes that Japan has a similar destiny with Britain which seeks to withstand the dominance of Western countries. Later in the novel, the Colonel, like young Akira who refers to his country as a "great, great country Just like England" (78), informs the protagonist that "if Japan is to become a great nation like yours, Mr. Banks, it is necessary. Just as it was once for England" (278).

Evil in the novel is thus represented by the financial profitability of the opium trade that informs the motivation of these empires. Ishiguro focuses on the British participation in the smuggling of opium that earns them huge profits and the various illegal custom dealing they resort to. Banks' mother stands in opposition to such illegal opium trade and denounces their enterprise as anti-humanistic "making vast profits importing Indian opium into China and turning millions of Chinese into helpless addicts" (288). Banks' father as one of the associates of the British company controls part of their business, thus adding to the process of colonisation and resulting economic exploitation. Inspector Kong beautifully summarises the socio-political anomalies of the regime: "... this city defeats you. Every man betrays his friend. You trust some-one and he turns out to be in the pay at a gangster" (204). Uncle Philip foregrounds the colonial interest of the British Empire in these economic configurations and says, "... we discovered that these people ... actually wanted the Chinese to be useless. They liked them to be in chaos, drug-addicted, unable to govern them properly. That way, the country could be run virtually like a colony, but with none of the usual obligations" (288).

Brian Finney, in this context, opines that the novel is "written for an international readership" and as such "oscillates between England, the old centre of empire and Shanghai where the Occident meets the Orient, itself the product of a hegemonic Western discourse" ("Figuring the Real" 2). According to Finney, the child's ideal of being protected in this enclave of colonial power is subverted as an illusion in which orphanhood becomes a trope for transnational identity ("Figuring the Real"

2). The protagonist gradually comes to a recognition that the "feared other" is placed within the self, discursively formed out of its own fear (Finney, "Figuring the Real" 2). In the words of Finney: "while attempting to foist onto the colonized the stigmas of eternal childishness, are in fact themselves childlike, having evaded the maturation by projecting the unacceptable within themselves onto the subjects of their colonial discourse" ("Figuring the Real" 2). History, in the novel, thus put to figurative use to reveal its origin in the personal and the psychological. The protagonist's quest for his missing parents is reminiscent of the "Western power's nostalgic attempt with the international settlement" on Shanghai to reinaugurate a "parental control over an aberrant nation" (Finney, "Figuring the Real" 3).

Brian Finney contends that in the novel, "personal and political subjection coincide repeatedly ... as do personal and political disintegration.... Fascism, like colonialism, is the imposition of parental discipline on adults discursively constructed as children" (3). The novel thus presents the post-imperialist trauma of the individuals which is further echoed by a similar anxiety traceable in the neo-colonial projects of the Western powers for dominance and economic exploitation. Banks, when encounters Mr. Lin as occupying his former family house as the head of his family, discovers in him an oriental representative—wild, untameable, waiting to be civilised that surrounds the supposedly civilised international settlement of his childhood which seems to give an outlet to his own colonial fantasies when the later reiterates: "of course it is quite natural. You wish to restore this house to just the way it was when you were a boy" (207). Ishiguro in *When We Were Orphans* builds an interestingly exotic and mysterious setting in the framework of a metropolitan city like Shanghai to deconstruct its status as *raison d'être*.

Banks, in Shanghai discovers that there is nothing in the world which can restore him to the utopian ideal of boyhood and that it is illusive to invert the idea of orphanhood. "He must recognize" as Tim Christensen observes, "that there is no self-evident truth of the self to be discovered in the place of his own subjective origins but a constitutive moment of difference from the self" (214) that leads him to the experience of his own psychic 'roots' in which his childhood can be viewed as an 'alien landscape' and in this critical nothingness, he must abandon the "myth of consciousness" in terms of both personal and national level as "pure and abstract, untarnished by its nebulous beginning" (Lane 19). This alien land of his childhood, in short, asserts "what we have learned from a narrative structured as a series of unstable, constantly self-displacing memories" (Christensen 214). Chu-Chueh Cheng traces a similar tendency of 'mythmaking-manoeuvre', also in Ishiguro's previous novel *The Remains of the Day*:

> The novelist cites *The Remains of the Day* (1989) and *When We Were Orphans* (2000) as examples: while the former capitalizes on "an international myth about the English butler and English country life", the later constructs Shanghai through "old Shanghai" stereotypes. To captivate an international readership, Ishiguro obviously puts into good use widely circulated images and perceptions.... The contour of a given culture is often constructed and perpetuated through cycles of imagination, distortion and replication. (3-4)

Similarly, Ishiguro's claim as an international writer addressing a global readership from the Western hemisphere, emphatically reflects a similar drive in his protagonist Christopher Banks' mission to actuate his global self in the essentialising ambience of Shanghai which he seeks to deconstruct. Christopher Banks revolts against this representational categorisations that contribute to the growth and perpetuation of national myths and the fabricated nature of these misconceptions.

The myth of England's self-proclaimed superiority and its ideology of the civilising mission assume a different turn in *When We Were Orphans*: Banks meticulously weaves an aura of Englishness around him, emulating the manners of the quintessential English detective Sherlock Holmes—confronts the Chinese localities as a world full of chaos where "dead bodies piled up everywhere, files buzzing all over them" (61) and where sinister forces lurking around the corner. As Cheng argues, "Envisioning China as the source of rampant crimes, Banks internalises the myth of the sinister oriental world, and worse yet, allows that misconception to dictate his professional judgment" which points out the conflation of two national myths in the unsophisticated vision he forms at personal level—"the barbarous and insidious China is disseminating vice worldwide and the civilised and moralistic England should come ashore to eradicate the evil and restore global harmony" (12).

In Banks' visionary Phantasm, China is projected as a symbolic equivalent of his own orphanhood which categorically needs the West's protection. Revealing the insignificance of Banks' innocence and Philip's pretence, the novel as Cheng argues, "undermines the myth of the White man's burden, that the enlightened British self is morally responsible for civilizing the barbaric Chinese other" (12). The discovery, on the part of Banks, however, is conditioned by two antagonistic formulae, namely, the moment when Colonel Hasegawa warns Banks of the disguised identification of the Japanese solider who is in fact a deserter wrongly recognised by Banks as his childhood friend Akira and the most disturbing moment of exploration that the Chinese warlord Wang Ku who takes his mother as concubine has been his real benefactor, all these years. These realisations liberate Banks from stereotyping, and from the strain of an elusive conception of orphanhood who finally learns to mitigate the tension between personal and national identification. The novel thus is a large scale experimentation with the markers and modalities of identification that create fixated entities and ideologies, in the perpetuation of national myths and ethnic stereotypes which he wants to deconstruct ironing out the discrepancies between facts and fiction. As Cheng insightfully observes:

> By juxtaposing the superficial resemblance and actual discrepancy between the factual and the fictional, Ishiguro exposes the falsity of stories one nation tells about itself and about others. Placed in contention, national fables betray the inadequacy of reducing a given society to an array of highly identifiable markers, scenery snapshots and ethnic stereotypes.

> The macroscopic approach Ishiguro takes in deriding national myths hence necessitates a microscopic analysis of how symbolic sights and characters collaboratively give intelligible physicality to an amorphous entity called "nation". (14)

'Orphanhood' for Banks then is a sense of utter homelessness which creates in the individual an anxiety to belong. Banks' sense of homeliness, childhood and parenthood disintegrate before him like his unpredictable memory. Banks believes, as his friend also shares with him, that his parent's discontent and their summative disappearance is somehow related to his being "not sufficiently English" (76). As Akira says, "I know why they stop, I know why ... Christopher. You not enough Englishman" (72) and admits his own situation as being the same for being "not enough Japanese" (73) which disappoint "our parents so deeply they were unable even to scold us" (73). By a methodical multiplication of these incompatibilities in the novel, Ishiguro universalises the theme of homelessness and challenges the stabilising contours of home and homeland. Banks' lack of English manners in his disposition forces him to reconfigure his identity according to the present need which makes him search his true personal and national identity in a problematic dialectics of belongingness. Thus, to be himself, he must alter a part in himself; to feel at home, he must search himself in a foreign land as Tim Christensen cleverly remarks: "Banks' home is always already—definitively—also a state of exile—it is a home that is not a home, or a home that is defined by its own absence, its meaning lying elsewhere—for Banks is English, despite being physically located in China and England is elsewhere" (214).

Banks' feeling of rootlessness leads him appropriating his sense of identification to a particular culture he feels inwardness with. Out of childlike curiosity, he asks Uncle Philip, "How do you suppose one might become more English" (76), to which the later admits the utter untranslatability of human self into a unified mode of life because the world has become increasingly multicultural in which every human being is bound to be "a bit of mongrel" presenting an eternal hybridisation of cultural consciousness:

> He gave a short laugh. Then he went on: But that's no bad thing. You know what I think; puffin? I think it would be no bad thing if boys like you *all* grew up a bit of everything. We might all treat each other a good deal better then. Be less of these wars for one thing. Oh yes, perhaps one day, all these conflicts will end, and it won't be because of great statesmen or Churches or organizations like this one. It'll be because people have changed. They'll be like you, Puffin. More a mixture, so why not become a mongrel? It's healthy.... People need to feel they belong. (76-77)

Banks feels the need to belong and his nostalgia for home is just a result of his "hybridity, a difference 'within', a subject that inhabits the rim of an in-between reality" (Bhabha, *The Location* 13) which reveals the unconditional polyvalence of 'homing desire' that informs the individual's sense of belonging. 'Home', for Banks is a state of perpetual exile and can be resurrected to vitality through the "Shards of memory" potentially having "numinous qualities" for transformation (Rushdie, *Imaginary Homelands* 12). In a most melancholic epiphany, Banks accepts and understands the true meaning of orphanhood as he declares: "for those like us, our fate is to face the world as orphans, chasing through long years the shadow of our vanished parents ... for until we do so, we will be permitted no calm" (313). In a similar fashion, Akira quotes the Japanese monk, "it was we children who bound not only a family, but the whole world together" (73) which can be called home.

At the end, Christopher Banks discovers that he is not only exiled from the protective bubble of his childhood but also from the predictable layers of his consciousness. He learns that a true return is a near impossibility and that identity can be reconfigured in relation to the changing contours of home and belonging. The individual's lived experience of the locality as Colonel Hasegawa quotes from a Japanese poet in the novel, "our childhood becomes like a foreign land once we have grown"

(297) which characteristically echoes Rushdie's belief that: "it's my present that is foreign and that the past is home, albeit a lost home in a lost city in the mists of lost time" (9). Ishiguro, like Rushdie, nourishes a similar tendency towards highlighting the metaphorical ambiguity of such entities as memory, identity and belonging which can be recontextualised with the shifting realities. In this critical diversity, Ishiguro's novels, which are claimed to be addressed to an international readership, serve as an onslaught to the rigidified bound of experience and an emphatic urge to "open the universe a little more" (Rushdie, *Imaginary Homelands* 21) to accommodate the cultural others.

Chapter 6
Featuring the Self: Hybrid Identities and the Idea of In-betweenness in Hanif Kureishi

> "Practices of representation always implicate the positions from which we speak or write—the positions of enunciation."
>
> —Stuart Hall, "Cultural Identity and Diaspora"

> "The author does not serve the reader with an easy solution to how identity is found, but more a true reflection of life itself, and that is what the book is all about. It is simply and convincingly a realistic account of a person's search for identity in today's multicultural Britain and all the complexity that comes with it."
>
> —Ulla Ambursley, *The Search for Identity in The Black Album*

> "The failure to grasp this opportunity for a revitalized and broader self-definition in the face of a real failure to be human, will be more insularity, schism, bitterness and catastrophe."
>
> —Hanif Kureishi, *My Beautiful Laundrette*

Britain, in the second half of the 20th century, has experienced an immense cultural transformation which involves the failure of an empire, large-scale immigrations from former colonies and a resulting diverse multicultural society that gradually seek to evolve a new reality of pluralistic cultural formations. Hanif Kureishi, the British novelist, screenwriter and filmmaker of

Pakistani and English descent, in this critical multifariousness, attempts to depict the hybridised positionalities of the immigrant subjectivities in his novels who inevitably experience an in-between perception of fragmented culturality as belonging to more than one cultures simultaneously. Kureishi is attentive to the factors that effectuate a fast transformation of the traditional notions of identity as fixed, essential and strictly homogenised which aim at recognising the migrant's experience of belonging and identification as shifting, fragmented and unmonolithic. The present chapter thus proposes to explore the disparate ways by which Kureishi deliberates a notional presentment of identities, explicitly infused and developed in his novels, as provisional and free-floating, eternally celebrating the deconstructive presence of hybridity in an in-between space of cultural diversity that point out the essential multivocality of all existence in a tentative, transcultural situatedness, perfectly balancing the local with the global in the cartography of unframable belongingness.

Kureishi's novels such as *The Buddha of Suburbia* and *The Black Album* are set in England which portray the individual's perceptions of cultural identity that is diasporic, heterogeneous and always in the making, informed by different cross-cultural connections. The second generation immigrants presented in the novels perceive their identities as a process of becoming rather than a state of being which undergo constant transformation in the formation of self-identification and belongingness. Karim Amir, the protagonist of Kureishi's debut novel, *The Buddha of Suburbia*, internalises in himself this impulse of change and shifting identification which is always on the move as Stefano Manferlotti beautifully put it: "a whole body that now rests and now runs, now flourishes and now decays, smiles and bleeds" (193).

Rather than representing identity in its essentialist denominations, Hanif Kureishi confronts the problematics of conveying identity as a complex thing and explores the countless ways of being "which is socially constructed and therefore always already provisional" in shifting relationships (Moore-Gilbert 128). His novels such as *The Buddha of Suburbia* and *The Black Album* celebrate hybridity and glorify it as a "radically deconstructive presence in a world obsessed with clear-cut definitions of cultural or ethnic identity" (Schoene, "Herald of Hybridity" 117). Kureishi expresses in one of his interviews that his characters are keen to break the fetters of tradition and cultural fixedness "struggling against an original sense of class that they're trying to throw off in the process of expanding their sense of the self" (Buchanan 112). Kureishi thus presents the struggle of these immigrants living in an alien society who strive to resolve their crisis of otherness that is the result of being suspended between two positions—the native culture and the host culture. Kureishi is a strong opponent of the fundamentalist ideologies of the Western culture that seeks to reduce identities and ethnicities to equivocal constants with changeless properties, in terms of cultural normativity, and stresses the fluidity of the subjective positions in relation to the cultural configuration that is never authentic or pure, subverting its apparent essentialist exclusivity.

Hanif Kureishi was born of bicultural parentage on 5 December 1954 in Bromley, England. His parents were liberal enough to allow him to choose a cosmopolitan lifestyle which is inspired further by his studying philosophy at King's College in London when he aspired to be a writer. Along with his literary pursuits he started writing plays to be performed in theatre. Later on, he took to screenplay writing in cinema strongly believing "that contemporary cinema must reflect social and political reality" (Kaleta 39). His first novel, *The Buddha of Suburbia* was met with great critical acclaim and was awarded with the Whitbread prize in 1990. The novel, modeled on the Bildungsroman genre, depicts the multi-ethnic Britain of the 1970s and tells the story of an Anglo Asian hybrid named Karim Amir who takes on a picaresque journey in quest of his own identity that reflects a "funny kind of Englishman, a new breed as it were having emerged from two old histories" (Kureishi, *The Buddha* 3). The novel is replete with autobiographical projections which reveal the author's mixed identity and acculturation having belonged to two different cultures simultaneously as Kureshi puts it: "I came from two worlds.... There was my Pakistani family, my uncles, aunts and so on. Then there was my English family, who were lower-middle or working class. My grandfather had pigeons and grey-hounds and all that. And having an Indian father ... finding my way through" (Leith 8). Karim in a similar fashion restages the essential drama of cultural hybridisation questioning the reductionist logic of Englishness which seeks to exclude the cultural other in the exclusionary politics of drawing difference between the insider and the outsider. Karim is disillusioned by his cultural mixedness and the complex unsettled position of his identity, seeks to reconfigure it by a performative perusal of the cultural codes and "celebrates the liberation and loss of self that he discovers in the maelstrom of a decayed physical and moral universe" (qtd. in Buchanan 160).

Similarly, Kureishi's *The Black Album* which seems to complement Rushdie's *The Static Verses*, in its fundamentalist undercuts, presents the cultural struggle of the protagonist Shahid, a university student who is torn between contradictory forces of liberal and conservative values which he tries to nourish throughout his life. He falls into a hopeless interracial love affair with his teacher Deedee Osgood, develops a flexible form of liberalism and religious tolerance, but at the end unwillingly forces himself to a fundamentalist group in the course of helping his fanatic friends. Like Karim, he is represented as a restless youth in the novel in search of his lost identity who "wants a new start with new people in a new place" (*The Black Album* 16). But unlike Karim, Shahid is presented as intellectually more sound and responsible than the former who likes "to be challenged intellectually and in every other way" (*The Black Album* 5). As powerfully observed by Holmes: "... it is through exercising his imagination as a budding artist rather than practicing his faith as a Muslim that Shahid ultimately seeks to find his identity as an adult" (305) that liberates him from the constraints of culture and the fetters of fundamentalism. His artistic ambition clears his vision to grasp the truth and by the novel's end, Shahid accepts the fluid, multiple nature of individual identity which dawns in him a new reality that "there was no fixed self; surely our several selves melted and mutated daily" (274).

The central theme of Kureishi's *The Buddha of Suburbia* is the question of identity and belonging. Karim's riveting journey into the postcolonial realities of Britain as a young man demonstrates the struggle for self-actualisation and finding a place in the society who doesn't have any compatible pattern to fit properly into a specific model of cultural configuration. The theme of self-refashioning and hybridisation, in the novel, question the very idea of categorisation and essentialist representation. Human mind is no more conceived as a unified being which can effectuate a stable, absolute form of consciousness. On the contrary, hybridity serves "as an assault on the 'Purities' claimed by either centre or margin" (Moore-Gilbert 196). Stuart Hall has argued that identity is not a stable entity and it ambivalently exists as a dialogic space between the self and the other in which identification is determined by the continuous exploration of oneself in relation to others:

> The English are racist not because they hate the Blacks but because they don't know who they are without the Blacks. They have to know who they are.... They are not Black, they are not Black, they are Indian or Asian, but they are not Europeans and they are not Frogs either and on and on.... And there is no identity that is without the dialogic relationship to the other. The other is not outside, but also inside the self, the identity. So identity is a process, identity is split. Identity is not a fixed point but an ambivalent point. Identity is also the relationship of the other to oneself. ("Ethnicity" 345)

Kureishi, in his novels, celebrates the fluidity of boundaries and the free-floating idea of identity as imagined constructions. Both Bhabha and Hall seek to subvert the essentialist model of identity that is assumed to be produced socially and culturally. Hall resists the determinist reductionism of the essentialist cultural representation and claims that cultural identity is a question of 'becoming' as well as of 'being', in the process the individual subjectivities present themselves onto others. Stuart Hall in his paper "Who Needs Identity?" argues that: "Identities are about questions of using the resources of history, language and culture in the process of becoming rather than being: not 'who we are' or 'where we came from' so much as what we might become, how we have been represented and how that bears on how we might represent ourselves" (4).

The meaning of cultural identity for Kureishi lies in the interactive process of cultural translation—the multiple ways in which the displaced individuals strive to relocate 'home' in diasporic imagination. Rushdie's idea of cultural negotiation is similar to the concept of 'routes' rather than 'roots' that James Clifford emphasises in the work *Routes* which proclaims the fluid notion of home and identity signalising the "multi-locationality across geographical, cultural and psychic boundaries" (Brah 194). The notion of 'routes' or 'translation' allows for a plurality of perceptions and heterogeneity of identifications because of its emphasis on multiple locations and journeys. It involves a fluctuating contextualisation that Rushdie calls "ambiguous and shifting ground" (*Imaginary Homelands* 15) or Homi Bhabha "liminal space" (*The Location* 5), which bring out the inevitable, non-essentialist conceptualisation of diasporic space where cultural hybridity becomes the defining principle. Stuart Hall in his paper "Who Needs Identity" questions the cultural identity of the indisposed diasporas combining the poststructuralist critical approaches with a philosophy of discursive identity formation which not only address the autonomy of the diasporic individual but also recognises the possibility of a multicultural negotiative atmosphere where identity becomes a construct in relation to the temporal as well as timeless attachment of the subjective positions to a particular socio-cultural discourse:

> I use 'identity' to refer to the meeting point or suture, between on the one hand the discourses and practices which attempt to 'interpellate', speak to us or hail us into place as subjects of social discourses and on the other hand, the process which produces subjectivities, which construct us as subjects which can be 'spoken': Identities are thus points of temporary attachment to subject positions that discursive practices construct for us. (5-6)

The amalgamated sense of identification often leaves the diasporan with a feeling of utter placelessness and triggers the creation of an in-between third space which is viewed as a productive condition for negotiation and articulation, a liminal space congenially appropriate for cultural translation. Bhabha in *The Location of Culture* develops the model of this 'third space' as an act of pure enunciation of cultural fragmentation. He focuses on the spatio-temporal dimensions of cultural analysis which defy the logic of synchronous presentation assumed by the traditional method of cultural evaluation. The evolution of the 'third space' therefore, destroys the symmetrical configuration of cultural formation as fixed and static. It deconstructs the historical identity of cultural identification as homogenising, unifying and absolute force. For this reason, Bhabha contends that the in-between third space occupied by the diasporic individual is stuffed with creative possibilities: "... it is the space of intervention emerging in the cultural interstices that introduces creative invention into existence" (*The Location* 8). Thus, diasporisation challenges the territorial form of nation-state and questions the rubrics of nation, nationalism and cultural homogenisation as Bhabha expounds in *Nation and Narration*:

> The marginal of 'minority' is not a space of a celebratory or utopian, self-marginalization. It is a much more substantial intervention into those justifications of modernity—progress, homogeneity, cultural organicism, the deep nation, the long past—that rationalize the authoritarian 'normalizing' tendencies within culture in the name of national interest or the ethnic prerogative. (Introduction 4)

The diasporic subjects are continually confronted with the problem of recollecting, rewriting and restructuring the fragmented shadows of a dislocated reality which should pilot them into permanence in the narrativisation of diasporic sensibilities. Thus, attempts are made at reinventing the lost selves in a permeable politics of cultural transaction in an alien ambience which by linking the past with present generates a new reality. The diasporic fiction in the borderline culture Bhabha writes:

> ... demands an encounter with 'newness' that is not part of the continuum of past and the present. It creates a sense of the new as an insurgent act of cultural translation. Such act doesn't merely recall the past as social cause or aesthetic precedent; it renews the past, refiguring it as a contingent 'in-between' space, that innovates and interrupts the performance of the present. (*The Location* 7)

The Buddha of Suburbia by Hanif Kureishi is an experiment in this differential diasporic sensibilities which demonstrate both the impact of race and class relations on the individual and how the colonial subjects are caught up in the ambivalence of colonial discourse and pushed into a new space, expressing themselves to be hybrid, ambivalent and in-between souls in the Bhabhasque dialectics of relocations of culture. The moral dilemma the protagonist faces in the novel reflects a deconstructive presence of two critical voices in the systematic consumption of centre as pure and essential. Karim must thrive on an acting career that manifests itself on his engagement in a multiplicity of fluid, shifting and imaginary selves to augment his process of self-actualisation. He must disguise and sell the essentialising stereotypes of cultural and ethnic identities which he believes to be a colonialist construct and can be reconfigured by non-essentialising and performative projections:

> The subject of the discourse of cultural difference is dialogical or transferrential in the style of psychoanalysis. It is constituted through the locus of the Other which suggests both that the object of identification is ambivalent and more significantly, that the agency of identification is never pure or holistic but always constituted in a process of substitution, displacement and projection. (Bhabha, *The Location* 162)

This temporal dislocation and double consciousness is representative of a postcolonial representation which seeks to bridge the gap between 'margin' and 'frontline' is central to Kureishi's migrant position that assumes symbolic reflection of a professional mutator, the "Everyman of the ... century" (*The Buddha* 141) who carries with himself immense possibilities of transcultural formations as he doesn't accurately fit into any of the given cultural configurations. Robert Young in *Colonial Desire: Hybridity in Theory, Culture and Race* claims this notion of hybridity to be an old concept generated in a number of socio-cultural debates in the 19th century which is tyrannously focused on colour as an obvious sign of racial difference only to disentangle the positive items of cultural fusion in an exclusionary dialectics of racism, associating this negatively with a supposed colonial desire, miscegenation and reduction of cultural essentialism:

> Hybridity ... works simultaneously in two ways: 'organically', hegemonizing, creating new spaces, structures, scenes, and 'intentionally' diasporizing, intervening as a form of subversion, translation, transformation.... Hybridization as creolization involves fusion, the creation of new form, which can then be set against the old form, of which it is partly made up. Hybridity as 'race-less' chaos by contrast, produces no stable form but a radical heterogeneity, discontinuity, the permanent revolution of forms. (148)

Robert Young regards this hybrid space as an influential weapon of discursivity to dehistoricise temporal and territorial essentiality of colonial discourse. But Bhabha, like Fanon, argues that hybridity is a necessary condition of coloniality. Cultural identity re-configures itself in this ambivalent space of enunciation in which there is no hierarchical systematisation, and the colonial presence registers a permanent split between reality as authentic and authoritative, and textuality as repetition and difference. Neutralising the claim of culture, Benhabib develops a complex model of dialogic culturality and subverting the strict internal homology of culture, she pleads for a "radical hybridity and polyvovality of all culture" and regards them as "multi-layered, decentred and fractured systems of action and significations" (26). Enacting a permeable pattern of culturalism, hybridity then turns into a non-instrumental ground for inverting the exclusionary politics of essentialism:

> ... hybridity turns into a difference-erasing concept, negating the foreignness of the foreigner, the otherness

> of the other. Indeed, this capacity to 'normalize' cultural difference, and thereby to neutralize the political claims of culture, explains its appeal: it subverts any normatively compelling non-instrumental grounds for preserving cultural differences and rescuing endangered cultural resources. Thus for those political theorists whose skepticism towards the political claims of culture inclines them to frame those claims as requiring citizens of multicultural democracies to choice between their 'rights' and their culture ... hybridity is the ideal conceptual tool for neutralizing those claims. (Kompridis 322)

Bhabha argues that cultures "are forms of representation" and therefore "have within them a kind of self-alienating limit" ("Interview" 210) which exposes the artificial arbitrariness of cultures as 'constructs' in which "the 'originary' is always open to translation, so it can never be said to have a totalized prior moment of being or meaning—an essence" ("Interview" 210). Bhabha with his model of hybridisation demonstrates that the postcolonial immigrant subjectivities have no need to either assimilate completely into the Western culture or to remain outside it. Contrarily, translation allows them to assume an in-between position which rejects the homologous binary oppositions between contraries "in favour of a more conjoined, 'hybridised' explanation of identity in which, as it were, forever the twain shall meet" (Sandhu 142). In this differential mutability, identity is reborn from "the great history of the languages and landscapes of migration and diaspora" (Bhabha, *The Location* 235). Bhabha views the border as a site eternally infested with a duality of disproportionate combinations creating in-between contrary identifications and belonging. This intermediate positionality proffers new complex forms of narrativisation disrupted by the possibility of cross-culturation:

> ... living at the border, at the edge, requires a new 'art of the present'. This depends upon embracing the contrary logic of the border and using it to rethink the dominant ways we represent things like history, identity and community. Borders are important thresholds full

> of contradictions and ambivalence. They both separate and join different places. They are immediate locations where one contemplates moving beyond the barrier. (McLeod 217)

Karim, The narrator-protagonist of *The Buddha of Suburbia*, is placed in such a borderline culture in the novel in which "cultural differences are not synthesized in to a new 'third term' but continue to exist in a hybrid 'third space'" (Thomas 63). The in-between positionality of Karim is made explicit in the very first sentence of the novel which reveals the "inescapable hybridity and intermixture of ideas" (Gilroy, Preface xi) that inform the identity of the diasporans torn between the two facets of cultural transformations:

> My name is Karim Amir, and I am an Englishman born and bred, almost. I am often considered to be a funny kind of Englishman, a new breed as it were, having emerged from two old histories. But I don't care—Englishman I am (though not proud of it), from the South London suburbs and going somewhere. Perhaps it is the odd mixture of continents and blood, of here and there, of belonging and not, that makes me restless and easily bored. (3)

It is evident from this statement that Karim vindicates his position as an Englishman in the British society but his use of the word "almost" invokes an uncertainty which points out to an inherent lack in him being a "new breed" who straddles upon two cultures simultaneously that makes him restless to belong. As Mark Stein observes, it is the impulse of being an "odd mixture" that drives him to appropriate himself to a dominant form of culturation and as he finds himself divided between "here and there", it activates a desire in him to belong somewhere which allows him to be "an Englishman with qualification" (116). Karim is aware of his proclivities towards Englishness despite his being of mixed origins which "emphasizes the condition of an ambivalent cultural attachment" that brings out the real significance of "the insider who simultaneously knows the perspective of an outsider" (Stein xiii).

This insider/outsider problematics permeates through the fabrics of the novel *The Buddha of Suburbia*. Kureishi is attentive to the differential attitude of the native and the immigrants living in Britain and the way they are biased against each other. Karim's uncle Anwar expresses disgust at the socio-cultural disparity in British society and comments, "'the whites will never promote us'.... 'Not an Indian ... they still think they have an empire'" (27). Karim, on the other hand, criticising the attitude of the South Asian people for the host country Britain, tells of Jamila's bias against her tutor Miss Cutmore: "She drove me mad by saying Miss Cutmore had colonized her, but Jamila was the strongest-willed person I'd met: no one could turn her into a colony. Anyway, I hated ungrateful people, without Miss Cutmore, Jamila wouldn't have ever heard the word 'colony'" (53). Kureishi in his novel thus seeks to discover this ambivalent relationship between the coloniser and the colonised which generates new realities of cross-culturation in a fast transforming globalised world.

Cultural hybridity, in the novel, seems to undermine the discourse of authenticity as a validating point for culturation. Being positioned with an ambivalent identity, Karim doesn't strive to confirm himself to any of the models provided by the society. Unlike Haroon and Anwar, Karim represents the second generation immigrants who was "born and bred" (3) in Britain and which makes him think that Englishness is natural to his character. Karim is not exposed to his father's culture and knows little about India. But at times he prefers his essential Indianness to other to capitalise on the situation which is easier for him to do being a nonconformist. To impress his friend Charlie who is inspired by Haroon's preoccupation with meditation and wisdom, he tells a lie that he performs "that meditation stuff every morning" (14). Shadwell's analysis of Karim in his theatrical maneuver is strongly guided by the visual presence of the racial sign as explaining his identity. The off-white color of his skin is enough for Shadwell to recognise him as the racial other. Shadwell, the director identifies Karim as an Indian fit for the role of Mowgli but not without reservation:

> 'What a breed of people two hundred years of imperialism has given birth to. If the pioneers from the East India Company could see you. What puzzlement there'd be? Everyone looks at you, I'm sure and think: an Indian boy, how exotic, how interesting, what stories of aunties and elephants we'll hear now from him. And you're from Orpington.... What a strange world? The immigrant is the Everyman of the twentieth century. (141)

The immigrant Everyman, however, is not selected for the role of Mowgli for his hybridised inclusiveness but for a certain kind of Indianness which Karim affects in his disposition as stereotyped by the Britishers like Shadwell and Pyke: "'In fact, you are Mowgli you're dark-skinned, you're small and wiry, and you'll be sweet but wholesome in the costume" (142-43). Shadwell is misguided by Karim's authenticity and fails to penetrate beneath the artificial exterior of Indianness which he later projects to the dramatic group to cover up the hybridised tension within. Shadwell reprimands Karim saying that he has been "cast for authenticity and not for experience" (147) which makes Karim exploit his stereotyped authenticity, performatively to thrive on his career whereas he is quite aware of the nonessentialist properties of his character. Similarly, Pyke interpreted Karim Amir as Indian, labelling him as 'black' before advising him that he must model his character on someone he knows from his own back-ground. Pyke and Shadwell apparently evaluate Karim as Indian based on the racial sign of skin color which they believe to be the prime totaliser of identity. But they soon understand that Karim doesn't speak Indian language and that he has not ever visited his supposed home country lead them to ostracise Karim's in-between position. Jamila and Haroon severely criticise Karim for his being looked like "a black and white Minstrel" attending the "bloody fucker Mr. Kipling pretending to whity he knew something about India!" (157). Karim again has to play the role of an Indian character when he has to imitate his father's friend Anwar. In the subsequent theatrical performances, Karim puts on several little scenes one of which is the one when he reacts madly against some imaginary British boys. Tracey, one of his colleagues, however, opposes to this stereotyped character saying that it will destroy the image of the immigrants in Britain as it seeks to perpetuate and project those stereotyped clichés which are strongly upheld by a given culture even though considered strange and funny:

> Your picture is what white people already think of us. That we're funny, with strange habits and weird customs. To the white man we're already people without humanity, and then we go and have Anwar madly waving his stick at the boys. I can't believe that anything like this could happen. You show us as unorganized aggressors, why do you hate yourself and all black people so much Karim? (180)

Tracey is mistaken in labelling Karim with the wrong category as he doesn't feel belonging to Indian people but the English: "a funny kind of Englishman" in search of "any kind of movement, action and sexual interest I could find, because things were so gloomy ..." (3). When Karim has to put on yet another performance, this time imitating Changez, he is again successful playing out some stereotyped aspects of the latter's character:

> At night, at home, I was working on Changez's shambolic walk and crippled hand, and on the accent, which I knew would sound, to white ears, bizarre, funny and characteristic of India. I'd worked out a story for Changez character (now called Tariq), eagerly arriving at Heathrow with his gnat-riden suitcase, having been informed in Bombay by a race-track acquaintance that you merely had to whisper the word 'undress' in England and white women would start slipping out of their underwear. (102)

The prejudiced perception of Karim by the white people leads him to a realisation of the multiple presentability of his hybridised self. Shadwell's suggesting of costuming brown cream over his skin implicates a tension that arises in the West to civilise the non-West by making them know themselves in a differential politics of 'otherness' and by preventing the 'other' to identify himself with a particular English identity.

Kureishi's dialectics of 'in-betweenness' allows the emergence of a new space which is permeated with the permeable interconnectedness of cultures through which Karim would maintain different discursive positionalities in the society. As powerfully observed by Berthold Schoene, it emanates "from *in between* the imperialist black vs. white rhetoric of racial segmentation, the unprecedented ambiguity of Karim's difference threatens to permeate the rigid structures of psychic and ideological Anglo-British territorialism" (qtd. in Romanow 88). Karim's performative enunciation of the identity reveals the discursive structure of culture which is constructed through racial signifiers. Karim's free-floating permeability with cultures is more a result of the fact that ethnicity to a large extent is a construct. As Schoene notes: "Karim is only ever true to his own proprioceptive sense of authenticity.... Any pre-packaged identity or definitive self-image are rejected as encumbrances obstructive to the free realization of his individuality.... The traditional concept of identity has become impractical to Karim" ("Herald of Hybridity" 120). Karim's rejection of a closed method of essentialist discourse inaugurates a new process of identity construction that supports a fluid notion of identity formation and cultural performativities. Karim later invents into himself another fictional character named Tariq which points out to the insignificance of English stereotypical assumptions and reflects the self-refashioning project of Karim who is successful in embracing any kind of cultural modifier that comes in his ways: "I became more energetic and alive as I brushed in new colours and shades.... I felt solid myself" (217). Karim knows well that identity like culture is a process and not a product which should be recognised and reinvented, investing new features into it as Karim remarks, "if I wanted the additional personality bonus of an Indian past, I would have to create it" (212-13). James Proctor argues in this connection that "his unstable, hybrid identity is not simply a product of ethnicity (of being Indian and English), but of locality.... Karim is a Chameleon ... he reinvents and repositions himself as black or white, as Asian or Cockney as the situation suits him" (153). In a number of situations in the novel, Kureishi demonstrates the fluid nature of identity in which characters are represented as 'constructs' open to shifting territoriality and reinscription.

The motif of newness depicting new forms of life permeates through the novel cutting across the stabilising boundaries of traditionality. Karim reflects: "I knew it did me good to be reminded how much I loathed the suburbs and that I had to continue my journey into London and a new life, ensuring I got away from people and streets like this" (101). However, escaping the old life is not informed with ease and he has to admit in the course of the Mowgli episode: "I wanted to run out of the room, back to south London, where I belonged, out of which I had wrongly and arrogantly stepped" (148). Karim's step mother Eva too nourishes such a desire to get out of the suburban realities but "she didn't realize it was in the blood and not on the skin; she did not see there could be nothing more suburban than suburbanites repudiating themselves" (134). One can trace a similar impulse in Kureishi himself when he says: "I wrote to become a writer and set away from the suburbs" (*Dreaming and Scheming* 13).

The novel *The Buddha of Suburbia* deals with the migrant situation of the post-colonial world and addresses the cultural and political issues of 1970s, focusing on the theme of rootlessness and lack of essence. The novel in its centrality depicts the ambivalent impulses of Karim. Also the novel portrays his father's relationship with the white lady Eva Kay who is a powerful presence throughout the novel influencing the lives of other characters. It is the self-reliant Eva Kay who injects the idea of impersonating an Indian mystic into the head of Haroon who finally falls in love with her to get away from the devastated suburban life. In Karim's case, she is an infinite source of inspiration for him which drives him further in his acting career. Karim is nevertheless fond of Eva, even if he is aware that she is the main reason behind his family's disintegration and the troubled marital life of his parents, only because she has introduced a new freshness into his suburban self. Karim rejects his younger brother Allie's statement when the later expresses his admiration for Karim's involvement in the soap opera saying: "... we can't pretend we're some kind of shitted-on oppressed people. Let's just make the best of ourselves" (268). Karim understands the complexity of such an engagement as it will make him re-enact the cultural stereotypes of Indianness which he himself suspects about. As Radek Glabažna argues:

> Allie feels that his self-understanding as a migrant, albeit a second-generation one, ties him down to a shabby world of inefficiency and self-pity—the main enemies of the Thatcherite political Philosophy—and would prefer to become a first class British citizen, even at the expense of his hybrid ethnic heritage. Karim is instinctively aware of the ambivalence of his brother's conviction, but chooses to ignore such doubts in the pursuit of a better life and game. For the role in the soap opera, he will be asked to enact the most rigid clichés about Indian identity and sell them convincingly to the consumers. (68)

Yet, at the height of this metamorphic projection, Karim has to impersonate a character modeled on Changez, a naive Indian with oriental exoticism in his disposition and after all a victim of racism by the white members of the society. He has been subject to frequent racial attack on the street:

> It was a typical South London winter evening—silent, dark cold, foggy, damp—when this gang jumped out on Changez and called him a Paki, not realizing he was Indian. They planted their feet all over him and started to carve the initials of the National Front into stomach with a razor blade.... The police, who were getting sick of Changez, had suggested that he'd laid down under the railway bridge and inflicted the wound himself.... There would be a fascist rally in the Town Hall; Asian shops would be attacked and lives threatened. Local people were scared, we couldn't stop it: we could only march and make our voices heard. (224-25)

The commercial ambition in Karim leads him to impersonate several selves without feeling a sense of inwardness into them as being markedly different from both the Indian and the British. He has not experienced overt racial discrimination like Changez, but still fails to grasp his true authenticity being posed in an in-between spatiality. He has multiple affiliations and loyalties as presented in the novel but his acting motif seems to be the central formulaic metaphor that permeates the novel both at literal and figurative level. As Glabažna astutely remarks: "his main loyalty lies with acting which turns out to be the central metaphor of *The Buddha of Suburbia*" (69). Karim's in-betweenness and internal bifurcation is symptomatic of the postcolonial anxiety that seeks to make coherent sense of the self out of the anomalous fermentation informed by the discursive constructs of colonial desire:

> The moral dilemma for Karim is of the same nature as the divide between the two critical voices with a defiant paradox sitting in the very centre of it: to sort out his chaotic life and create a more stable sense of self, Karim must embark on an acting career that is engaged with a multiplicity of fluid, imaginary selves. Moreover, in order to succeed and attract audiences, he must impersonate and sell essentialist stereotypes of cultural and ethnic identity that he knows to be partly a construct and product of colonialist discourse and partly performance. (Glabažna 70)

Karim's realisation of his artistic self is analogous to a similar impulse in the author himself as Moore-Gilbert contends that Karim's "trajectory towards a new life in the inner city reflects Kureishi's own similar journey" (14). Although critics have stressed his extensive integration into the mainstream of British social life, he still confronts the problematic feeling of racism in multiple form of cultural configurations which is duly reflected in his fictional projections, such as Karim Amir who admits in the very outset of the novel that although he is "an Englishman born and bred" is not at all "proud of it" since he fails to identify himself completely with the British culture (3). The multiplicity of experience which informs Karim's life signifies his "dispositional dimensions of life" (Butler and Spivak 4) which cannot confirm to the conventional conceptualisation of identity "as a normative imposition, suggesting coherence and consistency as indispensable constituents of personhood" (Schoene, "Herald of Hybridity" 121), and fails to encompass the overwhelmingly chaotic diversity of his life experiences. Berthold Schoene, in this context, argues that Karim's postcolonial identity "is never at one with itself but invariably overlapping, multiply mirrored, blurred" as he is "continually at risk of becoming a solitary freakishly shape—shifting nomad, haunted by rather than settled in culture" ("Beyond (T)race" 160).

This fluxing movement of the protagonist is an inherent characteristic of the immigrant as "the Everyman of the twentieth century" (*The Buddha* 141) which unsettles the essentialist notion of identity and culture and evolves a new hybridised condition for the modern man in an all-inclusive cosmopolity. As such, *The Buddha of Suburbia* as Mark Stein observes: "disrespects conventional boundaries and refrains from placing its characters exclusively within one type of formation, be it an ethnic group, a cultural group or a class. Instead, characters are 'afloat' within the orbit of divergent groups. Affiliation is actively sought and not inherited" (115). Kureishi in *The Buddha of Suburbia* deliberately draws a parallel between the world and a theatre in which "roles are learned, adopted and worked out through collaboration and negotiation ... within the wider social milieu of which the theatre forms part" (Moore-Gilbert 127). Another character that equates with the hybridized condition of Karim is Charlie who takes on the punk culture to invert his sense of Indianness with an authenticating air of Englishness, in an oversimplified but artificial manner. Karim can see through his artificial attire of authenticity: "He was brilliant: he'd assembled the right elements. It was a wonderful trick and disguise. The one flaw, I giggled to myself, was his milky and healthy white teeth, which, to me, betrayed everything else" (154). Charlie's taking his punk to New York can be viewed as a performative act of self-appropriation which in the process makes him even more original than the 'authentic' as sought by the cultural essentialists, for he has now acquired a cockney accent and won't anymore be deplored for his talking so posh. Karim thus notes, "He was selling Englishness, and getting a lot of money for it" (247). Bart Moore-Gilbert reflects upon the ontological incompleteness of these characters which "insistently presents identity as a developmental, unstable and shifting *process*, rather than a given stable *product*":

> Identity is in part the effect of dialogical interaction which always leaves the imprint of the interlocuted individual on the interlocutor. Karim and Charlie often act as a 'mirror' to each other ... which suggests their individual ontological incompleteness. Nor can identity ever reach closure through (solipsistic) self-reflection. Karim's self-narration splits him into observer and observed, a fracture which is also figured in his habit of looking into reflective surfaces, whether mirrors, shopwindows or the glass in underground trains. (127-28)

In *The Location of Culture,* Bhabha argues that "hybridity is camouflage" (193) relative to the "process of translating and transvaluating cultural differences" (252) which informs the life of the protagonist in *The Buddha*, for whom, theatricality is so natural to his character that he cannot do away with it. Karim while watching his mother reflects: "... she reminded me of the real world. I wanted to shout at her: Take that world away" (18). The theatrical world view nourished by Karim acts as a formulaic structure in the novel for the development of "the theme of self-transformation" (Stein 117). There are many characters in the novel who take to this art of acting at both literal and figurative level, symbolically creating rooms for reinvention and self-transformation. Haroon similarly assumes the performative individuality of an oriental preacher, Charlie takes to the punk culture as an ultimate resort to self-refashioning, Changez towards the end of the novel finds himself a changed man who learns to accept contradictions in life, and even Jamila, the most essentialist-looking individual in the novel, successfully reconfigure her identity in accordance to the shifting contextualities that life admits in its flow. As Alamgir Hashmi suggests: "... as the theatrical itself assumes a dimension of life, playing moves the plot, and searching for a character becomes both a structural and a symbolic device" (26). When, Karim is asked by the director: "... you have to be yourself. To make your not-self real you have to steal from your authentic self" (219), Karim cannot do so for he has no authentic self within but "oscillate between the self and its manifold disguises" (Schoene, "Herald of Hybridity" 119). Karim thus consciously detaches himself from the role he is playing and produces an appropriated version of individual identity on demand, rationalising his belief by recollecting the lines of a certain novel: "... dissimulating and silent for the sake of ambition, his pride often shattered, but beneath it all solid in his superiority" (qtd. in Kureishi, *The Buddha* 146).

In the novel, *The Buddha* Kureishi analyses the lives of the first-generation immigrants to Britain such as Haroon and Anwar who strictly adhere to their cultural values and traditional belief having a traditional history of their own. Haroon and Anwar, however, don't feel belonged to their 'roots' nor feel integrated to the British society. As a survival strategy, they recreate their own selves in the in-between liminality of colonial discourse which can be considered as an "interstitial passage between fixed identifications" (Bhabha, *The Location* 3) that promotes the emergence of a hybrid space celebrating differences without fixed hierarchies. Bhabha argues that identity is "never fixed", and cannot cohere into an "absolute form" which he believes to be "the contaminated yet connective tissue between cultures" as the representative of a 'partial culture' (Bhabha, "Culture's In-between" 54). Undermining the claim to cultural essentialism, Bhabha thus turns to Bakhtinian hybridism and its challenges to the totalising culturality:

> ... hybrid is not only double-voiced and double accented... but is also double languaged ... It is the collision between differing points of view on the world that are embedded in these forms ... such unconscious hybrids have been at the same time profoundly productive historically: they are pregnant with potential for new world views, with new 'internal forms' for perceiving the world in words. (Bakhtin 360)

Exemplifying Bhabha's argument, Haroon and Anwar find themselves in their respective in-between spatialities and vacillate eternally between home and host culture, performing multiple modalities of identity formation in an undeterministic performativity. As a first-generation immigrant, Haroon has to struggle to re-actualise his self-identification to be accepted as an Englishman. Having aristocratic roots, he doesn't look inferior to the British. Karim admires his father saying: "... like many Indians he was small, but Dad was also elegant and handsome, with delicate hands and manners; beside him most Englishmen looked like clumsy giraffes" (4). Haroon in his homeland has spent the colonial moments of oppression and believes the British to be a superior race having grand dispositions all round. This is the reason why he is utterly disappointed observing the scenario with ordinary peoples when he was sent to England for higher studies:

> Dad was amazed and heartened by the sight of the British in England, through, he'd never seen the English in poverty, as road sweepers, dustmen, shopkeepers and barman. He'd never seen an Englishman stuffing bread into his mouth with his fingers, and no one had told him the English didn't wash regularly because the water was cold—if they had water at all. And when Dad tried to discuss Byron in local Pubs no one warned him that not every Englishman could read or they didn't necessarily want tutoring by an Indian on the poetry of a pervert and a mad man. (24-25)

Both Haroon and Anwar reject the English socio-cultural values in favour of a performative diasporic identity. Their expectations about England after arriving there are shattered as a "freezing shock to both of them" (24). The essentials of English which Haroon has learnt before his arrival in Britain is of little use to him when he is confronted with the disturbing realities of the suburban culture in London. Haroon's confrontation with racism is related with his lack of professional success in London. He remarks: "The whites will never promote us.... Not an Indian while there is a white man left on the earth ... they still think they have an Empire when they don't have two pennies to rub together" (27). Racism and a continued indifference with the English cultural norms lead Haroon to give up his endeavour at assimilation and retreat into a constructed oriental identity as the exoticised Buddha of suburbia, as stereotyped by the Western discourse. He put on an inauthentic, constructed posture and concentrates on meditation practices as narrated in Buddhist texts and as conceptualised by the Western philosophy, and then enacts the performative transposition of an Indian stereotype: "... he was hissing his s's and exaggerating his Indian accent. He'd spent years trying to be more of an Englishman, to be less risibly conspicuous and now he was putting it back on spade loads" (21). Similarly, Anwar has also tried to adopt English ways and practices upon his arrival in England. Initially he doesn't attach much importance to his Indian roots and culture. He begins to frequent the prostitutes in Hyde Park who would call him "Baby face" for his plump cheeks (25) and drinks wine with Haroon. Anwar, however, faces extreme form of racism which drives and forces him back to Indian culture and religiosity when he starts behaving as if he is still in India. Karim reflects upon Anwar's confrontation with racism:

> The area in which Jamila lived was closer to London than our suburbs, and far poorer. It was full of neo-fascist groups, thugs who had their own pubs and clubs and shops. On Saturdays they'd be out in the High street selling their newspapers and pamphlets. They also operated outside the schools and colleges and football grounds, like Millwall and Crystal palace. All night they roamed the streets, beating Asians and shoving shit and burning rugs through their letter-boxes. Frequently the mean, white hating faces had public meetings and the Union Jacks were paraded through the streets, protected by the police. Here was no evidence that these people would go away—no evidence that their power would diminish rather than increase. The lives of Anwar, Jeeta and Jamila were pervaded by the fear of violence. I'm sure it was something they thought about every day. (56)

Anwar's bitter experiences of racism make him re-enact an extreme form of Indianism. When his daughter Jamila refuses to marry the man chosen by Anwar, he goes on a hunger strike and claims: "... if Gandhi could shove out the English from India by not eating, I can get my family to obey me by exactly the same" (60). Haroon, on the other hand, adapts to the English society far better than Anwar. At the beginning, however, he has to struggle to be accepted by the English society. Karim narrates that "he always carried a tiny blue dictionary with him, the size of a match box, making sure to learn a word everyday ... he'd look at me and say, 'you never know when you might need a heavyweight word to impress an Englishman'" (28). This pattern of assimilating into the English ways of life at the beginning is shared by both Haroon and Anwar which afterward is rejected by them in favour of an internal return to India. As Karim observes in the novel:

> May-be there were similarities between what was happening to Dad, with his discovery of Eastern philosophy, and Anwar's last stand. Perhaps it was the immigrant condition living itself out through them. For years they were both happy to live like Englishman. Anwar even scoffed pork pies as long as Jeeta wasn't looking.... Now as they aged and seemed settled here, Anwar and Dad appeared to be returning internally to India, or at least resisting the English here. It was puzzling: neither of them expressed any desire actually to see their origin again. (64)

Haroon and Anwar together challenge the Thatcherite notion of Britishness which seeks to reduce Britishness to a stable form of culturality in an exclusionary pattern of side-lining the migrants from the mainstream social lives of England. Haroon seems to incarnate a hybrid identity positioning himself as "the brown skinned Englishman" (Moore-Gilbert 47) affecting English habits with his job as a civil servant but doesn't abandon his Indian roots completely. Moore-Gilbert suggests that Haroon's cultural engagements make him to enact "a form of mimicry" because he can never fully eradicate his origins which implies that "the 'Englishness' he has espoused in public life is to some degree tactical" (132) and thus he becomes a "Muslim commodifying himself for white suburbanites searching for the 'inner-room' as an oriental Hindu 'Buddhist' Guru" (Yousaf, *Hanif Kureishi's The Buddha of Suburbia* 40). Bhabha in *The Location of Culture* argues that "mimicry emerges as the representation of a difference" (85) which is suggestive of a "double articulation" (122) involving a complicated process of reform, control and disciplining of desperate elements in multiple ways of appropriating the other as it visualises power. Mimicry, in this context, is "the sign of the inappropriate, however, a difference or recalcitrance which coheres the dominant strategic function of colonial power, intensifies surveillance and poses an immanent threat to both 'normalized' knowledge and disciplinary powers" (Bhabha, *The Location* 122-23). V.S. Naipaul writes in *The Mimic Man* that: "We pretended to be real, to be learning, to be preparing ourselves for life, we 'mimic men' of the New World, one unknown corner of it" (146). Haroon similarly thinks that with his pretentious version of Englishness he can stigmatise the effect of colonial discourse as Bhabha contends, "The menace of mimicry is its double vision which in disclosing the ambivalence of colonial discourse also disrupts its authority" (*The Location* 126). Haroon thus mimicking first the culture of the coloniser switches over to mimicry of the essential Indianness:

> ... the thing that made me realize that 'God', as I now called Dad, was seriously scheming, was the queer sound I heard coming from his room as I was going up to bed. I put my ears against the white paintwork of the door. Yes, God was talking to himself, but not intimately. He was speaking slowly, in a deeper voice than usual, as if he were addressing a crowd. He was hissing his s's and exaggerating his Indian accent. He'd spent years trying to be more of an Englishman to be less risibly conspicuous and now he was putting it back in spade loads, why? (21)

In refashioning himself as the "Buddha of Suburbia", as Wohlsein remarks, Haroon is successful in reconfiguring his identity which is after all "an invented identity and therefore highly hybrid—Haroon achieves two goals at a time. On the one hand, he has found a profession that he loves and is truly interested in, and, on the other hand he has found a way to be accepted by the white English" (144). Similarly, Anwar's abrupt re-assertion of his Muslim identity is a performative strategy to reconfigure his identity when he fails to integrate coherently to the British way of live. He finds himself in chaos and longs to belong. He was never a devout Muslim attending to his prayers regularly but soon realises that he must compensate his lack of belongings by identifying himself with Asian culture and the only way open to him is the religion through which he can performatively assert his presence. Karim satirically observes Anwar's pretentious allegiance to his religion which is far from being spiritual:

> For a few weeks he'd been visiting the mosque regularly, and now I occasionally went with him. The mosque was a dilapidated terraced house nearby which smelled of bhuna gost The floor was sprinkled with onion skins, and Moulvi Qamar-Uddin sat behind his desk surrounded by leather-bound books on Islam and a red telephone stroking the beard which reached to his stomach. Anwar complained to the Moulvi that Allah had abandoned him despite regular prayers and a refusal to womanize. (171-72)

Anwar's choice of Islam cannot be seen as an attempt to revive his spirituality but as a way to stigmatise the painful realities of living in a 'third space' and to stabilise his identity through religious connections. Jamila, on the other hand, doesn't need religion to reconfigure her identity, and rather represents the failure of the religious markers to put individuals in closed frameworks of fixities. Anwar believes that by marrying Jamila to a Muslim Indian like Changez will help her to retain her Indian roots and religiosity, disregarding the fact that she has already been exposed to the Western culture despite being born to an Indian family. She must actuate her individuality not by taking recourse to the religion but fighting against the discrimination and contradiction that she encounters by reading books and applying her intellection to the various problems of the world. It is however, interesting to note that Karim's father Haroon despite being a "charlatan" (22) as Karim calls him and a "complete phoney" (72) as regarded by Jamila, he is immensely successful re-inventing himself as a Buddhist preacher whereas Anwar's attempt to revive his individually through Islam dramatically fails in the process. His disillusioned desperation finally leads him to inaction and self-destruction:

> Uncle Anwar didn't sleep at all now. At night he sat on the edge of his chair, smoking and drinking un-Islamic drinks and thinking portentous thoughts, dreaming of other countries, lost houses, mothers, and beaches. Anwar did not work in the shop, not even rewarding work like watching shoplifters and shirt lifter. Jamila often found him drunk on the floor, rancid with unhappiness, when she went by to see her mother in the morning before work. (208)

Karim's Brother Allie is similar to his father in the performative task of mimicking a dominant presence. But what makes Haroon different from his son is his skin colour which is the prime signifier of racial difference. For this reason, he has to betray his coloured descent by innovating some striking features in his demeanour to invert the idea of otherness. Unlike Haroon, Allie faces no difficulty in adopting himself to the British society for his coloured descent resembles that of the white people. He, therefore, is keen to perfect the art of mimicry to the utmost height and is now no longer regarded as oriental or of mixed origin. Kureishi in these cultural ramifications challenges the static ideology of identification which is rather open to multiple refigurements transcending the dialectics of dominance and resistance. As Bronwyn T. Williams powerfully remarks, Kureishi's stance in the novels is:

> ... an attempt to disrupt the narrative forged to define the dominant culture, to hybridize the discourse, to reconfigure the concept of all cultural identities as fluid and heterogeneous. Instead of seeking recognition from the dominant culture or overcoming specific instances of political injustice ... endeavours to reconfigure these relations of dominance and resistance, to reposition both the dominant and the marginalized on the stage of cultural discourse and to challenge static borders of national and cultural identity. ("A State of Perpetual" 3)

Karim's hybridised position in the society makes him to experiment with different modalities of existence, but the race relation in Britain has also a strong effect on his mind: "... we became part of England and yet proudly stood outside it. But to be truly free we had to free ourselves of all bitterness and resentment, too. How was this possible when bitterness and resentment were generated afresh every day" (227). Certainly, there is disparity between Karim's state of mind and the state of affairs in a real society. Butler and Spivak in *Who Sings the Nation-State?* question this tension between the two:

> It makes sense to see at the core of this "state"—that signifies both juridical and dispositional dimensions of life—is a certain tension produced between modes of being or mental states, temporary or provisional constellations of mind of one kind or another, and juridical and military complexes that given how and where we may move, associate, work and speak. (4)

The juridical and military complexes as such have no effect on the personal situations of Karim as he is also an officially recognised British citizen, but certainly it is the social complexes that create a differential phenomenon of identification in which he is relegated to the periphery and appears as a recognisable image, yet ridiculous. According to Alaa Alghamdi, Karim's identifying with the cosmopolitan society in London offers a solution to this dilemma with which his character is originally presented—"that of being in-between, neither fully English nor fully Indian, but subjected to social forces which would discriminate against him and limit his exploration and self-expression" (89). For Karim, the 'third space' acts as a flexible model of belonging and justifies his claims on various relationships in London that appeals to his taste. Karim represents one of the travellers in the post-colonial world who in Phillips' words "wander freely among the noble of Europe's formerly all-powerful cities" (*The European Tribe* 120) and is open to be absorbed into any forms of culturality being unfirmly balanced "among the interstices between different cultures" (Stein 120). Karim, therefore, disregarding the life in the suburb happily celebrates his transformative movements and says: "... what I'd do there when the city belonged to me" (121).

The cosmopolitan society is diversified enough to eradicate the constraints that Karim is subjected to, living in the suburbs. As Alghamdi argues, Karim's hybrid culturality matters less in a cosmopolitan society like London "which has already embodied and absorbed inconsistent and diverse cultural norms and tropes" (89). The London society, however, doesn't demand the immigrants to fully identify themselves with it, accepting an already established, finite set of norms repressively, but "because the cultural practices are themselves contradictory, chaotic and diverse, the pressure to confirm is greatly diminished, and the social penalties for not doing so are likewise diminished" (Alghamdi 89). Alaa Alghamdi incisively observes that:

> The strength of the cosmopolitan setting, according to Kureishi, is that identification with it can liberate the postcolonial subject by engaging, rather than repressing, involving and multifaceted diversity. There is little pressure to conform within a truly cosmopolitan setting and consequently, identity is neither pre-ordained nor subject to rejection. The cosmopolitan setting is uniquely suited to post-colonial identity formation. (90)

Karim's cosmopolitan subsistence also helps him to experiment with different sexual experiences, being not content with anyone of the fixated polarities. Many passages in the novel are replete with sexual imagery that depicts the multifarious polyvalency of the protagonist's sexuality. Karim's sexual desires clarify the fact as Glabažna writes, "that Karim actually understands his sexuality as a mutable constellation of groundless performances" (73) in which 'hybridity', Moore-Gilbert argues, "is as much figured through Karim's bisexuality as through his mixed-race origins" (113). Karim himself admits his indiscriminatory sexual preferences saying:

> It was unusual, I knew, the way, I wanted to sleep with boys as well as girls. I liked strong bodies and the backs of boys' necks. I liked being handled by men, their fists pulling me, and I liked objects—the ends of brushes,

> pens, fingers—up my arse. But I liked cunts and breasts, all of women's softness, long smooth legs and the way women dressed. I felt it would be heart-breaking to have to choose one or the other, like having to decide between the Beatles and the Rolling Stones. (55)

Karim's sexual excess is interpretive of the failure to polarise his sexuality in any one mode as suggested by the socio-cultural ambience of the society. His desire equally for men and women highlights his performative proclivities towards a hybrid formation which is not guided by the homologous pattern of relationships, prefixed by a particular culture and society. The restless, multiple sexual encounters which Karim experiences are indicative of the lack of intimacy in those sexual ventures: "I had squeezed many penises before, at school. We stroked and rubbed and pinched each other all the time. It broke up the monotony of learning. But I had never kissed a man" (17). Karim's sexual encounter with his best friend Jamila is also devoid of love and intimacy and he is as confused as before questing in vain for the meaningfulness of these relationships. He thus reflects: "I was all pretentious, of course, and I learned nothing about sex, not the slightest thing about where and how and here and there, I lost none of my fear of intimacy" (52). Karim is also quite vocal with his sexual relationship with Eleanor which this time he identifies as love. But in Karim's world, even love is devoid of feeling and is reducible to a rational choice that is made for prosperity and progress: "I was always glad to get away now. I had a far more exciting project heating up over the other side of the river. I had chosen Eleanor to fall in love with and was making progress" (172). Love, according to Karim, is never complete and changes with shifting focus because it has nothing to do with feeling but futility: "So there it was. Helen loved me futilely and I loved Charlie futilely and he loved Miss Patchouli futilely, and no doubt she loved some other fucker futilely" (38). Radek Glabažna, therefore, suggests a Butlerian reading of the novel, so that one can see how Karim's new self is configured "through a variety of performances and is therefore just another performative category, alongside race and—Butler's chief concern gender" (73). Because for Judith Butler, "the fundamentalist reasoning of identity politics tends to assume that an identity must first be in place in order for political interests to be elaborated and subsequently, political action to be taken ... there need not be a 'doer behind the deed'. But that the 'doer' is variably constructed in and through the deed" (195). Karim is convinced, within the framework of Bhabha's theory, of the performative profundity of these categories which "produce its slippage, its excess, its difference" and his subversive activity thus dismisses all essentials as delusion that operates ambivalently in an "area between mimicry and mockery" (*The Location* 86). Karim can be considered as "a fictional counterpart of Homi Bhabha's theory of mimicry" (Glabažna 71) who seems to play out the philosophy of multiple, hybridised belonging which explicitly reveal the free-floating, variable performativity of identity as superficial and groundless. Karim's sexual (mis) adventures, in this sense, are performative acts which can never be measured by cultural standards and standpoints. Karim's mockery of an essentialised world of stabilising proclivities echoes Butler's account of the erratic identity roles that "the ontology of substances ... is not only an artificial effect, but essentially superfluous" (34):

> Karim's bisexual excesses are in perfect accordance with Butler's conviction that "if gender attributes and acts, the various ways in which a body shows or produces its cultural signification are performative, then there is no pre-existing identity by which an act or attribute might be measured". From a Butlerian scrutiny, the Buddha will indeed emerge as a novel stressing the performative character of gender and ethnicity—categories that we traditionally consider substantial and immutable. (Glabažna 73)

Karim's bisexual elementalities—his making love to men and women alike—is a significant marker of hybridity. He can't determine which he likes the most. As Rita Felski argues "... he exhibits no anxiety or guilt as he embarks on a series of affairs with men and women" (qtd. in Thomas 76). He is comfortably settled with his bisexuality and selects what suits him best in a specific context. Regarding the homosexual and bisexual overtones of Kureishi's works, Moore-Gilbert has said that "... the thematic of homo and bisexuality which run through Kureishi's oeuvre don't simply problematize dominant discourses of 'normal' and 'perverse' sexuality but of national belonging too" (199). Indeed, there is a parallel between how Karim fancies about both the sexes and his vacillating inclination towards both Englishness and Indianness.

Identity and belonging are the central concern of the novel *The Buddha of Suburbia*, but it is desirable to understand how the sense of identification is influenced by the disparate cultural factors of the age along with the development of the British society as highly multicultural and unnormative. With this regard, Bruce King has argued that the novel "is not primarily about identity, but about desire and liberation and their costs" and Karim "is not a product of cultural conflict like his father" but inevitably "a product of the cultural revolution of the 1960s of Pop music, instant fame, sexual freedom, drugs multiracialism, multiculturalism" ("Abdulrazak Gurnah" 89). As Ranasinha observes, "it is in this 'fringe world' of city culture that Kureishi's work is located, imbuing it with its distinctive metropolitan, hip quality" (15). Karim is inclined towards the pop culture and music; when visiting the pub with Haroon and Eva, he notices how young people are crazy about the latest fashion: "the little groovers talked esoterically of Syd Barrett. To have an elder brother who lived in London and worked in fashion, music or advertising was an inestimable advantage at school. I had to study the melody maker and New Musical Express to keep up" (8). He is more interested in music rather than studies and gets involved with a "pop-star school chum and becomes immersed in experimental theatre" (Kaleta 72). Apparently, the theme of music and popular culture in *The Buddha* is again reinforced by the influence of David Bowie who is an eternal source of inspiration for Charlie, the son of his father's lover Eva whom Karim admires, as Charlie is developed into a "Bowie-loving Bowie like character" (Kaleta 107):

> One of the boys was Charlie.... He looked less winsome and poetic now; his face was harder, with short hair, the cheekbones more pronounced. It was Bowie's influence,

> I knew. Bowie, then called David Jones, had attended our school several years before, and there, in a group photograph in the dining hall, was his face. Boys were often to be found in their knees before this icon, praying to be made into pop stars and for release from a lifetime as a motor-mechanic or a clerk in an insurance firm or a junior architect. (68)

Ruvani Ranasinha argues that Kureishi's concern over pop culture is strongly related to his multi-ethnic positionality as in the 60s and 70s "youth subcultures and ethnic cultures were both positioned in a marginal and contestatory relationship to the dominant culture" (16) and exist as subversive potentials to enunciate alternative traditions to the ethnic culture which is posed directly against the dominant mode of cultural presentation as holistic and pure. Ranasinha quotes Stuart Hall to demonstrate the tension between high culture and the informal youth culture:

> ... popular culture always has its base in the experiences, the pleasures, the memories, the traditions of people.... Hence, it links with what Mikhail Bakhtin calls 'the vulgar'—the popular, the informal, the undesired, the grotesque. That is why it has always been counterpoised to elite or high culture, and is thus a site of alternative traditions. And that is why the dominant tradition has always been afraid of it, quite rightly. (qtd. in Ranasinha 16)

Karim's hybridised personality doesn't seek an ethnic identity to self-actualise itself but he must be "immersed in youth culture that is itself a way of avoiding racialized environment" (Ranasinha 68). As Kaleta argues, the multiple engagements of Karim with different sexes and his involvement in the libidinous, temporary impulses as part of the popular subculture, "electrifies the social momentum reflected in pop music" (Ranasinha 81). Kureishi's *The Buddha of Suburbia* thus engages with the music and the fashionable development of the 1970s and traces its influence on the second-generation immigrants in the novel as Kaleta states: "it also gives us that decade without the contradictions, reservations or confusions experienced by living through it" (82-83).

Another second-generation immigrant who is strongly influenced by the cultural atmosphere of the seventies is Jamila who is firmly focused on his critical reading of the feminist writers like Germaine Greer and Kate Millet and thereby sharpening her intellectual consciousness. Jamila cannot be confined into a single mode of culturality or religiosity as her father Anwar wants her to be, for she is a freedom-loving individual and hates the culture of her parents. She regrets the patriotic authority of her father whose political orientation is shaped by the critical currents of the black power movements in America such as the works of Angela Davis and Malcolm X (68). She, therefore, engages herself in studying books and listening to music from a quite early age: "At the age of 13 Jamila was reading non-stop, Baudelaire and Colette and Radiguet and all that rude lot, and borrowing records of Ravel, as well as singers popular in France like Billie Holliday" (52). The novel thus depicts the cultural ambience of an particular moments in history, i.e. the seventies through the circuitous consciousness of the protagonist Karim Amir to describe how the popular sub-culture of the seventies inevitably informed the personal life of the individuals in that period. Kaleta thus describe the period as "a decade in which, in terms of religion and tradition, the deities of Asia give way to the gods of Empire and Rock, in which art's place in our pop culture world is questioned, and in which assimilation and identity collide" (84).

Brian Finney, in this context, claims that "the novel presents the pursuit of pleasure as it itself a way of freeing the self from the constraints of a racist, materialist and tradition-bound society" (*English Fiction* 125). His accomplishments and sexual involvements as described in the novel serve to a definitive end, that of reconfiguring his sense of self-definition. Karim's interest in "mysticism, alcohol, sexual promise, clever people and drugs" (15) is essentially an echo of his desire to rebuild himself with the image of his friend Charlie whom he looks for inspiration as incarnating the spirit of a fashionable London life. Karim is not the immediate product of the cultural conflict of the age like his father Haroon who migrated to Britain shortly after the independence and the partition in the 1950s, but is influenced by the later cultural expression of the multiracial Britain in the seventies, the imperial centre of city life marked by multicultural realities and diversification. Brian Finney contends that "if Karim learns anything in the course of this novel it is that seeking to fix one's sense of identity in any one position, whether that is national, ethnic, religious or political is self-defeating" (*English Fiction* 126) which leads him to the knowledge that identity is "something we stage" (*English Fiction* 132) and that "national identity is performed not inherent" (*English Fiction* 131). Karim's excessive fluctuation between internalising an exclusive form of Englishness and Indianness can be seen as reflecting this tension of mutable identification which makes him to choose things according to circumstances and selecting that only which suits best in a given context.

According to Kenneth C. Kaleta, Kureishi in his novels suggests that "the dogma of nationalism is in conflict with the reality of today's multicultural England" (3). Kureishi points out the need to reconceptualise the notion of nationalism in the present context as the world is evolving as an increasingly cosmopolitan society, and Britain in its present configuration must admit non-essentialist, unmonolithic model of identity construction and nationalistic representation. Kureishi in *The Buddha of Suburbia* then attempts to explore "a new way of being British" and in this process seeks to "reconfigure dominant, exclusive constructions of Britain in the context of large-scale post-war immigration" (Ranasinha 1). Kureishi's definition of nationalism is inevitably influenced by the racially charged atmosphere of the seventies:

> I think English literature has changed enormously in the last ten years, because of writers from my background—myself, Salman Rushdie, Ben Okri, Timothy Mo. You know, there are many, many of us, all with these strange names and some kind of colonial background. But we are part of English literature ... writing about England and all that implies. Whatever I've written about, it is all been about England in some way, even if the characters

> are Asian or they're from Pakistan or whatever. I've always written about England, usually London. And that's very English. Also the comic tradition, I think, is probably English, the mixture of seriousness and humour. Most of the pop music and the interest in pop music's a very English thing. Everything I write is soaked in Englishness, I suppose. (qtd. in Kaleta 3)

Analogously, Nahem Yousaf in his paper "Hanif Kureishi and 'the Brown Man's Burden'" observes that "Kureishi confronts the difficulty of being able to convey this 'complex thing', this 'fresh way of seeing Britain', and 'the innumerable ways of being' he perceives ..." (15). In Yousaf's view, *The Buddha of Suburbia* seeks to unravel the tension that informs the people's "recognition of Britain as a multicultural society and of Britons as racially diverse and culturally heterogeneous citizens" (*Hanif Kureishi's The Buddha of Suburbia* 27). Kureishi consciously engages, as it is claimed by him, in reconfiguring the notion of Englishness to reflect the hybrid realities of contemporary London:

> I stress that it is the British who have to make these adjustments. It is the British, the white British, who have to learn that being British isn't what it was. Now it is a more complex thing, involving new elements. So there must be a fresh way of seeing Britain and the choices it faces: and a new way of being British after all this time. Much thought, discussion and self-examination must go into seeing the necessity for this, what this 'new way of being British' involves and how difficult it might be to attain. (*Dreaming and Scheming* 55)

Kureishi in his essay "The Rainbow Sign" reflects upon his condition of an in-between positionality being straddled two cultures at the same time. He writes about his boyhood experiences growing up in London and his belated visit to his father's land Pakistan when he admits being forced into a "little identity crisis" (*Collected Essays* 11). He doesn't have any clear interpretation of his own 'homeland' and belongingness at that time, and is troubled by the anti-British remarks of his uncle living in Pakistan which makes him reintegrate his sense of belonging to Britain. His emphatic urge to belong somewhere is activated by the words of a relative when the latter tells to him: "... we are Pakistani, but you, you will always be a Paki—emphasizing the slang derogatory name the English used against Pakistanis, and therefore the fact that I couldn't rightfully lay claim to either place" (*Collected Essays* 12). Kureishi as a second-generation migrant has an underdeveloped sense of belonging to either places and sees the world differently than from his father who is a first-generation migrant having solidarity with and a feeling of rootedness to the native land. Kureishi as a young boy is puzzled by the racial remarks of his acquaintances and asks himself: "I wondered: did my uncles ride on camels? Surely not in their suits? Did my cousins, so like me in other ways, squat down in the sand like little Mowglis, half-naked and eating with their fingers" (*Collected Essays* 3). Kureishi consciously develops this 'Mowgli' theme in his novel *The Buddha of Suburbia* in which Karim, the protagonist has to struggle to produce a certain 'authenticated' version of Indianness on demand and that "his on-stage impersonations of the most stereotyped forms of Indianness do not mean selling himself or colluding with the enemy, but simply returning the colonial gaze by way of a complete mockery of these colonial clichés" (Glabažna 71). Karim, like Kureishi, acknowledges his mixed origin and understands the implication of those Eurocentric stereotypes on stage which reveals the downright and restricted vision of the colonial discourse. He cannot be made Indian by applying brown paint to his skin. He still sounds suburban even after affecting the metropolitan accent of Englishness in his speech as his girlfriend Eleanor complains him of. Kureishi's inclusion of the Mowgli episode in the novel is important because it once again points out his hybridised culturality, in which he must find out a negotiative strategy to overcome the tension. As Moore-Gilbert argues: "Just as Mowgli must negotiate between his identities as man and wolf-cub, so Karim is torn between different cultural identifications and, like Mowgli, he is in a process of maturation which involves choices between conformity to moral law and the promoting of nature" (125). In this case, the Indian identity is rather forced upon Karim who himself has never visited India before. He is identified in negative terms as the racial other of not being sufficiently white and hence is assumed to perfectly suit the role of Mowgli in his oriental quintessential behaviours. He is deliberately asked to be authentic which he is not. This exposes the insignificance of the stereotyped assumptions of the coloniser about the colonised in which they are systematically keen to generate a bias, appropriated picture of the orient as opposed and different from the occident. Franz Fanon in his book *Black Skin, White Mask* reflects upon this painful reality of identifying oneself with an entity one is not under the domineering gaze of the colonial desire:

> I had to meet the white man's eyes. An unfamiliar weight burdened me. In the white world the man of colour encounters difficulties in the development of his bodily scheme.... I was battered down by tom-toms, cannibalism, intellectual deficiency, racial defects.... I took myself far off from my own presence.... What else could it be for me but an amputation, an excision, a haemorrhage that spattered my whole body with black blood? (qtd. in Gibson 183)

The civilising mission of the coloniser is clearly reflected in Shadwell's words about Eva who introduces into this complexity the motif of rescue when the former remarks: "She's trying to protect you from your destiny, which is to be a half-caste in England. That must be complicated for you to accept—belonging nowhere, wanted nowhere. Racism. Do you find it difficult? Please tell me" (141). Ania Loomba claims that "colonial identities—on both sides of the divide—are unstable, agonized and in constant flux" (178). This constant change and instability inform Karim's fluctuating life and set him in eternal movement throughout: "I was not too unhappy criss-crossing South London and the suburbs by bus, no one knowing where I was. Whenever someone—mum, dad, Ted—tried to locate me, I was always somewhere else, occasionally going to a lecture and then heading out to see Changez and Jamila" (94). Karim's fluid individually thus unsettles the coloniser/colonised dialectics and allows the subaltern to speak. Karim's hybridised identity in this sense "displays the necessary deformation and displacement of all sites of discrimination and domination" (qtd. in Edwards 141).

Like Karim, Jamila is also mistaken for a "Paki" (53), but she can tolerate no insult smugly like Karim and strongly reacts to the insult on her heritage. On one occasion, she attacks a cyclist who hurls insults at her race when she is in the street with Karim. Ranasinha describes Jamila as "a committed feminist and antiracist" (61). Jamila is very different from other second-generation immigrants described in the novel with her strong sense of liberty and outstanding education that she receives under a missionary in London. Miss Cutmore is a librarian who was once a missionary in Africa who takes care of Jamila after her studies in school. Moore-Gilbert views Miss Cutmore as a representative of "the mission of social inclusiveness" (119) and with her missionary zeal, as Jamila mentions, seems to 'colonize' her with her strategy of assimilation for she thinks: "Miss Cutmore really wanted to eradicate everything that was foreign in her" (53) by teaching her how to make herself more of a European. But even after educating herself with all western ways, she is still seen as a 'Paki' in the eyes of the Britishers. The assimilative strategy of multiculturalism drastically fails here because Jamila's hybridity makes her life indigenously more difficult. Later in the novel, however, she dismisses her sense of 'being colonised' and makes her hybridity her strength. Töngür, in this connection observes that Jamila with her strength of character represents the "struggle against patriarchal and social changes" and with her in-between conditionality reaches a balance between her own sense of "cultural values and those of the British society" (101).

Anwar soon realises his daughter's strange behaviour and her growing tendency to become a European and decides to marry her to an Indian man named Changez. Her mind is full of revolutionary ideas; she loves her father but cannot marry a man she has never met in her life.

Yousaf suggests that "[t]his imposition of male power comprises Jamila's integrity" (qtd. in Buchanan 43), not her subordination. Like her daughter, Anwar's wife Jeeta too has to subject to the domestic violence in the hands of Anwar even if she understands that Anwar is deteriorating not only mentally but physically. Yousaf, in this connection, argues that "in Jamila and her mother we have two very strong women who are conscious of the roles assigned to them within a traditional working class family unit ... they choose to uphold a patriarchal structure that they know to be crumbling" (qtd. in Buchanan 43). Although living in London, Anwar is firmly grounded with the home culture and indeed returns to an imagined India of his own creation and holds onto the old ways. Jamila agrees to marry Changez only to save her mother Jeeta from her father's clutches. Susie Thomas argues that "Jamila outwits her father's attempt at patriarchal control, with her 'rebellion against rebellion' and arranges the marriage to suit her" (78). This specific incident delineating the patriarchal pressure points out to the larger colonial structure of patriarchal tradition which the domestic life is a part of. Ania Loomba has demonstrated the effect of colonialism on domestic sphere:

> Colonialism intensified patriarchal relations in colonized lands, often because native men, increasingly disenfranchised and excluded from the public sphere became more tyrannical at home. They seized upon the home and the women as emblems of their culture and nationality. The outside world would be Westernized but all was not lost if the domestic space retained its cultural purity. (168)

Jamila's marriage, like her life, is to be viewed as being inevitably influenced by her hybridity which is replete with disruptions and fluidity. The sexual negation in her married life makes her get "immersed in all aspects of life and political struggles in contemporary Britain" (Ranasinha 69). She happily embraces a communal life, bringing people together, consolidating upon socio-political activities and marches against racism. Jamila being "a woman who seeks political solutions" (Thomas 78) becomes the representative of the black community in London dreaming a utopian change in the politically motivated social life. For this reason, she takes to the "third space" of a larger commune life and "does not want to ditch her ethnic identity altogether" (Thomas 72). She is neither an Indian nor an English woman because "for Jamila, ethnicity is not an absolute and indivisible attribute to be defended at all costs, but constitutes the basis of mobilization towards determinate ends, the achievement of which will, by inference, depoliticize ethnicity altogether" (Moore-Gilbert 133).

Jamila's sexual life, like Karim's, is fraught with multiple movements and disruptions. She is comfortable making love with both men and women alike. When Simon leaves for America making her pregnant, she develops an intimate relationship with Joanna (273). So, like his in-between raciality and ambivalent culturality, her sexuality is also equally informed by hybridised relationships and affiliations which make her heterosexual and at times lesbian. Changez thus remarks: "Jammie loves two people, it's simple to grasp. She loves Simon, but he isn't here. She loves Joanna, and Joanna is here" (273). Changez is chosen primarily for his Muslim 'authenticity' by Anwar so that he can fulfil his dream of seeing his grandchildren fathered by Changez, but to his great displeasure, all his dreams are shattered as Changez turns out to be a lazy, crippled man having a marked interest for Conan Doyle's detective stories. From his habits of reading, one can infer that he is not altogether ignorant of the critical current of the intellectual world he inhabits. His experience of the English culture has started even before arriving in London. His interest in overcoat and detective stories which he asks for as his dowry reveals his colonial influence when he was staying in India. Changez's assimilative process of acculturation is started quite early in his life in India when he is exposed to the colonial discourse. As Ashcroft, Griffith and Tiffin rightly observes:

> Hybridity occurs in the post-colonial societies both as a result of conscious moments of cultural suppression, as when the colonial power invades to consolidate political and economic control, or when settler-invaders disposes indigenous peoples and force them to 'assimilate' to new social patterns. It may also occur in latter periods when patterns of immigration from the metropolitan societies and from other imperial areas of influence (e.g.

> indentured labourers from India and China) continue to produce complex cultural palimpsest with the post-colonized world. (*The Post-colonial* 183)

Changez and Haroon both come under this critical assumption developed by Ashcroft, Griffith and Tiffin because the process of hybridisation is actually started in the homeland in both the cases, which is rather accelerated throughout their life in England. Changez is presented as a naive character when he is first introduced in the novel having no fantasies about the Western culture. It is unacceptable for him that Haroon should leave his wife and Karim should fall in love with several women at a time. He regrets: "Oh God, this whole country has gone sexually insane.... Your father should go back home for some years and take you with him. Perhaps to a remote village" (97). Later development of a "sexual promiscuity" (Loomba 107) in his character is traceable upon Karim's bringing of the books of Harold Robins to him. He starts searching for sexual opportunities and finally ends up sleeping with an Asian Prostitute namely Shinko without feeling a grain of remorse. He tends to rationalise his condition by saying to Karim: "Karim, all my entire problems are solved! I can love my wife in the usual way and I can love Shinko in the unusual way" (101). He never feels regretful of his betrayal to his wife, but when he discovers Karim and his wife Jamila sleeping naked to each other on the bed, instantly condemns Jamila of "adultery, incest, betrayal, whoredom, deceit, lesbianism, husband-hatred, frigidity, lying and callousness as well as the usual things" (134), forgetful of his own guilt and misgivings. He is vacillatingly torn between two extremes—the call of the Koran and the new found liberties and sexual pleasures in the West. His hybridised positionality in the society already makes its presence felt through his life as he becomes "increasingly open to the new roles and identities which are thrust upon him" (Moore-Gilbert 128).

Changez's national identity is another point of concern in the novel about which he seems to be eternally confused throughout. After Anwar's death when Jamila chooses to join the commune, there are many option open to him but he chooses to follow Jamila and embraces a Western solution to his problem. He likes the liberty and enjoyment the Western society offers and even urges his people to get assimilated into the Western culture, but when things become darker, his sense of insecurity again forces him into enunciating an authentic version of Indianness which he thinks to be the only remedy against instability. On one occasion, he blames Karim for deserting him and his people and solicits him not to leave his "own people behind" (136) which indicates his personal connectedness with the people of his own culture. Later in the novel, however, we discover a marked shift in his tone as he is describing about his people and their failure to inculcate the Westernised lifestyle living in England which reveals a Eurocentric proclivity in his demeanour:

> 'Look at that low-class person' he'd say, in a loud voice, stopping and pointing out one of his fellow countrymen. Perhaps a waiter hurrying to work or an old man ambling to the day centre, or especially a group of Sikhs going to visit their accountant. 'Yes, they have souls, but the reason there is this bad racialism is because they are so dirty, so rough looking, so bad mannered. And they are wearing such strange clothes for the Englishman, turbans and all. To be accepted they must take up the English ways and forget their filthy villages! They must decide to be either here or there. Look how much here I am! And why doesn't that bugger over there look the Englishman in the eye! No wonder the Englishman will hit him'. (210)

Changez here grossly overlooks his own hybridised condition of in-betweenness and the degree of frustration resulting from such unbelongingness one may experience to "decide to be either here or there" (210). He wants to see himself completely anglicised but is ironically ignorant of his own difficulty to strike out such a negotiation. He fails to penetrate beneath the surface reality that the role of the imaginary character such as Tariq that Karim seeks to emulate on the stage is but a simulation of his own character which explains his inability to see the truth after a prolonged process of anglicisation of his being in the Western society. This is yet another form of colonisation that thrives on disseminating a Eurocentric discourse in the postcolonial world that assumes a rationalised pre-eminence of all that is 'occidental'. Internalising this logicism of colonial discourse, Changez embraces the Western culture and seeks to lose his Indian authenticity by deploring his own culture and glorifying the Western values. Till the end of the novel, Changez is presented as a confused character, eternally experimenting with his incarnated version of Englishness which makes him a mimic man, forever preventing his movement towards the 'third space'. Unlike Karim and Jamila, he is deliberately described in the novel as one who fails to hear his own voice and becomes crippled by his own values.

Conversely, Karim, from the very outset is content with his in-between positionality even if he acknowledges his proclivities towards a certain kind of Englishness which he needs to make progress in his life. His nickname 'creamy' as Buchanan suggests, "enable him to pass for something other than a Pakistani" (45) and even in his daily habits, Englishness is quite manifest and natural on his part when, on one occasion, he says, "I loved drinking tea and I loved cycling. I would bike to the tea shop in the High street and see what blends they had" (62). But when situation demands, he never hesitates to bring out his authenticated version of Indianness that he has so scrupulously internalised in himself from the second hand sources. During his hey days in the suburbs, he uses his Indianness to achieve things he wants like winning Charlie's love by impressing him with his oriental Indianness. But things change dramatically for him on his arrival in London and he begins to deny his Indianness to be like an Englishman, to accentuate his acceptability in the society. As Bhabha argues in *The Location of Culture*, "For identification, identity is never a priori, nor a finished product; it is only ever the problematic process of access to an image of totality" (73). Analogously, Karim believes that his identity is never original and that even if he sees himself as an Englishman, he realises that there is another piece of him which he must attend to. At the funeral of his uncle Anwar, a great emotional discovery dawns upon him and he feels that he betrayed an obvious urge of Indianness inside him by not acknowledging his Indian roots:

> But I feel, looking at these strange creatures now—the Indians—that in some way these were my people, and that I'd spent my life denying or avoiding that fact. I felt ashamed and incomplete at the same time, as if half of me were missing, and as if I'd been colluding with my enemies, those whites who wanted Indians to be like them. Partly I blamed Dad for this. After all, like Anwar, for most of his life he'd never shown any interest in going back to India.... So if I wanted the additional personality bonus of an Indian part, I would have to create it. (212-13)

The realisation of this 'lack' makes him a truly hybrid character. He is one step closer to meet the other missing part of his self: "a strong experience of Indianness that would help him round up the fragments of his de-centred self into a unified whole" (Glabažna 69). In this poignant epiphany, he discovers that he will completely be himself by embracing the hitherto neglected part of Indianness in him, even if he is aware that the gap between him and the Indian culture is indeed unbridgeable. He can never be a complete Englishman as his mother encourages him to be nor can he be a real Indian as Jamila and Changez want him to be. He learns to exist in suspension that is in the 'third space' which "is defined by its location in a unique spatial condition which constitutes it as different from either alternative" (Grossberg 359). "The hybrid", which summarises Karim's condition, therefore, as Papastergiadis contends, "is not formed out of an excavation and transferral of foreignness into the familiar, but out of this awareness of the untranslatable bits that linger on in translation" (194). Karim, the protagonist of the novel, in a similar manner stands suspended between his notions of Englishness and Indianness. As Paul Gilroy argues in *The Black Atlantic*: "The contemporary black English, like the Anglo-Africans of earlier generations and perhaps, like all blacks in the West, stand between (at least) two great cultural assemblages, both of which have mutated through the course of the modern world that formed them and assumed new configurations ... black and white" (1). The emergence of this newness in cultural identification challenges the traditional configuration of class identity to which Karim rivetingly seeks to belong. The novel thus deals with the in-between problematics of Karim's experience as he "sees himself as consisting of two halves, a conception he introduces in the opening paragraph. This raises the question of how these two halves interact, how they feed upon each other, and in how far they remain irreconciled to each other" (Stein 121). According to Schoene, Karim, in the novel, rejects the notion of identity as "normative imposition" (121) and seeks to command "ethnic roles like masks" (Stein 142) embracing his hybrid identity which he understand as "fluid, contingent, multiple and shifting" (McLeod 225) which makes him a true representative of the Bhabhasque dialectics of the "Third Space":

> A willingness to descend into that alien territory ... may reveal that the theoretical recognition of the split-space of enunciation may open the way to conceptualizing an international culture, based on the exoticism and articulation of culture's hybridity. To that end we should remember that it is the 'inter'—the cutting edge of translation and negotiation, the in-between space—that carries the burden of the meaning of culture. It makes it possible to begin envisaging national, anti-nationalistic histories of the 'people'. And by exploring this Third Space, we may elude the politics of polarity and emerge as the others of our selves. (38-39)

Karim's chaotic movements throughout the novel can certainly be traced somewhere in between these polarities that challenge the stable notion of identity and "must necessarily dismiss all essentials as illusion" (Glabažna 7). He deliberately moves away from the constraints of categories and presents his identity in its most ambiguous and complex form. His freedom that results from his hybridity allows him ample scope to experiment with a variety of heterogeneous selves, defying even the framework of freedom itself. As Schoene contently observes:

> Karim aims to struggle free of society's restrictive frame of Bildung and its manipulative power of inscription. Karim will not relinquish his vague idea of who he might be only because his particular sense of self is not listed

> in society's catalogue of traditional identities. Karim is free continuously to reinvent his identity which—due to the creamy colour of his skin, his nomadic lifestyle and bisexual inclinations—remains ultimately unintelligible within the framework of the society he inhabits. (119)

Similarly, in his novel *The Black Album,* Kureishi focuses on the hybrid potentialities of the second-generation immigrants in Britain whose cultural identities can be perceived as hybrid and relational which subverts the conceptualisation of identity and community as pure and essentialist. *The Black Album* seeks to uphold a sense that the individuals have no place in the society whose identities are strongly rooted in a particular belief system. The novel depicts the multicultural realities of Britain which celebrate cultural diversity and encourages a diasporic formation that is hybrid, metamorphic and fluid. Kureishi, in this novel, doesn't attempt an essentialised definition of the black British experience, but rather challenges the static borders of national and cultural identity. As Bradley Buchanan contends:

> ... thc ccntral features of Kureishi's depiction of English life are arguably not based on stable racial or ethnic identities but instead on the blurring of class boundaries, the rise of feminism, the emergence of gay and lesbian movements, and the institutionalization and the commercialization of youth culture and popular music, as well as an increased awareness of the arbitrariness and contingency of identity (be it racial, religious, or cultural). (14)

The novel accordingly seeks to reconfigure the topography of English cultural landscape and social spaces challenging the monolithic concept of racial, cultural and national identity.

Kureishi's *The Black Album* with its interpretive framework brings out the significance of the concept of plurality and cultural hybridity as against the radical, fundamentalist thought and belief system. The multiple and the unstable are presented as necessary ontological conditions that inform the lives of the diasporic subjects with multi-dimensional engagements and affiliations. The novel thus deals with the protagonist Shahid's problematics of choosing a self-conscious lifestyle that is neither apathetic nor fundamentalistic. He is torn internally between two extremes of his desire—embracing the Muslim radical fundamentalism by joining the Riaz group or by pursuing an open, heterogeneous model of cultural liberalism with the pleasure-loving principle of his teacher Deedee. Ruvani Ranasinha observes that "the choice is personified somewhat schematically between Shahid's Asian neighbourhood, Riaz, a mature student and stern leader of the young Muslims ... and his white, liberal ex-hippie tutor Deedee Osgood who offers him sex, raves, ecstasy and postmodern uncertainties" (84). Shahid finds himself eternally suspended between these two positions—the Muslim friends of his college such as Riaz, Chad and Hat who resist the white supremacy and strongly react against racism and Deedee who is a freedom-loving individual, strongly grounded in the expressive culture of the West.

As depicted in the novel, Shahid and his brother Chilli grow up in a middle-class family in the country side of Kent. They have nourished different world views with them. Chilli's concern is primarily focussed on the conflictual pattern of generational representation, while Shahid's engagements are centred mainly on liberalism and literature. The title of the novel indicates an association with the lost album of the American musician Prince, the release of which was banned in 1987 and was only illegally available to the public. Shahid is a big fan of Prince and wants to emulate him. The title of the novel evokes an opposition to censorship and seeks to celebrate racial difference and cultural hybridity. Deedee Osgood makes an explicit reference to the musician Prince: "... he's half black and half white, half man, half woman, half size, feminine but macho, too" (25). Thus, the title of the novel itself introduces the theme of hybridity into the novel. In spite of the development of a cosmopolitan culture in Britain with its multicultural presentment, Shahid has to confront the stigma of racism which activates a sense at urgency in him to belong:

> Everywhere I went I was the only dark-skinned person. How did this make people to see me? I began to be scared of going into certain places. I didn't know what

> they were thinking. I was convinced they were full of sneering and disgust and hatred. And if they were pleasant, I imagined they were hypocrites. I became paranoid. I couldn't go out. I knew I was confused.... I didn't know what to do. (19)

After his father's death, Shahid moves to London where he gets admittance in a university in London and meets Riaz, a Muslim student and his next-door neighbour. He never compromises with his circumstances and aims to consolidate his identity in a multicultural society like London. His ideas keep oscillating between liberalism and fundamentalism. He criticises Deedee when the later calls Riaz an extremist by saying: "Some people have anger and passionate beliefs. Without that nothing could get done, do you have anger and passionate beliefs?" (110). Shahid is troubled by such a remark and linking this with racism, he replies: "The thing is, Deedee, clever white people like you are too cynical. You see everything and rip everything to shreds but you never take any action. Why would you want to change anything when you already have everything your way? We are the victim here!" (110). Deedee being an experienced person, inspires Shahid to inculcate liberalism in his attitude rather than the radical fundamentalism as professed by his friends.

Like Karim of *The Buddha*, Shahid can also be described as a restless youth who "wants a new start with new people in a new place" (16). Although he is dissatisfied with the education system in the school where "books are stuck down the throats like biscuits" (74), he is attracted by the pleasure and intellection which arts and literature would provide because "he wants to be challenged intellectually and in every other way" (5). Also his father's lifestyle proves to be very influential and leaves an indelible mark in his individuality. His father doesn't embrace the traditional life of an immigrant Muslim as expected by others but becomes an assimilated citizen of Britain who rather "hated anything old-fashioned, unless it charmed tourists. He wanted to tear down the old; he liked progress" (39). He has no sympathy for Shahid's literary pursuits which he thinks lead but to poverty. Shahid, however, still feels deeply rooted to his own culture and at a crucial moment of his emotional development admits "that papa was wrong and find his own direction, whatever that is" (76). Chilli, his brother serves as a living antithesis to his father. He is neither professional nor hardworking like his father and can safely be described as the 'playboy of the Western world' whose "relentless passion has always been for clothes, girls, cars, girls and the money that bought them" (41). He has an aggressive approach towards finding his own place in the society and engages himself with criminality, drugs and becomes more extroverted and outgoing than his younger brother Shahid. He is ambitious and fashionable hanging around places to find drug dealers, Italian girls, French croupiers and wears Boss suits, Calvin Klein with Al Pacino as his role model. Establishing himself as a successful businessperson in England, he intends to move to USA. Chilli rejects the tradition and religious duties of his father's generation and doesn't like to inherit them which are for him old-fashioned and humourless: "'You see them, our people, the Pakis, in their dirty shops, surly, humourless, their fat sons and ugly daughters watching you, taking the money.... The new Jews, everyone hates them. In a few years the kids will kick their parents in their teeth. Sitting in some crummy shop, it won't be enough for them'" (201).

It is evident from Chilli's speech that he wants to follow a Westernised lifestyle strictly different from the old ways of living a religious life as a devoted Muslim.

It is, however, surprising to note that despite being brought up in such an open culture, Shahid as a young man should indulge in religious fundamentalism. It can be interpreted as the result of constantly being afflicted with the threat of racism and discriminatory humiliation for being the racial 'other'. Emrys Jones, with this regard, opines that the "threatening situation in which immigrants find themselves has had the effect of strengthening their communal identity. In London, as in many other cities, this tension has led to open conflict on numerous occasions, which in turn, has highlighted the existence of racial prejudice" (188). The novel is set in the chaotic ambience of religious agitation on the part of immigrant Muslim in the multicultural Britain, disrupted with multiple tensions of racial, cultural and religious differences. It was a period of great cultural unrest when Thatcher's policies were being questioned and criticized as being potentially opposed to a truly multicultural Britain. The assimilationist pattern of multiculturality could no more hold any relevance for a densely hybridised society like Britain and helped formation of cultural and racial stereotypes as McLeod in *Beginning Postcolonialism* has observed: "Oriental peoples often appeared in Western representations as examples of various invidious racial stereotypes" (44).

British political philosopher Bhikhu Parekh believes that the sense of belonging among individuals of a multicultural society like Britain cannot be developed as basing on a particular ethnicity or a shared culture as it is too complex for a shared commitment to the political community (*Rethinking Multiculturalism* 342). The ideals of a political community should not contradict the individual's commitment to its continuing existence and lived experience of belonging and well-being. In a multicultural society, the members may markedly differ in interests and "might criticize the prevailing forms of government, institution's policies, values, ethos and dominant self-understanding in the strongest possible terms, but these should not arouse or provoke charges of disloyalty so long as their basic commitment to dialogue is not in doubt" (Parekh, *Rethinking Multiculturalism* 342). The contradiction of multiculturality is obvious when a "wider society" seeks to define its "common good" in a demeaning and "exclusive manner", patronises some and dismisses others neglecting the individual ethos (Parekh, *Rethinking Multiculturalism* 342). Regarding the dismissed and the neglected, Parekh writes that "Although such individuals are free in principle to participate in its collective life, they often stay away or ghettoize themselves for fear of rejection and ridicule or out of deep sense of alienation" (*Rethinking Multiculturalism* 342). The "cultural liberty" enjoyed by the cultural or ethnic groups as put by Amartya Sen "focuses on our freedom either to preserve or to change priorities" whereas "valuing cultural conservation" provides "support for the continuation of traditional lifestyles by new immigrants in the West" which comprise the prime problematics of multiculturalism (113).

Multiculturalism based on cultural conservation is focused upon the essentialist theory of authenticity which views culture as holistic realities, monolithic in forms. It suffers from the drawback of depoliticising the differences by celebrating cultural diversity rather than emphasising the transformative struggle against domination or racism which seems to be content with contradiction rather than evoking real desire for the elimination of differences.

Multiculturalism with its policy of 'cultural conservation' is severely criticised in Britain after a group of Muslim population in Britain protested against Rushdie's allegedly blasphemous seminal novel *The Satanic Verses* in 1989 and burnt copies of the book in public. In his book from *Fatwa to Jihad* Kenan Malik argues that:

> The celebration of difference, respect for pluralism, avowal of identity policies—these have come to be regarded as the hallmarks of a progressive, anti-racist outlook and as the foundation stones of modern liberal democracies. Yet there is a much darker side to multiculturalism, as the Rushdie affair demonstrated. Multiculturalism has helped foster a more tribal nation and, within Muslim communities, has undermined progressive trends while strengthening the hand of conservative religious leaders. While it did not create militant Islam, it helped ... create for it a space within British Muslim communities that had not existed before. (4)

With regard to the novel *The Black Album*, Chris Weedon observes that "It is a novel about second generation Pakistani in London and engages with questions of identity through a radical contrast of lifestyles ranging from affluent westernised middle-class living, through Muslim fundamentalism to serious involvement in drug culture" (142). Apart from these, the novel raises the issue of multiculturalism where the second-generation immigrants in Britain confront the Western rage and racist reference against them. Kureishi deals which the issue of racism and the resulting chaos that emerges from this continued discrimination against these immigrants and ethnic communities. Experiencing constant and prolonged racial discrimination, they develop strong solidarity and brotherhood to resist the racist and physical attack from the British people through their fundamentalist ideals as a weapon to fight against racism.

After joining the college, the protagonist of the novel finds himself divided between two affiliative positions—his love for liberalism and the urge to be integrated with the Riaz group supporting fundamentalism as a kind of shield to resist racial humiliation. He starts a love affair with his college teacher Deedee Osgood who believes that "all limitations are prisons" (25) and at the same time joins the fundamentalist group headed by Riaz. The novel describes Shahid's escape from his Thatcherite family members through his literary pursuits which is eventually influenced and shaped by his consciousness of racism and his study of colonial literature. He desires to become a writer to address the matters like racism and national belonging in his writing. Liberalists in the novel like Deedee Osgood and her former husband Dr. Andrew Brownlow further act as catalysts to accentuate Shahid's inculcation of an liberal and progressive attitude towards life. Shahid's conflictual evolvement of the dualistic dichotomy between Islam and the liberal outlook of the Western culture finds a parallel in Kureishi's own struggle of a similar pattern of in-between positionality which makes Ruvani Ranasinha to remark: "Kureishi avers that notions of Asian and British that cannot be defined separately. His protagonists live the potentials and experience, the pitfalls of mixing and métissage emphasizing the precarious ambivalent nature of all cultural translation. His work parodies the idea of homogeneous, distinct, racially distinct communities" (13). Though Kureishi was born and bred in an Islamic family, he has little knowledge about Islam before he takes to writing but later becomes attentive to contemporary issues and finally in the novel *The Black Album* he takes up problems such as Muslim fundamentalism versus progressive liberalism in London. Mohammad Siddiqui informatively remarks:

> Going beyond a vague and clichéd east-west encounter—a recurring theme in British and American

> fiction especially in the works of writers like E.M. Foster and Pearl S. Buck—Kureishi specially takes up the issue of Muslim fundamentalism in what turns out to be a pseudo progressive multicultural London. Writing in postcolonial context, Kureishi is obviously aware of the issues of racial prejudice and lack of communication between the looked down upon Pakis and the complacent English. (111)

At the outset Shahid feels more like an Englishman and when Riaz tells him that they are fellow countryman, Shahid replies "well ... not quite" (2). His mixing with the fundamentalist group makes him question his identity and belonging and he becomes suddenly conscious of the configuration of race and religion in Britain. He confesses his gradual awareness of his Indian roots to Riaz when he meets him for the first time. His studying Black literature clears his vision and activates an urge in him to belong. But when the crucial moment comes to join the fundamentalist group of Riaz he makes another confession:

> I wanted to be a racist ... my mind was invaded by killing-nigger fantasies ... of going around abusing Pakis, Niggers, Chinks, Irish, any foreign scum. I slugged them under my breath whenever I saw them. I wanted to kick them up the arse. The thought of sleeping with Asian girls made me sick.... I wouldn't touch brown flesh, except with a branding iron. I hated all foreign bastards.... I have wanted to join the British National Party. (11)

Shahid's mystification about his identification is an outcome of the kind of education he receives in his family. His father has been a rich businessman who lives during Thatcherism and embraces an occidental lifestyle. He is a man who always wants to impart newness into his life: "the furniture was replaced every five years and new rooms were necessarily added" (39). His first literary effort at writing a story named "Paki Wog Fuck Off Home" (72) is very unfavourably received by the family. His father rejects it straightaway saying "This artist type are always poor—how will you look relatives in the face" (75)? His mother states that "people don't want this hate in their life" (73). His mother self-consciously pretends that 'racism' indeed doesn't exist in England even when "Shahid vomited and defecated with fear before going to school, or when he returned with cuts, bruises and his bag slashed with knives" (73). From the family, therefore, he learns nothing about religion as is evident from the following passage:

> In Karachi, at the urging of his cousins, Shahid had been to the mosque several times. While their parents would drink boot leg whisky and watch video sent from England, Shahid's young relatives and their friends gathered in the house on Fridays before going to pray. The religious enthusiasm of the younger generation, and its links to strong political feeling, had surprised him. One time Shahid was demonstrating some yoga positions to one of his female cousins when her brother intervened violently, pulling his sister's ankles away from her ears. Yoga reminded him of 'those bloody Hindus'. This brother also refused to speak English, though it was, in that household, the first and common language; he asserted that Papa's generation, with their English accent, foreign degrees and British snobbery, assumed their own people were inferior. (91)

Shahid's brother Chilli gets completely Westernised—clad in Armani's suits, smokes Marlboros and wears Ray-Bans sunglasses and reacts strongly against racial attacks: "... when the National Front Yelled, 'Get back Pakis!' Chilli, wearing a mink-coloured suit, had annoyed everyone by taking out his wallet, waving it at the racists and shouting, 'Get back to your council flats, Paupers!'" (139). Zulma, like her husband Chilli, chooses a Westernised mode of life and disapproves of Shahid's joining the fundamentalist group headed by Riaz:

> 'I'm explaining that religion is for the benefit of the masses, not for the brain-box types. The peasant and all—they need superstition, otherwise they would be living like animals. You don't understand it, being in a civilized country, but those simpletons require strict

> rules for living, otherwise they would still think the earth sits on three fishes ... but these mind-wallahs must know it's a lot of balls.... These madmen are becoming far too mad. It makes the derangement seem general. (186)

Shahid's friend Straper is yet another example of composite cultural identity. Although being grounded in the British society, he empathises with the Asian people but dislikes persons like Chilli who have made himself "too fucking Westernized" branding that as "the wrong turn in" (195) of his life. He says to Shahid that he himself is also discriminated against like Shahid and his fellow Pakis who are equally "a problem for this world" (144). Straper's case seems to universalise the stigma of racism which is why when he is asked by Shahid of the whereabouts of the racist, he doesn't give a straight answer and replies that to "find someone who hates another race" is sufficient "to knock on any door" (144). He has sympathy for the Riaz group and is really impressed by their achievement, describing them as 'pure' especially the way they save Chad's life from drug addiction (144). Riaz's main accomplice Chad represents the strictly defined world of religion and any deviation from the religious life is abhorrent to him. Chad hates art and literature in all forms and even criticises Riaz's decision of writing a book about Islam describing him as "too frivolous, too merry" (58). Chad is full of suspicion about Shahid's affiliation to the Riaz group and advises him to stay away from the pleasure of the senses, saying "pleasure and self-absorption isn't everything" otherwise man would be reduced to "become beasts" (128). He is aware of the Britain's imperial projects in the past which the nation is still boasting about but is blind to the same process of marginalisation his own religion is perpetuating among its members. Chad while talking with Shahid mentions the story of a girl condemning Deedee for giving her protection in her own house who "was forced to say that religion treats women as second-class citizens" to which Chad reacts by saying: "... would I dare to hide a member of Osgood's family in my house and fill her with propaganda? If I did, what accusations? Terrorist! Fanatic! Lunatic! We can never will. The imperialist idea hasn't died" (229). As stated by Deedee, Chad's present cultural make up is essentially an outcome of his past experience with racism and a continued sense of unbelonging which gets his soul lost in translation:

> He used to be called Trevor Buss.... He was adopted by a white couple. The mother was racist, talked about Pakis all the time and how they had to fit in.... He'd seen English country cottages and ordinary English people who were secure, who effortlessly belonged. You know, the whole Orwellian idea of England.... The sense of exclusion practically drove him made. He wanted to bomb them.... When he got to be a teenager he saw he had no roots, no connection with Pakistan, couldn't even speak the language. So he went to Urdu classes. But when he tried asking for the salt in South hall everyone fell about his accent. In England white people looked at him as if he were going to steal their car or their handbag ... but in Pakistan they looked at him even more strangely.... Trevor Buss's soul got lost in translation, as it were. Someone said he even tried the Labour Party, to try to find a place. But it was too racist and his anger was too much.... It was fermenting and he couldn't keep it under. (106)

Chad's in-between condition of (un)belongingness is evident in Deedee's speech and the way he moves from one place to another in his quest for identity. He indeed wants to preserve his religion and culture which he feels to have been blurred by the wild weather of multiculturalism, and wants to be a God-fearing creature for his fear of condemnation. He thus narrates his feeling to Shahid: "'They are existing at the lowest level! And we think we want to integrate here! But we must not assimilate, that way we lose our souls. We are proud and we are obedient. What is wrong with that? It's not we who must change, but the world!' ... 'It's hellfire for disbelievers, you know that'" (81).

Shahid, on the other hand, is forever confused about his loyalty and affiliation. Deedee who represents the world of Englishness is an inexhaustible source of inspiration for him with her liberal outlook and strong sense of freedom and imagination, and at the same time he feels himself drawn towards the undercurrents of fundamentalism exhibited by the Riaz group for the thinks, at times, that it's only by reviving his strong sense for Islam through which he can re-establish his sense of belonging:

> The problem was, when he was with his friend their story compelled him. But when he walked out, like someone leaving a cinema, he found the world to be more subtle and inexplicable. He knew, too, that stories were made up by men and women; they could not be true or false, for they were exercises in that most magnificent but unreliable capacity, the imagination, which William Blake called 'the divine body in every man.' Yet his friends would admit no splinter of imagination into their body of belief, for that would poison all, rendering their conviction human, aesthetic, fallible. (133)

But Chad has no doubt, whatever, of the fundamentalist project of Riaz and feels a complete surrenderance to Riaz's cause, trusting him unquestionably to have fighting for the whole Muslim community. His excessive submissiveness has made him "a dog without a master" (218) when Riaz is not with him. Chad begins to doubt Shahid's loyalty towards Riaz and hates his effortless life and his inclination towards pop culture and music which he identifies as a threat to the Islamic culture (19). Chad suspects Shahid's promising words which he believes to be useless because they cannot be translated into action when situation warrants: "'Because you are always talking, never taking action. And you know why? Because you had an easy life! That shit you tol' me the first day, you invent it to make yourself interesting! Oh, yeah, I know how much you are a liar. Action will be taken'" (219).

Hat, like Chad is fully content living a religious life as prescribed by Islam and supports Riaz's cause being a part of that fundamentalist organisation. He also suspects the indifferent attitude of Shahid and doubts his sincerity towards the ideal of political Islam which they themselves are practising:

"What's the problem, Shahid, boy? A few of us notice you get moody. Someone said you hiding something" (168). Hat warns Shahid against doubting the authenticity of Islam: "Good. But our religion isn't something you can test out, like trying on a suit to see if it fit! You gotta buy the whole outfit" (235). Like Chad he rejoices at Riaz's condemnation of the homosexuals but likes to spare them on certain condition: "homosexuals should be beheaded; though first they should be offered the option of marriage" (119). Tahira too is deeply influenced by Riaz's philosophy and supports the latter's cause and his book-burning demonstration wholeheartedly. She comes to the aid of Riaz when they decide to raise their voice against Deedee Osgood for intervening in the book burning protest. She feels that Deedee is up against the whole Muslim race in suppressing a minority cause: "And today she has prevented us from free expression. Isn't that racist censorship" (229)?

Deedee, unlike Riaz and his friends, favours imagination and free thinking and therefore deplores Riaz not for his racist overtones but because he is "devoid of doubt" (110). Thc in-between condition of suspicion, disbelief and uncertainties then for Deedee is not a weakness in the individual but a blessing in disguise which lead most to the clarity of vision and grasping of truth. Deedee traces Riaz's growth of religious sentiments which fall into sharp contrast with that of his father's: "Riaz was kicked out of his parents' house for denouncing his own father for drinking alcohol. He also reprimanded him for praying in his armchair and not on his knees. He told his friends that if one's parents did wrong they should be thrown into the raging fire of hell" (109).

Shahid's liberal views of art and literature come into clash with the discourse of Islamic fundamentalism which Shahid later wants to profess being influenced by the Riaz group of friends. Shahid internally divides himself into two halves—one part must go with Deedee with her pleasure-seeking principles which would lead him to become a real Britisher and the other must feed on the spirit of Islamic fundamentalism to give him a real taste of Islamic identity. Kureishi, in the following passage beautifully sums up Shahid's ambivalent condition of in-betweenness:

> The silence of his room felt unnatural and oppressive. It seemed like days since he'd been alone. Who would be solitary if they could avoid it? He had been resisting his own company, running from himself. It wasn't mere boredom he feared; the questions he dreaded were those that interrogated him about what he had got into with Riaz on one side, and Deedee on the other. He believed everything; he believed nothing. His own self increasingly confounded him. One day he could passionately feel one thing, the next day the opposite. Other times provisional states would alternate from hour to hour; sometimes all crashed into chaos. He would wake up with this feeling: who would he turn to be on this day? How many worrying selves were there within him? Which was his real, natural self? Was there such a thing? How would he know it when he saw it? Would it have a guarantee attached to it? (147)

Being entangled between fundamentalism and liberalism, between the Western culture and Indian ways of living, Shahid finds himself in between the contradicting polarities of uncertainties which accentuate the search for his true identity. Regarding Shahid's dilemma, R.S. Godlasky states that "Hanif Kureishi's characters are never quite sure who they are. Caught between the often conflicting cultures of Britain and Asia, they seem to suffer the problem of that many second-generation British Asians face—they lack a definite identity" (2). The continued encounter with racist aggression in the dominant white society makes Shahid feel turning out to be a racist himself. He begins to reflect upon his own position in the society racially and nationally which he thinks to be the outcome of the way the white have treated the minorities for centuries: "It been the longest, hardest, century of racism in the history of everything. How can you not have picked up the vibe in this distorted way? There's a bit of Hitler in all white people—they've given that to you. It's all they ever done for us" (12). Shahid, like Chad, starts thinking that they must stand united against this oppression by consolidating the ethos of Muslim fundamentalism to challenge the assumptions of the Western world. Kureishi emphasises this connection of the *The Black Album* with "white racism, separatism and Muslim militancy" (Ranasinha 82). Kureishi thus observes: "Muslim fundamentalism has always seemed to me to be profoundly wrong, unnecessarily restrictive and frequently cruel. But there are reasons for its revival that are comprehensible.... It is constraining, limiting, degrading, to be a victim in your own country. If you feel excluded it might be tempting to exclude other" (qtd. in Ranasinha 83).

Shahid is not adopted by either of the culture he likes to belong. His accent betrays him unredeemably wherever he goes. He realises the harsher realities of the outer racist world coming in contact with "people whose eyes burned with blame and resentment" (136). His presence in Britain with a Paki background is unwelcomed and threatening as inferable from the dramatic incident when he is attacked by a white woman and her daughter: "'Paki! Paki!'. She screamed. Her body had become an arched limb of hatred with a livid opening at the tip, spewing curses. 'You stolen our Jobs! Taken our housing! Paki got everything! Give it back and go back home!'" (139). Kureishi's characters such as Karim and Shahid are indeed fictional projections of a similar racially charged atmosphere that informs Kureishi's adolescent life in Britain with his own mixed cultural background (Kaleta 19). Kureishi writes: "When people insult you, when friends of yours become skinheads and go out Paki-bashing and you don't have anyone to talk to about your feeling and you're far too nervous to confront your friends directly, you have to express yourself somehow" (qtd. in Kaleta 19). This is what Shahid exactly does to overcome the trauma of 'otherness' and racial discrimination, but the urge to belong sometimes underscores his belief in the world of imagination and he feels inclined to relocate his sense of identity in the Islamic community represented by the Riaz group playing on the logicism of political Islam. In the novel, Kureishi presents political Islam that is initiated by Riaz and his friends as a concrete response to the continued racial aggression they are deliberately exposed to. Chad finds security and feels a sense of belonging joining the community and declares: "No more Paki. Me a Muslim" (128). For Chad and Riaz, fundamentalism serves as a cohesive force for group solidarity which redefines their sense of identity and belonging. Ranasinha argues in this context that fundamentalism as presented in the novel works as a weapon to fight racism and can be viewed as giving security to their community feeling and "the assertion of an Islamic identity as a positive identity for Asian Youth" (86).

Another character in the novel who has shown a marked interest in literature and liberalism apart from Deedee and Shahid is the estranged husband of Deedee Mr. Andrew Brownlow who argues with Riaz in the presence of Shahid that religious faith is but "the slave of superstition ... existing in an imaginary realm ruled by imaginary being" (97). His ideas are apparently inspired by Bertrand Russell when the former quotes: "The whole conception of God is a conception derived from the ancient Oriental despotism" (96). He feels that:

> Since then often the people-me-felt abandoned in the universe. Atheism can be a terrible trouble, you should know. Having to invest the world with meaning. Would be marvellous to believe that soon after death by cancer one will slip—I mean, sip—grapes, melon and virgins in paradise. Paradise being like Venice. Without the smells or early closing. Heaven, surely, as someone said, was man's easiest invention. (96-97)

Brownlow in his aggressive anti-religious stance seems to create a dichotomy between the Eastern spiritualism and the Western liberalism associating the conception of God with "oriental despotism" (Curtis 67) and grossly overlooks the fact that the values of liberalism itself is derived from the principles of Christianity. His inability to respect other's point of view and branding religion as mere superstition demonstrate his failure to contribute to the cause of a multicultural society as he claims in the novel helping the Riaz group. Kureishi is conscious of this fact and makes Riaz square Brownlow's assumptions balancing it with his fundamentalist counterarguments:

> But you are a little arrogant.... Your liberal belief belong to a minority who live in northern Europe. Yet you

> think moral superiority over the rest of mankind is a fact. You want to dominate others with your particular morality, which has—as you also well know—gone hand-in-hand with fascist imperialism.... This is why we have to guard against the hypocritical and smug intellectual atmosphere of western civilization. (98-99)

Equally with Riaz, Chad too effaces his British identity completely and rejects the life of pleasure and self-absorption. He is suspicious of extreme individualism and liberalism manifested in the Western mode of life especially in the pop culture of the West and hates music and literature of the postmodern. As Maria Degabriele astutely remarks: "Kureishi represents this Islamic rejection of pop culture and postmodernity as something that is founded on a rejection of Western imperialism" (19). In contrast to Chad, Shahid, although being deliberately allured by Deedee with 'the secrets of desire' and sexual pleasure which liberalism has offered to him, he is at the same time critical of the one-dimensional identity of his friend Riaz. The fundamentalists fail to realize that there are "innumerable ways of being in the world" (*The Black Album* 274) and that identity, ethnicity and culture are all "fluid, contingent, multiple and shifting" constructions generating "the possibility and necessity of creating a new culture" (McLeod 225). Kureishi obliquely hints at the danger of acknowledging identity as absolute and presents the ambivalent feeling of his protagonist Shahid in criticising his friend Riaz:

> Shahid watched the man he had wanted as his friend and who like him but with less reason, seemed strangely out of place here. Riaz loved 'his people', but, unless offering assistance, he appeared uncomfortable with them. Riaz had little: no wife or children, career, hobby, house or possessions. The meaning of his life was his creed and the idea that he knew the truth about how people should live. It was this single mindedness that made him powerful and, to Shahid now, rather pitiful. (173-74)

Deedee's presence in Shahid's life relieves his pressure of conflictual configuration of identity when he is surrounded with contradiction and uncertainties. Kureishi himself admits that: "I am interested in people who liberate other people.... She liberates his sexuality, and she also frees him from fundamentalism, she shows him a way out, a way through this tangle of drugs and religion" (Kumar and Kureishi 128). Shahid and Deedee cross every limit of restrictive frameworks prescribed by the society and culture, breaking the boundaries and barriers of racial and religious institutions. Deedee seems to be an adaptation of Haroon's character in *The Buddha of Suburbia* preaching all "limitations are prisons" (25). Kaleta writes "Shahid finds Deedee his dream lover—knowing, inventive and erotic; and, likewise, Deedee finds Shahid her dream lover—devoted, innocent, and prolific" (124). At one point Shahid, influenced by the ideals of Deedee Osgood even decided to breakup with his fundamentalist friends, but another moment finds himself again devoted to Deedee Osgood's liberal policies and sexual fantasies. For Shahid, Deedee becomes a means to get away from the problematic politics of identification and belonging and to pursue a liberal mode of life. Deedee inspires in Shahid an artistic approach to life doing disparate experiments with their sexual selves. In the words of Holmes, "what Deedee encourages in Shahid is a continuous reshaping of the sex in erotic and artistic play" (Holmes 306). In his quest of his sexual identity, Shahid at length, takes to crossdressing to explore the female side of his hybrid soul: "For now she refused him a mirror, but he liked the feel of his new female face. He could be demurred, flirtatious, teasing, a star; a burden went, a certain responsibility had been removed. He didn't have to take the lead. He even wondered. What it might be like to go out as a women, and be looked at differently" (117).

By cross-dressing they discover in each other the presence of themselves, exploring the heterogeneous sexual proclivities of their selves in which "the dynamics of sexual power have been clearly exposed" (Kaleta 132). Shahid's brother Chilli's sexual propensity, on the other hand, is markedly different from Shahid who in his adolescent days keeps competing with his father in various sexual adventures, affecting certain machoistic mannerism. Chilli, after discovering his brother's affair with

Deedee Osgood interrogates Shahid: "'Ah-ha. Class pussy. How old is she'" (40)? He starts giving advice to his brother: "... people know within two minutes if they want to fuck someone. Within an hour they know if they want to be with them. You want her—then take her" (45). Kaleta writes, "Chilli's plight as an assimilated dreamer is quite clear. He sold himself out to live on Easy Street" (143).

Shahid is not constraint by the formulaic patterns of restraint imposed by the society or religion upon individual, and out of curiosity, he seeks to explore his sexual self in all its multicoloured hues. Kaleta contends that "Shahid wants to believe in something; he is searching for something to believe in. Pledging his love to Deedee on a train carrying them away from the seething streets of London, Shahid chooses at that time to believe in love. That choice compels him to embrace the present" (143). Shahid chooses to enjoy the present life with Deedee "until it stops being fun" neglecting the call of the Riaz group which will again put him into dreadful uncertainties (276). It is this influence of the sexual self which makes him alter the content of Riaz's manuscript which he is asked to type, according to his own sexual fancies. According to Holmes, "Shahid's writing is sexually explicit, reflecting his ongoing uninhibited activities with his lover Deedee Osgood" (302). He wants to live and realise his hybridised self through literature and art and "it is through exercising his imagination as a budding artist rather than practising his faith as a Muslim that Shahid ultimately seeks to find his identity as an adult" (Holmes 305). Shahid struggles to become an artist and views literature as a means to overcome the contradictions and uncertainties of life. Poetry infuses beauty into life and makes it worth living. It is this ideal which leads Shahid to transmute the political content of Riaz's writings into wonderful poetry. Kaleta suggests: "When Shahid transforms Riaz's writing into poetry rather than transcribing his political tract, he turns the fundamental political observations into poems so lush that he gets erection" (139).

Shahid is depicted throughout the novel as a wavering, irresolute person: "... one day he can passionately think one thing, the next day the opposite" (147). He identifies the fundamentalist group of friends as his own people and can't break away from them. Sometimes he experiences "a lack of faith" and then learns to be patient and let things move as it is for he believes, "understanding will certainly follow" after that (96). Shahid's search for artistic freedom and cosmopolitan lifestyle makes his association with the fundamentalist group physically untenable. Holmes observes that "it is Shahid's insistence on the freedom of the imagination that finally causes the split between him and Riaz's group" (304). Shahid and Riaz together represent the age-old conflict between art and morality. For Shahid art is a liberating impulse, boundless and unrestricted but for Riaz morality is fixed and unquestionable, otherwise chaos will let loose in the world. Riaz and Chad seek to alter an essential reality of the world and choose to live their life with illusions, thriving on their straightjacketed religious ideals being afraid of seeing the truth with an open mind. Iain Chambers' observation, with this regard, may complement Shahid's final decision to break away from his fundamentalist friends:

> If you live in a black-and-white world, and prefer the security of an abstract utopia to the potential of the present, then contemporary popular culture merely seems to be the predictable product of capitalism and consumerism ... of Britain 'going down the drain.' Yet self-righteously to castigate this culture and its forms of consumption is to miss the point. Mentally to extract ourselves from it, to turn our back to what is actually happening, is to live an intellectual lie. (*Popular Culture* 190)

Shahid in his search for identity discovers that there is no morality underneath to make life meaningful. Ironically, it is this morale of life that leads him to the realisation of his identity "as fluid, uncontained, always in the process of becoming" (Weber 125).

The second-generation immigrants depicted in the novel have revealed a marked tendency towards embracing the city life as Ball suggests that "their urban existence involves not a hardening around the past but rather discovery, emergence, risk and real-world conflict" (225). Shahid's father as a Thatcherite can be described as living the "philosophy of individualism and self-advancement" (Gunning 74) and nourishes an innate desire to tear down the 'old' for the sake of achieving 'newness' in life which implies his attempts to uproot himself completely from his native culture and embracing an assimilated immigrant culture in the West. Shahid reflects on his father's cartography of his native place when the latter visits back to Pakistan after a long stay in England: "The place enraged him: the religion shoved down everyone's throats; the bandits, corruption, censorship, laziness, fatuity of the press; the holes in the roads, the absence of roads, the roads on fire. Nothing was ever right for papa there. He liked to say, when he was at his most depressed, that the British shouldn't have left" (107). The first-generation Asian immigrants represented by Shahid's father move to England primarily to "make an affluent and stable life in a country not run by tyrants" (53), but living in London society is not easy for them and is contrasted with the open, heterogeneous, instable city life which is embraced by the second-generation immigrants such as Shahid, Chillie and Chad. Shahid's uncle Asif acknowledges the contradictions that inform the so-called multicultural society of England and regrets the way they are rejected by the dominant culture in the complex process of assimilation. It is difficult for him to live in a place that doesn't thrive on "intelligence, initiative, imagination, and in which most endeavour bogged down into hopelessness":

> 'It's easy for people, especially if they're young,' he said,
> 'to forget that we've barely arrived over in England. It takes several generations to become accustomed to a place. We think we're settled down, but we're like brides who've just crossed the threshold. We have to watch ourselves, otherwise we will make up one day to find we have made a calamitous marriage.' (54)

After his father's death, Shahid finds his home as "cruelly archaic" (26) and searches for a mode of liberation to get away from the frigid sub-urban realities. Literature provides him, in the first place, an outlet to address his inner fragmentation as Maria Degabriele observes that the texts read by Shahid trigger in him an "emerging sense of identity that stands in difference from and resistance to the dominant White English culture" (2) which he thrives to re-actualise. After coming to London and having developed contradictory patterns of emotions that pull him in two opposite directions, Shahid begins to evolve a sense of the place which he inhabits. In the multi-ethnic London, place assumes a complex and alternative form. Here, even the mosque itself which is considered one of the holistic categories of Islam is presented in its non-essentialist, multi-cultural, diversified manifestations and projectiles:

> Arranged on three floors, the rooms of the mosque were as big as Tennis courts. Men of so many types and nationalities—Tunisians, Indians, Algerians, Scots, French—gathered there, chatting in the entrance, where they removed their shoes and then retired to wash, that it would have been difficult, without prior knowledge, to tell which country the mosque was in. Here race and class barriers have been suspended. There were businessman in expansive suits, others in London Underground and Post Office uniforms; bowed old men in salwar kamiz fiddled with beads. Chic lads with ponytails, working in computers, exchanged business cards with young men in suits. Forty Ethiopians sat to the side of one room, addressed by one of their number in robes. (131-32)

Here the mosque itself represents the non-fixative model of hybridity at the centre of the "limitless city" (57) of London, densely diversified and unmonolithic so that everyone lives side by side in peace and harmony. London as a metropolis offers a heterogeneous urban experience where belonging can be provisional and informed with ease and that "in London, if you found the right place, you could consider yourself a citizen the moment you went to the same local shop twice" (193). Shahid, with these cosmopolitan realities, sticks to his own belief system and seeks to define his own sense of Britishness, reconfiguring it with the model of the postmodern sub-culture represented by the metropolitan city life, characterised by its relational and unfixed categories and concepts. As Bald observes:

> Unlike their parents, young male and female Black British are averse either to harmonizing their voices with those of the Anglos in a chorus written by the latter, or to playing only the music of the lands of their origin. Instead, they see themselves engaged in making a postmodern music of discordant notes and multilingual voices. From such music we can expect a re-articulation and reconfiguration of the discourses of identity. (86)

Shahid opts for the pop culture of the 1980's England "where fragmentation, change, undecidability are the norm" (Degabriele 29) rather than exceptions and with his firm assertion, "I can't be limited" (272) embarks on a riveting journey with Deedee Osgood keeping his options open with his liberalism and individualism. His search for the situatedness of his self, paradoxically engages him with multiple identity performances, and in contrast to Riaz's assertion of his feeling alienated in England, Shahid claims: "There's nowhere else I will feel more comfortable" (175). Shahid's claim points out a similar belief in Kureishi himself when the latter says that the second-generation immigrants belong to Britain even amidst the harsh realities of racism and multicultural possibilities and not to the culture their parents belonged to: "for me and the others of my generation born here, Britain was always where we belonged, even when we were told—often in terms of racial abuse—that this was not so" (*Collected Essays* 48). Shahid's involvement in the pop culture and his passion for Prince introduces in the novel the theme of fluidity and hybridity in which identity can only be experienced in terms of perpetual movements and unpolarised mixing. The transitory, heterogeneous nature of the youth culture are being indicated and integrated into the life of the protagonist as when he makes a reference to the musician Prince and his lost album. As Kaleta suggests, "Prince is the idol of the novel's characters" because he represents a bunch of contradictions in himself which makes him truly hybrid (141). The novel also refers to a whole range of popular youth culture and art:

> There were many Matisses—he liked to think that Matisse was the one artist about whom nothing bad could be said; Blu-tacked up were Liotard's portrait of Mary Gunning, Peter Blake's *Venice Beach* meeting of himself, Hockney and Howard Hodgkin, several Picassos, Millais's strange *Isabella*, a photograph of Allen Ginsberg, William Burroughs and Jean Genet, Jane Birkin lying on a bed, and dozens of others which he had torn from his bedroom and brought to London. (19-20)

The influence of the popular youth culture is clearly visible in Kureishi's writing which is an indispensible feature of postmodernity. The emphatic presence of pop culture in the novel exists as a vital strategy to subvert the fixated boundaries of the absolute categories and radical essentialism. In an interview by Amitava Kumar, Hanif Kureishi expresses his interest in the popular youth culture:

> When I wrote that (*The Black Album*), I was involved with dance music, house music, and a new drug called Ecstasy, which I loved. Every ten years there had been a revolution: in the sixties, it was LSD and psychedelic music, in the seventies it was punk and speed and heroin, and in the eighties it was dance music and Ecstasy. So *The Black Album* kind of came out of all that. Also my own life was falling apart. I was very involved in drugs and all kinds of dissident sexuality. ("A Bang and a Whimper" 126)

Similarly, in the novel the protagonist Shahid takes to popular culture as a means to subvert "all the conventions—what some discourses would call the moral foundation—of the traditional British family" (Ball 236). Jago Morrison rightly observes that in Kureishi's fiction "there is a continuing interest in visual effect, in fashion and particularly in music" (180).

Shahid's love for music is explicitly described in the novel on several occasions, one of which is when he is with Deedee in the Orkneys. He hesitates at first being in such a place forbidden by his religion, recalling his mother's words, "'wrong things', pop music and drugs, in the way adults discussed wine or literature'" (56) but soon comes under the exhilarating spell of music playing in the background:

> Suddenly Shahid was hearing something that made his knees bob. Was it the Doors? No, crazy, it was something new, the Stone Roses or Inspiral Carpets, one of those Manchester guitar groups. Whoever it was lifted him. Music could act like an adrenalin injection on him, and he wanted to go woo-woo-whoa for being here with his lecturer who was talking him out.... When he stopped trying to hold himself together, he realized he was liking this. He was certain now that he wanted to be here. Yes, this wasn't too bad. (58)

Shahid later admits that he cannot live without music although he understands that it may clash with the principles laid down by the Islamic Shari'ah law. Shahid even begins to frequent those fashionable places of London replete with "ruined woman", "vodkas and orange" and "beer" which are strictly prohibited by Islam:

> Many of the men were bare-chested and wore only thongs; some of the women were topless or in just shorts and new tops. One woman was naked except for high heels and a large plastic penis strapped to her thighs with which she duetted. Others were grabbed in rubber, or masks, or were dressed as babies. The dancing was frenzied and individual. People blew whistles, others screamed with pleasure. (59-60)

London, for Shahid, represents the transnational space of an all-inclusive cosmopolity where he can experiment with his multiple hybridised self without being threatened by the stabilising essentialities of monocultural configuration. Shahid's position demonstrates the possibility of transnational models of belonging where the dominant narratives of class, identity and home crumble into nothingness and challenge the absolutism of 'roots' with the contingency of 'routes' (McLeod 200-16). The novel *The Black Album* captures this tension between 'roots' and 'routes' and traces its development in the consciousness of the protagonist Shahid who grows up in London and attaches a lot of importance to the pop culture like Kureishi himself. Ranasinha remarks that Kureishi's writing are inevitably "immersed in popular culture" which fall into sharp contrast with the "more narrowly literary writings of earlier writers from a postcolonial background" (15). Ranasinha adds:

> For Kureishi, Pop was the 'first sort of common culture that was ever aware of. His texts are permeated by transatlantic youth culture, not the Bollywood films informing Rushdie's novels or Meera Syal and Gurinder Chadha's *Bhaji on the Beach* (1993). Kureishi breaks the conventions of realism but not by using 'Asian' influences. This 'Englishness' redefines expectations about the writing and culture of minority artists. (15)

Similarly the novel's title *The Black Album*, playing on the spirit of the popular youth culture seeks to redefine 'Britishness', claiming its Black roots which is never static and must subject to the inter-cultural cross-fertilisation of belonging and rootedness. Kureishi's novels such as *The Buddha of Suburbia* and *The Black Album* are permeated with the powerful, exhilarating melody of the pop culture. As Ranasinha claims, in these two novels, the "'visceral', 'sensual' pop songs are invoked to register the 'exhilaration' and 'momentary but powerful impulse' 'the teenage sexual longing' of his libidinous fictional protagonists" (16). London in its postmodern uncertainties thus gives Shahid enough scope for non-meta-narrative transcultural experimentations because he rejects ideas that require strict definitions of boundaries and borders—"he makes a choice not to commit" (Kaleta 147) to the accepted dogma of culture and religion. He finally selects a position which may capture this idea of multiplicity with the assertion "I can't be limited" (272), break away from Riaz group and continues his Journey with Deedee guided by the ever-shifting ideals of identification.

The novel *The Black Album* is set in the late 1980s, at the time when Ayatollah Khomeini, the Iranian spiritual leader issued a fatwa against Salman Rushdie demanding death punishment for him. The novel can be considered as a fictional response to the ban of Rushdie's book *The Satanic Verses* in particular and to censorship in general. Rushdie's invisible presence is perceptible from the very beginning of the novel. Shahid relates his experience of reading *Midnight Children* to Riaz and asks if he has read it to which Riaz replies: "I found it accurate about Bombay. But this time he has gone too far" (9). Later alluding to Rushdie's *The Satanic Verses*, Riaz says: "I am telling you that it is not ourselves in general, not the people, but the mind of the author that we are being informed of. That is all one man" (183). Similarly, Chad's reaction to the book echoes Khomeini's death threat to the writer: "... that book been around too long without action. He insulted us all—the prophet's wives, his whole family. It's sacrilege and blasphemy. Punishment is death" (169). The idea of killing a person for writing a book is abhorrent to Shahid: "... would you kill a man for writing a book" (173)? Riaz justifies Chad's observation saying that punishment is a necessity to put the anarchic elements in check otherwise evil will let loose in the world:

> Are you not with your people? Look at them, they are from villages, half-literate and not wanted here. All day they suffer poverty and abuse. Don't we, in this land of so-called free expression, have to give them a voice?... We cannot just forsake our people and live for ourselves.... If we did, wouldn't that mean we had totally absorbed Western morals, which are totally individualistic. (173)

The fundamentalists, however, misread the material which they interpret as too liberal and too individualistic to give a voice to the minority. The allegedly blasphemous book, as Kureishi exemplifies in *The Black Album*, was regarded by many fundamentalist Muslims around the world as offensive and an attack to the Islamic faith although Rushdie, in the meantime, wrote a letter to the then Prime Minister of India Rajiv Gandhi in October 1988 following the imposition of a ban in India claiming "that the book isn't actually about Islam, but about migration, metamorphosis, divided selves, love, death, London and Bombay." Defending his position against the provocation and censorship Rushdie regrets:

> This is, for me, the saddest irony of all; that after working for five years to give voice and fictional flesh to the immigrant culture of which I am myself a member, I should see my book burned, largely unread, by the people it's about.... I tried to write against stereotypes; the Zealot; protests serve to confirm, in the Western mind, all the worst stereotypes of the Muslim world. (qtd. in Ratti 159)

Riaz begins to ignite the minds of the group against such writers who according to him misrepresent Islam in the name of storytelling saying: "as one would deprecate a disrespectful nature in another person, it is impossible to see how such a spectacle could be valued as literature.... After all, for what higher purposes can such literature possibly exist" (183)? Riaz vehemently criticizes the author citing examples with sensitive content to aggravate the rage:

> 'We are discussing here the free and unbridled imagination of men who live apart from the people'.... 'And these corrupt, disrespectful natures, wallowing in their own Juices, must be caged' as if they were dangerous carnivores. 'Do we want more wild lions and rapists stalking our streets? After all,' he went on, 'if a character comes into your house and spits out that your mother and sister are whores, wouldn't you chuck him from your door and do bad things to him? Very bad things?' There were many smiles. 'And isn't this what such books do?' (183)

That *The Black Album* is written as a response to the fatwa issued against Salman Rushdie is further substantiated by the protest headed by Riaz and the involvement of the group in bombing of a bookshop selling *The Satanic Verses*. Riaz tells Shahid that the only punishment he would want to give is: "Stone dead. That is the least I would do to him" (172). For Riaz, the Western ideal of individuality and liberalism is a threat to the sacred image of Islam which must be fought against:

> Must we prefer this indulgence to the profound and satisfying comforts of religion? Surely if we cannot take the beliefs of millions of people seriously, what then? We believe nothing! We are animals living in a cesspool, not humans in a liberal society.... To me these truths are about the importance of faith and concern for others are deeper than the ravings of one individual imagination: Up to a point. And then no further. Is there one society in which any individual can be allocated unlimited freedom? Anyhow, we must now move forward.... We have to discuss what action we will be taking against the book. (184)

Kureishi admits to his integrating the theme of Rushdie affair in the novel which he wanted to experiment in his screen play *My Beautiful Laundrette* but later considers it to be a major theme to be taken up in his second novel *The Black Album*, in which he will be engaging the clash between the Islamic fundamentalism and the postmodern culture of hybridity that stand in opposition to each other:

> The fatwa against Rushdie in February 1989 reignited my concern about the rise of Islamic radicalism, something I had become aware of while in Pakistan in 1982, where I was writing *My Beautiful Laundrette*. But for me, that wasn't the whole story. Much else of interest was happening at the end of 80s: the music of Prince; the collapse of Communism and the "velvet revolution"; the rise of the new dance music, along with the use of a revelatory new drug, ecstasy; Tiananmen square; Madonna using catholic imagery in 'Like a Prayer'; postmodernism, "mash-up", and the celebration of hybridity—partly the subject of *The Satanic Verse*. (Kureishi, *The Guardian*)

Chad and other members of the Riaz group decide to start demonstration against the book in public places as well as in the college premise. Shahid hesitatingly agrees to the decision and accompanies them when Deedee Osgood emerges to interfere with the students' demonstration and urges Riaz to pore over the book once before forming any assumptions thereof. Riaz responds by saying: "... is the free speech of an Asian to be muzzled by the authorities?... Are the white supremacists going to lecture us on democracy this afternoon? Or will they permit us, for once, to practice it" (224)? Deedee wants to prevent Shahid from the blunder he is going to commit by joining the friends in their book burning demonstration. Shahid's role, to a large extent, in the event is ambivalent and he fails to share their emotional vigour. He finds himself again in an in-between space of contradicting affiliations and loyalties in which he is unable "to tell the sane from the mad, wrong from right, good from bad" (220). He begins to reflect:

> Where would one start? None of this would lead to the good. But what did? Who knew? What would make them right? Everything was in motion; nothing could be stopped, the world was swirling; its compasses spinning. History was unwinding in his head into chaos, and he was tumbling through space. Where would he land? If the security guard had asked him to add two plus two, what would he have answered? (220)

Shahid cannot be with them any more for he doesn't share their religious fervour and "ecstatic rigidity" (225) and stumbles through his in-between space of uncertainties and placelessness, perpetually swinging between liberal individuality and orthodox fundamentalism.

Shahid tries in vain to "evade their eyes" (225) while his people are rejoicing triumphantly over the book burning event. Kureishi describes Shahid's irresolute move amidst the burning scenario:

> Shahid looked away immediately, with a guilty expression, as if he weren't enjoying it as much as he should. He wanted to appear neutral but knew that wasn't possible. It wasn't as if he felt nothing, like many of the people looking on. If anything; he felt ashamed. He was someone who couldn't join in, couldn't let himself go.... The stupidity of the demonstration appalled him. How narrow they were, how unintelligent, how ... embarrassing it all was! (225)

After the burning of the book, Shahid is awakened to the reality that "This destruction of a book—a book which was a question—had embodied an attitude to life which he had to consider" (227). He entertains ideas to terminate his connection with Riaz and his fundamentalist ideologies:

> He was mounting the stairs when, nearing his floor, he heard familiar voices. He cursed. Some of them must have gathered in Riaz's room. He started to turn round. He would get out. He had left the posses. He hadn't made a decision: the alliance terminated the moment Hat soaked the book in petrol. He had been taught much about what he didn't like; how he would embrace uncertainty. May be wisdom would come from what one didn't know, rather than from confidence. That's what he hoped. (227)

Shahid's reaction to the book-burning event comprises Kureishi's critique of religion, within the limiting universe of fundamentalist discourse, in the present context, which far from being a faith related to one's spirituality, is reduced to a communal feeling which can be viewed "as an ideology, as a system of authority, a kind of business" (qtd. in Thomas 102) indicative of "the failure of our most significant attribute, our imagination" (Kureishi, *Collected Essays* 103). Progressive liberal individualism of Shahid thus triumphs over his tendency for fundamentalist commitment. He feels that the amorphous ambiguity of imagination is far more acceptable than the contemptuous clarity of one's cultural and religious identification leading to a constricted cosmology of perception. Kureishi is understandably attentive to this tension between the fundamentalist constraints and imaginative propensities of a writer which he confesses in an interview to Colin McCabe:

> Well, I like to think that I do, and also in the film "My Son the Fanatic", I like to feel that, in so far as I can, the characters are sympathetically portrayed. And that this is an argument worth having and there are points on both sides. But I suppose that in the end I would betray the fact that I don't like fundamentalists, and fundamentalists don't like writers. So, you know, there

> is going to be a kind of animosity between us from the start. (McCabe 54)

This then explains Shahid's responsibility, his commitment towards the society in the way he distances himself from his fundamentalist friends and embraces a liberal, imaginative outlook towards life. He can't be too religious, devoid of doubts like Riaz. He must choose a self out of the several options available to him that thrives on uncertainties rather than be reduced to any definite dogma which may fit into the prescriptive framework, chalked out by any society, culture or religion. This is the reason which is why Shahid when asked to type the "original manuscript" (233) that has been given to him "in good faith" (234), cannot but dilutes the religious fervour of the draft by secular, deceptively sexual content:

> He had begun typing Riaz's work in good faith, but there were certain words, then phrases and verses, he couldn't bring himself to transcribe. Once he'd begun not transcribing, he'd got carried away. He'd been enjoying himself with Deedee; It seemed natural to express the puzzle of this wonder.
>
> Shahid said, 'It was a celebration'.
>
> 'Of what yaar?'
>
> 'Passion.' (234)

Clarifying Hat's puzzlement Shahid says, "'I wouldn't put them into print! I wouldn't mix it up with religious words'" (234). Shahid calls this harmless alteration, a passionate celebration of his feeling which will lead him to liberation—to be released from all exclusionary essentialities of life, accepting a life in movement—a life that is manifested in multiple, hybrid positions and proclivities. Shahid asserts to himself, "I can't be limited" (272) and turns his back permanently on the fundamentalist ideologies of his friends, and join hands with Deedee in their "new adventure" (276) which will usher them into a land of unprecedented liberty where heterogeneity is the rule rather than exception. Eventually Shahid, as Weber observes, "rejected both deadly bourgeois lifestyle and fanatic intellectualism in the name of the capricious, fluid, playful imagination" (129).

Shahid's relinquishment of the "ecstatic rigidity" and embracing a life of uncertainties and fragmentations can be viewed as his transition from the in-between space to a hybridised position which unsettles the "'universalist' or 'essentialist' ways of thinking, by means of a characteristically subtle, dense and metaphorically slippery rhetoric" of representation (Walder, *Post-colonial Literatures* 79). Shahid, at length, realises the limitless possibilities of his sense of identification and belonging:

> He had to find some sense in his recent experiences; he wanted to know and understand. How could anyone confine themselves to one system or creed? Why should they had to? There was no fixed self; surely our several selves melted and mutated daily? There has to be innumerable ways of being in the world. He would spread himself out, in his work and in love, following his curiosity. (274)

Karim in *The Buddha of Suburbia* and Shahid in *The Black Album* thus represent the idea of an in-between space which symbolises social encounters and cultural permutation and that "this interstitial passage between fixed identifications opens up the possibility of a cultural hybridity that entertains difference without an assumed or imposed hierarchy" (Bhabha, *The Location* 4). Both protagonists, Karim and Shahid find themselves in an ambivalent position of perpetual permeability which allows them to experiment with their fluid, relational, shifting selves without being content with an essentialist, homogeneous model of belonging and identification. Kureishi with his "narrative of the self" (qtd. in Davis, *Understanding* 181) explores the multiple modalities of cultural configuration which is formed, reformed and transformed continuously in the fleeting multiplicities of variable existentialities.

Hanif Kureishi, in his novels thus attempts to resituate the unbridled voice of the black British in a cosmopolitan context of transcultural representation in which diaspora identities "are constantly producing and reproducing themselves anew, through transformation and difference" (Hall, "Cultural Identity" 55). As Kobena Mercer summatively puts it: "Within the British context, the hybridised accents of black British voices begin to unravel the heteroglossia, the many voicedness of British cultural identity *as it is lived*, against the centrifugal and centralizing monologism of traditional versions of national identity" (qtd. in Pascual 60). In this dichotomous fragmentation of the cultural space, "the immigrant" as Kureishi feels "is the Everyman of the twentieth century" (*The Buddha* 141) who is the true "representative of the movements and aspirations of millions of people" (Borderline 4) living in this densely diasporising world where hybridity is the rule rather than an explicative exception.

Chapter 7

Reconfiguring the Inner Landscape: Self-refashioning and Belongingness in Romesh Gunesekera's Novels

"It is normally supposed that something always gets lost in translation; I cling, obstinately, to the notion that something can also be gained."

—Salman Rushdie, *Imaginary Homelands*

"It is within the 'ordinary' processes of memory that the self is continuously created and destroyed."

—Nicola King, *Memory, Narrative and Identity: Remembering the Self*

"Memory is identity.... You are what you have done; what you have done is in your memory; what you remember defines who you are; when you forget your life you cease to be, even before your death."

—Julian Barnes, *Nothing to be Frightened Of*

Romesh Gunesekera, in his novels, seeks to represent the process by which the diasporic subjects are able to nourish and sustain self-images of survival in an alien environment, traversing the restrictive rigidity of identity and belonging, in which the notion of 'home' becomes an emotional construct rather than be circumscribed by territorial borders, national identity and monocultural rootedness. Gunesekera's novels allow us to re-examine the dynamics of cultural representation enacted through multiple diasporic movements across the globe that is informed by various postcolonial upheavals which collapse the spatial and temporal boundaries of identification and help evolve a reconfigurated version of identity, focussing on the idea of self-refashioning, to resist cultural, ethnic and racial marginalisation. In this narratological domain, memory plays a pivotal role in shaping and reshaping of one's belongingness connecting the fragmented diasporic past with a yet unsettled presence. The present chapter thus demonstrates the manners in which the novelist, in his first two novels such as *Reef* and *The Sandglass*, explores this idea of deterritorialisation and the resulting rhetoric of refashioning with great poetic subtlety and depicts the ambiguity of displacement while exposing the intrinsic insubstantiality of homeland and monolithic belongingness in the narrative of the sequestered self.

Romesh Gunesekera was born to a Sinhalese Christian family in Sri Lanka in 1954 where he spent his early childhood before migrating to Philippines at the age of twelve. He moved to England in 1972 where he lived and worked since. Thus, in his first seventeen years of life, he grew up in three different countries. As Gunesekera reflects, "At that time it was a bit unusual. But it is the way a lot of people are beginning to live, and it's not only the rich. Because of migrant labour, because people are on the move all the time, a huge part of the global population now has the experience of growing up in one place and living in a very different place" (Sengupta). Gunesekera broke into the literary scenario with his book *Monkfish Moon* (1992), a collection of short stories dealing with the ethnic and political tensions that had unsettled Sri Lanka since independence in 1948. Since then he has published many novels and short story collections such as *Reef* (1994), *The Sandglass* (1998), *Heaven's Edge* (2002), *The Match* (2006), *The Prisoner of Paradise* (2012), and *Noon Tide Toll* (2013), and has received a lot of awards and prizes for his literary pursuits. *His Monkfish Moon* fetches him the Commonwealth Writer's Regional Prize in 1993. *Reef* is the most acclaimed novel which was shortlisted for the *Guardian* fiction prize and the Man Booker Prize in 1994. His works primarily draw upon the ever-confounding issues of home, immigrant experiences, the unsevered connection between the time past and the time present, and the problematics of nostalgia and loss.

Romesh Gunesekera in his fictional manoeuvres has tried to revive alternative ways of seeing and living the world, seeking anchorage in a foreign land in a diasporic situation which enables the characters to rethink the notion of nationalism, home and belongingness. Gunesekera as a diasporic writer seeks to recreate and reconfigure the inner landscape of belonging once uprooted from his original homeland "for it is through a journey into the incommensurable spaces within memory itself that these writers enact individual passages, which can no longer be sustained by the recognition of any easily identifiable or firm boundary lines whether of tradition, language, place or time" (Nasta 212). As identity is firmly grounded in the vast abysses of our psychic process, memory plays a crucial role in individuation and self-identification of the diasporic subjects. It assumes an emotional dimension and moves beyond the merely spatial and temporal boundaries. As Rosemary Marangoli George has powerfully claimed:

> Today, the primary connotation of 'home' is of 'private' space from which the individual travels into the larger arenas of life and to which he or she returns at the end of the day: And yet, also in circulation is the word's wider significance as the larger geographic space where one belongs: country, city, village, community. Home is also the imagined location which can be more readily fixed in a mental landscape than in actual geography. The term 'home country' suggests the particular intersection of private and public and of individual and communal that is manifest in imaging a space as home. (9)

Susheila Nasta describes writers like Gunesekera as "birds of passage" (212) whose locations are always in a state of flux, refigured and reconfigurated by the confluence of individual and collective memories and desires projected into the obsequious phenomenon of time. Seeking to cartograph the modalities of home from a range of possible locations both within and without England, Gunesekera steps into an unexplored landscape of mind untrodden yet by the contemporary writers of diaspora by "'making memory' itself the subject of fiction" (Nasta 213) and re-articulation of identity: "In so doing, the sounds of their voices echo like those of migrant birds, whose perennial flights into other skies mark and name the permeable boundary lines of those immigrant histories which have always existed, to evoke the title of Paul Gilroy's most recent study of 'homelessness' and diaspora, 'between camps'" (Nasta 212-13).

In his novels such as *Reef* and *The Sandglass* Gunesekera successfully explores the idea of reterritorialisation from the fragmented condition of the lived reality in terms of emotional reconstruction of home, subverting the assumed spatial and temporal borderlands. These novels prefigure a diasporic condition which connects the immigrant perceptions of the host land with loss and nostalgia of the homeland, integrating the disjunctions, compressions and conflictions of the past with the present, to reconfigure the inner landscapes of the protagonists as liberating ways of survival away from the original home of rootedness. It presents an amalgamated experience of multiple consciousnesses informed by the inherent ambivalences in the individual cultural spaces which symbolise the shifting idea of identity within the differential matrix of language that is indelibly coloured with fractions of mutilated memory. As Nasta contends:

> ... the multiple layers of a diasporic subjectivity are inscribed through a precarious journey into the gaps within the symbolic realm of discourse itself, where writing becomes the 'territory of loss and memory' and the act of narration enables the possibility of a 're-return to selfhood through [a] dialogic and interrogative encounter', that is both a confrontation with an 'internal/ external other' as well as the 'site' of an existential and 'unfulfilled journey home'.... Although echoes of home are still discernible in these texts, the lines of their cultural and linguistic parameters constantly shift as their chimeric contours flow in and out of other landscapes, other histories which reconfigure and

disrupt the longing for such stable anchorage points. (214)

Gunesekera's debut novel *Reef* tells the moving story of Triton, a young and efficient chef who is steered into the service of Mister Salgado, a marine biologist and a Sinhala intellectual, experimenting with the movement of the sea and the disappearing reef which poses a threat to the equilibrium of the island. The narrative unfolds itself in flashbacks as Triton gives vent to his imagination from his current stay in England where he has immigrated to establish himself as a restaurateur to the memorialisation of his childhood in Sri Lanka. Through these characters and the political instability that informed the lives of the islanders, the novelist tells the tragi-comic story of a lost Eden and a young man coming to terms with his own destiny. In course of time, Triton becomes indispensable to the Marine biologist Salgado and in the 70s when the latter is forced into exile amidst the mounting threat of Tamil terrorism; it is Triton who must accompany him wherever he goes. After twenty years of his stay in London which is described quite briefly by Triton, he meets one Tamil refugee at a gas station and is pleased to narrate the ten years of his engagement with Mister Salgado in Sri Lanka. Just as Salgado engages himself with the observation of the vanishing coral reef, Triton busies himself in mastering the art of cooking. He is instinctive and creative and his cooking experiments with different foods and delicacies become an expression of his own identity. After the departure of Salgado's house boy and cook it is he who has to perform everything from cooking to managing the house as a butler, and to please his master and his ravishing mistress Miss Nilli who provides a contrast to the gloomy interior of Mr. Salgado's house which is partially dispelled by her arrival. Triton's identity is bound up with Mr. Salgado's. He wants to groom himself in the image of his master and to see him satisfied is his greatest pleasure. So, being pleased with Triton's meat patties and his cashew-studded love-cake, Nilli lavishly praises Triton for the treat which is yet followed by a relishing encomium from Mr. Salgado in the praise of his cook which is an immense delight to the young boy: "'Triton made it.' Mr. Salgado said. *Triton made it*. Clear, pure and unstinting. His voice at those moments would be a channel cut from heaven to earth right through the petrified morass of all our lives, realizing a blessing like water springing from a riverhead, from a god's head. It was bliss. My coming of age" (64-65).

Triton closely watches his master Mr. Salgado and with some carefully manoeuvred training, he is now in a position to learn everything which his master willing to teach: "... I watched him, I watched him unendingly, all the time, and learned to become what I am" (43). Neil Gordon identifies the ways Triton gradually subsumed into the personality of his master Mr. Salgado:

> He learns his habits, the intimate details of his tastes for clothes and food; watches his work, listens to his conversations with his friends. When Mister Salgado travels on his marine studies, Triton travels with him. When ultimately, Mister Salgado will go into exile, Triton will go with him. And when Mister Salgado falls in love with Miss Nilli and so undergoes the great—the only—sentimental education of his life, Triton, never transgressing his observer's distance falls in love with her too.

Triton in his self-refashioning like the coral reef raises himself from ordeal to glory and becomes a favourite of his master, unperturbed by the bloody political and ethnic violence that has afflicted the serene life of the beautiful island since the late 1950s: "All over the globe revolutions erupted, dominoes tottered and guerrilla war came of age; the world's first woman Prime Minister—Mrs. Bandaranaike—lost her spectacular premiership on our small island, and I learned the art of good housekeeping" (45). Triton's journey is a passage from the primitive country side to the complexity and satisfaction of a highly civilised world where people engage themselves with reading books, discuss the state affairs, enjoy the sundry delicacies of the world and travels to London. Richard Eder in "Cooking up a Storm" observes that "Triton's reverence for his work and his master is the page's reverence for the knight he serves and for the order of chivalry that mastered the universe until the coming of the crossbow" (1). Although Triton becomes Salgado's alter-ego, in the new land, to which they migrate; while the master is attentive to his exiled existence, the servant learns to adjust himself to the new environment and carves out a new identity and home of his own. Whereas Salgado has to return to the island defeated, "summoned by a desire to hold on to a lost dream and memory of a lost love" (Nasta 214), Triton, the orphaned figure, successfully integrates himself to the new society he seeks to be assimilated with: "It was the only way I could succeed: without a past, without a name, without Ranjan Salgado standing by my side" (180). Triton is wholeheartedly committed to his survival in the host land and attempts to transmute his makeshift existence by an alternative dream, and transforms his tiny snack shop into a big Sri Lankan restaurant and becomes a leading restaurateur at Earls Court in London.

Introducing the role of memory in the refurbishment and refashioning of individuality, Ranjan Salgado, at one point in the novel alerts Triton of its omnipotence: "You know Triton ... we are only what we remember, nothing more ... all we have is the memory of what we have done or not done; whom we might have touched; ever for a moment" (180). Triton is able to construct a home for himself in the host land. While Salgado is forced to return to his promised homeland trapped by his memory, Triton uses his memory as a survival strategy to reconfigure his inner self as a step towards erecting his 'imaginary homeland'. However, Salgado's longing for his homeland inspires and activates Triton's legacy of nostalgia in a highly symbolic patterns of diasporic existence who can never escape the backlash of memory and the call of the collective unconscious. As Salman Rushdie writes in his novel *Shame*:

> All migrants leave their pasts behind although some try to pack it into bundles and boxes—but on the journey something seeps out of the treasured mementoes and old photographs, until even their owners fail to recognize them, because it is the fate of the migrants to be stripped of history, to stand naked among the scorn of strangers upon whom they see the rich clothing, the brocades of

> continuity and the eyebrows of belonging. (Rushdie, *Shame* 63-64)

Sharanya Jayawickrama in his paper "Consuming Desire: Identity and Narration in Romesh Gunesekera's *Reef*" contends that "the dynamics of investment and/or exploitation of cultural images and markers in the text engage with certain niches of desire in the global market while complicating notions of identity as Gunesekera writes from both the Sri Lankan diasporic imaginary and the South Asian British experience" (10) and his writing offers us a consideration of the cultural poetics inaugurated through diasporic texts and positioning of the writers of the diaspora across the globe. Gunesekera as a diasporic writer recreates in his fiction a Sri Lanka of the mind through his memory and imagination, even though he employs a foreign language and maintains strategic distance from his homeland as well as from the host land, "repatriating the skills and tactics they mastered in England to give new dignity and authority to their homelands" (qtd. in Jayawickrama 16).

According to Jayawickrama, there are elaborate suggestions in the novel of the desire for authenticity which can alternatively be replaced by a consumerist allure of the exotic. As Triton prepares the crab recipe stuffing it with onion and parsley and cheddar cheese, he muses: "... deep inside the stuffing I would bury a seeded slice of green chilli stepped in virgin coconut oil" (120). His culinary art is authentic and unadulterated in comparison to the intensely spicy and cheaply flavoured cuisine of the huge restaurants in the world: "Lemon and a dash of Brandy from the bottle Mister Salgado got at Christmas from Professor Dunstable would make it exceptional and, I was sure, better than she had ever had at some stuffy hotel restaurant" (120). Triton's early response to this increasingly consumerist culture, however, positively reappears at the closing pages of the novel as he is developed into a restaurateur of the metropolis from a local cook of the island. As Jayawickrama observes:

> In the age of the cheap package holiday and the vulgarization of local art forms into the souvenir, tourism transmutes the desire for the 'authentic' cultural experiences/image/motif into the commercial

> allure of the exotic, which is often largely irrelevant to the contemporary life of a society ... the exercise of consumer desire in the global marketplace discovers the authentic and the exotic as interchangeable categories. (11)

The 'authentic' with the diasporic writers thus becomes a site of ambivalent impulses, instincts and desires within that cultural environment as Tim Brennan argues that such diasporic author admits a "flirtation with change" (3) by shrouding the real conflicts and traumatic encounters for a more palatable and de-politicised discourse of cultural differences and incompatibilities.

Ranjan Salgado who enjoys a sophisticated position in his native place finds England to be an unfavourable place for survival and fails to integrate himself with the new reality that has dawned upon him. London as a postmodern metropolis ceases to privilege the grand narrative, where the mini-narrative takes the centre-stage, which serves as a carnivalesque deconstructing the higher stands in the hierarchy and opens up a diasporic space to be confronted with. With his so-called refugee existence and expatriation, Mister Salgado sees his dreams shattered before the emerging consumerism and commodification of organic authenticity:

> I used to plan it in my head: how I'd build a Jetty, a safe marina for little blue glass-bottomed boats, some outriggers with red sails, and then a sort of floating restaurant at one end. You could have produced your finest Chilli crab there, you know, and the best stuffed sea-cucumbers. Just think of it: a row of silver tureens with red crab-claws in black bean sauce, yellow rice and squid in red wine, a roasted red snapper as big as your arm, shark fin and fried seaweed. It would have been a temple to your gastronomic god, no? I thought of it like a ring, a circular platform with the sea in the middle. We could have framed for the table and nurtured rare breeds for the wild. A centre to study our prehistory. We could have shown the world something then, something really fabulous. What a waste. (177)

Jayawickrama observes that Salgado's "grand vision combines conservation and consumption" which serves as "a productive pathway into the very roots of their history as well as a refuge through which they could participate obliquely in the life of the island" (11). Triton, however, learns to accept his diasporic presence and recognises the futility of nourishing such dreams of the past and embraces the new life the host land has to offer:

> The nights were long at the Earls Court snack shop with its line of bedraggled, cosmopolitan itinerants. But they were the people I had to attend to: my future. My life would become a dream of murky hair, smoky bars and garish neon eyes. I would learn to talk and joke and entertain, to perfect the swagger of one who has found his vocation and, at last, a place to call his own. The snack shop would one day turn into a restaurant and I into a restaurateur. It was the only way I would succeed: Without a past, without a name, without Ranjan Salgado standing by my side. (180)

Triton thinks that erasing the claims of the past by being nameless is a step towards merging into a diasporic cosmopolity which resists the sustenance of authenticity. For Triton, to exist without a past is a means of survival in a foreign land like England which eases and diminishes his oriental connections. In the words of Jayawickrama "the 'cosmopolitan' becomes a deferral of particular identity in favour of an undefined sense of belonging" which rather needs "a dilution and consumerization of the identities and sense of history imagined in youth" (12). Triton at this crucial point summarises his definition of the diasporic self: "I was learning that human history is always a story of somebody's diaspora: a struggle between those who expel, repel or curtail—possess, divide and rule—and those who keep the flame alive from night to night, mouth to mouth, enlarging the world with each flick of a tongue" (174).

In the diasporic setting of England, the immigrants have to shed their petty differences in order to cope and survive with the new found world because the reaction is not against a particular place but a virtual space in the mind which is to counter and this space as Triton acknowledges is "without a past, without a name" (180). While Salgado returns to his native land with his dreams shattered, Triton devises and discovers new modes of existence to survive in a new alien surrounding. On Salgado's departure from England, Triton wonders as to whether the sea there, "shimmering between the black humps of barnacled rocks, mullioned with gold bladder wrack like beached wholes ... snuffling and gurgling" is the same as the "coral spangled south coast back home" (172). An inquisitive Triton questions Salgado: "'Do all the oceans flow one into the other? Is it the same sea here as back home'" (172)? Salgado replies that "'The earth has spun with its real stars under a beautiful blue robe ever since the beginning of time. Now as the coral disappears, there will be nothing but sea and we all return to it'" (172). Triton's curiosity is proverbial: "... are we not all refugees from something? Whether we stay or go or return, we all need refuge from the world beyond our fingertips at some time" (174). According to Susheila Nasta, this deconstruction of the essentialist cultural and national myths "sets up an implicitly radical dialogue with the landlocked binaries of a colonialist historiography" (215). As Jayawickrama, in this context, astutely remarks:

> The future requires new modes of connection and habitation as a requisite of survival in a global environment—the "enlarging" of the world is enacted within the local and personal interrelations that constitute human history and that alter identity. Gunesekera employs potent images of food in his text to hint at authenticity yet manipulates these same markers to show that identity is more reliant on adaptation, on allowing different flavours to mix and combine anew. (12)

According to Nasta, the line taken from Shakespeare's *The Tempest*, "of his bones are coral made" that serves as the epigraph of the novel "signals Gunesekera's broad metaphysical concerns: a preoccupation with the effects of the passage of time, of loss, and the role of the imagination in the transformation of individual human lives" (215). The novel in its core introduces the note of "universal permeability" between cultures and spaces "linking the two worlds of London and Sri Lanka in Triton's developing consciousness, a space where ideas can 'flow freely' as stories and memories germinate like seeds and migrate from one mind to another" (Nasta 215). The metaphor of the coral reef is thus central to the developing tensions in the novel and one of the unifying features in the text which proffers "connections and reconstitution" (Nasta 215), creating an impression of continuity with change and eternal transformation of ideals that inform the life of the common humanity. As Richard Eder rightfully observes:

> Coral is Salgado's passion and the book's central metaphor. A coral reef is alive, but only at its skin. Its billions of tiny organisms multiply and build on the surface, leaving their calcified bodies as the reef's mass. The violence of politics and change, in this image, destroy the living integument while seeking to give it more vital forms. Civilization is at the surface, not deep down; destroy the surface and the life that preserves it will die. Gunesekera's point, like his coral, is not calcified but alive. (1)

Mr. Salgado strives his best to restore the fast vanishing reef but to no avail owing to the internal strife and disequilibrium that inflict the country's public life. The reef itself works as a metaphor for Sri Lanka herself which once used to be a peaceful country, remarkable for her beauty and grandeur, is now torn within by the incessant political strife and disruption. The reef becomes a suggestive symbol not only of an "irreparable human loss" but also a constitutive impulse of self-refashioning in the transformative politics of a fragmented diasporic past "creating a palimpsest of a diasporic history built on the remembered stories of individual lives, which mutate and transform like polyps on the Sri Lankan reef" (Nasta 215). Ranjan Salgado thus regrets:

> You see this polyp is really very delicate. It has survived aeons, but even a small change in the immediate environment ... could kill it. Then the whole thing will go. And if the structure is destroyed, the sea will rush in.

> The sand will go. The beach will disappear. That is my hypothesis. You see, it is only the skin of the reef that is alive. It is real flesh: immortal. Self-renewing. (48)

As Salgado leaves his land and takes up a modest job in England, he finds his friends being killed amidst the developing violence in Sri Lanka. His life changes significantly but there is not an end to all his hopes. Mr. Salgado wanders between his deep concern for the coral reef and the enveloping tension in the political life of Sri Lanka. Like his master, Triton too is threatened by the growing strife and forces of displacement that infiltrate the feudal glory of his kitchen and may end his career as a chef. But he accompanies his master and migrates to England and continues to serve Mr. Salgado. Encouraged and inspired by his master, he looks forwards to build up his snack shop into a big restaurant in the near future. Like the polyps, the rich but fragile culture, which the two have known and were born into, is at the verge of utter imperilment and has perished in violence, with the distorting web of change, but there is an impulse of the eternal renewal ever glowing in their souls which will exacerbate a sense of strongly cemented belongingness to the human world wherever they go. Life must continue to exist and prosper howsoever much modification it has undergone through. Susheila Nasta has delicately summed up this established parallel between the coral reef and the human life proposing a 'fluid terrain' on which migrant histories and individual identities are constantly made, unmade and remade:

> As Gunesekera is keen to show us the umbilicus of language, symbolic vessel of the human imagination, is like the skin of the reef itself: a delicate container not necessarily punctuated by arrivals or departures, or by willed acts of physical emigration or immigration, whether from the histories of diasporas lived within or imagined outside his native Sri Lanka. It is, rather, a fluid terrain defined by the 'sea in our loins', a space which calls, as Ian Chambers has put it, for a 'dwelling in language', rather than in 'place', where the shifting boundaries of time and geography enable the creation

> of migrant histories and identities that are 'constantly subject to mutation.' (216)

The sea in the novel proves to be a powerful metaphor of a mysterious body of water which has an identity of its own. A history of its own. Seas are the connective links between oceans, and its waves have their own ebb and flow like the fluctuating destiny of man. The sea signifies universal togetherness and oneness and defies man's persistent claim on clearly demarcated boundaries with fixed territorialities. Mr. Salgado is attentive to this fact when he says: "'You remember, all one ocean, no? The debris of one man floats to another. The same little polyp grows the idea in another head'" (176). The sea and the reef also serve as effective means for Triton to connect with his master and to get closer to his metaphysical concerns. Triton is gradually drawn towards the wilderness of the sea, feels its mysterious power and expresses his fascination for it: "I looked up again, I would glimpse the sea between the trees bathed in a mulled gold light. The colour of it, the roar of it, was overwhelming. It was like living inside a conch: the endless pounding. Numinous. You couldn't get away from it. No wonder Mister Salgado said the sea would be the end of us all" (60).

Triton, after reaching London, reflects on the difference and otherwise between the seas and realises that his own acquaintance with the sea in Sri Lanka is not different from that of its presence near London. Mr. Salgado, on the other hand, identifies an impossibility of a reconciliation of the images of the past and that of the present: "The urge to build, to transform nature, to make something out of nothing is universal. But to conserve, to protect, to care for the past is something we have to learn" (178). But he recognises the vigour and vitality of imagination: "'It's your imagination,' he said, 'It is not get poisoned in this place.' As if we each had an inner threshold that had to be breached before our surrounding could torment us" (176).

He acknowledges the purity of the sea, undiluted yet by the fear of anxiety and the forces of uncertainty. The safest way one can trace the elegance of the sea and the coral reef is through the journey by mind to the sea of imagination: "In our minds we have swum in the same sea. Do you understand? An imagined world" (176). For Triton, past is like a dark demon lurking in the background of presence and to live in the present one must kill the demon of the past: "I went to classes and other libraries, night and day, for almost all the years we spent in London together; broke all the old taboos and slowly freed myself from the demons of our past: What is over is over forever, I thought" (175-76).

Though Triton and Salgado both leave their native land as refugees, Triton is happy to feel utterly at home in England for his life in the homeland has offered an unengaging past and a bleak future for him. Mr. Salgado, in contrast, has nourished a hope to return in spite of the worsening political life of the island nation. "In the end, belonging has to do with people you're with—not with places," says Gunesekera in one of his interviews, and alienation ... "has nothing to do with being in a different country" (Hussein). Diasporic identity carries with it an ambivalently amorphous condition of being an ambassador and a refugee at the same time: While one needs the projection of one's culture and the capacity to augment its understanding, the other seeks out refuge and projection and connects positively, with disparate relationships, to the host culture. Triton's using of his culinary skill in London to earn his living makes him an ambassador of Sri Lankan culture and his seeking shelter in London by properly integrating himself to a foreign culture makes him a refugee in the host country. He is a "syncretic border intellectual" (97) as described by Abdul JanMohamed in his "Worldliness-Without-World" who can feel at home in both culture strategically mingling and synthesising features of both home and host cultures. Mr. Salgado, on the other hand, drastically fails to assimilate himself in the host culture and suffers emotional isolation owing to his rigid rootedness in the native culture. As Charu Mathur argues: "Although educated in England, Mr. Salgado's position as an exile now is indicative of an enforced isolation that results in an emotional withdrawal from the host country. Since geographic displacement is not the only kind of dislocation, the territorial acceptance or rejection of "home" is governed by mental and emotional markers" (25).

Islands like Sri Lanka have always been spaces informed by continuous arrivals and departures which effectuate a radical and regular transformation of places as diasporic topographies. An Island which encounters natural catastrophes such as cyclones, tsunamis, wars, earthquakes; the humanity at large is at stake and is highly affected by diseases and other health hazards. An Island can also be a site of easy conquest by the West for its natural beauty, exoticism and other distinctive features which give it a status of a microcosm of the world. Writers like Gunesekera thus seek to treasure the aesthetic aura of the islands with all its natural grandeur and beauty. In the Western mindscape, however, the island is a symbolic paradise which turns into the tropes of exploitation altering the placidity and stability of the islander's life. The historical fragmentations fill the island with social, political, ethnic and religious strife and dismantle the core culture of the place when the islanders are forced to adopt and are equipped to adapt to new conditionalities offered by the present life which leave them in a historical and cultural void. The candour of colonialism gradually opens up the option of migration, and the islanders, torn by the repeated historical fragmentations, resort to a nomadic itinerary which may fulfil their dreams and aspirations albeit in a new land of acculturation. It is their haunting colonial histories of displacement and uprootedness which make them live suspended between two worlds—the homeland and the host land. As in *Reef*, Triton, the cook and Mr. Salgado, the marine biologist plan migrating to London due to the political unrest in Sri Lanka which ends in a civil war unsettling the serene life of the island. The place can no longer offer a peaceful haven for the citizens living on the land. The image of the reef acts as a repertoire to witness the gradual erosion of the land, both physical and cultural. Socio-political tension and intolerance disrupt the island's unity and add to the fragility of the nation as a whole. The reef which acts as a protective shell for the island resisting the upsurge of the sea is largely threatened due to bombing, netting, mining, large-scale fishing and global warming. The physical delicateness of the reef is associated with the vulnerability of the islanders who know that once the connection is lost, it will be quite difficult to bring it back to its original stature. The unsettled ideology of the islanders thus helps effect immigration to other lands. The summative nomadism then can be viewed as an outcome of the fragmented self of the island and its inhabitants, its general life and culture. Therefore, "Ethnic and class conflicts which have threatened to rend Sri Lanka apart in the past few decades, are a central concern in Gunesekera's fiction" (Garner). However, Gunesekera's accessibility to the socio-political realism of the native land is limited in the sense that he has maintained a spatial distance from them. This is the reason which is why some critics attack his expatriate cultural experience and perception of Sri Lanka and his projection of it with "selective historicisation and exoticism" (Huggan 30).

'Culture' has recently been defined as "a way of being, relating, behaving, believing and acting which people live out in their lives and which is in a constant process of change and exchange with other cultures" (Tilbury and Wortman ix). This idea of culture is appropriately worked out in Gunesekera's island setting in his novel *Reef* which portrays the islanders' struggle to keep their distinctive cultural features amidst fragmentation and chaos. The novel employs the various food tropes which are important markers of a given culture. Triton's experiment with various foods which parallels the marine biologist Salgado's experimentation with the coral reef, as the island's gastronomic conventions carries with them a uniqueness is not to be found in any foreign cuisine. Triton, who gradually masters the culinary art of the island, is an agent of fusion and synthesis. He transfers that indigenous art and culture to an alien space which opens up a way to assimilation from the apparent fragmentation.

Food acts as a distinctive marker of cultural practices and an expression of identity as it entails mixing, synthesis and assimilation and thereby supports hybrid culture and multicultural possibilities. Gunesekera, in his novel *Reef*, beautifully executes the narrative of food to evoke a distinctive sense of the island's identity in the aroma and flavour associated with those foods that establish the connection between the islanders with the island, and which cannot be severed fully even though the individuals leave that land and settle elsewhere in the world. This implies that the traditional eating habits and culinary mores are carriers of cultural values which are practised by a particular community. Triton's acquaintance with the ingredients and his subsequent engagement in the culinary business in London purports his self-expression and refashioning of his self in a foreign setting, as he must add new ingredients and flavours to the already existed culinary art which he has mastered in his native land, to be acceptable to the foreign people. The novelist is thus keen on developing and executing the food trope as an urge to preserve the island's distinctive identity and culture but at the same time to assimilate the foreign cultures. The fusion that is resulted from the intersection of the two cultures—Eastern and Western—highlights the notion of the "confluence of cultures" (Sheehan and Morrison) which helps Triton identify himself as a part of that foreign reality, exacerbating his present position to serve at the table as a culinary artist. In this cultural process of assimilation, Triton brings home the point that like the mixing of food, people can also be harmoniously blended and mingled into one and that identity can be reconfigured and belongingness can be re-established even in an alien world such as England. The manner in which Triton is able to stuff and cook a typical Western turkey to perfection using the indigenous ingredients, "decorated it with temple flowers and some left-over Christmas tinsel" (*Reef* 79) suggests that cultural fusion and assimilation are no more unproven facts. Shyama Ramsamy in her paper "Island life: Comparative analysis of V.S. Naipaul's *Mystic Masseur* and Romesh Gunesekera's *Reef*" has beautifully summed up this idea of multicultural reciprocation through food between cultures and traditions:

> The act of mixing two completely different cuisines stresses on the idea that the hybrid identity can be useful at times. The promises of a recreated space, identity and culture are not void. Moreover, food ... holds a pertinent cultural bearing in the sense that it brings together at

> one table in a specific place people of manifold beliefs, traditions, cultures, identities, thus, adding to the idea of multicultural social meeting and gathering to enjoy a similar food. The mixture of cooking fashions result in Triton's success as a chef and restaurateur par excellence whereby he has been able to lock a fixed acknowledged identity in the cosmopolitan adopted city. (3)

Hence, indigenous art can be used in a different perspective to cater to the need of the foreign audience. Triton, like Karim of *The Buddha,* becomes the emblem of cultural fusion who knows it very well how to synthesise two diverging cultures in one. His preparation of the Christmas turkey, in this context, supports the thesis that migrant writers like Gunesekera can reconfigure their inner landscape in the process of self-refashioning and assimilate the gift of the West to refurbish their distinctive and unique indigenous cult. As in an interview Gunesekera has pointed out, "culture is not contained, it's all over the place" (Erney) which is enduringly encapsulated in his elegant and moving novella *Reef.*

Susheila Nasta's analysis of *Reef* highlights a diasporic sensibility that permeates Gunesekera's fiction by "vividly dramatizing the difficulties of imposing a false historiography on the discursive discontinuities of diasporic lives" (27). The coral reef emphasises Triton's initial awe and admiration for his master's passion and wisdom about marine life, but later he criticises it as an alternatively purported history of a nation and its hierarchies as experienced by the subaltern: "To him there were no boundaries to knowledge. He studied mosquitoes, swamps, sea corals and the whole bloated universe ... he wrote about the legions under the sea, the transformation of water into rock—the cycle of light, plankton, coral and limestone—the yield of beach to ocean" (24) is his early acclamation to Mr. Salgado's erudition which is cut short by a tinge of irony in his previous statement about him: "Although he had been to the best of Colombo's schools, Mister Salgado regarded himself as largely self-educated" (24). Salgado's indifference towards the conservation work is apparently fuelled by his contact with Miss Nilli whom he falls in love with. Triton wryly comments: "She brought out the urban socialite in him and shrouded the scholar" (119). Mr. Salgado, however, attends the inaugural ceremony of the irrigation project which indicates co-optation into the governmental project. As Triton muses, "It was a bubbly world of gaiety that seemed to belong to a previous more frivolous generation. At the *kadé* on the main road the talk was on the need for revolution, or for a return to traditional values ... but in our house none of that mattered" (83) ironically demonstrates that the privileged semi-feudal lifestyle of the upper Sri Lankan society are far removed from the impoverished lifestyle of the poor classes represented by Triton. The narrative signifies that at the extreme limits of the elite and the subaltern voice is situated the silently suffering reef. In spite of Salgado's support of the irrigation project, it seems that he is yet to comprehend the real problem of his country. He entertains his guests at the Christmas party by re-telling the great biblical flood which to him is not as exotic as the monsoon rain of Sri Lanka. It is not only a postmodern attack on the concept of Biblical meta-narrative as providing source for history but also an exposure of the contemporary construction of Buddhist and Tamil meta-narratives which are co-opted as its alternative. When Salgado's friend asserts that Sri Lanka is "Buddha's special haven", he cynically replies: "choose a religion, pick up your fantasy. History is flexible" (85) which criticises the derivational politics of postcolonial historiography. Associating Sri Lanka to a past paradise, at length, Salgado's exoticism here tantalises his guests with a picture of his country's commonly purported Edenic past. He reflects on the regenerative feature of the sea and is optimistic of another renaissance in his country which will be instrumental in creating a new world for Sri Lanka and its inhabitants which shows his comfortable combination of the zeal for conservation and commercialisation of a utopia. The novelist, in the narrative, is not concerned with recreating an island paradise, the utopia of the mind, but is attentive to the exoticised anxiety which is hard to resist by the individual in a densely diasporising society. As Susheila Nasta contends:

> Gunesekera does not dwell on painting the exotica of a lost paradise whose beauty ... poignantly overshadows

> the bloody realities of a violent civil war, but examines instead the gaps, paradoxes and delusions which have led to the hollownesses at the centre ... whether set in London or Sri Lanka—the tragic epiphanies of individual lives occur in counterpoint with the haunting and beautiful landscape of an island which is not 'exoticized', but exists instead as a source of subliminal anxiety, always out of the reach. (226)

The novel concerns Triton's emotional development and his search for identity in the backdrop of the social and political changes that take place in his island home. Triton's initial experience with the evil of the society is first seen to be manifested in the character of Joseph, his serving counterpart in the house of Salgado. Triton says: "Even in Mister Salgado's house deceit had found a nest, especially in the head of his servant Joseph" (8). As one day, Joseph returns home after drinking a whole night; he is fined by Salgado and driven out of his home. This is a major development in the character of Triton as he is now the soul caretaker of the entire house and is ready to shoulder all household responsibilities. He wants to improve his culinary skill and starts cooking elaborate meals as his master desires. The Christmas dinner is a crucial event in Triton's life and his mastery in cooking is at once recognised and appreciated by all guests. Triton's casual trip to the sea with Salgado's friend Dias marks another significant development in his character as he begins to figure out the socio-political changes around him. Triton narrates his perception of the sea life: "I felt the sea getting closer; each grain of sand closer to washing the life out of us ... it made me feel helpless" (60). Triton's continual maturity is delineated in his conversation with Miss Nilli. Triton's interacting with Nilli is his first experience ever speaking to a woman who feels her presence on Salgado's house to be a positive sign which corresponds to the changes that occur on his arrival, and the huge changes that inform the world outside Salgado's house. Triton as a young house boy holds his Prospero-like master with utmost reverence and is spellbound by Salgado's knowledge. Triton's cognitive detachment from the public sphere and his emotional isolation remind us of the butler-narrator Stevens of *Remains of the Day* by Kazuo Ishiguro who believes in extreme dedication and sincerity to his master. Triton, like Stevens, never questions his servitude or Salgado's integrity as a marine biologist. When the guests of the table are discussing the state policies that privilege the upper class at the cost of downgrading and curtailing the rights of the lower classes, he regards their talk as irrelevant. When interrogated by Wijetunga, a Marxist supporter about "the crisis of capitalism, the history of social movements and the future shape of Lankan revolution" (111), Triton expresses his innocent aloofness by replying: "But I am only a cook" (111). Only towards the closing pages of the novel we are allowed a glimpse of his full maturity when he braces himself up to face the world all by himself "without Ranjan Salgado standing at my side" (180).

In proximity with Salgado, Triton begins to observe the destructive, suicidal practices of coral bleaching. On the periphery of Salgado's research station at Yala, he is frightened to notice "skull-heaps of petrified coral—five-foot pyramids beside smoky kilns—marking the allotment of a line of impoverished lime-makers, tomorrow's cement fodder, crumbling on the loveliest stretch of the coast" (59-60). When he visits the fish market with Nilli to buy some exotic fish for her dinner, the latter is horrified by a nauseating scenario of death that pervades the market place: "... outside a man was filling an unmarked van with baskets of dead fish. Small pieces of bleached white coral decorated the municipal parking lot" (118). The reef is being used to meet the requirements of the impoverished social classes who can't compete with the global market. Mister Salgado as a scientist looks forward to creating costal refuges to save the ultramarine world from the imminent danger: "'If only we could make the whole coast life Yala. A sea sanctuary, with not a soul there. A real refuge'" (161). He regrets the wasteful outlook of the populace: "'But the trouble is all these people. People who want to live just for today. Let tomorrow take care of itself, as if nothing ever matters but their own moment of passion'.... 'The thing you have to learn is to let what will happen, happen, I suppose. Not to struggle, not for anything'" (162).

To protect the coral reef and to restore the ecological balance is his distant dream. He says to Triton: "I can see it like a dream, you know, painted in my head" (161). The formation of sanctuaries, however, does not take into account the economic policies underlying the capitalistic exploitation and disruption of natural resources. It also fails to address the structural inequalities resulted from the creation of the sanctuaries which make the poor costal people to mindlessly destroy their immediate environment. Salgado is guilty of re-enacting a neo-colonialist ideology in his project of preserving the reef as Sharae Grace Deckard argues: "Salgado's fantasy of preserving the sanctity of the entire coastline by expelling its indigenous inhabitants is dangerously similar to the discourses of purity and ethnic exclusion used in nationalistic rhetoric to construct the idea of Sinhalese or Tamil homelands and to expel ethnic 'others'" (166). This contradiction in his disposition is readily visible when, despite his scientific rationalism and logicism, he cites the Buddhist myths of Sri Lanka as a "paradise of demons" to project an imaginative cartography of the island's disruption:

> Africa, the whole of the rest of the world, was part of us. It was all once one place: Gondwanaland. The great land mass in the age of innocence. But the earth was corrupted and the sea flooded in. The land was divided. Bits broke and drifted away and we were left with this spoiled paradise of *yakkhas*—demons—and the history of mankind spoken on stone. (84)

Salgado predicts in a gloomy manner the eventual despoilment of the island's reef and the coastline resulting in the total submersion of the land: "And if the structure is destroyed, the sea will rush in. The sand will go. The beach will disappear" (48). Deckard cogently relates Salgado's discourse of imagined endangerment of the island to the social panic resulted by the growing currents of Marxist and Tamil insurgencies, inaugurating the politics of belongingness as reviving the nations homogeneity and essentialist propaganda:

> Salgado's "toxic discourse" of reef endangerment and environmental flooding is correlated with the social

> panic caused by the rising tides of insurgency by Marxist revolutionaries and Tamil secessionists. Encircling the island, restraining the sea's violence, the reef is integrated into rationalist and liberationist notions of insularity, which imagine Lanka as a homogeneous, bounded entity, belonging to one people or the other, obscuring its true geographical origin as an island among islands, connected in a land bridge to the sub-continent. The reef thus becomes an ambivalent symbol in which the signifiers of ecological crisis and class inequalities are repressed and overwritten with the signifiers of ethnic violence and political conflict. Ironically, as coastal erosion increases, the political rhetoric of insularity intensifies. (167)

The themes of birth, death and rebirth are central to the imagery of the reef which works as the central metaphor of the text. The Reef's refashioning of itself finds a parallel in Triton's reshaping of his destiny and is echoed in the evolutionary idealism of a nation which is always in the making. According to Deckard, "The novel's repeated imagery of coral 'skull-heaps' reinforces the association between the trope of the dying reef and human death" (167). Triton too, in the narrative, discovers a similar note in the tidal wave of the forest when he remarks: "The whole country had been turned from jungle to paradise to Jungle again, as it has been even more barbarically in my own life" (15). Triton, again refers to the myth of the murderer prince Ahimsaka, later comes to be known as *Anguli-maala* who thinks that by killing he will do good to the world and "become a wise and righteous king and sit on a golden throne" (166). Ahimsaka's delusion is clearly reflected in the regenerative dialectics of Wijetunga who claims that: "Our country really needs to be cleansed, *radically*. There is no alternative. *We have to destroy in order to create....* Like the sea. Whatever it destroys, it uses to grow something better" (111).

Triton nourishes a fantastically fabulous picture of the reef in his head which is eventually influenced by Salgado's luminous description of the wonderful reef. But when he sees the reef for the first time in his life, he is terrified by its diffusive profusion: "I was frightened by its exuberance" (176):

> It was a jungle of writhing shapes, magnified and distorted, growing at every move, looming out of the unknown, startling in its hidden brilliance. Suspended in the most primal of sensations, I slowly began to see that everything was perpetually devouring its surroundings. I swam into a sea of sound; my hoarse breathing suddenly punctuated by clicking and clattering, the crunching of fish feeding on the white tips of golden staghorn. My own fingertips seemed to whiten before me as trigger-fish, angel-fish, tiger-fish, tetrons, electrons and sandstone puffer-fish swirled around me, ever hungry. (176-77)

According to Deckard, "this Darwinian image of a "devouring reef" is invested with a radical alterity that signals the threat posed to Sri Lanka's culture and environment by the modernizing schemes of global development" (168). Triton's vision of the reef as primeval, exuberant and encompassing destroys Salgado's artificial design of controlling the forces of nature and preserving Sri Lanka's island paradise myth associated with his so-called "erotic sea" (130). The metaphor of consumption, moreover, "implies that the country is devouring itself, feeding on political myths of paradise and islandness which can only lead to violence" (Deckard 168). As Wijetunga, at a point in the narrative, warns against the tourist culture flourishing in Sri Lanka in favour of an indigenous tradition—pure and monolithic in essence: "All they see is packets full of foreign money. Coming by the plane-load. Don't they realize what will happen? They will ruin us. They will turn us all into servants. Sell our children" (111).

Gunesekera, in the novel, has thus exposed the myths and fantasies associated with the island as a paradise in which its purity is retained beyond disruption: "... remember this was also known as the Garden of Eden. It panders to anyone's chauvinism, you know: Sinhala, Tamil, aboriginal" (85). As Deckard astutely observes:

> The temporal-spatial "breach" provoked by Triton's encounter with the Tamil refugee precipitates his return, in memory, to the island of his childhood. As he narrates his transition from solipsism to political disillusion, it is tempting to view Triton as cast out from the paradise of childhood harmony with his culture and environment. Throughout the text, Sri Lanka is represented by the characters as an endangered or already-spoiled paradise, with the reef as the anti-paradisal figure signifying political and ecological anxieties about the erosion of a nation-state. (261)

Gunesekera admits that the idea of 'lost paradise' as recreated in *Reef* is one of his "central obsessions": "That sense of a lost paradise is something I have ... because that's how people look at the past—often, though not always, however traumatic the past might be, actually the loss of it is even more traumatic" (qtd. in Hall "A Voyage around the Author"). Nevertheless, the lines adopted from Shakespeare's *The Tempest*—"of his bones are coral made"—which prefaces the narrative is suggestive of transformation rather than of loss. It focuses on the regenerative properties of the elements rather than their imperilment against the distorting web of time. Illuminating on this theme of transformation, Sharae Grace Deckard refers to a passage in which Hannah Arendt contrasts the historical thinking of Walter Benjamin to pearl-diving:

> Like a pearl diver who descends to the bottom of the sea, not to excavate the bottom and bring it to light but to pry loose the rich and strange, the pearls and the coral in the depths, and to carry them to the surface, [Benjamin], delves in to the depths of the past—but not in order to resuscitate it the way it was and to contribute to the renewal of extinct ages. What guides this thinking is the conviction that although the living is subject to the ruin of the time, the process of decay is at the same time a process of crystallization.... (qtd. in Deckard 171)

Gunesekera as a diasporic author acknowledges the power of memory and its therapeutic effect on the diasporans, because to retrieve time is to integrate a thread of lost consciousness to one's idea of identity and belongingness. As the novelist relates in one interview: "What runs deeper is a sense of identity and difference—the whole notion that no one ever really belong in one place. Even animals migrate" (Hussein); analogously, Triton's voyaging back into his own past is an attempt to reconfigure his inner landscape, to integrate a lost thread to his present consciousness, to encounter the remote richness of his unexamined past. In the words of Deckard:

> Triton's plunge into memory leads him to re-examine all that was rich and strange about his past, but also to realize that his childhood had been a period of ignorance, rather than paradisal innocence. Unlike Salgado, who choose to return to the "far-away house of sorrow", Triton does not try to recapture paradise lost, but rather to seize agency in the present. He rejects originary myths in favour of a historical consciousness of dispossession and resistance: "Human history is always a story of somebody's diaspora" (174). The decay of his former self crystallizes his new identity as a "cosmopolitan itinerant without a past, without a name" (180). Therefore, in *Reef,* Gunesekera uses the paradise motif to criticize ... demystify national myths of the island and demystify the migrant's memory of the homeland. (171)

Reef, the lyrical novel can appropriately be termed as a novel of memorialisation, articulated through a voyage of discovery into a lost home which suggests a metaphorical journey towards self-fulfilment and search for identity. On being asked by Rocio G. Davis about the role of memory in his works in one interview, Gunesekera says, "our imagination is fed by the past, by the impressions we remember, the things we've heard and seen.... The novel is about a man who is trying to tell the story of his life (Triton). He is trying to understand who he is, how he has come to be what he is, which means, in a sense, exploring memory, trying to understand memory". In his interview with Rocio G. Davis, Gunesekera reflects upon the ways Triton "functions as an artist" in the narrative and thus *Reef,* the novel, can safely be described as a *Künstlerroman* which traces the growth and development of the protagonist's destiny as an artist. Gautam Kundu rightly observes that:

> ... Triton pursues his culinary skills diligently, fruitfully, and with an aesthetic care and attention to detail that are analogous to a painter working on her palette or of a writer finding his distinctive "voice". Underscoring the cook/"artist's" emerging "voice" is Triton's stream of memory, which according to the author, serves a Proustian function of setting into motion the process of remembering.... What Triton remembers most, through, and with deep regret and nostalgia, is a certain sense of wholeness he associates with his "homeland's" mythical past and its prelapsarian beauty and innocence, which are now lost in Sri Lanka's "fallen" state of confusion and chaos. (94)

The novel records the artists' struggle to erect a 'home' in the adoptive country. Triton gradually learns to cook and eventually becomes an extraordinary chef. He remembers his childhood innocence and waywardness of the youth, and recounts his instinctive desire to experience "Mister Salgado's famous ocean and the life beyond our garden gate" (62). The novel is replete "with sumptuous fare, from tiger prawns to rum soufflés, whose cook, like Prospero, is both magician and artist. 'Food is everything to Triton—his art, his vocation, his identity'" (Jaggi). The novel thus concerns Triton's recapturing of the lost time which has grown hazy with experience is an important marker of identity enhancing self-actualisation. As Gunesekera asserts: "In the sense that writing is to retrieve the past and stop passing of time, all writing is about loss. It's not nostalgia, in the sense of yearning to bring back the past, but recognition of the erosion of things as you live" (Jaggi). Illuminating on the relationship of memory to identity, Gunesekera says that recreating the lost time may not make up a biographical portrait of the protagonist but is psychologically important for him:

> ... The book is about identity, gaining a voice, finding a voice, which to me again is linked with the whole idea

> of an artist. It is an artistic enterprise, which is about finding a voice ... that actually we are all artists, we are all artists of our own lives ... and then we recreate it in our memory. There is a creation and a recreation process ... that birth of the artist, the birth of the voice, to me paralleled this idea of a child becoming an adult.... Triton becomes an artist in the sense of becoming a cook, a chef, very much in the way a painter finds his palette and a writer finding his voice. (Davis, "We are All Artists")

According to Robert Winder, "Triton's servility is a metaphor of the East's relations to the colonial West. But the new life of the island is an ugly cocktail of bad politics and violence": "Down on the beach, the bodies of men and boys who had disappeared from their homes, who had been slaughtered and thrown in the sea, were washed in by the tide. Every morning they reappeared by the dozen: bloated and disfigured, rolling in the surf" (166-67). But just as the waves of the sea move washing over the reef, depositing coral for the fish to make them survive, so there are tides in a nation's life operating upon the sundry affairs of men. When Triton steps outside his domesticities, he must confront "the exact ebb and flow of the whole cluster of galaxies" (78). When he prepares the most perfect dishes; it is his manner of navigating "every possible channel" (79) into the minds of the guests present at the table. Each single event and experience in Triton's life in the old home is a stepping stone towards self-actualisation as he matures from his boyhood to adulthood. Nilli, for Triton, is the brightest fish in the sea feeding on the reef. She gleams with the sunshine, and her suitcase is the source of immense curiosity for him. He stares her ceaselessly, speechless and out of breath and her feminine fervour is minutely described by him with intense clinical details:

> Her ears moved too when she spoke. They were larger than I expected. Each with two symmetrical wrinkles where they joined her neck and the outer edges curled in like the edge of a puppadum when it hits hot oil. My instinct was to press the ears back with my hands

> and keep the entrances to her soul open like the lips of a glazed pink conch. (89)

Then by degrees the life of the reef begins to overshadow the life of the house and guests start flooding into it and "invade in shoals" (90) "to enjoy their wanton adulation" (91) and the tension that engulfs the island breaks in like a stormy, roaring sea. The sea is like destiny, the harbinger of both renewal and decay: "We have to destroy in order to create ... like the sea. Whatever it destroys, it uses to grow something better" (111). Thus the metaphor of the reef amidst the stormy, violent sea in its silent suffering parallels the potency of the West Wind in "Ode to the West Wind" by P.B. Shelly which acts both as a 'destroyer and the preserver' bringing about the germs of new life up on the earth. The image of the reef in the sea acts as the source of regeneration and renewal. It is the source of life, and death. As Charu Mathur in her paper "Home as an Emotional Construct" writes:

> The vulnerability of the island mirrors the vulnerability of "homes". Where is home, asks Gunesekera, for people who hover between a Sri Lanka that no longer embraces them and an England that they are reluctant to embrace? The colonial tension having been transferred to the post-colony, there is a preoccupation with the process of self-preservation through the act of transformation that determines the immigrant's relationship with the homeland. (28)

Melanie A. Murray in her book *Island Paradise: The Myth: An Examination of Contemporary Caribbean and Sri Lankan Writing* contends: "The erosion of the reef by the sea can be read as a warning against the erosion of cultural identity in the context of civil war" and the search for tranquility in the novel "takes place in *Heaven's Edge* within an imaginary site and indicates an unsettled disposition relative both to Gunesekera's diasporic identity and, more specifically to disturbances in Sri Lanka ... the meaning of home becomes a fictional creation" (98). Triton and his mentor Salgado in the novel can be considered as orchestrating the author's cultural hybridity—a diasporic sensibility which reflects the tensions between homeland and host land, settlement and dispersal. According to Avtar Brah, "diasporic journeys are essentially about settling down, about putting roots 'elsewhere'" (182) and thus register a 'homing desire' in the migrant individuals, perpetually critiquing the discourses of the fixed origins. Triton, after migrating to England, activates his exilic memory and imagination, and remembers his life with Salgado in Sri Lanka as an act of recreating a lost home in an adopted country. Triton resorts to creating an imaginary homeland for survival at a metaphorical level whereas Mr. Salgado, the marine biologist and scientist, is entrusted with the recuperation of life under threat, at a literal level, by protecting the coral reef from erosion. Tariq Zazeel in his paper "Unpicking Sri Lankan 'Islandness' in Romesh Gunesekera's *Reef*" argues that Salgado attempts to map the "island-ness" of the land by a fixed scientific discourse of the coast, which is a perception of the "island-ness" that does not acknowledge the internal borders but "smooth(s) over the gaps" (590). His scientific rationalism is the result of his internalising a Western discourse, "a modernity rooted in Sri Lankan's colonial experience" (Murray 98) which crumbles into insignificance through Triton's memory. Triton can be seen as contesting this "island-ness" perception of Salgado through his diasporic memory that is "remoulded through the post-colonial experience of immigration" (Zazeel 584). Triton's retrospective reconfiguration of an imaginative topography is essentially coloured by a drift of the diaspora as he is attentive to the limitation and insularity of his homeland whereas Salgado is primarily guided by his rational logicism which he inherits from the enlightenment. This tension in the text is beautifully analysed by Melanie A. Murray:

> Triton can see the limitation (the very 'insularity') of the island; his narrative suggests that he is ultimately felt confined by it. Salgado represents a discourse of enlightenment, of scientific rationality. He aims to preserve the 'island', whereas Triton feels threatened by 'island-ness', which is subverted through his imagination. Salgado's concern is with the preservation of the coral reef while Triton conjures up predatory images that

> frightened and overwhelm him. These images can be understood as omens of the impending war. The two perspective—of Salgado as pragmatic intellectual and Triton as imaginative and creative—reveal contrasting yet complementary positions and convey the tension between striving to preserve the island and feeling confined by it, a tension between 'home' and 'dispersal'. (99)

Salgado's mapping of the island as remote and insular is associated with the coloniser's narrative control of the island which is challenged by Triton with his predatory metaphors of fish and deconstructs the myth of paradise in the backdrop of political upheaval and ethnic strife that plague his homeland. *Reef*, the novel delicately presents the rifts and dichotomy between the two locations—England and Sri Lanka—the two homelands of Triton to nourish a diasporic consciousness which explains "*how* and *why* originary absolutes are imagined" and "what the search for origin signifies" (Brah 197). The idea of return, therefore, is not a significant theme of the narrative fostered by Mr. Salgado at the end of the novel, but that the notion of home is exposed as an imagined relationship sustained with the world by the individuals. As Murray asserts: "This ongoing process, by drawing in multi-locational attachments, helps to constantly refine and revise the diasporic experience as always being in motion" (101).

By describing the island as a microcosm of the universe, Gunesekera ironically challenges the European narratives of the 'discovery' which consider islands as timeless and ahistorical. This is, however, achieved by an early allegorical depiction of the island as an Edenic site, and then by focusing on its vulnerability to violence and cultural erosion resulting by the civil war and political tension. Thus, "Allusions to both Western and Eastern myths are used in a creative syncretism indicative of Gunesekera's cultural hybridity" (Murray 106). Gunesekera's cultural hybridity enables him to revision and transform the narrative, creatively merging the tradition of the East and the West—literary or otherwise, and thereby opens up the way to regeneration like the endangered reef of the novel. As Murray rightly observes:

> Gunesekera's voyage is still in process; his representations contest fixed origins and advocate change, while also lamenting the loss of (Edenic peace).... The gap, or breach, between fiction and reality is self-reflexively exposed; [he] convincingly advocates the need to connect mixed cultures and histories while creatively linking and transforming his mixed cultural heritage. His work, the achievement of a diasporic writer, celebrates movement and flux, acknowledging a shifting environment symbolized by the sea. (106-07)

Gunesekera's diasporic consciousness is thus a combination of nearness and distance, indifference and involvement nourished through a plurality of experience which provides a formal position to the migrant for survival. The coexistence of parallel homes effectuates in him a complex sense of home that subverts any temporal or spatial boundaries. This kind of migrant, as Sonia Floriani believes, "aims to double the here and now of his life, and reassess the elsewhere and then" (80). For Triton, as for Gunesekera himself, home is not to be found only here or only there, in Sri Lanka or in England, but in both these places. Triton thus performs the role of a "marginal man" explained and elaborated by Robert E. Park who is:

> ... a cultural hybrid, a man living and sharing intimately in the cultural life and traditions of two distinct peoples; never quite willing to break, even if he were permitted to do so, with his past and his traditions, and not quite accepted, because of racial prejudice, in the new society in which he now sought to find a place. He was a man on the margin of two cultures and two societies, which never completely interpenetrated and fused ... historically and typically, the marginal man [is] the first cosmopolite and citizen of the world. (qtd. in Floriani 80)

The 'marginal men' such as Triton and Gunesekera are thus cultural hybrid, who are not only enriched by curiosities and creative capabilities but also characterised by a certain sense of restlessness and inner conflicts, for whom the notion of home is always having multiple modalities and unfixated conditionalities, and identity accordingly can be reconfigured, refashioned altering the inner landscape of the mind.

In his second novel, *The Sandglass,* Gunesekera in a Rushdian fashion portrays memory as fragmented, the mirror which is broken—mutilated beyond repair and flawed by an elliptical narrativisation—yet instantiating the ways to the recognition that "it is perhaps only memory that is left to define the migrant's true home" (Nasta 228). The complex time-scales of the novel helps Chip, the narrator to unravel his reminiscences of the seventeen years he has known the Ducal family. The narrative opens when Prins, the eldest son of Pearl Ducal returns to London for his mother's funeral in 1993. In an attempt to decipher the truth behind the mysterious death of his father Jason Ducal, Prins reflects on his fragmented past with the company of the narrator who strives to bridge up the gaps with bits and pieces from the history of the three generations of the Ducals with the rivalling Vatunases, intricately integrated into the lives of the Ducals. Pearl has shifted to London long years back and passes her time desultorily in a dingy flat, living an unexcited life. The mysteries surrounding Jason Ducal's death in the homeland prove to be a constant pull on characters such as Chip and Prins who set out to disentangle the rift between Ducals' unanswered and untold histories.

The novel meticulously knits together the fragments of memory that slip into the untrodden landscapes of the curious mind. Chip becomes a moving symbol of the endless quest for identity, endeavouring to explore the unity from a long aborted diasporic past in an orphaned ambience of eternal anomaly. Characters in the narrative move endlessly between homeland and host land, entailing a fluid itinerary of diasporic existence. Pearl, after spending forty years of her life in a yellowing flat in London, still craves for homely sentiments and shares with Chip stories from her Sri Lankan home. Despite temporary consolation and release from the political feud and social turmoil of the homeland, through the life that is lived in London,

Sri Lanka remains the most promised land for the dislocated characters which enamours them forever. Prins hoping to enact a new home in the lost city returns "to his dreamland by then, thoroughly fed up with his mother, his brother, the family and England. He had gone promising never to come back: an emigrating immigrant" (82). The novelist in delineating the diasporic life of the protagonist reflects on the difficulties a diasporic artist encounters in the recreation of home and home culture in addition to the danger of dislocation in the adaptive host land.

The father-son relationship in the novel which enables Prins to revisit and rediscover his past can be seen as a projection of a similar impetus that attracts the inmates to their dream land home country, inescapably in transformative reveries. The novel answers the ways memories are reshaped and handed down in diasporic families and in which identifications are reconfigurated, re-enacting the consuming process of remembering and redefining the tentative terrains of belonging, to exacerbate their hybrid identities and ambivalent situatedness.

It is Chip, the confidante of Pearl, who is entrusted with the duty to weave the various interconnected fragments of reality into a meaningful totality that inform the lives of the Ducals. The narrative, however, at every point, integrates the personal lives of the characters with the larger colonial history of the post-independence Sri Lanka. Disguised with this tension in the surface, the novel addresses a totally different concern in the framework as Chip, at one point, in the novel indicates this concealment frustrating the reader's initial appreciation of the text: "The Imagination is our most molested flower, he wrote, so easily crippled in a heartless paradise" (185).

Analogously, Prins' thirst for a diasporic reclamation of the long lost past which combines the private life with the political history of Sri Lanka is challenged at every steps in the novels, eluding a permanent solution to his problems:

> You know, nothing really fits. That's the trouble. It all pretends to fit, like someone has constructed it all for us to see exactly how the thing works, but really it is

> done to hide everything. To lead us completely in the wrong direction. I feel I have been given a puzzle with a ready-made solution to divert me from something else which I must not discover. (249)

The various narrative techniques employed by Chip as a narrator lead to the creation of the "surrogates for his representations of a past lost" (Nasta 228) and dawn a realisation upon him about the "rooms of memory" they have spawned (Nasta 226). Gunesekera's larger concern in the novel, in this manner, combines a highly suggestive mode of representation of a parentless, undecided projection as a symbol of the diasporic existence. Susheila Nasta in this connection writes:

> *The Sandglass* seems to 'fit' with a number of features characteristic of the late twentieth-century novel of diasporic reclamation. For it is a novel which painstakingly charts the history of a life knitted together by the fragments of memory and the previously 'untold' stories of a diasporic past. It is a past which is meticulously reconstructed, covering two countries, the dynamic histories of two families, and stretching by the end across three generations.... Chip becomes the repository for a quest, which only seems to relate obliquely to his own location and the 'orphaned fragments' of his 'aborted past'. (229)

Gunesekera, thus continues to explore the multiple modalities of diasporic narrativisation and its indispensable connection with memory and its complication. The novel is replete with migrants and the descendants of those migrants who are in the quest of excavating their familiar histories and to re-actuate their lost sense of belonging and identification. Chip is strongly obsessed with unravelling the personal history of Pearl and her exile to England after the feud with the neighbouring Vatunases. Prins, similarly, is consumed by the desire of returning to his homeland and restoring his abandoned family home, Arcadia. After Pearl's death, Prins returns to England temporarily to perform the funeral rites and Chip gets an opportunity to disclose the complicated story of the Ducal family. The compact timeline of the action comprises a place in London over the course of a day, which is repeatedly disrupted by digressions and diversions into the temporal past, traversing the geographical setting of an immediate London, thus, diffusing the borderlines of memory and topography that promote the impulse of return. Chip's "productive confusion" in this context "is combined with a growing anxiety to attempt to move outside the limitations imposed on his story by the relentless passing of time" (Nasta 230). Susheila Nasta astutely observes:

> We are given an insight into this process by the novel's persistent exposure of the impossibility, either for Pearl's generation or that of her children, to ever realize the Utopian promises of their displaced 'dream lines'. Jason's 'Arcadia' becomes a 'mausoleum', a 'teardrop' like Sri Lanka itself, situated on the edge of unresolved ethno-religious histories. Moreover, as we see through the narrative's progressive destruction of the various other fictional houses it builds—whether Prins's Shangri-La, Pearl's flat in 'England', or Ravi's failed attempt to find an 'imaginary homeland' in America (a homeland built on the poetry of Longfellow, Whitman and Ginsberg)—such individual co-ordinates of diaspora cannot be sustained. And whilst Gunesekera is clearly playing in the novel on subverting the received images of what some have perceived to be an irresponsible use of an 'orientalist exotica', he does so in a self-conscious manner which does not succumb to the notion of Sri Lanka as either a 'poisoned paradise' or a 'latter-day derivative of the colonial construction of 'Ceylon as Eden'. (230)

Stuti Goswami in her paper "Silence in The Sandglass: Reading through the Meshes of Time, Memories and Silence" observes that the novel presents a cluster of contradiction—"many questions are picked up, a few are prodded, and none resolved ... many spaces are left unanswered: silences consumed in greater silences". It addresses a number of problems but "gaps unfilled sans an anchor in the past, weightless" (Goswami). Indeed, the novel leaves entangled a lot of problems without suggesting a solution thereof. Chip as a narrator has to find out a coherence among these entangled threads. The mysterious death of Jason Ducal in 1956, Pearl's younger son Ravi's quest for a dreamland in the United States, and his suicidal attempts in Pearl's Almeida Avenue flat, Prins' emulation of his father's opportunistic propaganda and the furthering of his interest in the production of a local whisky branded as Ambrosia are some of the unattempted questions left unanswered by the composite framework of the novel which serves as one of the contributory elements of these emerging gaps in the text. The character of Prins, in this regard, is drawn upon certain ambivalent conditionalities which inform his life with the anxiety of a transactive encounter with the deadened past. Although he wants to probe into the mysteries surrounding his father's murder, he finds himself at loss owing to his affrighted, sudden discovery of the truth about the past. Nasta, in this context, meaningfully argues that:

> For Prins, despite his curiosity about his father's death, is also portrayed as a character who fears the secrets of the past, a counter point to Chip, who needs to carefully rework and re-examine the 'density' of the material which surrounds him but constantly eludes him. Instead, like his rival, Dino Vatunas, Prins is keen to sell the present: 'the paradise experience between death camps and suicide bombers who didn't care', mysteriously disappearing by the close, like his father before him. (229)

Pearl's husband Jason's purchasing of Arcadia, a grand mansion once owned by an English Captain bears symbolic overtones: "He called it Arcadia ... and had built the house as a kind of homage to a suppurating colonial dream: the dream of a voyage of adventure" (23). The house stands for the Captain as a nostalgic erection of a lost empire, but for Jason, it embodies the reveries of postcolonial privilege and prestige. The dismantling of the colonial hierarchies in a post-independence Sri Lanka, yet effectuates the marginalisation of other minority groups. Jason, at this point, is promoted to the post of the Vice-President of a British owned tea company.

Jason's big mission, here, suggests a progressive transition from the lowest strata of colonial hierarchy to the height of the elite group under the Sinhalese nationalist government: "Jason seems to have become a true colonial: a man obsessed with place and status—geographical and social. Only once assured of his own place in the murkiness of the universe could he bring order and shape to life around him" (23-24). Jason and his contemporaneous thus "emulated the vanities of their pre-war colonial masters, trying to transform themselves into brownskin imperial successors" (103). Jason's possession of the grand Arcadia, however, soon invites the ire of Esra Vatunas who cannot resist the magnificence of the house, adjacent to his own mansion Bellevue, and begins a saga of feud which ranges from controversy over land to economic rivalry as time moves on. Pearl, on the other hand, doesn't subscribe to the world view reflected in the demeanour of Jason, and is horribly troubled by the queer unease of the possession:

> She said she felt reluctant to challenge Jason's well-being with her unease, but she knew she did not want to die in this house of his. 'I could feel something pushing me or pulling me out of his Arcadia. But looking at Jason, I could see that he felt the opposite. He wanted that house to be his whole life: the place where he would die'. The incompatibility still disturbed her. (25)

Arcadia tends to limit the free flow of Pearl's life, but Jason is steadily absorbed into it as if the spirit of Arcadia has delved deep into his marrows. Jason moves higher in the ladder of his professional success which gradually opens up the rifts between the couple. Enmeshed with his new job and enamoured by a prosperous future, he fails to comprehend the growing distance between the two. Jason buys a distillery and lunches his own brand of whisky when a mishap occurs—Jason Ducal dies in an accidental firing by a man, most likely hired by Esra Vatunas. Soon after Jason's death, the project is taken over by Esra who runs the business with roaring success. Pearl seeks refugee in England leaving her three children to be taken care of by a relative in Sri Lanka, who gradually migrates to England, to live with their mother. When Prins returns to London, Anoja is already dead delivering a baby named Naomi. These initial years of Pearl's life in London is almost shrouded in mysteries and silences and Prins' final departure for Sri Lanka to revive the lost dream of his father brings the role of Chip to the foreground, who is left behind with pearl, to fill the black spaces of their respective trajectories. One can map the growing importance of Chip's role in Pearl's exilic life as he becomes "the one who was there, willing to share the reality of her words and peek into another world" (8) and as pearl recounts the happenings of those early years in England act as "an invisible eavesdropper in the twilight of a camphoric age" (10).

The urge to belong to a land by possessing it characterises the impulse of almost all the characters in the novel. Pearl, however, sells Arcadia as she believes the land having "a propensity to fester. Rent, don't own, stay free, was her maxim, even when she was eventually rooted to her Almeida Avenue flat in a country determined to make democracy permanently indebted to private ownership" (89). The conflictual manoeuvring between the two houses, namely Arcadia and Bellevue, suggests a microcosm of the wider and wilder socio-political tensions promoted by the privileged elite section of the Sri Lankan society: "That was when the big shots were laying down all these bloody laws of self-interest.... The rules by which we have been stomping over each other for forty years.... Now I am having to reconstruct the whole concertina: nothing remembered, nothing forgotten and everything up for grabs" (97). The novel also narrates the ever-altering political geography of the island in which new realities are dawned with each shift in colonial and postcolonial configuration. The land possessed by the Vatunas is represented as queer shaped, weirdly plotted into lands simulating the shapes of genitals: "the bizarre idea of using his family tree to make procreative sculptures out of his property.... He wanted testicles for one, a vulva for another, a lingam for a third, swollen glans and so on" (28).

This "lewd land-map" (28) and his early wills of "reproductive drawing" (28) at a metaphorical level suggest an eroticisation of the island as an object of desire, a possessive obsession for a Promethean Paradise, to feel at home, and at the same time a patriarchal upper hand in the subordination of the land as representing feminine paraphernalia. The young Esra, however, has a modified version of this feminine paradise when he describes his vulva-shaped estate as "the imprint of a divine hoof as God cantered to heaven from the island" which neatly "obscure(s) the secret lasciviousness of his father's vision" (29). According to Deckard, "this religious fantasy obscures the land's libidinal history beneath a narrative of purity which ascribes authority to its owner, mirroring the way in which post-independence nationalists created sterilised myths of a 'Pure' homeland" (173).

Prins seeks to recreate and revitalise the unfulfilled dream of his father's enterprise by attempting to regenerate Sri Lanka's economic glory. His neo-colonial financial pursuit in Sri Lanka is inseparably aligned with his personal nostalgia for the homeland and to establish his sense of belonging to a lost home which can again be reconfigurated with the existing connections. He is catapulted to success in the initial attempts in the first ever boom of tourism industry in Sri Lanka and becomes the General Manager of a group of luxurious hotel owned by Gold Sands Enterprises. Built around the idea of providing exotic experiences to the foreign tourists, the hotels are named after the paradisiacal loci-Shangri-La, New Arcadia to attract the fascination of the visitors. Prins, however, soon comes to realise the ill effects of the luxury tourism in the land with its insensitivity towards environmental hazards and retrograde unsustainability: "'... sex, sun and sand. There's no damn future in it.' He could see it even then, sex would turn unsafe, the sun would become cancerous, and the sand slowly slip into the sea leaving behind only a squalid line of tarted-up pleasure domes" (103). But he cannot abandon his dream of reclaiming his umbilical home culture, physically his father's estate and the Arcadia of his childhood—the plundered paradise he seeks to regain in the transformative rhetoric of self-identification, reconfiguring the inner landscape of the mind. He reminisces with nostalgia the most curious moment of his childhood to be the one when he plays delightfully with a toy gun in the ambience of bright fanciful colours. The memory of the incident yet again is fraught with a sense of guilt compounded by a dark shadow: "And then this shadow that kind of gooks everything and makes it dark. Then it gets dimmer and dimmer and disappears. But I feel guilty. Like I shouldn't remember. Some crushing sense of guilt. Not that I was doing any thing. Not even playing with myself. I don't think that sense of guilt is on the boy there: me. But it somehow washes over it all" (77). Sharae Deckard has linked this guilt to Prins' repressive resistance to violence:

> Prins' feeling of complicity with the exploitative dynamics of tourism, industry, and social corruption is projected into his personal past, the toy gun a repressed signifier of the violence resulting from his economic activities and a harbinger of his father's death and his own. He comes to see the civil war as caused by monolithic, immovable forces, shadows overhanging his existence which he can neither escape nor alleviate. (174-75)

Prins associates the disorientation of his family to the possession of the house Arcadia: "'It was the eight years in that house. Arcadia. Can you imagine? They move into this house and it becomes a mausoleum. I was born in a *mausoleum*. May be it should have been called that: Château Mausoleum" (78-79). Troubled and haunted by a sense of dislocation and decadence, he is thwarted at every attempt to preserve the house of memory he has spawned. At the end of the narrative, Prins like "the innumerable ones who vanish younger and younger with apparently increasing brutality all over the world" (247) disappears into nothingness following the footsteps of his father almost like assassinated: "It made me aware for the first time of the density of what surrounds us, the transformations that take place in our lives, the capricious acts of disappearance performed every day" (248). The corrupt promises of reviving a lost paradise—the dream of Arcadia—finally usher in death and gloomy isolation. The dream land of fantasy is bound to become a mausoleum having no one to share your sorrows. It activates a recognition of the irretrievable erosion of momentous life as one lives in his/her re-configurated home. Analogously, to the fate of the Ducals the Vatunases' house, Bellevue encounters a similar deterioration in the ambience of a desolate graveyard:

> Behind the facade dressed in filigree, its last walls were no more than a day away from the ball and chain of the giant crane poised over it, but it still looked huge and grand and desolate. Its garden, and the gardens of the houses in its ploughed-up wings, had been reduced to a sea of scalloped grey earth, a graveyard of incurable dreams. (277)

Chip, with his final version of the vision of New Arcadia, combines the commodification of the grand image of the house along with a nostalgic reconstitution and reworking of the mythical metaphors of the island that proves to be futile in the face of global economic imperative which shatters Prins' illusions of paradise and progress. Deckard, in this context, astutely observes that "while mourning the loss of Prins, Chip is nonetheless sceptical of nostalgic narratives which mythologize past, and capable of imagining a more humane future. His invocation of Dawn, Pearl's newly-born granddaughter, replaces the false image of regeneration, the capitalist New Arcadia with a humanist new dawn" (176). Chip thus ends the novel with a final vision of New Arcadia urging the drive towards a better world:

> In one corner of the vast plot of Vatunas land, on the footpath that would have once skirted Prins's home boundary, a large hoarding proclaimed the future: 'The New Arcadia'. The proposed flagship hotel of the Great Sands Corporation, the reconstituted hotel chain that Prins had worked for and Dino now ran, regenerating the whole of the Vatunases' land in its own name. There was an artist's futuristic drawing of an elegant garden hotel, shimmering in glass, with bougainvillea cascading over every recessed balcony and a column of starred features in bold red letters: air-conditioned honeymoon apartments, fantasy love suites, and Eros cinema and a subterranean ice rink with a Japanese snow machine. I stood in front of it waiting for Prins to rise, bucking again, out of the disputed ground of his imagined world to free the future from the shadows of the past. I wanted to hear him, or pearl again, or the voice of the last of

> her displaced dreamline, Dawn, spin us forward from this hurt earth to a somehow better world. (277-78)

The attempt to re-establish a lost home is central to the thematic framework of the novel. *The Sandglass* portrays the vain attempts of the two neighbouring but rivalling families, the Ducals and the Vatunases. Jason Ducal, driven by his self-interest and profited by the withdrawal of the British from Sri Lanka is able to buy a magnificent house in Colombo "where no Ducal before him had ever dreamed of owning one" (22). Jason Ducal views his house Arcadia as a large ship and from the bridge of which he can map his unprecedented progress. Arcadia, ironically, in its form is tear-shaped like the country itself. Adjacent to this big house lies the property of the Vatunases: "... the result of a deep and intense relationship between the sleeping earth and the ambitions of a line of modern dynasts. And for the Vatunases, from the first to the last, land defined everything the shape of their lives, the shape of their bodies and their heads and the shape of their dreams" (22). *The Sandglass*, Gunesekera's most ambitious work, thus presents with great delicacy, his preference for the exposition of an emotional truth which explicitly resonates throughout the framework of the novel:

> Sri Lanka compels the leaving of it. Nor for nothing is it "tear-shaped", fecund and beautiful, it is the putative site of the Garden of Eden, of the Paradisiacal Atlantis, from which humanity was exiled. Even those who stay there are forced, by the uncertainties and cruelties of its unflagging civil war, to live in a kind of exile. With its tainted, blood-stained past, stretching for back beyond the British occupation, and its unpredictable future, it would seem unable, in any satisfying sense, to provide a home for its inhabitants. (Binding)

The family histories of the Ducals and the Vatunases are integrated together with great emotional concern for the places and events that influence their fragmented lives. Chip, the narrator has left Sri Lanka some years before and doesn't have a place of his own in his own country, and comes to

London in 1975 to lodge with Pearl, Prins' mother. Pearl's name itself is indicative of the lost grandeur of Sri Lanka, famous for its pearls, and is equated with it in her loveliness. Chip, after meeting Prins, who has arrived in London to perform his mother's funeral, intimately evokes the scenes of the past "pixel by pixel" in his memory (75). Prins treats London as the place of his exile not only because his connection with the homeland but for a culminating relationship with a Vatunas daughter Lola, but after returning to Sri Lanka, he finds no peace, externally or internally. He is greatly obsessed by the undeciphered mystery of his father's death but later on gives in to entrepreneurial activities which often come to be clashed with his spiritual adventure into the unexplained entanglement of the universe. In one of his notebooks that is left behind, he records his thought thus: "The imagination is our most molested flower ... so easily crippled in a heartless paradise" (185). Prins' story in the novel is drawn as a close parallel to his father Jason who, like him, has to experience a similar encounter with the obscure fate. When Chip revisits his homeland Sri Lanka, he fails to find Prins—nobody knows his whereabouts and this rapid descent to obscurity is emblematic of his "heartless paradise" (185) which he tries in vain to reform. But those, who are living away from the homeland as a kind of refugee in the host land for a bright future, are not happy either. Nothing is more pathetic in the novel than the silenced, tragic life of Ravi, Prins' brother who embraces the petty obscurities of his life in such an undramatic manner that it hardly deserves the name: "He not only tried not to make any impression in his daily life, but he tried to undo all past impressions.... He had been so meticulous over his exit that after he passed away not even a single letter arrived for him to remind anyone of his curtailed life" (85). Chip's character as the narrator of the novel is to be contrasted with the character of the narrator/protagonist Triton of Gunesekera's first novel *Reef*, who, in his narrative, for the most part, is ignorant, with his proverbial innocence of the metaphoric implications of the incidents he describes. Chip, on the other hand, is doomed with a clearer foresight and awareness and is too anxious to underscore the dictate of the fate and circumstantial conditionalities. He, therefore, is far less an autonomous character than Triton being unable to be content with an oblique method of narration which may impair the readers' emotional response to situations and relationships projected in the novel:

> Yet this is also part of the novel's point: only the oblique is possible for these confused heirs to a former imperial possession. *The Sandglass* is a novel of true distinction, the work of a profoundly honest mind, one utterly unconcerned with the authorial self, intent instead on the lot of fellow humans and its meaning. He wants, in the words of the beautiful close to his novel, "to free the future from the shadows of the past", to be spun "forward from his hurt earth to a somehow better world." (Binding 278)

The novel's action comprises a day and a night in London where Chip, the narrator, a Sri Lankan immigrant lives with many other Sri Lankan immigrants, with profound longing and nostalgia for the lost home they have left behind in the mist of an irretrievable time. The incident and stories they narrate and share with each other essentially lead home in the backdrop of the complicated tumultuous fabric of the post-independence Sri Lankan history. The characters thus continue to live in the Sri Lanka of their minds and it is their memories of the lost land which make them survive and nourish whether they are in home or elsewhere. Story-telling becomes one of their most fitting surviving strategies to connect with their diasporic past. Suvir Kaul in his review of Gunesekera's *The Sandglass* incisively argues that:

> While a few of Gunesekera's characters are larger than life figures, *The Sandglass* is very often about those who 'leave hardly a trace behind', except in the memories of those who survive them. As in Amitav Ghosh's *The Shadow Lines*, story-telling and memories become specially urgent for diasporic sub-continentals who are all tied to people and the past via the umbilical cord of personal narrative. Both novels feature male narrators who are in crucial ways understudies to older, more

> restless men, which means that the narrative is often at once removed from the events it features.

Gunesekera then achieves a rare technical competence with his creative vitality, projected on the characters and events providing the audience a critical distance from which to view and judge and this distance promotes highly reflective and meditative interpretations, presented with a profusely textured prose, chiselled with powerful emotions and fecund memorialisation, without lapsing into cheap sentimentality. The narrative seeks to chalk out the narrator's "sense of accelerating loss for what is behind us—the lost opportunities, the unregainable past—and fear for what lies ahead" (220). For Chip, the narrator, Britain presents a life of regularity that exists in the veritable planes of the immediate presence, but ironically enough both 'time past' and 'time future' are rooted in an incurable anxiety worked out on a remote island, once regarded as home. Gunesekera thus confidently presents a moving story of the human weakness and waste and the existential catastrophes that overwhelm the individuals and nations in their diasporic quests for belonging and self-re-actuation. As Suvir Kaul contends: "Gunesekera is free of the self-conscious insistence (made popular by our magical realists) that the realities of the subcontinent are so unique that they demand exaggerations of novelistic form and character, Gunesekera's vision is more sparse and economical, his canvas less cluttered but his achievement is wide-ranging, as is his quiet, questing talent." Chip thus admits that he "wouldn't know what was going on anywhere at the best of time" (70) albeit he is the one to patch the fragments of reality into a meaningful coherence, finally fails magically and muses. "I wanted to live in hope as much as in truth" (277).

S.W. Perera's critique of Gunesekera is remarkable in situating the novelist in the context of what he regards as "the Lankan fiction of diaspora" ("Images of Sri Lanka" 64) which placed him by the side of other diasporic writers such as Michael Ondaatje, Shyam Selvadurai and A. Sivanandan et al. He is, however, suspicious of Gunesekera's project of communicating Sri Lanka to the West as destructively contributory to the national culture of Sri Lanka. Gautam Kundu in his essay on

Romesh Gunesekera argues that Perera like Ranasinha who accuses Gunesekera as "myopic and orientalist" in his approach to his former homeland "is critical of Gunesekera for enforcing orientalist notions of the other as exotic, mysterious, and, in the end, unknowable" (qtd. in Kundu 97), but in his later article on *The Sandglass*, he is less critical of the novelist's fascination for exoticism and "recognizes the difficulties an expatriate artist faces in her depiction of 'home' and 'home culture' plus the perils of expatriation itself, as the artist struggles to create for herself a 'a new home' in the adoptive country" (98). Perera in his article "The Perils of Expatriation and a 'Heartless Paradise': Romesh Gunesekera's *The Sandglass*" astutely observes that:

> The sandglass marks an extension to and a continuation of Romesh Gunesekera's *Reef*. The author provides a complex study of the perils of expatriation through the suggestion that assimilation, even marrying into British Stock, is the way forward for immigrants. The 'Fallen Paradise' offers nothing but corruption, violence and chaos. Gunesekera's ambivalence towards Sri Lanka disallows, rather than enables, the creation of sophisticated fiction. (94)

Minoli Salgado in his book *Writing Sri Lanka: Literature, Resistance and the Politics of Place* observes that "critical evaluations of Romesh Gunesekera's novels have been entangled in this invidious scripting of exoticism in a multitude of contradictory ways. His texts have been read to be in the service of exoticism, to work or subvert or redeploy exoticist impulses, and to affirm a diplaced or deferred exoticism in its perceived representation of the nation as a past paradise" (148). According to her, the recreation of Sri Lanka as a lost paradise comprises a "multitude of registers" ranging from the mythological to the stereotypical discourse of the Western outlook and tourist documents—"all of which work to commodify the country in Manichean terms. Paradise is, after all, the Garden of Eden, 'the abode of the blessed', 'a region of supreme bliss', a state of supreme felicity', a pleasure ground—a sexy and spiritual sell" (148). The idea of displaced exoticism in relation to the representation of past paradise, and the emotional registers evoked in the text point out to Gunesekera's reworking of the cultural coding in the structural and thematic frameworks of his novels which serves to explain the writer's apparent alienation from the homeland and the summative anxiety resulting thereof.

Critics thus question the author's cultural legitimacy in his various distortions of cultural tropes which serve as a basis containing "a universalizing representationalist assumption of mimesis, authenticity and truth telling in its reading of fictional representation" (Salgado 149). Minoli Salgado, at this point, quotes Ruvani Ranasinha as the latter assumes:

> Gunesekera and other expatriate Lankan writers have been viewed as preferred insiders and initiated informants in the affairs and culture of the East and their expatriation has conferred upon them the writerly virtues of detachment and objectivity. The acclaim these writers receive legilimizes and maintains the authority of stereotyped, unchanging ideas about the orient. (qtd. in Salgado 149)

Salgado argues that such a reading of Gunesekera as suggested by Ranasinha is both reductive and misleading. It is reductive in the sense that it fails to comprehend the very exoticism that nostalgia and stereotyping serve to reflect—the "radical uncertainty of cultural reclamation" (Salgado 149) which informs the works of the novelist. Above all, it is misleading as it assumes that the readerships beyond Sri Lanka are "equally bound to a purely representationalist reading of the text" (Salgado 149).

The novel focuses on a retrospective reconstitution of the various exploits of the two families—the Ducals and the Vatunases, recollected through the conversations between Chip and Pearl which are telescoped into a span of 24 hours, leading to a thickening sensation of the distant past, running parallel with the immediate past of the characters, experienced as British immigrants within the structural framework of Pearl's funeral. The novel with its careful manoeuvring of juxtapositions, of the intricately complex actions and mediations liberate "the historical narration from spatial and temporal mooring"

(Salgado 153). According to Minoli Salgado "History is spatialised, levelled into simultaneity and space temporalised, marked by the vicissitudes of an emergent time, so that both are rendered inherently provisional and unstable. It is a context in which dwelling is permanently displaced, making settlement permanently temporary" (153). Analogously, Chip, the narrator of the novel, is constantly on the move, unsettled in his linear narrativisation of the events. His momentary residence with his adopted mother Pearl is repeatedly destabilised by Prins' episodic visits and re-visits and excludes him from his so-called settled lodging. Minoli Salgado thus reflects up on the deliberately deferred conditionality of all 'homes' which are rooted not in the recreation of the past but in the anxiety registered by an inevitable loss:

> Home is therefore not a space that is deferred into the provisionality of the future or past, nor is it merely a mobile habitat, but rather it is located as a dwelling place marked by its imminent loss. It is haunted not by the ghosts of a knowable past, but by the spectre of inevitable loss in a way that projects the future proleptically into the present. The condition of predictive loss is reinforced by a narrative trajectory in which disrupted histories are shown to refuse to relinquish their secrets: the exact circumstances surrounding Jason Ducal's death and Prins' disappearance remaining unknown at the novel's close. It is a context that serves to present memory as 'a material force' in the mediation of competing temporalities. (153-54)

Gunesekera's reconfiguration of memory as a 'material force' to be utilised as the reconstitution of exilic space effectuates an imaginatively allegorical reclamation of the lost land as a re-inscription of the island nation. The regeneration of the island is then spatially understood in the connections and contrasts established between the exoticist and erotic mapping of the land inscribed by the Ducals and the Vatunases respectively. Pearl's imaginative reconstruction of Arcadia is thus mediated through her husband Jason's colonial desire for "place and status—geographical and social" (23). Arcadia becomes a dwelling place of the thwarted desires of the displaced diasporans with their colonial connections, "meditating these forms of territorial reclamation through the spatio-temporal idiomatics marked by the mobility of temporary habitation. 'Arcadia' as a pastoral idyll is thus unequivocally situated as the fantasy of the displaced subject, clearly located within an aesthetics that foregrounds its decontextualized, disembedded status" (Salgado 154). Gunesekera resists the exoticising impulse of mapping the margins and rather addresses the cultural disruptions and insecurities resulting from the combination of colonial, postcolonial and migrants' metaphorical mensuration of the land. The eroticism grounded in Vatunas' notion of territoriality, on the other hand, although rooted in a territory of desire does not not merely resort to an imaginative recreation but is clearly based on the material condition of immediate exploitation. The rapacious territoriality of Buttons Vatunas moves beyond the benign cultural mimicry of his counterparts, hence, "while his contemporaries emulated the vanities of their pre-war colonial masters, trying to transform themselves into brownskin imperial successors, Esra turned himself into a full-blown emperor" (103). Minoli Salgado in this context, concedes that:

> *The Sandglass* thus sets into operation a contrastive dynamic of competing models of territoriality in which the territorial dispute between neighbours has a subliminal allegorical resonance with contemporary territorial debates. By distinguishing between the imaginative reclamation of territory and the material conditions of its effects, Gunesekera splits the scripting of exoticist readings of land into the simulated dehistoricized registers of fantasy, and the active conquest, control and consumption of territory—between, in other words, the spectacle of compensatory retrieval and its active, brute enforcement. (155)

Gunesekera's enterprise, in this manner, seeks to destabilise the historical registers and foregrounds the spatio-temporal incommensurability of the migrant's position, and dislocates the imaginative territoriality into a point beyond the mere historical reclamation. The idea of home and belonging in this deterritorialised dialectics as Nasta suggests reveals "a preoccupation with the representation of an interior landscape of desire, a longing to enter the symbolic as a narrative journey" (213). Diasporic writing as exemplified by Gunesekera then is the expression of an immediate impulse to re-enact and reconstitute a diffused cultural order. As judiciously claimed by Minoli Salgado:

> Gunesekera's work reminds us that writing is not simply a place to live—a refuge from the violent clash of incommensurable realities—but also constitutes a regenerative means of addressing social and cultural disjunction. In displacing the past the novel also displaces destiny, opening the door for a future outside political violence in a para rational logic that works alongside real political events. For as Andre Brink has suggested, 'only by dreaming and writing the impossible can life be made possible once again'. (165)

The novel *The Sandglass* portrays the complexity and multiple modalities of 'home' that is reconfigured through a summative negotiation of identity in relation to the lives lived in England and Sri Lanka. Gunesekera's writing is characterised by a haunting flavour of the home country which activates in the diasporic individuals a sense of longing that forces them to revive and re-establish their urge of belonging to re-actuate their idea of identification. The characters in *The Sandglass* at different levels are engaged in enacting their respective imaginary homelands through the meshes of memories and simmering silences that are left unanswered or deferred in a differential equation of redefining the lost sense of identification as "unravelling the ways in which the discontinuities of time past and time present collapse spatial and temporal boundaries" (Nasta 216).

The Sandglass literally refers to a mechanical device to measure the flow of time which comprises two inverted glass bulbs vertically joined by a narrow passage through which sand trickles at a certain pace from the upper bulb to the lower one. When all the sand is accumulated in the lower bulb, the sandglass is inverted and the process of measuring time beings anew. The hourglass thus concretely suggests the time present as being between time past and time future. It becomes a symbol to recapture time—it not only symbolises the manner time fleets but also the common everydayness of life which acts as a connective link between the past and the present through the "repetitive experiences, attitudes and practices that both maintain themselves and alter across the wider stretches of time that make up ... human history" (Mulhall 178). As Susheila Nasta writes for the British Council in *Home Truths*:

> ... Gunesekera's major preoccupation ... is less with questions of psychic or physical displacement engendered by his character's diasporic histories than with exposing the artist's dilemma of representing such histories, caught as they are through memory and filters of the lens of time. And if, as is the case in *The Sandglass* the borders between time and space appear to be indistinct, this is not only due to Gunesekera's deliberate refusal to set up such artificial divisions, but also due to the narrative's implicit interrogation of how the process of writing from memory itself blurs such categories. (231)

According to Stuti Goswami, Chip, the narrator serves as "the negotiator between the past and the present, to weave the diverse memories into one tapestry. And yet, the swirling eddies leave gaping holes in the tapestry—manifested through the silences—leaving much of the answers, if not all to (the reader's) speculation." Prins' reconstitutive recollection of the past thus exemplifies these gaps in memory as he acknowledges: "Trouble is, when I look back I see him and everything else through so many filters. Nothing you can be sure of, you know. It makes it all very difficult. I have to build it up, pixel by pixel in my mind" (75). There are, therefore, rifts between Prins' memory of Pearl's life and Chip's re-telling of their family history as both are immersed in their own world of memory and silences. Chip admits that he knows much more than what Prins does, yet he maintains silence as Pearl has wished before her death: "But the Pearl he remembered was rather different from the one I had come to know" (7). The sandglass of narration as endeavoured by Chips thus "becomes the symbolic frame which signifies the novel's main subject. It is an image that acts both as a 'metaphor' for the passage of time and the need for the artist to capture that moment in the present, in what Gunesekera has called a continuous reworking of the 'process of transformation'" (Nasta 231).

The emotional ambience which environs the characters modulates memory in a transformational idiomatic of incoherent juxtaposition as the elemental aspects of the personal memories of pearl that encompass much of the Ducal's history cannot be put together nor can it be retrieved in the time's limiting frame are symptomatic of the gaps or silences in the memories as a form of metaphorical amnesia. But as Goswami has warned against any essentialist representation of memory as regular flow in the consciousness of the individual, "these memories do not flow in a continuum. Rather, these are episodic memories—gleaned from different sources at different times in different ways—that Chip tries to chip into bigger picture". The temporal schema of representation thus moves back and forth in time blurring the specificity of reference, underlying an 'everydayness' indelibly coloured by Pearl's life—"the apparent stasis, the almost mundanity of her knitting at her armchair, her butter rice, the fluorescent haze of the television's drone and bits and pieces from the past that the narrator Chip weaves together ... it was Chip, and Chip alone, who has always been a part of 'everydayness' of Pearl's life" (Goswami). Remembering which is akin to knowing, therefore, turns out to be a mode of re-living, a re-enactment of the experience of the past which is subdued by the distorting waves of time. Goswami thus points out to the differential matrix of incomprehensibility registered in the autobiographic memory as an integral phenomenon coalescing the past, present and future:

> In this flitting, much knowledge is lost. The gaps are glaring. At time, characters attempt at least, think of stopping time. As if, reading, writing, even not uttering anything would stop, albeit for a while, the flow of time, the indelible, incessant advances of time. The past—the 'what-has-been' becomes a befuddled dark matrix of incomprehensibility, for someone or the other

> has always kept the lights out. The future exists for the sake of itself, with a hollowed out present and none knows that the characters are unable to move forward—paralyzed by the past (Pearl), drawn back by the past (Prins), unaware of the future. After all, the past though not something under the present's control, but definitively constitutive of who (or what) it is.

The sandglass then becomes a fitting metaphor to represent these changes wrought in the memories of these diasporans desirous of a narrativised reclamation of the past as suggested by Gunesekera himself: "Sand is free moving, opaque and porous ... glass is hard transparent and non-porous. But there is a point, albeit at a different melting point when they are one and the same" (qtd. in Nasta 231). Stuti Goswami rightly observes that:

> ... the sand dunes, like rolling sea waves in the upper glass bulb reflect the paradox that besets the novel. The paradox of infinitude within a glass case. Of life's finitude. Of silence in ripples across a miniature desert. The paradox of the offspring of the Ducals recounting borrowed memories of the history of the Vatunases, who probable had, and has a hand at the steady deterritorializing of the Ducals from their land with an outsider sharing, storing and recounting memories of the Ducals—the paradox of a witness—an eye—of just one eye that sees—only partially—and that is silent (silenced) as in this work that can only see but not speak, for it is immersed in the sand.... Like the two glass cases joined by the aperture, the past and the future connected by the present. But, as in *The Sandglass*, the three realms (dimensions) transient, ever changing ever flitting.

Thus, towards the end of the novel "Chip is less concerned with the material details of the stories which perpetually run through his hands than with the artistic questions raised by the act of mediation itself" (Nasta 231). Chip's futile attempts at optimisation over the birth of Pearl's grandchild which he interprets to be the prelude to a new 'dawn' in the initiation of a "somehow better world" (278) serves to be a forced closure because the narrative which seems to be a reworking of reclamation turns out to be "a series of stories which melt into a predictable quest for place, we see that place is no convincingly determinant" (Nasta 231). Analogously, Chip's recurrent quest for refilling the gaps and silences in Pearl's life history is equated with his "repressed narrative of his own psychic survival" (Nasta 231) and perhaps, in turn, counterbalances a similar narratological impulse in the writer himself echoing his own survival strategy, at a metaphorical level. As regard Chip's own connection to the stories he describes, jotting and appropriating the fragments of other people's lives effectuates the emergence of yet another story untold and highlights the implicit germ of a narrative within a narrative. Moreover, the manner in which Chip emphasises the channelisation of his substances through the narrow passage of the sandglass helps "assuaging his longing to capture the realities of a world forever remade in 'the capricious acts' of disappearance which occur every day, we gain an insight into the complexity of Gunesekera's own task as a writer and his attempts in this novel to celebrate the 'resilience of all stories, even ones of disappearance to make new'" (Nasta 232). As suggested by Pearl in the chapter 'Darkness': "You see clearly only when it is empty, no? You can't look back until it is, but by then it's over. Empty. Gone. You have to turn yourself upside down and start all over again" (159).

The novel thus seeks to address the complexities informing the notion of home and belonging that is viewed as a transformative negotiation of identity in relation to the experiences and emotions encountered in Sri Lanka and England. The fractured memories of a diasporic past and a desire to reinvent colour the displaced lives of the individuals in their restless quest for self-re-actuation. Memory and desire, therefore, play an important role in the process of individuation and are intricately interlinked with one another as Uma Parameswaran argues: "... both occupy the same space and evolve to the centre; but the centre is located in a sense of exile, in a place that never was and hence the perpetual interplay, and endless torment" (*Writing the Diaspora*

321). Prins Ducal's life is endlessly tormented not because he arrives in London to accomplish his mother's funeral but by the unaddressed questions of the past which he seeks to unravel with his friend Chip. Chip, on the other hand, is tormented with the secrets which he keeps about Ducals family and is painfully encountered with the task of chronicling the bits and pieces which vaporously exist in the mist of his mortal mind. There is strong emphasis on the flitting movements of time as the spatial displacements wrought the lives of the characters with alternation beyond repair and an isolated Pearl feels "the world ... did not change much from place to place; not as much as it changed with passing time. It's time that wreaks havoc with us, you know. Plays hell with everything" (51). Her rejection of the homeland is triggered by the temporal and emotional isolation that trapped her life with a hostile ambience and her questing for a new life in England is essentially motivated by an innate urge to belong—to feel at home in London where she spent the happiest moments of her life with her husband. Pearl's shifting to London is a manipulative strategy to disown a strained past and to reclaim the cherished 'island' of the mind. As Chip, at one point, in the novel, introduces the theme of reclamation establishing a parallel between Pearl and Ravi's idea of immigration: "That was how Pearl came to England. In love with a shadow in her head that she couldn't quite focus on until she got here. Perhaps Ravi was simply repeating her own journey to England, but with different co-ordinates" (64). In Pearl's life, however, the political turmoil of the land, which results in the mysterious accidental killing of her husband Jason, registers an emotional calamity in her life which furthers her dislodging from the homeland and seeking refuge in England. On the other hand, Prins' rejection of the 'mother' for the sake of the 'motherland' embodies his quest to unravel the mysteries of a strained past troubling him endlessly as an inferno of his questing mind, allied with an economic concern to cash on the constricted condition in his homeland "by making money out of painting, tourism out of terrorism" (41). As Prins put it: "You have to escape and go where you can find yourself, or you stay and transform what is around you until it becomes your own" (37).

Unlike Prins', the predicament of Ravi is instituted by a physical isolation and emotional ostracism which he encounters in his long stay in America. His brown skin and appropriated English accent turn out to be the White Man's Burden which shock and startle the Americans he confronts: "My brown skin face was a bit of shock.... It was extraordinary.... In this country, it is my skin that people notice, that goes in front of me, everywhere. People look at me and they see darkness first. Even my shadow seems darker to them than theirs" (65). Ravi's 'Trishanku' like position lands him nowhere—A Sri Lankan by birth, living in London and then migrating to America—fragments his person into multiple consciousnesses—each of his roles being incompletely realised as "unfinished identities" (qtd in Braziel and Mannur 50). As Charu Mathur in his paper "Home as an Emotional Construct" observes:

> This results in a consumptive uncertainty regarding the construction of selfhood. The ambiguous identity leads to a hazy relationship with location so that the feeling of belonging becomes problematic. Ravi's passion for collecting travel tickets is indicative of this unstable relationship with land while his reluctance to leave "home" reveals a fear of dislocation. Ultimately, finding no place where he could feel at "home", he gets his own ticket out of life. "It's a question of memory ... should we remember things as a way of learning, or forget them as a way of healing?" Wonders Gunesekera. (30)

Gunesekera thus crowds his novels with people seeking anchorage in a new land where they can feel at home restructuring their idea of home in the dialectics of territoriality. Spatial and cultural boundaries are traversed to find an enunciative space—the 'third space', to use a Bhabhasque register of discursivity—that mediates the national and the diasporic while addressing the situatedness or otherwise of cultural determinants which reinstate and redefine the divergent contours of home and belonging. Minoli Salgado emphasises this mediation as revealing "the resistance of the nation to openness while simultaneously insisting upon its subjection to transactional practices":

> In the fields of literary and cultural analysis, such mediations demand a form of deterritorialization that is based upon our ability to re-situate ourselves—to move into dislocated spaces and find alternative origins and sites of belonging in them. It also requires us to both resist and acknowledge the centrality of closure; to retain an enduring belief that it is both necessary and possible to reclaim our multiple pasts without being claimed by them. (172)

Reconfiguring identity in terms of homing and belonging thus involves a series of subtle negotiations, moving back and forth in emotional allegiances and memories, pushed and pulled by multiple influences from multiple places, value systems and culturalities which inform the lives of the diasporans, with a certain fluidity in which they find themselves perpetually deferred from the lands of their origins—their respective so-called comfort zones. Gunesekera's protagonists therefore, keep on asking the Rushdian question: "[Is] it possible to be—to become good at being—not rootless, but multiply rooted? Not to suffer from a loss of roots but to benefit from an excess of them?" (Rushdie, *Joseph Anton* 72). As Charu Mathur powerfully feels:

> The "home" is structured on new linkages and circumstances of habitation as a requisite for survival. It exists on a constantly shifting axis driven by a desire to reshape whilst exposing the fictionality of all "homes". The territory of "home" is circumscribed as much by mental geography as by its representation in spatial and temporal terms. In Gunesekera's work, there is movement well beyond the stereotypical vision of a narrative of reclamation to a foregrounding of the impact of troubled Sri Lankan history and the rooms of memory they have spawned. The fundamental concern is a need for constant deferral, for "home" is an emotional construct constituted by memories and

> desires that question their own terms of reference and making of history. (30)

Gunesekera, in his novels, thus problematises the concept of diaspora by deconstructing the binaries between the home and the world, linking the global with the local in the differential dialectics of a cosmopolitan culture to engender the boundaries of home with an increasingly porous and shifting structure. As Nasta meaningfully argues: "… the sandglass is a potent symbol both for death and for life, for absence and presence, a conduit by which the artist can briefly hold the transformations wrought in human lives by passing of time. For the act of writing 'flashes up' its own revelation when they are least expected, lunching the writer and reader alike into a differently framed space" (232). Self-refashioning in this narrativised space becomes an act of evolving permeable relationships with the perceived world and beyond, and to exacerbate the inner landscape of mind with a contextual reconfiguration of cultural coordinates in the fluid poetics of transactive transformation.

Chapter 8
Conclusion

The representation of 'home' in the cartography of belonging is a much debated issue in the contemporary society as the world has witnessed unprecedented transnational flows of people across the globe in the last few decades. The migratory propensities of the human society trigger a re-assessment of the notions of home and belonging which includes reconfiguration of borders and boundaries that are continuously negotiated in a fluid poetics of unsettled identifications. Home has ceased to become a geographical entity and turns out to be an emotional site marked out by tangential locations and permeable connections across borders. The location of the self is thus disrupted beyond retrieval which interrupts and transforms the conventional spatial layouts of belonging, evolving a provisional concept of identity, which is far from being implanted in a territorial rootedness, is constantly challenged by the ambivalent nature of its very existence and its intersectional positionalities. Cultural identities, in these diasporic encounters, share a fluid space of shifting locations which transcends the nativistic politics of retrospective reclamation in the articulation of a solid, pure and stable identity. Identity, then, is a relational concept, multiple in its configuration that exists and develops in relationship with others in a socio-cultural context. Being situated at the border, the diaspora thus is exposed to the narrative of the diverse cultural groups and necessarily influences and transforms the modalities through which we seek to explore the ways of dwelling in this shared space of identification.

The basic premise which motivates this study involves an interrogation of the significance, relevance and capacity of a place to become home, with its informing features of collective memory and cultural identification and a summative explication of the notion of home and belonging as a response to the questions: "Where is home? Where do we belong? What constitute our sense of home or else homelessness? How does one relate the experience of diaspora as a contributory force to the formation of 'home' or 'homeland'? I would like to sum up by stating that the spatial parameters of home, both as fixed and liminal, problematises the rhetoric of identity formation and the supposed land of identification. Home tends more towards a range of fluid locationalities as the diasporans seek to embrace multiple possibilities, complex and innumerable ways of being and becoming and a permanent process of movement and change.

Identity, therefore, is not a stable and immutable entity admitting the possibility of a single, fixed sense of belonging, rather it becomes a construct which is an evolving process of maintaining identification beyond the limits of time and space in order to live with a difference which entails a transcendence from the clearly demarcated borders and boundaries of belongingness. According to cultural theorists, a fully unified, complete and coherent identity is a myth as it is formed and transformed constantly in relation to the ways individuals are represented and addressed within the framework of cultural configurations which environ them. Stuart Hall believes that identity in the postmodern world has becomes a "moveable feast" because "within us are contradictory identities, pulling in different directions, so that our identifications are continuously being shifted about" ("The Question" 277).

The transformative dynamics of locations and territories of the contemporary world no longer bind the people to a single particular space. The perception of disruption from a particular location constitutes the general texture of eternal human existence in a diasporic migratory reality because the privileged role assumed by 'home' doesn't comprise the prime goal of all human activity but becomes its essential condition and hence the perpetual movements and ceaseless commencements. The study of the space, therefore, is considered as one of the important determinants of identity drawing significant academic and critical intellections. In the everydayness of life itself, the two terms such as 'place' and 'space' are often used interchangeably, although there is important distinction between the two. 'Place' is said to be a concrete manifestation of the abstract idea called 'space'. The undifferentiated spatial entity is gradually assigned the status of a place as we tend to be familiarized with it and endow it with significance and value. As Yi-Fu Tuan argues, "if we think of space as that which allows movement, then place is a pause; each pause in movement makes it possible for location to be transformed into place" (6). I am, in this study, inclined to agree with Yi-Fu Tuan's opinion that space is necessarily associated with movement and place with relative stasis which makes me emphasise throughout my research that the relocation of the self is more focused on the socio-cultural space rather than a physical setting called place, delimited by the fixated premise of stability and security.

In the socio-cultural space of human society, 'personal space' is culturally conditioned and is highly dependent on the existing contextualities. Securing the sovereignty of that space and to prevent any transgression, definitive boundaries are erected to confine and construct it as 'home'. The mere possession of the territorial right over a place, however, does not ensure the construction of a home because the boundaries which premise a space do not entail a physical space but a cultural and psychological space which connotes ownership and belonging, and home is not a mere site for comfort and security but a vital point in which one negotiates the experience of belonging and unbelonging. Home, thus, becomes a significant determinant of identity in which belonging turns out to be an important qualification to determine the distinction between those having 'home' and those who are deprived of it. Home, in the words of Buechner then is "a place you feel you belong, and which in some sense belongs to you" (7).

The discourse of home also includes another important element: 'memory' whereby one reconciles the perception of nostalgia and resistance both at individual and collective levels as the real landscapes are inevitably intertwined with landscapes of memory. Landscape as a definitive product of mindscape points out to the nexus between place and memory which suggests that history is narratological, a product of the things being reminded and thus historical or collective memory is viewed as the product of external programming in which "personal memories have been reshaped into collective memories by forms of political intervention ... in landscapes, particularly through 'official' acts and objects of commemoration" (O'Keeffe 6). There is, therefore, the necessity to restate or redefine the notion of place-identity which are created for different reasons by different individual at different times, proffering a confluence of different narratives and thus are "user determined, polysemic and unstable through time" (Ashworth and Graham 3). The imagined past, interspersed through these narratives, provides resources for the imagined future, and collective memory or heritage becomes imbued with the imagining of the past and is more concerned with meanings and values than realities or actualities of the places. The transformed realities of the places thus help disowning or forgetting an unpleasant past that serves as a burden of the present, involving positive recreation of the present from the imaginary past that actually never was.

In the contemporary world of increasing globalisation, the notion of home as a stable and fixed location has changed to represent a state of constant flux characterised by instability rather than permanence, perpetually recreated and reconfigured in the migratory process of dislocation and its summative re-plantation of individual identity and belongingness. With the experience of dislocation and fragmentation, the conventional home of stability and physical centeredness assuming an unified, absolute reality becomes fractured and disrupted which anchors the individuals in eternal transit "between a plurality of life-worlds but come to be at home in none" (Nigel and Overing 160). The notion of home at once becomes a normative, spiritual and cognitive experience which correlates the metaphysical sense of homelessness with a sense of personal estrangement on the level of consciousness. Being 'homeless', therefore, according to this view, is not so much about movements or the fluidity of socio-cultural time and space but that "one is at home when one inhabits a cognitive environment in which one can undertake the routines of daily life and through which one finds one's identity best mediated—and homeless when such a cognitive environment is eschewed" (qtd. in Etoroma 103). The construction and enactment of home, both behavioural and ideational, thus is contingent up on the migratory process in which individuals deliberately operate as 'transnationals', traversing and transgressing the assumed socio-cultural borders of stabilising boundedness and imagine new possibilities of belonging on their way. Home, therefore, is not a fixed place of identification or belonging but rather "a constantly negotiated space between self and location" (qtd. in Sojka 521). Negotiating the tension between the stasis of the remembered home and the mobilised reality of the physical home left behind, consequently, lands these dislocated diasporans in a 'third space' which emerges out as an in-between space of cultural translation, markedly different from either alternatives of identifications. This 'liminal', in-between space is a highly reactive site of symbolic interaction, bridging the gaps and incongruities between the antagonistic binarism of the contraries which "prevents identities at either end of it from settling into primordial polarities" (Bhabha, *The Location* 5). This interstitial passage between fixated belonginess, according to Bhabha, "opens up the possibility of a cultural hybridity" (*The Location* 5) which necessarily foregrounds the significance of the 'threshold' existence implicating the indefiniteness of all home-making projects.

The meaning of home for these displaced diasporans then lies in the interactive process of cultural translation—the diverse ways whereby they strive to relocate 'home' in diasporic imagination. Salman Rushdie's idea of cultural negotiation echoes the concept of 'routes' rather than 'roots' that James Clifford emphasises in his work *Routes: Travel and Translation* which proclaims the fluid notion of home signalising the "multi-locationality across geographical, cultural and Psychic boundaries" (Brah 194). The notion of 'routes' or 'translation' as home or homing desire allows for a plurality of perceptions and heterogeneity of identifications because of its stress on multiple locations and journeys. It involves a fluctuating contextualisation that Rushdie calls "ambiguous and shifting ground" (*Imaginary Homelands* 15) or Homi Bhabha's "liminal space" (*The Location* 5) which points out to the inevitable non-essentialist conceptualisation of diasporic space where cultural hybridity becomes the defining principle.

The evolution of the 'third space' destroys the symmetrical representation of cultural formation as fixed and static. It deconstructs the historicity of cultural identification as homogenising, unifying and absolute force. For this reason, Bhabha contends that the in-between third space occupied by the diasporic subjectivities is stuffed with creative possibilities: "It is the space of interaction emerging in the cultural interstices that introduces creative invention into existence" (*The Location* 12). Diasporisation thus challenges the territorial model of nation-state and questions the rubrics of nation, nationalism and cultural homogenisation.

The postmodern thinkers Giles Deluze and Felix Guattari in *A Thousand Plateaus* seeks to recast this multiplicity of cultural representation with the rhizomatic theory of difference in which the world is no longer viewed as being comprised of distinct entities—aggregative and integrative—rather a fundamental saturation of difference becomes an essential condition for the possibility of the phenomena. Diaspora like rhizomes defies the dimensions of over simplification—on one hand, it focuses on the lines of articulation, of sedimentarity, strata and territories—on the other, it attends to the lines of flight, movements of deterritorialisation and destratification. It is territorialisation which constantly replicates the possibilities for deterritorialisation. Every rhizome in this irrepresentational disruption "contains lines of sedimentarity according to which it is stratified, territorialized, signified, attributed, etc. as well as lines of deterritorialization down which it constantly flees" (Deluze and Guattari 9). The diasporic individuals, like rhizome, in their search for a home, are thus endowed with a double perspectives of performative negotiations which entail an attempt at reproduction and reinvention of cultural determinants in which both points of departure and arrival are always in a constant flux, transgressing the stable and frivolous physicality of longing and belonging.

In Chapter II of this book, therefore, I have attempted an in-depth, comprehensive analysis of the diverse modalities of 'home' to explore and highlight the multidimensional contours and contents of diasporisation in the process of restoring the unselved souls in their respective reconstituted home which celebrates the fluidity of boundaries and the free floating idea of identity as imagined construction.

In the present research, two texts each of three authors are selected for close reading and analysis with a purpose to determine the perspective in which these fictional works deal with the construction of identity with reference to the conceptual analysis of home and belonging. The authors selected for theoretical and textual analysis namely Kazuo Ishiguro, Hanif Kureishi and Romesh Gunesekera have, in their works, seriously engage the problem of home, identity and belonging in different cultural contexts and thus the present study is particularly attentive to their projection of fictional 'home' in their literary works with a view to conceptualise the ethos of home in the framework of fragmented cultural space. The novelists discussed in this book are widely different from one another in their thematic presentations and narrative techniques, yet they, in their peculiar ways, seek to dramatise the perception of home and homing possibilities in their fictional works. The quest for home thus is a common motif in all the six novels selected for consideration in the research.

Chapter III of this study titled "(De)constructing Diaspora: A Study in Composite Identities" looks into the diverse aspects of diaspora in diaspora studies and criticism and the process whereby diaspora in the recent years has developed numerous connotations, including the relevance and efficacy of the term in the contemporary globalised world. The chapter also addresses composite identity formation of the diasporic subjects as a result of the ceaseless process by which the individuals find themselves continuously in a disconcerted space of multilocational belonging, nourishing contrary and ambivalent viewpoints simultaneously for survival in an alien ambience.

The chapter seeks to deconstruct the dominant models of fixity and boundedness within diasporic formations in the framework of transcultural representation which impact and shape the process of identity formation, subverting the fixed and stable notion of diasporic community, that radically challenges the reductive dialectics of methodical homogenisation.

The term 'diaspora' now is applied as a 'metaphorical label' for exiles, expatriate, refuges, immigrants, homeless or rootless individuals who are displaced from their original homelands and settled elsewhere in the globe. The term, in its recent usage connotes the 'deterritorialised' or 'transnational' people across the border of nation-states. Diaspora according to Leela Gandhi can be viewed "as a theoretical device for the interrogation of ethnic identity and cultural nationalism.... Not surprisingly, diasporic thought finds its apotheosis in the ambivalent, transitory, culturally contaminated and borderline figure of the exile, caught in a historical limbo between home and the world" (131-32). The movement from the familiar to the alien registers in the diasporans a traumatic sense of homelessness and the continued confrontation with disillusionment leaves them in a social, cultural and psychological void. Being constantly shifted between two psychological planes, they create a condition of living with duality developing dual perspectives and visions—the hope to return to the homeland and the desire to assimilate in the host land. This double consciousness of attachments and affiliations makes the diasporans stay suspended midway between contradictory positions like the mythological king 'Trishanku' of the Indian epic *Ramayana*, who was destined to move embodied to paradise but had to settle midway between the earth and the heaven, serves as an appropriate metaphor for the postmodern condition of migrants inhabiting the contested glocalised space of cultural fragmentation.

Home, therefore, is a series of emotionally charged mental images that the diasporans sustain and eulogise in their alienated space which is never a natural one as they have to negotiate between the overwhelming categories of attachments and identifications. This problematic space of divided loyalties has been a key focus in the recent diaspora studies. Against the historical prototype of the dispersed Jewish diaspora, the emphasis in the new discourse of diaspora has been increasingly on the positive dimensions of a transnational existence and cosmopolitan configuration that thrive on inclusiveness and enhance the lives of the marginalised. The creation of these multiple diasporic possibilities proliferates into the general condition of human life which is not territorialised in a single place. This lure of revisionary deconstructivism also reflects the eluding and enigmatic conceptualisation of the term as a constitutive aspect of human life and belongingness. For this reason, diaspora can be viewed as a concept that functions as a catalyst for interdisciplinary research pursuits which has the capacity to reveal and bridge the gap between theory and praxis. Diaspora, in this epistemological dialectics, interrogates the very nexus between conceptualisation and condition, breaking free from the bounds of a close system. The term diaspora has been derived from the idea of the scattering of seeds and as such it "must be allowed to take root, transplant, cross-fertilize, rather than fossilize" (Fernadez 7).

The notion of diaspora revolves round an inevitable duality, split or fragmented identities between multiple cultural references the diasporic subjectivities are exposed to. Epistemological diasporisation, in this sense, evolves dual points of references between the homeland and the host land where all knowledge becomes constructs, effectuating a 'split-epistemology' produced by the intersection of both structural and cultural conditions, inhabited by a specific diaspora. Thus, the multicultural domain, as exemplified in this book, in the case of Asian diaspora in Britain, works through a 'diasporic epistemology' of cultural contestation which exposes the redundancy of the cultural knowledge and other forms of hegimonising and ethnocentric modalities. Clifford refers to this spatial virtuality as "contact zones of nations, cultures and regions" ("Diasporas" 303) that views diasporic perception as transitional connection between belonging and unbelonging, disrupting the fixity and fetishism imposed by ethnic systematisation of human subjects.

This postmodernist model of diaspora connotes a condition rather than being definitive of a community. This condition not only displays a strong proclivity towards multiple journeys and localisation but also exhibits a subversive impulse of disrupting the boundaries of the binaries. It perpetuates a differential redefinition of cultural accommodation and syncretism, filtering out the pitfalls of essentialism and stereotypical reductionism. The substantiality of hybridity is thus reasserted, by the recreative 'third space' which is presented as a mode of articulation in the performative dialectics of engendering reflective possibilities and exists as an "interruptive, interrogative and enunciative space of new forms of cultural meaning and production blurring the limitations of existing boundaries and calling into questions established categorizations of culture and identity" (Meredith 3). Stuart Hall, like Bhabha, thus analyses cultural identity as a relational and interactive entity—"fluid, contingent, multiple and shifting" (McLeod 225) which can be contrasted with the 'border lives' of Bhabha in which concepts are overlapping, hybridised in shifting subjectivities that promotes the necessity and possibility of replicating new cultural landscapes for these displaced diasporans. Human subject is no longer viewed as grounded in a fixed identity but rather is a discursive effect generated in the act of enunciation. Diasporisation and hybridity then share the commonalities—the denial of the essentialist positions of home and belonging, purity and inherent authenticity of cultural constants. Diasporic composite formation thus takes up the virtual 'third space' as an incontrovertible 'in-between' position that challenges fixity, authenticity and fetishism of monolithic cultural configuration. The actualisation of 'self' as well as 'other' is believed to be constructs on the same ground and allows an unprecedented cosmopolitan nomadism which perpetually dynamicises the idea of belonging and rootedness.

The next important topic for discussion in my research comprises the notion of Englishness and the politics of belonging in a multicultural society such as England. Chapter IV of this dissertation thus focuses on the developing sense of belonging among the immigrants subjects in Britain which is viewed as an ongoing process of redefinition that involves the rhetoric of inclusion and exclusion in a wide variety of cultural groups inextricably knitted together. The chapter seeks to address questions such as: What is Englishness? Is there any quintessential definition of Englishness which may circumscribe the race with holistic exclusionary properties as a site for resistance? How does immigration status in England affect people's sense of belonging? How far multiculturalism as a policy and philosophy is successful in abandoning the myth of monocultural nation-states? What actually comprises the right to cultural maintenance and community formation in an open environment like England? These questions are vital and relevant in the framework of my research because England serves as a common location not only for the novelists such as Kazuo Ishiguro, Hanif Kureishi and Romesh Gunesekera but also for the protagonists in the selected novels who are forever attentive to the multicultural diversity of England in the quest for their respective homes, carving out a place and identity for themselves in the alien land of diasporisation.

Englishness can safely be theorised in Foucauldian terms as the product of a particular discursive field in which various socio-cultural institutions play crucial roles. England is one of the societies in which the idea of cultural and ethnic diversity, the question of multiculturalism and the discourses on nation and identity have gained currency in recent decades. Attempts have been made to redefine the hegemonic discourses of culture, nation and identity including the critiques of Western colonialism to the struggles of the diasporic peoples in the land of the white majority. A central phenomenon in this counter-hegemonic discourse has been challenging the dominant narratives of history, ethnic and cultural stereotyping and white supremacy. These challenges are important factors in the current debates about Englishness and the forms of identity and belonging these conceptualisations of Englishness enable, preclude and admit. Cultural critics have pointed out that the myth of homogeneity attached to the idea of Britain as a nation was both the result of the imperialist agenda and the evolution of a Eurocentric modernity that was unable to hold the true spirit of an inevitable immigrant past. The essentialist myth of Englishness is long endured but exists with an intercultural diversity and racial mixture that heterologically informed the British life. For the last few decades, "Englishness has often been constructed as a heterogeneous, conflictual composite of contrary elements, an identity which is not identical with itself" that focalises the inner dissonance of the ruptured self of England divided within itself for it cannot be presented and characterised by "an essential core identity from which the other is excluded" and it is this non-fixedness that "enabled it to be variously and counteractively constructed" (Young, *Colonial Desire* 3). England by the end of 20th century, as a post-imperialist nation, was fast losing its hold on a sense of coherent national identity as the significant presence of the diasporic others in the cartography of its national history exposes its faltering myth of Empire and its declining fantasy of the invented Englishness which apparently problematises and complicates the linear historicity of the Western modernity itself. A new world order thus begins to emerge in Britain which seeks to reconstitute the rigid socio-cultural configurations of belonging, inverting the traditional conception of Englishness by introducing to it a permeable pattern of rediscovering the self and national identification.

The supposedly homogeneous combination of a nation then is a myth which can never be translated into reality. As Robin points out, "the imagined unity of the [English] nation has always struggled to cope with actual diversity and difference" (486) that is suggestive of a movement from the nationalistic to an urban framework of representation, in this case, the city of London as the centre of global transactive interactions which replaces the conventional model of cultural cohesiveness with a hybrid system of multiple projectivities. The city of London then can interestingly be presented as having dual functions and is viewed as a metaphor for the nation that incubates new cultural formations disrupting the old forms of stabilised cultural configuration. London as the home of many disparate ethnicities becomes multifarious and multi-dimensional in its referentiality and while 'nation' proffers "stability and continuity the city offers important possibilities for cultural unsettling and transformation" (Robin 491).

New forms of belonging are thus evolved out from this multicultural realities represented by metropolitan city life and the densely diasporised cultural space in which new modes of identifications are worked out with a reconfigurated version of Englishness which involves an imagination of openness and an all-inclusive cosmopolitan vibrancy.

England at this crossroad of belonging confronts with the necessity to redefine its core culturality and the premises of nationalistic identification when the idea of multiculturalism is rethought in the framework of a multi-ethnic Britain as proposing ways to eliminate racial discrimination and the integration of the racial others into mainstream life of the nation. The need to address the race-relations and ethnic diversity in Britain was one important aspect of the Parekh Report entitled *The Future of Multi-Ethnic Britain* published by the Runnymede Trust in October 2000. The report champions the vision of multiculturalism and attacks the essentialised conceptualisation of the community and the self and aims at forging a new national narrative claiming that Britain is not only a "community of citizens" but also a "community of communities" in which difference and diversity are always welcomed and celebrated (Parekh, Preface viii). The commission on *The Future of Multi-Ethnic Britain* scrupulously distances itself from the homogenised, bounded and monolithic notions of community invoked in the earlier approaches to multiculturalism and proposes a balance between cohesion, equality and difference, seeking to evolve an anti-essentialist model of an all-inclusive Britishness which fosters an understanding that all identities are in a process of transition, and pursing a pluralistic vision of human culture.

The new vision of multiculturalism presented by the commission aims at subverting the container model of the nation-state underscoring the need of core values pertaining to Englishness, Britishness or whiteness and proposes a common belonging with "shared cultural meaning" (Parekh, *The Future* 16) and stature which emphasises social cohesivity with an eternal disregard for "the oppressive uniformity based on single substantive culture" (Parekh, *The Future* 56). The notion of belonging in these critical cross-cultural connectivities thus critique "the myth of homogenous and monocultural nation states" when advocating the rights of minorities in an alienated foreign atmosphere (Castles, *Ethnicity and Globalization* 5). There is, therefore, no strict relationality between the individual and the nation, the ethnicity and the nationality because created nations are "imagined political communities" and are both "limited and sovereign" (Anderson 6) for ideas can serve as powerful basis of social action and reaction. The notions of 'nation' and 'nationality', above all, are modern constructions.

Chapter V of the present study titled "Identity, Memory and the Shifting Contour of Home" is entirely devoted to the textual analysis of Ishiguro's two novels such as *The Remains of the Day* and *When We Were Orphans* in which the novelist exquisitely extrapolates the cross-cultural sensibilities of the immigrant subjectivities to a grander scale of post-war global dispersion. Ishiguro, as a 'multicultural personae' in the post-war Britain, attempts to invert the status of diasporic bewilderment in an alien land with the native's local contentment in the host land, with a deeply-seated sense of estrangement which is viewed more as a result of internal dislocation rather than an alienation inflicted from without. Ishiguro challenges his reader's expectations by pondering the issue of diasporisation outside the conventional framework of alien location and racial identification. His cultural critique operates in a subtle mechanism of tactical intricacy whereby he deliberates the construction of a discursive site which dexterously transfers to the English context a formulaic pattern of Japanese way of life in the meticulous implementation of highly formal exterior to conceal tensions, fragmentation and self-deception. Unlike Kureishi and Gunesekera, who seek to portray the diasporic sensibility of the characters directly in the form of territorial dislocations and the resulting nostalgic enunciation in the process of self-actualisation in an alien ambience, Ishiguro "depicts diaspora as a tragedy more communal than individual, a disjunction more historical than geographical, and most noticeably, a phenomenon more global than regional" (Cheng). Ishiguro's ambivalent position allows him a dual perspective of transformative transaction with a fragmented past in which memory plays a pivotal role in reconfiguring the identities of the individuals, retrospectively rendered through the fragile fragments of a dynamicised memorialisation.

Ishiguro's awareness of his cultural bifurcation and his perception of 'not quite' belonging to either of the culture makes him a homeless writer who has "no clear role, no society or country to speak about, Nobody's history seems to be my history" (Vorda and Herzinger, "An Interview" 83). To be denied having any clear role in history is to negate the very premise of identification and hence the need to recollect those memories of the past and to recreate their ambience through fictional projections. The narrative itself, therefore, serves as a retentive mechanism to capture the remains of the past, to refashion a Japan of the mind which is now possessed only in fragments as a "shaky edifice we build out of scraps" (Rushdie, *Imaginary Homelands* 12) as representing the narrative of the homeland: "I just invent a Japan which serves my needs. And I put that Japan together out of little scraps, out of memories, out of speculation, out of imagination" (qtd. in Mason 9). His novels then are ceaseless experimentation of validating his experience to recollection in the preservation of his imaginary homeland.

Ishiguro's *The Remains of the Day* thus focalises this Japanese subtlety in the person of the narrator/protagonist Stevens, who, in his recollections of his years of services at Darlington Hall, reveals an exquisite Japanese mode of life in his hyperactive attention to individual detail, his pride in his profession of butlership, his rigorous insistence on performing duties restraining his emotional propensities, his unshaken faith and loyalty to his master are some of the prominent aspects of Japanese collective consciousness. Stevens' unwavering sense of 'dignity', moreover, which allows him to remain emotionally unmoved in his confrontation of his father's death, is essentially a Japanese ethical code subtly transmuted into the character of an English butler who appears more English than many English gentleman. Stevens' notion of dignity which he seeks unwaveringly to uphold throughout his life even provides a parallel which equates the ethical codes of chivalry in the medieval ages with that of the Samurai Warrior in a Japanese context.

The novel is an extended experimentation in the poetics of identification reconfigured by the fragile fragments of memorialisation. The entire novel is constructed around the motif of a journey—Stevens' real journey has a metaphorical parallel in the trip his mind takes to the narrative residues of the past—in which his recollection is purposive of the prefigurement of his life as well, for the butler generates a view version of his past life that is more acceptable to him than his real-life story. To impart his existence a substantial novelty, he narrates his life history in a manner that conceals the "terrible mistakes" (239) of his life. He must revisit his past—the untrodden spots of his emotional life—to evaluate the meaningfulness of his present life. His contemplation on the meaning of butlership thus is a way to justify his life in Darlington Hall as his identity is grounded and built on the dignified position he holds in the service of his lord. In his opinion, greatness in a butler "has to do crucially with the butler's ability not to abandon the professional being he inhabits" (42). He compares the English butlers with the continental ones who have the tendency to deviate at slightest provocation. Yet it is his obsessive longing for this kind of greatness and dignity which shatter his possibility of retaining his romantic love. Shrouding his true self within this professional function, he drives Miss Kenton to marry another man. Miss Kenton recognises Stevens' pretensions: "Why, why, why do you always have to pretend" (153) and reveals his greatness to be a masquerade, a lie, a reluctance and inability to see the truth. His ideal that in his service to a great gentleman like Lord Darlington, he is serving the whole humanity falls into insignificance as his master himself with his old-fashioned idea of chivalry is secretly involved in the cause of Munich and Nazi appeasement. His profound confidence on the ideal of dignity begins to crumble which reveals that there is no greatness to have, in subordination, for which he has sacrificed his own growth and development as a human being and as an emotional creature.

Stevens' quest for his identity thus is a cumulative process which involves the combination of his disparate engagements with the various issues the novel seems to address, including his conceptualisation of 'dignity', his repressive ideology of self-denial, his reconciled critique of the twilighted existence of the British Empire and the notion of Englishness which are intricately related with the idea of home in the reformulative dialectics of identity and belongingness. Ishiguro in *The Remains* subverts the stereotyping assumptions and attitude related to the idea of English butlership and English gentleman to demonstrate the hollowness of these fixed categories and how they fall an easy prey to the misguided ideal of their respective lives which are indelibly coloured by their individual experience of the national history. This is also no coincidence that the novel begins with the summer of 1956, the time of Suez Crisis which witnesses the gradual declining of England as an Empire. Darlington Hall symbolises Englishness, tradition and aristocratic propensities. Stevens' nostalgic memorialisation of the lost grandeur can be compared with the present status of the estate which is handed over to an American named Mr. Farraday is suggestive of the growing American influence.

Indeed, Britain finds in Stevens a parallel of its rationalising proclivities towards the error of the past in rewriting the histories of its dismantled Englishness. The disruption of Stevens' proud world of butlership and the magnificent Darlington Hall thus coincide with the final glow of Britain's supposedly glorious imperial enterprises. Stevens with his unreliable reminiscences presents the unreliable configuration of historical engagements in the catastrophic development of Britain's omnipotent imperiality. The historical allusions in the novel unfold a larger theme of negotiative encounter between the past and the present which happens to be a principal concern for the immigrant authors in Britain.

The myth of Englishness takes a different turn in Ishiguro's *When We Were Orphans*. From his childhood days in Shanghai, Christopher Banks construes through the mysteries of Conan Doyle detective stories an imaginary homeland permeated with "the air of English lanes and meadows" crisscrossed by "foggy streets" (62). His decision to become a detective is certainly motivated by his desire to be sufficiently English and his firm belief that the mythical Englishness which he wishes to subscribe to is to be properly manifested in the aura and mission of the fictional Sherlock Holmes. Envisioning China as the root of all evils, he internalises, the myth of a sinister and barbarous Oriental World which must be rescued by the civilised and moralistic England to restore global harmony. Banks' proverbial innocence considers China as an infant who is in the dire need of the West's protection, but to his utter amazement, he discovers that it is he who is prematurely deprived of the parental care and guidance—disillusioned and bewildered in the Oriental World. His moral confidence that he will bring peace and order by "rooting out evil in its most devious form" (31) that threatens "to put civilization to the torch" proves even more infantile than the land he vows to guide to safety from apparent collapse. Challenging Banks' immaturity and Uncle Phillip's hypocrisy, the novel subverts the myth of the White Man's Burden that the civilised, enlightened British self is entrusted with the moral responsibility to civilise the primitive Chinese Other. The pomposity of the benevolent paternalism, however, is later deflated as filtering out of Banks' delusions when he confronts the essential facts in their manifold disguises. Banks' proud, detective world deteriorates into dust when he is enlightened with the truth by Colonel Hasegawa that the Japanese soldier, whom he mistakes for his childhood friend Akira, is in fact a deserter. Even a more mortifying fact, for the proud detective is that Wang Ku, the Chinese Warlord, has been his benefactor for all these years, paying for his expenses on his stay in England, and that the evil actually does not lie in the Oriental China but emerges from the very West.

The novel *When We Were Orphans* is an imaginary experiment with private memory—the undeciphered past of the protagonist—in search for a lost identity and 'home' in the actualisation of the self. Although it is understood that nostalgia may bring misery, "Ishiguro also demonstrates that it can serve as a foundation for imagining a world better than one's present" (Weston 337). Banks thus dwells on his memories to unravel his true identity and the source of his orphanhood which continues to poison all his remaining life. Ishiguro's protagonists including Stevens and Banks must experience the cathartic effect of a reconstitutive memorialisation which leads them to a summative confrontation with the obvious realities which have so far eluded their grasp. James Procter contends that "All of Ishiguro's novels to date, narration is, at least partly, a therapeutic process, the novels are not attempts to render the past convincingly, but rather to pursue how individuals interpret and construct that past" (qtd. in Abdulgawad 5). Ishiguro in *When We Were Orphan* thus explores the idea of fragmentation which struggles to arrive at a modest sense of identity and positionality in terms of psychic displacement in the global and domestic spheres.

As the title of the novel implies, Banks is not the only orphan present in the story and that there is a general proliferation of orphans in the texture of the work. Banks is not only orphaned at a younger age, he later adopts Jennifer who also is orphaned at the same age. Sarah, the only woman, he loves also lost her parents in her childhood. Moreover, Mr. Lin, the owner of his family house in Shanghai also relates to the condition of orphanhood when he talks of an orphan girl adopted by his father who is treated by his son as sister. The entire texture of orphanhood finds a succinct expression in the response of Sarah Hemmings when the later is inquired about her parents by Banks: "It seems like forever", she says and adds: "But in another way, they're always with me" (48). The motif of orphanhood then becomes a common condition for the whole humanity and through its metaphorical multiplication transforms into a collective experience.

Banks, like Ishiguro, is a "cultural amphibian" (Buendia 27) who straddles two countries and two cultures simultaneously. Banks at a tender age is being transported to England from Shanghai when Colonel Chamberlain reassures him that he is finally going home which makes him burst into tears: "As I saw it, I was bound for a strange land where I did not know a soul, while the city steadily receding before me contained all I knew" (30). Banks is deprived and displaced not only from his childhood security but also from his homeland of identification.

At the end, he realises that the narrative of 'return' is a near impossibility as Colonel Hasegawa illuminates quoting from a Japanese poet: "Our childhood becomes like a foreign land once we have grown". Banks is inevitably estranged from both his old and new lives. Banks' orphanhood not only reflects a movement away from his childhood and homeland but also exemplifies a similar journey on the part of the novelist away from the narrative realism of a detective plot. The mythic voyage Banks embarks to the heart of his dark fantasies finds an analogue in Ishiguro's journey as a novelist "*closing in on some strange, weird territory* that for some reason obsesses me" (Vorda and Herzinger 84). The novelist's obsessive return to this territorial and temporal domain is an experiment "to write out of something that is unresolved somewhere deep down" (Vorda and Herzinger 85) which echoes a similar impulse in Banks' compulsive obligation.

The condition of orphanhood in the novel thus becomes a trope for transnational identity. The protagonist gradually comes to a recognition that the 'feared other' is placed within the self, discursively formed out of its own fear (Finney, "Figuring the Real" 2). Orphanhood for Banks is a sense of utter homelessness which registers in the individual an anxiety to belong. Banks' sense of homeliness, his childhood and the scientific precision of his professionalism disintegrate before him like his unpredictable memory. By a systematic duplication of these incompatibilities, Ishiguro seems to universalise the theme of homelessness and challenges the essentialising contours of home and belonging. Like Stevens of *The Remains of the Day* who finally realises the significance and efficacy of the bantering skills, Banks in a most melancholic epiphany understands and accepts the true meaning of orphanhood as he declares: "for those like us, our fate is to face the world as orphans, chasing through long years the shadow of vanished parents ... for until we do so, we will be permitted no calm" (313). In a similar fashion, Akira quotes the Japanese monk: "It was we children who bound not only a family, but the whole world together" (73) which can be called home.

Next, in Chapter VI of this book, I have attempted a detailed study of Hanif Kureishi's two novels namely, *The Buddha of Suburbia* and *The Black Album* in which the novelist is particularly attentive to the factors that demonstrate a fast transformation of the conventional notion of identity as fixed, essential and strictly homogenising to an ontological stance of hybridised cultural formation, focusing on the in-between existential reality of the immigrant subjectivities, fostering ambivalent perceptions of a fragmented cultural space. The protagonists of the novels under consideration such as Karim and Shahid find themselves forever suspended in an in-between position of contradictory emotions whereby a sense of utter rootlessness and a lack of essence of any kind is strongly registered in their individual psyches. Both the protagonists view migrancy as a metaphysical condition of life which obscures and dislocates the very idea of the unified self, and the multiplicity of being that is focalised through their dispositions offers intriguing points of intellection on the issues of hybridity and its relation to the provisional theatricality of identity and belonging. Karim and Shahid as hybrid diasporans exhibit in their characters an aura of restlessness and embrace a life in movements, struggling against the constraints of authenticity in a society that is preoccupied with clear-cut absolutes and exclusive positionalities.

Karim of *The Buddha of Suburbia* thus recognises his hybrid heritage and thrives on an acting career which significantly manifests his "dispositional dimensions of life" (Butler and Spivak 4) which cannot be translated into a traditional mode of identification as a normative position suggesting consistency and coherent constituents of personhood. Shadwell is totally mistaken into believing that Karim is not cast for his experience but for his authenticity: "In fact, you are Mowgli, you're dark skinned, you're small and wiry, and you'll be sweet but wholesome in the costume" (142-43). There is no doubt that the authenticity, Shadwell is questing for, emerges from the oriental stereotype of Indian boy—dark, exotic and speaking an Indian accent. Authenticity here then becomes an excuse for continued stereotyping. It's a strategy to control the conceptualisation of the orient. Karim at a point in the novel, therefore, lets the audience see through his performative projections and discover the invention behind his theatrical performance of Mowgli: "I sent up the accent and made the audience laugh by suddenly relapsing into Cockney at odd times. 'Leave it out Bagheera', I'd say" (158). Karim's apparent dilution of the stereotype exposes the incongruity of his role and reveals the discursive structure of culture which is constructed through racial signifiers. Karim's free-floating permeability with cultures is more a result of the fact that ethnicity to a large extent is a construct. As Schoene pertinently observes: "Karim is only ever true to his own proprioceptive sense of authenticity.... Any pre-packaged identity or definitive self-image are rejected as encumbrances obstructive to the free realization of his individuality.... The traditional concept of identity has become impractical to Karim" ("Herald of Hybridity" 120).

Karim's rejection of a closed model of essentialist discourse inaugurates a new process of identity construction that supports a fluid notion of identity formation and celebrates the glorified omnipresence of man's hybrid nature. Karim later invents into himself another fictional character named Tariq which again points out to the insignificance of English stereotypical assumptions and reflects the self-refashioning project of the protagonist who is successful in embracing any kind of cultural modifier that comes in his ways: "I became more energetic and alive as I brushed in new colours and shades.... I felt solid myself" (217). Karim knows well that identity like culture is a process and not a product which should be recognised and reinvented, investing new features into it, as Karim later remarks: "If I wanted the additional personality bonus of an Indian past, I would have to create it" (212-13). James Procter argues in this connection that "his stable, hybrid identity is not simply a product of ethnicity (of being Indian and English), but of locality ... Karim is a Chameleon ... he reinvents and repositions himself as black or white, as Asian or Cockney as the situation suits him" (153). In a number of situations in the novel, Kureishi demonstrates the fluid nature of identity and belonging in which characters are represented as 'constructs', open to shifting territoriality and re-inscription.

Yet, the search for a foundation makes Haroon, Karim's father, to give up his attempts at assimilation and retreat into a constructed oriental identity as the exoticised Buddha of Suburbia as stereotyped by the Western discourse. He is placed at another extreme against Eva's son Charlie who takes to punk culture and "was selling Englishness, and getting a lot of money for it" (247). Haroon, on the other hand, prefers to sell his Indianness donning the mask of a religious preacher leading meditation and yoga sessions. It is, however, the height of irony, that his followers are deceived by him as he consciously affiliates himself to a cultural legacy, obviously gathered from the London bookshops, that all his ideas are borrowed "from this books on Buddhism, Sufism, Confucianism and Zen which he had bought at the Oriental bookshop in Cecil Court" (5). Karim's career, in this sense, resembles his father's as both rely upon theatrical enunciation of their performative identities in reinventing Asian personalities for the consumption of their occidental audience. This new identity has been successfully perpetrated as there is an 'audience' that opens itself up to it which necessarily echoes Bhabha's conceptualisation of the colonial dependence: "It is as if the very emergence of the 'colonial' is dependent for its representation upon some strategic limitation or prohibition *within* the authoritative discourse itself" (86). The coloniser's ideological gaze on the exotic 'Other' equates Haroons' being and Haroon simply confirms to these prefigured ideas. Haroon's performative engagement with an exoticised Indian, with his oddly brewed cocktail of Eastern mysticism, demonstrates the constructed, fabricated notion of authentic, essentialist, ethnic and racial identity rendered almost null through the power of parody.

However, one should not overlook the important difference that informs the characters of Haroon and Karim. While Haroon believes that it is only through an authenticated version of a singular position (Indianness) that he can survive and succeed in an alien ambience, Karim is reluctant to take up any of the position available to him and celebrates the herald of hybridity recognising the fluidity of subject position, being perpetually dissatisfied with society's restrictive frame of bounded singularity. Karim is convinced of the performative profundity of these categories which "produce its slippage, its excess, its difference" (Bhabha, *The Location* 86) and his subversive activity thus dismisses all essentials as delusion that operates ambivalently in an "area between mimicry and mockery" (Bhabha, *The Location* 86). Karim can be represented as a fictional embodiment of Bhabha's theory of mimicry that seems to play out the philosophy of multiple, hybridised belonging which explicitly reveals the free-floating, variable theatricality of identity as superficial and groundless. Karim's sexual adventures, similarly, in this sense are performative projections which can never be measured by cultural standards and viewpoints. Karim's mockery of an essentialised world of monolithic absolutes echoes Butler's account of the erratic identity roles that "the ontology of substances ... is not only an artificial effect, but essentially superfluous" (34).

Shahid, the protagonist of *The Black Album*, on the other hand, is portrayed as intellectually more sound and responsible than Karim who wants "to be challenged intellectually and in every other ways" (5) and therefore suffers more than the latter. After his father's death he seeks to break away from his family to begin a new life in the city, away from the disheartening suburban realities: "The city would feel like his; he wouldn't be excluded; there had to be ways in which he could belong" (16). Shahid's in-between position allows him to live with a duality: he permanently oscillates between two sets of values and contradictory emotions provided to his being by his black friends and his white lover. Deedee, his lover, helps fostering in him an open, liberal outlook towards life while his fundamentalist friends constantly influence him to adopt the conservative religious values prescribed by Islam. Shahid feels that he has got multiple selves in himself and attempts to make a choice: "Which was his real, natural self" (147). He begins to experiment with several extremes at hand and even considers becoming a racist: "I wanted to be a racist ... my mind was invaded by killing-nigger fantasies" (11). The next moment he finds himself confronting another extreme of his character by joining the book burning demonstration with his fanatic friends as an act of protest against religious transgression, grooming himself as a hardcore fundamentalist.

Gradually, he feels that there is something missing in his life: "I kept thinking there was something I lacked" (10) and consequently he aspires to carve out a place for himself grounding his faith in religion. Even if he gets involved with the Muslim fundamentalist friends headed by Riaz, he is never fully committed to their enterprise. An eternal conflict between his writing ambition and religion informs his psychological disposition which serves as a stepping stone towards his maturity. He experiences a transition from his Pakistani ancestry to his oft-desired identity as a Briton. He begins to explore different domains of understanding such as race, religion, culture, etc. to find his place in the society he lives. He recognises the fact that identity is inevitably about transformation, growth and development and by the end of the novel he is mature enough to admit: "There was no fixed self; surely our several selves melted and mutated daily? There has to be innumerable ways of being in the world" (274).

Kureishi, in *The Black Album* presents the fundamentalist Muslim student's militancy as a concrete response to ethnic and racial discrimination. A fundamental assertion of Islamic identity seems to provide a positive identity for these Asian youth. As Chad abhorrently declares: "No more Paki, me a Muslim" (128). The pursuit of fundamentalist principles, in this sense, is an attempt to define one's identity for people like Chad and Riaz. Chad admits of finding stability in joining the group of the Muslim friends. Chad was adopted by white parents and his longing to belong stems from his sense of insecurity as explained by Deedee: "The mother was racist, talked about Pakis all the time and how they had to fit in" (106). Chad can clearly see that he has no proper connection to either Pakistan or Britain and his in-between existence leads him to search for stability in his life which makes him compare his position with those in the society "who effortlessly belonged" (106). Chad's character can be contrasted with that of Haroon whose constant subjection to racial discrimination enables him to take up specific position in the society to bring out to the fore the authenticity of his disposition.

The novelist deliberately depicts the Muslim fundamentalism practised by Riaz and his group to which Shahid seeks to belong in opposition to the liberal individualism of the West defended by Shahid's lover Deedee Osgood. The characters in the novel thus stand for conflicting forces and belief systems: "... democracy and freedom of speech versus authoritarianism and censorship; Shahid's love for literature and his delight in imaginative exploration, pitted against the group's dogmatism and resistance to art" (Ranasinha 90). By representing these contradictory impulses in continuous opposition, Kureishi undertakes to proliferate the binary patterning between anti-intellectualism and the free, open analysis of Western rational but liberal thought. Shahid is thus perpetually torn between the appeal of religious conservatism and the emphatic claims of subjective imagination. Shahid contemplates and mediates a position between these extremes and finally subscribes to neither views. He embraces a hybrid cultural identity which violates bounded rootedness and absolutist perceptions of existence. Like his fictional counterpart Karim of *The Buddha*, Shahid tends to occupy a liminal in-between space which is permanently unsettled and unfixed and where heterogeneity is the rule rather than exception. He asserts to himself: "I can't be limited" (272) and "rejected both deadly bourgeois life style and fanatic intellectualism in the name of the capricious, fluid, playful imagination" (Weber 129). Shahid's rejection of the "ecstatic rigidity" and embracing a life of uncertainties and fragmentation can be viewed as his transition from the in-between space to a hybridised position which unsettles the "'universalist' or 'essentialist ways of thinking, by means of a characteristically subtle, dense and metaphorically slippery rhetoric" of representation (Walder, *Post-colonial Literatures* 79). He eventually realises the limitless possibilities of his sense of identification and belonging. In the narrative of his sequestered self, he explores the multiple modalities of cultural configuration which is formed, reformed and transformed continuously in the fleeting multiplicities of variable existentialities. Following his curiosity, Shahid appreciates that his place in British Society in terms of ethnic, racial and national affiliation doesn't necessarily preclude a definite and clear role.

Chapter VII of this book titled "Reconfiguring the Inner Landscape: Self-refashioning and Belongingness in Romesh Gunesekera's Novels" examines the cultural dynamics of the displaced diasporans enacted through multiple diasporic movements across the globe in quest for the lost home in which memory plays a significant role bringing about a symbiotic confluence of the time past and time present which helps evolve a reconfigurated version of identity in the discourse of home and belonging. Gunesekera in his fictional manoeuvres seems to suggest that feeling at home is essentially a subjective and culturally determined link to the imaginary, and the memory of home is recreative of the inner poetry of the private self which is evoked by emotion and not by factual recollections. Identity, in the framework of Gunesekera's novels, becomes an unsettled entity marked out by the discontinuities of time and space in which, through the ambiguity of displacement, the diasporans are able to reconstruct the inner landscape of mind to perpetrate their sense of belonging, disrupting the idea of the bounded rootedness and homogenised belonging.

Gunesekera's debut novel *Reef* tells the elegant and moving story of the young chef Triton who forsakes his father's home to work as a houseboy for the marine biologist Mr. Salgado in Sri Lanka. The narrative unfolds in flashbacks as Triton gives vent to his imagination from his present stay in England to the memory of his past ten years of life in Sri Lanka. Memorialising his early years in England, he recalls an encounter with a woman who inquires him that whether he is a refuge fleeing Africa to which Triton readily replies, "I am an explorer on a voyage of discovery" (174). This sense of discovery permeates through the life of Triton and involves also his re-visioning the experience of the past in which he successfully grooms his character in the image of his master whom he emulates. He contemplates the banishment of the wicked houseboy Joseph from Salgado's house and "imagine a star-chart in the sky that would cause the fall of Joseph" (11). When Joseph vanishes into the town, Triton is pleased that "some miracle whereby my wishes had been picked up by the spirits of the city" (30) has occurred and believes that surely "the gods had intervened on my behalf" (31). After the departure of Salgado's houseboy and cook, it is he who has to perform everything from cooking to managing the house as a manservant and to please his master and his ravishing mistress Miss Nilli who provides a contrast to the gloomy interior of Mr. Salgado's house which is partially dispelled by her arrival. Triton closely watches his master Mr. Salgado and learns everything which his master willing to teach: "I watched him, I watched him unendingly all the time, and learned to become what I am" (43). He becomes an alter ego of his master and gradually gets accustomed to his life and manners. When Salgado decides to migrate to England, Triton must follow him in his journey to the new land. But whereas Salgado is attentive to his exiled existence in the foreign land, Triton, the servant, is able to erect an identity of his own in the alien ambience and transforms his makeshift existence to a successful restaurateur. While Salgado has to return to his homeland defeated "... summoned by a desire to hold onto a lost dream and memory of a lost love" (Nasta 214), Triton, the orphaned figure, profitably integrates himself to the new society he seeks to be assimilated with: "It was the only way I could succeed: without a past, without a home, without Ranjan Salgado standing by my side" (180). Triton is capable of moulding not only the flavours and taste of his dishes through his culinary skill but also his diasporic existence in England and forms a world of his own for his survival. The rhetoric of re-fashioning inevitably informs his migrant self but Salgado, his master is essentially bent by the desire to return, burdened by the sense of his exilic memory. The memory of the past which enriches Triton's diasporic existence negatively reacts with Salgado's identity augmenting his movement back to the home country that makes him recognise the all-encompassing omnipotence of memory: "We are only what we remember, nothing more ... all we have is the memory of what we done or not done?" (190).

Salgado, however recognises the productive vitality and vigour of imagination: "'It's your imagination', he said, 'It is not get poisoned in this place.' As if we each had an inner threshold that had to be breached before our surrounding could torment us" (176). The safest way one can trace the elegance of the sea and the coral reef is through the journey by mind to the sea of imagination: "In our minds we have swum in the same sea. Do you understand? An imagined world" (176). For Triton, past is like a dark demon lurking at the corner of presence and to live in the present one must kill the demon of the past: "I went to classes and other libraries, night and day for almost all the years we spent in London together; broke all the old taboos and slowly freed myself from the demons of our past: What is over is over forever, I thought" (175-76). Disowning one's own past is thus viewed as a strategy to reconfigure the present, and being subdued by one's past memory is forever to poison life obstructing actions in the present.

The line taken from Shakespeare's *The Tempest*, "of his bones are coral made" which epigraphs the novel points out to the novelist's boarder metaphysical concerns with the disrupting effects of time and space and the role of imagination in the reconfigurement of individual identity. The novel in its core introduces the note of "universal permeability" between cultures and spaces "linking the worlds of London and Sri Lanka in Triton's developing consciousness, a space where ideas can 'flow freely' as stories and memories germinate like seeds and migrate from one mind to another" (Nasta 215). The metaphor of the coral reef is thus central to the developing tensions in the novel and one of the unifying features in the text which entails "connections and reconstitution" (Nasta 215), creating an impression of continuity with change and perpetual transformation of ideals that inform the life of the common humanity. The reef itself stands for a constitutive impulse of self-refashioning when Salgado reflects up on its replicative power of metamorphosis: "You see, it is only the skin of the reef that is alive. It is real flesh immortal self-renewing" (54).

The sea itself happens to be a permanent influence upon the life of the characters, necessarily linking their past with the present. It becomes a powerful metaphor of a mysterious body of water having an identity of its own. Seas are viewed as connective links between oceans and its waves have their own ebb and flow like the fluctuating destiny of man. The sea signifies universal togetherness and oneness which defies man's persistent claim on clearly demarcated boundaries with fixated territorialities. An inquisitive Triton asked Salgado: "'Do all the oceans flow one into the other?' 'Is it the same sea here as back home?'" (172). The all-encompassing universality of the sea connecting the continents is reasserted, when later, in the novel Salgado remarks: "You remember, all one ocean, no? The debris of one man floats to another. The same little polyp grows the idea in another head" (176). Metaphorically, the sea seems to level every difference whether one is at home or in a alien land. Salgado, however, recognises the impossibility of a reconciliation of the images of the past with that of the present: "'The urge to build, to transform nature, to make something out of nothing is universal. But to conserve, to protect, to care for the past is something we have to learn'" (178). Unlike Salgado, who makes up his mind to return to the "far away house of sorrow" (180), Triton chooses not to recapture a lost paradise, but rather to seize the opportunities at hand in the immediate presence. Triton dismisses all originary myths about homeland in favour of a historical consciousness of dislocation and resistance: "Human history is always a story of somebody's diaspora" (174). The decomposed polyps of his mind crystallises his former self into a new identity—a "cosmopolitan itinerant without a past, without a name" (180). The novelist, in the framework of the coral reef thus "demystify national myths of the island and demystify the migrant's memory of the homeland" (Deckard 171).

Similarly, in Gunesekera's second novel, *The Sandglass* the characters are forever trapped in the vast plane of uncertainties between the homeland and host land, between the mysteries of the past and an ever unreliable present. The novel seeks to represent the complexities and ambiguities related to the idea of home and belonging through the negotiation of identity in relation to the various engagements in England and Sri Lanka. Prins Ducal arrives in London to attend his mother Pearl's funeral and with the accompaniment of Chip, Pearl's confidante, attempts to dig out the mines of an hitherto neglected past to disentangle the mysteries surrounding his father Jason's sudden death in the homeland Sri Lanka. Pearl, by then, has spent forty years of her life in an old flat in London, obsessed about her fragmented past and passing her time desultorily in isolation and feeding Chip's enthusiasm with stories and anecdotes of her homeland to an extent that Chip himself is able to enact his own mental journey to the unrecovered past he is a part of. Although London provides them a temporary release from the feud and fragmentation of the homeland, Sri Lanka continues to be a permanent influence enamouring the inmates to return to the promised land of origin. Following his dream, "Prins had gone back to his dreamland by then, thoroughly fed up with his mother, his brother, the family and England. He had gone promising never to come back: an emigrating immigrant" (82). Chip, the narrator of the novel, is entrusted with the responsibility of keeping Ducal's secrets, who, with his bits and scraps of memory, chronicles the happening of the four generations of the Ducal family intricately connected with the rivalling Vatunases. He, however, recognises the fragile fluidity of memory while building his stories of the past from the second hand information supplied to him by Pearl: "Trouble is when I look back I see ... everything ... through so many filters. Nothing you can be sure of.... It makes it all very difficult. I have to build it up pixel by pixel, in my mind" (75).

As exemplified in the title itself, the novel *The Sandglass*, in filtering the events of the four generations through the narrator's consciousness, hangs a moral on the passing of time. Although spatial dislocation registers a change in the life of these diasporans, Pearl strongly feels that "the world ... did not change much from place to place, not as much as it changed with passing time. It's time that wreaks havoc with us, you know. Plays hell with everything" (51). The accidental murder of his husband Jason which is an outcome of the violence and bloodshed rampant in the homeland and the ensuring antagonism with the Vatunas's land surrounding Jason's Arcadia makes her flee to London where she believes to have spent her happiest moment with Jason. Pearl's shifting to London, which can be seen as a strategy to disown or reject a troubled past in the tear-shaped homeland, is inevitably governed by her temporal and emotional associations rather than any forms of territorial displacement. London is the place where she feels she belongs. Chip thus narrates: "That was how Pearl came to England. In love with a shadow in her head that she couldn't quite focus on until she got here" (64). Conversely, Prins' rejection of his 'mother' for the sake of 'homeland' is necessarily motivated by his desire to cash on the troubled and strained condition of the motherland "by making money out of paintings, tourism out of terrorism" (41) as he believes: "You have to escape and go where you can find yourself or you stay and transform what is around you until it becomes your own" (37) for "we are all artists of our own lives" (Davis, "We are All Artists"). Unlike Prins' and Pearls', the predicament of Ravi is instituted by a physical isolation and emotional ostracism which he encounters in his long stay in America. His brown skin and lack of English accent turn out to be the White Man's Burden which baffles the expectation of the American he meets: "People look at me and they see darkness first. Even my shadow seems darker to them than theirs". Ravi's amphibian-like positionality makes him belong to none of the places he is familiar with. As Chip says: "Perhaps Ravi was simply repeating her (Pearl) own journey to England, but with different co-ordinates" (64). A Sri Lankan by birth, living in London and then migrating to America fragments his person into multiple consciousnesses—each of his roles being incompletely realised as "unfinished identities" (qtd. in Braziel and Mannur 50). The fluidity of these movements and shifting identification dilute the sanctity and holistic notion of home which makes Nasta comment: "Although echoes of home are still discernible in these texts, the lines of their cultural and linguistic parameters constantly shift as their chimeric contours flow in and out of other landscapes, other histories, which reconfigure and disrupt the longing for such *stable* anchorage points" (Nasta 214).

The sandglass thus becomes a potent symbol to recapture time from "the orphaned fragments of [an] aborted past" (*The Sandglass* 2) which not only represents the manner time fleets but also the common everydayness of life that acts as a connective link between the past and the present through the "repetitive experiences, attitudes and practices that both maintain themselves and alter across the wider stretches of time that make up ... human history" (Mulhall 178). Gunesekera's experiment with diasporic sensibility, in this manner, seeks to unsettle the historical registers and focalises the spatio-temporal incommensurability of the migrant position, and dislocates the imaginative territoriality into a point beyond mere historical reclamation. The idea of home and belonging in this deterritorialised dialectics, as Nasta suggests, reveals "a preoccupation with the representation of an interior landscape of desire, a longing to enter the symbolic as a narrative journey" (213). Diasporic writing, as evidenced by Gunesekera, then is the expression of an immediate impulse to re-enact and reconstitute a diffused cultural order, reconfiguring that inner landscape of mind through the immutable interplay of the fractured memories and desires.

The writers discussed in this book have projected in their novels diverse possibilities of diasporic formations in which discourses about home and belonging assume new status and meaning in the reconfigurement of individual identity in the adopted land of diasporisation. Each of the writers is particularly attentive to the manners the diasporic subjects are able to cope and construct images of their respective imaginary homelands as a strategy to perpetrate their sense of belonging, traversing the putrid premises of racial and cultural marginalisation. Although these writers are markedly different from one another in style and subject matter, nonetheless, forging a new home and identity in a foreign land becomes a common concern for these novelists under discussion, and therefore, they deliberately seek to present their novels in such contextual realities which offer them rooms for transformation. The theme of transformation permeates through the lives of all the protagonists in the novels under discussion which makes them come out as saner and more sensible individuals at the end. Stevens thus contemplates the true meaning of his life, questioning his past services and loyalties, restructuring his old ideals and sensibilities when he discovers the 'evening' as the best part of the day: "I should adopt a more positive outlook and try to make the best of what remains of my day" (257). The meaningfulness of Stevens' entire life has been reduced to this few moment of truly personal meditation in which he is allowed a glimpse of the real meaning of human life: "... in bantering lies the key to human warmth" (259) which at once transforms him from an analyst to an enthusiast. Similarly, Christopher Banks realises at the end that "orphanhood becomes a central metaphor for universal trauma" (Zinck 147) and the individuals in the present cultural configuration of the world "must face the world as orphans" (*When We Were Orphans* 168). Accordingly, Karim's experimentation with several selves dawns in him a new reality that there is no essence in the world and that being engaged with a multiplicity of fluid, imaginary selves will finally liberate one's soul from a bounded society "obsessed with clear cut definitions of cultural or ethnic identity" (Schoene, "Herald of Hybridity" 117). On the other hand, Shahid, torn between the hopeless, orthodox, fundamentalist ideas and liberalist humanism of the West comes to an understanding that the "purity" claimed by either centre or margin is originally a 'myth' because "there was no fixed self; surely our several selves melted and mutated daily" (274). In a similar fashion, Triton of the novel *Reef* transforms his makeshift existence into a successful restaurateur in the city of London, disowning an aborted past of utter fragmentation and is convinced of the re-vivifying dynamism of metamorphosis: "We have to destroy in order to create.... Like sea. Whatever it destroys, it uses to grow something better" (111). While his master drastically fails in his mission in the West, Triton, the servant feels utterly at home in England and prospers as he recognises the role of reconfiguration and refashioning in the narrative of his dispossessed self unlike Salgado who stresses the symbiotic syncretism of a mesmeric memory and its fragile power. Like Triton, Chip is optimistic of a new world order to emerge over the sordid gloom and thus sees the birth of Pearl's granddaughter Dawn as precluding the dawn of a new light, emblematic of her name which will "spin us forward from thus hurt earth to a somehow better world" (177-278).

The rhetoric of return or reclamation of a lost world, however does not always hold true in the lives of the characters and protagonists discussed in this dissertation. Miss Kenton, at a point, in the novel, warns Stevens of the irretrievable propensities of temporality when she says: "there's no turning back the clock" (*The Remains* 239) which deprives him of his "vain hope of undoing the past" (Lodge, *The Art of Fiction* 156) and makes him negotiate with his feelings. Banks' capricious mooring over the planes of Shanghai and war-torn battlefields to unravel the mysteries of his orphanhood and to recover the lost dream of family home rather lands him in a fresh realization of the harsher realities of his life to have discovered that his whole life has been squeezed into an object of an act of philanthropy by the warlord Wang Ku who has kidnapped his mother. Banks has huge "regrets for what could have been and not what could be" which makes him "visit his mother after more than thirty years to check that dream is the imperfect of dreams" (Vinet 143). Banks' suffering and trauma unlike that of his mother's is, therefore, more intensified being always in proximity with that loss. Kureishi's characters, on the other hand, such as Anwar and Asif rely heavily upon the cultural heritage of the past to which they seek to return but are apparently thwarted at crucial points in their lives which make them rethink the meaningfulness or otherwise of their hyphenated existence in the host land. Anwar's bitter experience of racism makes him re-enact an extreme form of Indianism, and his strict adherence to the traditional values blindly forces him to marry his daughter Jamila to a misfit named Changez whom he thinks to be well-grounded in the Indian ways of life. On his daughter's refusal to marriage he claims: "If Gandhi could shove out the English from India by not eating, I can get my family to obey me by exactly the same" (60). Similarly, Shahid's uncle, Asif acknowledges the contradictions that inform the so-called multicultural society of England and regrets the way they are rejected by the dominant culture in the process of assimilation: "We think we're settled down but we've just crossed the threshold. We have to watch ourselves, otherwise we will wake up one day to find we have made a calamitous marriage" (54). In the novel

Reef, while Salgado recognises the power of memory in the act of reclamation: "We are only what we remember" (180) and returned defeated to his promised land of origin, Triton feels his dislocation as a blessing in disguise and thus furthers his development capitalising on the situation because he is extraordinarily attentive to bury the dead past with the sands of a productive presence for "In the end, belonging has to do with people you're with—not with place" (Hussein) you are implanted in, with a fixed, unalterable rootedness.

Being unable to streamline themselves into the core values of the host culture, the diasporans thus feel obliged to experiment with a variety of roles and opportunities the West has to provide them for. Christopher Banks takes up the role of a master detective "to root out single-handedly all the evil in the world" (16-17) because only by being a detective, as he thinks, can solve the mystery surrounding his orphanhood and that it serves as a gateway to enter into the past and his universe of Englishness, which seems to offer a solution to his earlier wonderment: "How do you suppose one might become more English" (76). It's the same coordinates which motivate Haroon to feign mystic catering to the British sensibility and later makes Anwar to frequent the prostitutes in Hyde Park and to drink wine with Haroon. Karim and Shahid, however, take this trans-cultural role-playing to newer and greater heights as they are not to become complacent in any of the roles assumed by them or provided by the English society, and choose the life of cosmopolitan itinerants, emphasising the catachrestic notion of an appropriated Englishness that "lacks a true referent in a transnational, diasporic world" (Williams, "A State of Perpetual") which brings out the transplanted nature of their identity which is aptly conversant with the diverse cultural codes of the West. This rhetoric of refashioning augurs well in the case of Triton as his paradise is regained after a continued odyssey from the country setting through his development of culinary skills in Salgado's house to the city of London where he establishes himself successfully as a restaurateur. Prins' rejection of the mother in favour of the motherland, however, replicates the dream of his father Jason, "a truly colonial: a man obsessed with place and status—geographical and social" (23-24) is primarily motivated by the material benefits to be gained cashing on the trouble situation in the homeland which can be viewed a yet another forms of neo-colonialism perpetuated by the West.

In all the novels under discussion, the transnational metropolis of London serves as a congenial setting for the protagonists, which provides them ample scope for experimentations with their multiple selves. "English cites," says Baucom, "are certainly places in which the nation's cultural identity continues to be refashioned" (191) which helps evolve "a more pluralized and relational concept of place-identity" (qtd. in Ball 69) for these displaced diasporans in quest for their re-formed and reconfigurated 'homes'. Hence, London acts as a dynamic, heterogeneous space which is endlessly in motion, undergoing change and transformation. London, in the novels, is presented as a centre of social and cultural encounters, saturated with energy and possibilities, and through its desperate links and interconnections, inaugurates an open and porous space of belonging where identity is better realised in its manifold movements across bounded categories rather than strictly fixated stabilising boundaries.

For Christopher Banks, London is the place of 'social connections' where one can stay "well connected" (5) "linking oneself with 'society' at large" (12) and thus favour the moulding of his person into a renowned detective of the contemporary England. Moreover, the city of Shanghai acts as an another London for Banks which is keen to stigmatise and blur the borderline between the privileged and the oppressed, the centred and the marginalised, fostering a sense of inclusivity and cultural erosion that certainly helps him to embark on his father-rescuing mission. He hopes that his success in Shanghai will serve as being 'triumphant memory' for his step daughter Jennifer on his return to England. For Karim of *The Buddha*, London is "a house with five thousand rooms, all different" (126) and where life was bottomless in its temptations which falls into sharp contrast with the life in the suburb where "security and safety were the reward of dullness" (8). The heterogeneous, multicultural space provides him a pluralistic perception of the world which doesn't force him to be a part of any pre-defined cultural or social groups. London, for Karim, is full of sensations, excitements and opportunities and thus becomes his most favourite and familiar place where he feels he belongs to: "... my favourite city, my playground, my home" (196). The theatricality of experience later manifested in Karim's disposition supports his reference to the city as a 'playground'. This transnational 'contact zone' provides Shahid, the protagonist of *The Black Album*, a vision to perceive his hybrid culturality in relation to the divergent sensations and influences it projects on to its inhabitants. It is the city life and its cultural venues which are amply exploited by Shahid and his lover Deedee that make him turn his back permanently on the fundamentalist ideals of his fanatic friends and embrace the liberal views of the West with its emphasis on freedom of speech and tolerance. The open culture of the London city, moreover, supports his theory of the "innumerable ways of being" (274) following which he now will "spread himself out, in his work and in love" (274). Similarly, Triton in the novel *Reef* succeeds primarily because he is particularly alive to the cosmopolitan realities of London which proffer plurality, transformation and development. Triton, with his culinary skills, necessarily inculcates the tactics of "mixing and mestigge" (Ranasinha 13) in his character that gradually prepares and propels him to shed his longing for authenticity and to embrace the consumerist culture of the metropolis which helps him to become a successful restaurateur in a foreign land. London as a postmodern metropolis, thus, ceases to privilege the grand narratives and opens up a passage for the mini narratives to the take the centre stage which exist as a carnivalesque, deconstructing the higher strands in the hierarchy that helps effect the construction of a diasporic space to be identified with. In the words of Jayawickrama, "'the cosmopolitan' becomes a deferral of particular identity in favour of an unidentified sense of belonging" which rather needs "a dilution and consumerisation of the identities and sense of history imagined in the youth" (12).

Diasporic writing is inevitably about movement rather that settlement. The novels discussed in this book are thus replete with motifs of movement which explicitly engage our attention in a range of diverse diasporic possibilities that emerge out of such movements—physical, psychological and temporal. The protagonists of these novels continually forge for themselves "itinerant cultural routes" which will take them both imaginatively and physically to many places and into contact with diverse culturalities living in the society, away from the enrooted security and fixity of identification and belonging, establishing an uninterrupted relationship between past and present because "the grounded certainties of *roots* are replaced with the transnational contingencies of *routes*" (McLeod 215). Forgoing new narratives for themselves, the protagonists in these novels thus move away from the totalising or holistic notion of identity and location and seek to exacerbate their identities in movements and transition challenging the traditional ideas of fixity and rootedness. Ishiguro's *The Remains of the Day*, in this respect, is constructed around the motif of a journey—Stevens' real journey through the West countries has a metaphorical parallel in the trip his mind takes to the narrative residues of the past, in which his recollection is purposive of the prefigurement of his life as well, for the butler generates a new version of his past life that is more acceptable to him than his real life story. The novel is an extended experimentation in the poetics of identification reconfigured by the fragile fragments of memorialisation. Stevens' present sense of alienation can be understood through an evaluative journey into the collusive caves of memory and those who transport more of their past lives into their lived presence "both confirm their own identity and enrich the present with the past's amplified reduces" (Lowenthal 198). Stevens' traumatic experience of the self is a summative, unremitting process of revision, emphatically tracing the deferred tendencies of memorialisation that challenges the homogeneity and fixity of self-identification. Stevens' psychic movement into his past life thus enables him to generate a re-configurated version of identity for himself, for the formation of identity is a continuous process of presenting and representing one's individuality to oneself and to the world around. In *When We Were Orphans*, on the other hand, Ishiguro seems to multiply movements in the texture of the protagonist's narrative which features a multiplicity of movements and transpositions across the globe that tend to unsettle the notion of home and national belonging. Banks' career as a detective is emblematic of perpetual movements which also entails revisiting the unsolved mysteries of the past through the distorting web of memory. After his parents' disappearance, Banks is transported to England from Shanghai to which he returns again as a detective to solve the mysteries of his orphanhood. Even after his long stay in England, he can't adapt to the English ways of life owing to his attachment to the former land and later admits: "... all these years I've lived in England, I've never really felt at home there" and that "the international settlement ... will always be my home" (301). But the new Shanghai, Banks returns to, ceases to be an equivalent to his former home and his multiple movements across borders and boundaries register a sense of homelessness and fragmentation in him. The fragmented sense of utter homelessness inhabits the memory of Banks when he says towards the end of the novel: "... there are those times when a sort of emptiness fills my hours" (368) that demonstrate the ways in which the fragmented experience of the world is subtly inculcated into the life of the modern man pointing out to the impossibility to evolve a central metaphor to represent this essential human condition.

Similarly, Karim Amir, the narrator/protagonist of *The Buddha* recognises his hybrid potentialities early in the novel describing himself as "a funny kind of Englishman" in search of "any kind of movement, action and sexual interest I could find, because things were so gloomy" (3). Karim's first movement in the novel is an attempt to escape the shabbiness of the suburbia where "people rarely dreamed of striking out for happiness" (8). Karim's restlessness throughout the novel which sometimes amounts to madness is the result of this impulse of change and shifting identification which makes him always on the move through the city as Manferlotti beautifully puts in: "a whole body that now rest and now runs, now flourishes and now decays, smiles and bleeds" (193). Constant change and instability inform Karim's fluctuating life and set him in perpetual movement throughout: "I was not too unhappy criss-crossing South London and the suburbs by bus, no one knowing where I was. Wherever someone—mum, dad, Ted—tried to locate me, I was always somewhere else" (94). This fluxing movements of the protagonist is an inherent characteristic of the immigrant as "the Everyman of the twentieth century" (141) which subverts "the essentialist notion of identity and culture and evolves a new hybridized condition for the modern man in an all-inclusive cosmopolity. For Karim, the 'third space' acts as a flexible model of belonging and justifies his claims on various relationships in London that appeals to his taste. Karim represents one of the travellers in the post-colonial world who in Phillips' words "wander freely among the noble of Europe's formerly all-powerful cites" (*The European Tribe* 20) and is open to be absorbed into any forms of culturality, being comfortably balanced "among the interstice between different culture" (Stein 120). Karim, therefore, rejecting the life in the suburb, happily celebrates his transformative movements and says: "What I'd do there when the city belonged to me" (121). Karim's acting career doesn't allow him to settle in any fixed roles or locationalities which always demands action and movements rather than passivity or stasis. Karim's endless journey through the realities of 1970s Britain as a young man demonstrates the struggle for self-actualisation and finding a place in the society who doesn't have any compatible pattern to fit properly into a specific model of cultural configuration.

Karim's hybridised identity and its summative liquidity of movements and perceptions, in this sense, "displays the necessary deformation and displacement of all sites of discrimination and domination" (qtd. in Edward 141). Likewise, being entangled between fundamentalism and liberalism, between Western culture and Indian ways of living, Shahid finds himself in between the contradicting polarities of uncertainties which accentuate the search for his true identity. Shahid opts for the pop culture of the 1980's England "where fragmentation, change, undecidability are the norms" (Degabriele 29) rather than exceptions and with his firm assertion: "I can't be limited" (272), embarks on a riveting journey with Deedee Osgood to exploit the city's cultural venues and their divergent sensations. His search for the situatedness of his self, paradoxically engages him with multiple identity performances, and in contrast to Riaz's assertion of his feeling alienated in England, Shahid claims: "There's nowhere else I will feel more comfortable" (175). Shahid's involvement in the pop culture and his passion for Prince, the musician and composer, moreover, introduces in the novel, the theme of fluidity and hybridity in which identity can only be experienced in terms of perpetual movements and unpolarised mixing. London as a metropolitan city offers Shahid numerous conflicting strands to experiment with, and thus makes him reflect that "there are innumerable ways of being in this world" (274) and that it is difficult to cling to any clearly defined positions or perceptions of life prescribed by the contemporary society. He rather ponders over the chaos and ambiguity loosed upon his fluctuating mind: "He believed everything, he believed nothing ... one day he could passionately feel one thing, the next day the opposite. Other times provisional states would alternate from hour to hour; sometimes all crashed into chaos" (147). Thus, characters such as Karim and Shahid take to a life of eternal movements and transformation, and the metropolis as a multicultural site and a transnational space offers them limitless scope and possibilities to forge the narratives of their respective selves which are always "on the move and on the make in the metropolitan cityscape" (Ball 224), inaugurating a dynamic process of continual development, negotiation and change.

Analogously, Triton's life is marked out by multiple journeys and movements throughout—first from a humble life in a country setting through the grandeur and sophistication of Salgado's house in Sri Lanka to the multicultural, cosmopolitan realities of English life in the metropolis. In the narrative, Triton acts increasingly as an artist moulding and devising new ways of belonging and dons several roles in several positions as people change their clothes. He comes out successful in all identity roles assumed by him because his vision of the world is essentially prospective unlike his master's which is necessarily retrospective, forcing him unconditionally to return to the native land. Salgado is undoubtedly a man of the past and hence his movements throughout are regressive, in contrast to Triton's whose eyes are steadily fixed upon the diverse possibilities the future has to offer to him. Triton nourishes a fantastically fabulous image of the reef in his head which is eventually influenced by Salgado's luminous description of its wilderness. The reef in its perpetual movements towards transformation finds an analogue in the person of Triton who likes never to look back and thus disowning the past, easily integrate himself in the general life of the host country. In this respect, the reef's refashioning of itself is suggestive of Triton's transformative reshaping of his destiny and is echoed in the evolutionary idealism of a nation which is always in the making. Triton, in the novel, discovers a similar tendency in the tidal wave of the forest when he remarks: "The whole country had been turned from jungle to paradise to jungle again, as it has been even more barbarically in my own life" (15).

The sea with its moving body of water and endless waves continues to be an inexhaustible influence on the psyche of Triton tempting him to be creatively in constant motion. Like the provisional identity of Triton, the sea has an identity of its own—capricious and always in the move—celebrating its movements forever that sounds eternity. Triton tries to comprehend the enormity of the sea and its all-encompassing power of reconnection which bridge the gap between the homeland and the host land and imagines a connected world linked through the liquidity of the seas: "The sea shimmering between the black humps of barnacled rocks ... snuffing and gurgling" seems exactly the same as "our coral-spangled south coast back home" (172).

In a similar fashion, Gunesekera, in *The Sandglass* seems to suspend his characters eternally into a transformative dynamics between the land of origin and the adopted land of identification. Almost all the characters featured in the novel inviolably migrate in quest of their lost identities to re-actuate. Movements become a harbinger of change. Thus, Prins Ducal, who has already returned to his homeland, is again called back to England, to perform the funeral rites of his mother Pearl, who, dissatisfied with her life in the island, permanently established herself in London. Ravi, Pearl's another son, migrates to America and returns defeated having suffered the predicament of emotional ostracism in an exilic situation which dislocates him not only from the land but from life itself. Although Chip, the narrator travels to Sri Lanka late in the novel, his journey for most part is psychological, disentangling the threads of a fragmented temporality, building an integrated reality "pixel by pixel" (75) in his memory to reconfigure the "orphaned fragments" (2) of his dilapidated past. Chip becomes a moving symbol of the endless quest for identity, endeavouring to explore the unity from a long aborted past in an orphaned ambience of eternal anomaly. The novel thus meticulously knit together the fragments of memory that slip into the untrodden landscapes of the curious mind. The idea of home and belonging, in this deterritorialised dialectics, as Nasta suggests, reveals "a preoccupation with the representation of an interior landscape of desire, a longing to enter the symbolic as a narrative journey" (213).

Remembering, then is not a passive act but is akin to knowing, a movement towards reinvention which turns out to be a mode of re-living, a re-enactment of the experience of the past, subdued by the disrupting waves of time. The sandglass becomes a potent symbol to represent these changes wrought in the memories of these dislocated diasporans, desirous of a narrativised reclamation of the past as suggested by Gunesekera: "Sand is free moving, opaque and porous ... glass is hard, transparent and non-porous. But there is a point, albeit at a different melting point when they are one and the same" (qtd. in Nasta 231). The sandglass of narration as endeavoured by Chips thus "becomes the symbolic frame which signifies the novel's main subject. It is an image that acts both as a 'metaphor' for the passage of time and the need for the artist to capture that moment in the present, in what Gunesekera has called a continuous reworking of the 'process of transformation'" (Nasta 231).

All the three authors discussed in this book are, therefore, particularly attentive to this rhetoric of transformation and change, subtly integrated and worked out into the lives of the protagonists in quest for their respective 'homes'. The protagonists such as Stevens, Banks, Karim, Shahid, Triton, Chips, et al. emphatically acclaim themselves as "hybrid cosmopolitans" (Friedman 409) and are blessed with the knowledge that "all forms of culture are continually in the process of hybridity" (Bhabha, *The Location* 211) admitting a free play of the supposedly cultural constants or holistic essence. The discourse of home thus involves a radical redefinition place and time, exposing the transgressive tendencies of the so-called rigidity of cultural or national boundaries and its interruptive interiority. Desire for a home then is a symbolic force based on the lived experience of the locality beyond the rigidified limit of perception in the present contextualities.

Summing up, the idea of 'home' has ceased to be a fixed place, invested with the tonality of security and stability, but a constantly negotiated space between the seminality of the self and the liquidity of the location. Home as a determiner of identity lacks any strictly primal place of identification, and it is precisely this indefinitive quality of home that simultaneously serves to 'mythify' and 'demythify' this conceptualisation as provisional and relative and as an almost universalised entity of utopian longing and belonging. Home no longer denotes simply one place, but locations. It is the place where one rediscovers new ways of being and belonging, ironing out the frontiers of difference. Confrontation of dispersal and fragmentation becomes a part of the process in the construction of a new world order in the making. When the 'homing desire' of the individual is allied with a deep feeling of waste and a sense of irrevocable displacement, home ceases to be a place anymore and becomes an emotion. Home, in this sense, transcends the physical limits of fixed borders, boundaries and nationalities and gets metamorphosed into a non-spatial entity spawned by the silenced memories and unspeakable desires of the past. The projection of these multiple homing possibilities proliferate into the general texture of human life where home becomes a dynamic space of contestation and nomadised dispersion, augmenting a narrativised confluence of the past and the present which interrogates the hegemony of the closed system and homogenised perception. In this de-politicised framework of homing possibilities, diasporic writers such as Ishiguro, Kureishi and Gunesekera scrupulously deliberate the fictional presentment of this universal migrant condition which seeks to endow the marginalised and the displaced a voice and a place in this utterly placeless and muted world of fragmented affiliations and relationships. These writers, in their cartographies of 'home', thus enunciate a redemptive oasis of multicultural identifications—as a discursive site replete with formative possibilities—celebrating the free-floating provisionality of identity, reconfigured through the fragile fluidity of memory in the narrativised relocation of the self, in which multiplicity, mobility and uncertainties are rules rather than exceptions that eternally unsettle and dynamicise the notion of home and belonging.

Bibliography

PRIMARY SOURCES

Gunesekera, Romesh. *Reef*. New Delhi: Penguin Books, 2014. Print.

_____. *The Sandglass*. New Delhi: Penguin Books, 1999. Print.

Ishiguro, Kazuo. *The Remains of the Day*. New York: Vintage, 1993. Print.

_____. *When We Were Orphans*. London: Faber and Faber, 2012. Print.

Kureishi, Hanif. *The Black Album*. London: Faber and Faber, 2010. Print.

_____. *The Buddha of Suburbia*. London: Faber and Faber, 2009. Print.

SECONDARY SOURCES

Abdulgawad, Elnady. "Domesticating the English Novel: The Character of the Butler in Kazuo Ishiguro's *The Remains of the Day*." *Academia.edu*. N.p., n.d. Web. 19 Apr. 2017.

Abu-Shomar, Ayman. "Critical Spaces of Diaspora for Liquid Post-modernity; Editorial." *Academia.edu*. N.p., n.d. Web. 07 Apr. 2017.

Achebe, Chinua. *Home and Exile*. Oxford: Oxford University Press, 2000. Print.

Adorno, Theodor. *Minima Moralia: Reflections on a Damaged Life*. London: Verso, 2005. Print.

Agnew, Vijay. "A Diasporic Bounty: Cultural History and Heritage." *Diaspora, Memory and Identity: A Search for an Identity*. Ed. Vijay Agnew. Toronto, Buffalo and London: University of Toronto Press, 2005. 171-86. Print.

_____. "Introduction". *Diaspora, Memory and Identity: A Search for an Identity*. Ed. Vijay Agnew. Toronto, Buffalo and London: University of Toronto Press, 2005. 3-17. Print.

Ahmed, S. "Home and Away: Narratives of Migration and Estrangement." *International Journal of Cultural Studies*, 2.3 (1999): 329-47. Print.

Al-Taee, Nasser. *Representations of the Orient in Western Music: Violence and Sensuality*. Burlington, USA: Ashgate Publishing Ltd., 2010. Print.

Alghamdi, Alaa. *Transformations of the Liminal Self: Configurations of Home and Identity for Muslim Characters in British Postcolonial Fiction*. Bloomington: I. Universe, 2011. Print.

Alibhai-Brown, Y. *After Multiculturalism*. London: The Foreign Policy Centre, 2000. Print.

Althusser, Louis. *Essays on Ideology*. London: Verso, 1984. Print.

Anderson, Benedict. *Imagined Communities: Reflections on the Origin and Spread of Nationalism*. London: Verso, 1998. Print.

Ang, Ien. "Together-in-Difference: Beyond Diaspora, into Hybridity." *Asian Studies Review*, 1-13, Web. 09 Apr. 2017.

_____. *On Not Speaking Chinese*. New York: Routledge, 2001. Print.

Appadurai, A. *Modernity at Large: Cultural Dimensions of Globalization*. Minneapolis: University of Minnesota Press, 1996. Print.

Armbruster, H. "Homes in Crisis: Syrian Orthodox Christians in Turkey and Germany". *New Approaches to Migration? Transnational Communities and the Transformation of Home*. Ed. N. Al Ali and K. Koser. London/New York: Routledge, 2002. 17-33. Print.

Ashcroft, Bill, Gareth Griffiths, and Helen Tiffin. *The Post-Colonial Studies Reader*. London: Routledge, 2006. Print.

_____. *The Empire Writes Back: Theory and Practice in Post-colonial Literatures*. London: Routledge, 2002. Print.

Ashworth, G.J. and B. Graham. "Senses of Place, Sense of Time and Heritage." *Senses of Place: Senses of Time*. Ed. G.J. Ashworth and B. Graham. Aldershot: Ashgate, 2005. 1-15. Print.

Assman, Jan. "Collective Memory and Cultural Identity." *New German Critique*, 65 (1995): 123-33. Print.

Bachelard, Gaston. *The Poetics of Space*. Boston: Beacon Press, 1994. Print.

Bakhtin, M.M. *The Dialogic Imagination: Four Essays*. Trans. Caryl Emerson and Michael Holquist. Astin: U of Texas Press, 1981. Print.

Bald, Suresht R. "Negotiating Identity in the Metropolis: Generational Difference in the South Asian British Fiction". *Writing Across Worlds: Literature and Migration*. Ed. Russell King, John Connell and Paul White. London and New York: Routledge, 1995. 70-88. Print.

Ball, John Clement. *Imagining London: Postcolonial Fiction and the Transnational Metropolis*. Toronto: U of Toronto, 2004. Print.

Bammer, Angelika, Introduction. *Displacements: Cultural Identities in Question*. Ed. Angelika Bammer. Bloomington and Indianapolis: Indiana University Press, 1994. xi-xx. Print.

Barker, Chris. *Cultural Studies: Theory and Practice*. London: Sage, 2003. Print.

Barth, Fredrik. *Ethnic Groups and Boundaries: The Social Organization of Culture Difference*. Long Grove: Waveland Press, 2006. Print.

Bates, Karen G. "Interview with Kazuo Ishiguro." *Conversations with Kazuo Ishiguro*. Ed. Brian W. Shaffer and Cynthia F. Wong. Jackson: Univ. Press of Mississippi, 2008. 199-220. Print.

Baucom, Ian. *Out of Place: Englishness, Empire, and the Locations of Identity*. Princeton: Princeton University Press, 1999. Print.

Baumann, G. *Contesting Culture: Discourses of Identity in Multi-Ethnic London*, Cambridge: Cambridge University Press, 1996. Print.

_____. *The Multicultural Riddle*. London and New York: Routledge, 1999. Print.

Bauman, Zygmunt. *Identity: Conversations with Benedetto Vecchi*. Malden: Polity Press, 2012. Print.

Benhabib, Seyla. Preface. *The Claims of Culture: Equality and Diversity in the Global Era*. Princeton, N.J: Princeton UP, 2002. i-xiv. Print.

_____. *The Claims of Culture: Equality and Diversity in the Global Era*. Princeton, N.J: Princeton UP, 2002. Print.

Bentley, Arthur Fisher. *The Process of Government: A Study of Social Pressures*. New Brunswick, N.J: Transaction Publication, 1995. Print.

Berberich, Christine. *The Image of the English Gentleman in Twentieth-century Literature: Englishness and Nostalgia*. Aldershot, Hampshire, England Burlington, VT: Ashgate, 2007. Print.

Berlin, I. *The Crooked Timber of Humanity: Chapters in the History of Ideas*. London: Fontana Press, 1991. Print.

Bhabha, Homi K. "Culture's In-between." *The Question of Cultural Identity*. Ed. Stuart Hall and Paul Du Gay. London: Sage, 1996. 53-60. Print.

_____. "DissemiNation." *Nation and Narration*. Ed. Homi Bhabha. Hove, United Kingdom: Psychology Press, 1990. 291-322. Print.

_____. "Interview with Homi Bhabha: The Third Space." *Identity, Community, Culture, Difference*. Ed. J. Rutherford. London: Lawrence and Wishart, 1990. 207-21. Print.

_____. Introduction. *Nation and Narration*. Ed. Homi Bhabha. Hove, United Kingdom: Psychology Press, 1990. 1-7. Print.

_____. *The Location of Culture*. London: Routledge, 1994. Print.

_____. "The Manifesto." *Wasafiri*. Volume 14.29 (1999) 38-40. *Taylor and Francis Online*. Web. 18 July 2017.

_____. "The Third Space: Interview with Homi Bhabha". *Identity: Community, Culture, Difference*. Ed. J. Rutherford. London: Laurence and Wishart, 1990. 207-21. Print.

Binding, Paul. "Books: A Tear-shaped Homeland." *The Independent*. Independent Digital News and Media, 21 Feb. 1998. Web. 11 May 2017.

Birke, Dorothee. *Memory's Fragile Power: Crises of Memory, Identity and Narrative in Contemporary British Novels*. Trier: WVT Wissenschaftlicher Verlag Trier, 2008. Print.

Bizzini, Silvia Caporale. "Recollecting Memories, Reconstructing Identities: Narrators as Storytellers in Kazuo Ishiguro's *When We Were Orphans* and *Never Let Me Go*." *Atlantis: Journal of the Spanish Association of Anglo-American Studies*, 35.2 (2013): 65-80. Print.

Blunt, Alison, and Robyn M. Dowling. *Home*. New York: Routledge, 2006. Print.

Boas, Franz. *The Mind of Primitive Man*. London: Macmillan, 2011. Print.

Bracken, Christopher. "Postcolonialism." *Encyclopedia of Semiotics*. Ed. Paul Bouissac. New York: Oxford University Press, 1999. 504-23. Print.

Bragg, Billy. *The Progressive Patriot: A Search for Belonging*. London: Transworld, 2007. Print.

Brah, Avtar. *Cartographies of Diaspora: Contesting Identities*. London: Routledge, 1996. Print.

Braziel, K. and Mannur, A. *Theorising Diaspora*. Oxford: Blackwell Publishing, 2003. Print.

Brennan, Tim. "Cosmopolitans and Celebrities." *Race and Class*, 31.1 (1989): 1-19. Print.

Brocklehurst, Helen, and Robert Phillips. Introduction. *History, Nationhood and the Question of Britain*. Ed. Helen Brocklehurst, and Robert Phillips. Houndsmill, Eng.: Palgrave Macmillan, 2004. i-xxiv. Print.

Brooker, Peter, and Peter Widdowson. *A Practical Reader in Contemporary Literary Theory*. London: Prentice Hall, 1996. Print.

Brown, Bill. "Thing Theory." *Critical Inquiry,* 28.1 (2001): 1-22. Print.

Brown, Gordon. "Speech to the Fabian New Year Conference, London, 2006". *British Political Speech | Speech Archive*. Web. 11 Apr. 2017.

Bruner, Jerome. *Actual Minds, Possible Worlds*. Cambridge: Harvard University Press, 1986. Print.

_____. "The 'Remembered' Self." *The Remembering Self: Construction and Accuracy in Self-Narrative*. Ed. Ulric Neisser and Robyn Fivush. New York: Cambridge University Press, 1994. 41-54. Print.

Buchanan, Bradley. *Hanif Kureishi*. New York: Palgrave MacMillan, 2007. Print.

Buechner, Frederich. *The Longing for Home*. San Francisco: Harper Collins, 1996. Print.

Buendía, Felipe. *Cultural Producers and Social Change in Latin America*. New York, NY: Palgrave Macmillan, 2014. Print.

Butler, Judith, and Gayatri Chakravorty Spivak. *Who Sings the Nation-state? Language, Politics, Belonging?* Oxford: Seagull, 2007. Print.

Butler, Judith. *Gender Trouble: Feminism and the Subversion of Identity*. New York: Routledge, 2011. Print.

Byrne, Bridget. "Crisis of Identity? Englishness, Britishness and Whiteness." *Empire and After: Englishness in Postcolonial Perspective*. Ed. Graham McPhee and Prem Poddar. New York: Berghahn Books, 2007, 139-57. Print.

Caputo, John D. and Jacques Derrida. *Deconstruction in a Nutshell: A Conversation with Jacques Derrida*. New York: Fordham University Press, 1997. Print.

Castles, Stephen. *Ethnicity and Globalization: From Migrant Worker to Transnational Citizen*. London: SAGE, 2000. Print.

_____. "Migrant Settlement, Transnational Communities and State Strategies in the Asia Pacific Region." *Migration in the Asia Pacific: Population, Settlement, and Citizenship Issues*. Ed. Robyn R. Iredale, Charles Hawksley, and Stephen Castles. Cheltenham, UK: Edward Elgar, 2003. 3-26. Print.

Chambers, Iain. *Border Dialogues: Journey in Postmodernity*. London: Routledge. Print.

_____. *Popular Culture: The Metropolitan Experience*. London: Routledge, 1986. Print.

Chatarji, Partha. *The Nations and its Fragments: Colonial and Post-colonial Histories*. Princeton: Princeton University Press, 1993. Print.

Chatman, Seymour. *Coming to Terms: The Rhetoric of Narrative in Fiction and Film*. Ithaca and London: Cornell University Press, 1990. Print.

Cheng, Chu-chueh. "Chic Clichés: The Reinvention of Myths and Stereotypes in Kazuo Ishiguro's Novels." *EnterText* 5.3 (n.d.): 1-39. PDF file.

Christensen, Tim. "Kazuo Ishiguro and Orphanhood." *The AnaChronist* 13 (2007): 202-16. Web. 25 Apr. 2017.

Clifford, James. "Diasporas." *Cultural Anthropology,* 9.3 (1994): 302-38. Print.

_____. "Mixed Feelings." *Cosmopolitics: Thinking and Feeling Beyond the Nation*. Ed. P. Cheah and B. Robbins. Minneapolis: University of Minnesota Press, 1998, 362-70. Print.

_____. *Routes: Travel and Translation in the Late Twentieth Century*. Cambridge, MA: Harvard University Press, 1999. Print.

Cohen, Robin. "Solid, Ductile and Liquid: Changing Notions of Homeland and Home in Diaspora Studies." *Transnationalism: Diasporas and the Advent of a New (dis)order.* Ed. Eliezer Ben Rafael and Yitzhak Sternberg. Leiden, Boston: Library of Congress Cataloguing, 2009. 117-34. Print.

_____. "Diaspora and the Nation-State: From Victims to Challengers." *International Affair (Royal Institute of International Affairs)*, 72.3 (1996): 507-20. Print.

_____. *Global Diasporas*. Seattle: University of Washington Press, 1997. Print.

Collymore, Tawnee. "Towards a Diasporic Epistemology: How Filipino Canadian Young Men Make Sense of Educational Success and Failure." *T Space Repository*. N.p., 01 Nov. 2012. Web. 07 Apr. 2017.

Connor, Steven. *The English Novel in History, 1950-1995*. London, New York: Routledge, 1996. Print.

Crang, P., C. Dwyer and P. Jackson. "Introduction: The Spaces of Transnationality". *Transnational Space*. Ed. P. Crang, C. Dwyer and P. Jackson. Abingdon, New York: Routledge, 2004. 1-23. Print.

Curtis, Michael. *Orientalism and Islam European Thinkers on Oriental Despotism in the Middle East and India*. Cambridge: Cambridge University Press, 2009. Print.

Dalai, P. *Poetics of Polyglossia in the Island Diaspora: A Reading of K.S. Maniam's The Return*. 2006. Print.

Davies, Carole Boyce. *Black Women, Writing and Identity: Migrations of the Subject*. London: Routledge, 2002. Print.

Davis, Helen. *Understanding Stuart Hall*. London: Sage Publications, 2004. Print.

Davis, Rocio G. "We are All Artists of Our Own Lives: A Conversation with Romesh Gunesekera." *Miscelanea: A Journal of English and American Studies,* 18 (1997): Web. 10 May 2017.

Dayal, Samir. "Diaspora and Double Consciousness". *The Journal of the Midwest Modern Language Association*, 29.1 (1996): 46-62. Print.

Deb, Kushal. *Mapping Multiculturalism*. Jaipur: Rawat Publications, 2002. Print.

Deckard, Sharae. *Paradise Discourse, Imperialism, and Globalization: Exploiting Eden*. New York: Routledge, 2010. Print.

Degabriele, Maria. "Prince of Darkness, Priestess of Porn: Sexual and Political Identities in Hanif Kureishi's *The Black Album*." *Intersections: Gender and Sexuality in Asia and the Pacific*. N.p., n.d. Web. 04 May 2017.

Deleuze, Gilles and Felix, Guattari. *A Thousand Plateaus*. Trans. Brian Massumi, London: Athlone Press, 1988. Print.

Dennett, Daniel. *Consciousness Explained*. London: Penguin, 1992. Print.

Derrida, Jaques. *Margins of Philosophy*. Trans. Alan Bass. Chicago: University of Chicago Press, 1982. Print.

D'hoker, E. "The Unreliable Ripley: Irony and Satire in Robert Mcliam Wilson's *Ripley Bogle*." *Modern Fiction Studies*, 52.3 (2007) 460-77. Print.

Dirlik, Arif. *Global Modernity: Modernity in the Age of Global Capitalism*. Boulder, Colo.: Paradigm Publication, 2007. Print.

Dunlop, Rishma. "Memoirs of a Sirdar's Daughter in Canada: Hybridity and Writing Home." *Diaspora, Memory and Identity: A Search for an Identity*. Ed. Vijay Agnew. Toronto, Buffalo and London: University of Toronto Press, 2005. 115-50. Print.

Dyer, Richard. *White*. London: Routledge, 1997. Print.

Eagleton, Terry. *Ideology: An Introduction*. New York: Verso, 1991. Print.

Easthope, Anthony. *Englishness and National Culture*. London: Routledge, 1999. Print.

Eber, Dena Elisabeth and Arthur G. Neal. "The Individual and Collective Search for Identity." *Memory and Representation: Constructed Truths and Competing Realities*. Ed. Dena Elisabeth Eber and Arthur G. Neal Bowling Green, OH: Bowling Green State U Popular, 2001. 169-82. Print.

Eder, Richard. "Cooking up a Storm: A Servant Keeps It Together in a Disintegrating World", *REEF*, Romesh Gunesekera (The New Press). *Los Angeles Times*. 19 Feb. 1995. Web. 09 May 2017.

Edwards, Justin D. *Postcolonial Literature*. Houndmills, Basingstoke: Palgrave Macmillan, 2008. Print.

Elgrably, Jordan. "Home or the Loquat Tree." *Jordan Elgrably*. N.p., 17 Nov. 2013. Web. 22 Apr. 2017. <http://jordanelgrably.com/blog/2015/6/10/home-or-the-loquat-tree>.

Eliot, T.S. *Selected Essays*. London: Faber and Faber Ltd., 1976. Print.

Eriksen, T.H. "Creolization and Creativity". *Global Networks,* 3.3 (2003): 223-37. Print.

Erney, Hans-Georg. ""Culture is not Contained, It's All over the Place." An Interview with Romesh Gunesekera." *Romesh Gunesekera*. N.p., 4 Oct. 1996. Web. 10 May 2017.

Etoroma, E.E. "Finding Home." *International Journal of Diversity in Organisations, Communities & Nations*, 6.3 (2006): 103-10. Print.

Fanon, Frantz. *Black Skin, White Masks*. New York: Grove, 1967. Print.

Farrier, David. ""The other is the neighbour": The limits of dignity in Caryl Phillips's A Distant Shore." *Journal of Postcolonial Writing,* 44.4 (2008): 403-13. Print.

Favell, A. "To Belong or not to Belong: The Post-national Question." *The Politics of Belonging: Migrants and Minorities in Contemporary Europe*. Ed. A. Favell and A. Geddes. Aldershot: Ashgate, 1999. 209-18. Print.

Featherstone, Simon. *Englishness: Twentieth Century Popular Culture and The Framing of the English Identity.* Edinburgh: Edinburgh U Press, 2009. Print.

Feigenbaum, Janet. "How We Tell It and How It Was." *The Times Literary Supplement*, 30th October 1998. *JSTOR*. Web. 25th July 2015.

Felski, R. "The doxa of difference." *Signs,* 23.1 (1997): 1-22. Print.

Ferguson, Niall. "Why We Ruled the World | Niall Ferguson | Journalism." *Niall Ferguson.* N.p., n.d. Web. 15 Apr. 2017.

Fernadez, J. *Diasporas: Critical and Inter-disciplinary Perspectives.* Oxford: Oxford University Press, 2009. Print.

Feuchtwang, Stephan. "Racism: Territoriality and Ethnocentricity." *Antiracist Strategies.* Ed. Alrick Xavier Cambridge and Stephan Feuchtwang. Aldershot: Avebury, 1990, 3-90. Print.

Finney, Brian. *English Fiction since 1984: Narrating a Nation.* New York: Palgrave Macmillan, 2014. Print.

_____. "Figuring the Real: Ishiguro's When We Were Orphans." *Jouvert*, 7.1 (2002): 1-32. Web. 22 Apr. 2017.

Floriani, Sonia. "The Homeless Self: Migrants, Space-time and Biographical Strategies." *Imagining Home: Migrants and the Search for a New Belonging.* Ed. Diana Glenn, Eric Bouvet, and Sonia Floriani. Kent Town, South Australia: Wakefield, 2011. 67-84. Print.

Foucault, Michel. "What is an Author?" *Aesthetics, Method and Epistemology: Essential Works of Foucault, 1954-1984.* Vol. 2. Ed. James Faubion. London: Penguin, 2000, 205-22. Print.

Friedman, Jonathan. "Indigenous Struggle and the Discreet Charm of the Bourgeoisie." *Journal of World Systems Research,* 5.2: 409, n.d. web. 16 July 2016.

Furst, Lilian R. "Memory's Fragile Power in Kazuo Ishiguro's *Remains of the Day* and W.G. Sebald's *Max Ferber*". *Contemporary Literature,* 48.4 (2007): 530-53. Print.

Gallix, Francois. "Kazuo Ishiguro: The Sorbonne Lecture." *Conversations with Kazuo Ishiguro.* Ed. Brian W. Shaffer and Cynthia F. Wong. Jackson: Univ. Press of Mississippi, 2008. 135-55. Print.

Gandhi, Leela. *Post-Colonial Theory: A Critical Introduction.* India: Oxford University Press, 1998. Print.

Garner, Gary N. "Conflict and Confusion in Sri Lanka." *Cultural Survival.* N.p., n.d. Web. 09 May 2017.

Geertz, C. *Works and Lives: The Anthropolist as Author.* Cambridge: Polity Press, 1988. Print.

Gellner, E. *Nations and Nationalism.* Oxford: Blackwell, 1983. Print.

Genette, Gerard. *Narrative Discourse—An Essay in Method.* New York: Cornell University Press, 1980. Print.

George, Rosemary. *The Politics of Home: Postcolonial Relocations and Twentieth-century Fiction.* Los Angeles: U of California P, 1996. Print.

Gervais, David. Preface. *Literary Englands Versions of 'Englishness' in Modern Writing.* Cambridge: Cambridge UP, 2008. i-xiv. Print.

Gibson, Nigel C. *Rethinking Fanon: The Continuing Dialogue.* Amherst, NY: Humanity, 1999. Print.

Gikandi, Simon E. *Maps of Englishness: Writing Identity in the Culture of Colonialism.* New York: Columbia University Press, 1997. Print.

Giles, Judy, and Tim Middleton. *Writing Englishness 1900-*1950: An Introductory Sourcebook on National Identity. London: Routledge, 1995. Print.

Gilroy, Paul. *The Black Atlantic*: *Modernity and Double Consciousness.* London: Verso, 1993. Print.

_____. "Diaspora and the Detours of Identity". *Identity and Difference.* Ed. K. Woodward. London: Sage, 1997, 299-343. Print.

_____. *Postcolonial Melancholia.* New York: Columbia University Press, 2005. Print.

_____. Preface. *The Black Atlantic*: *Modernity and Double Consciousness.* London: Verso, 1993. ix-xi. Print.

_____. *There Ain't No Black in the Union Jack.* London, Boston: Unwin Hyman, 1991. Print.

Glabažna, Radek. "Theatre of Identity." *Moravian Journal of Literature and Film,* 2.1 (2010): 65-77. Print.

Glyn, Anthony. *The British: A Portrait of the People.* London: Penguin, 2007. Print.

Godlasky, R.S. "Revising Englishness: Embracing hybridity in Hanif Kureishi's *The Black Album.*" *Journal of Commonwealth and Postcolonial Studies,* 13.1 (2006): 1-16. Print.

Gordon, Neil. "REEF." *Boston Review.* New Press, Apr.-May 1995. Web. 14 May 2017.

Goswami, Stuti. "Silence in the Sandglass." *Academia.edu.* N.p., n.d. Web. 11 May 2017.

Graver, Lawrence. "What the Butler Saw." *The New York Times.* N.p., 8 Oct. 1989. Web. 01 June 2017.

Graves, Benjamin. "Homi K. Bhabha: The Liminal Negotiation of Cultural Difference". Web. 12 Apr. 2017.

Grillo, Ralph D. *Pluralism and the Politics of Difference: State, Culture, and Ethnicity in Comparative Perspective.* Oxford: Clarendon, 2004. Print.

Grossberg, Lawrence. *Bringing it All Back Home: Essays on Cultural Studies.* Durham, NC: Duke UP, 1997. Print.

Gunning, Dave. *Race and Antiracism in Black British and British Asian Literature.* Liverpool: Liverpool U Press, 2010. Print.

Gupta, Akhil, and James Ferguson. "Beyond "Culture": Space, Identity, and the Politics of Difference." *Cultural Anthropology,* 7.1 (1992): 6-23. Print.

Gurnah, A. "Writing and Place". *Wasafiri,* 19.42 (2004): 58-60. Print.

Gutmann, A. Introduction. *Multiculturalism and 'The Politics of Recognition'.* Ed. A. Gutmann. Princeton: Princeton U Press, 1994. 1-25. Print.

Hafezi, Mohamed H. *Toward a General Economy of Travel; Identity, Death and Memory.* Diss. University of Florida, 2004. Web. 07 Apr. 2017.

Halbwachs, Maurice. *On Collective Memory*. Trans. Lewis A. Coser. Chicago: The Univ. of Chicago Press, 1952. Print.

Hall, Catherine. "British Cultural Identities and the Legacy of the Empire." *British Cultural Studies: Geography, Nationality and Identity*. Ed. David Morley and Kevin Robins. Oxford: Oxford University Press, 2001, 27-40. Print.

Hall, Sarah M. "A Voyage around the Author: Interview with Romesh Gunesekera." *Bloomsbury Author Information*. N.p., 19 Feb. 2007. Web. 10 May 2017.

Hall, Stuart, "Fundamentalism, Diaspora and Hybridity." *Modernity: An Introduction to Modern Societies*. Ed. S. Hall, D. Held, D. Hubert and K. Thompson. Oxford: Blackwell Publishing, 2007, 629-32. Print.

_____. "Conclusion: The Multicultural Question." *Un/settled Multiculturalisms: Diasporas, Entanglements, "Transruptions"*. Ed. Barnor Hesse. London: Zed Books, 2000, 209-41. Print.

_____. "Cultural Identity and Diaspora." *Identity and Difference*. Ed. Kathryn Woodward. London: Sage Publications, 1997, 51-59. Print.

_____. "Ethnicity: Identity and Difference." *In Becoming National: A Reader*. Ed. Geoff Eley and Ronald Grigor Suny. New York: Oxford University Press, 1996, 339-49. Print.

_____. "New Ethnicities". *Black British Cultural Studies: A Reader*. Ed. Houston A. Barker Jr., Manthia Diwara and Ruth H. Lindeborg. Chicago: U of Chicago, 1996, 163-72. Print.

_____. "Reinventing Britain." *Wasafiri*, 29 (1999): 52-62. Print.

_____. "The Local and The Global: Globalization and Ethnicity." *Dangerous Liaisons: Gender, Nation, and Postcolonial Perspectives*. Ed. Anne McClintock, Aamir Mufti, and Ella Shohat. Minneapolis, MN: University of Minnesota, 2010, 173-88. Print.

_____. "The Question of Cultural Identity". *Modernity and its Futures*. Ed. Stuart Hall, David Held and Tony McGrew. Cambridge, UK: Polity Press, 1992, 274-316. Print.

_____. "The Spectacle of the 'Other'". *Representation: Cultural Representations and Signifying Practices*. Ed. Stuart Hall. London: The Open University: Sage, 1997. 223-90. Print.

_____. "Who needs Identity?" *Questions of Cultural Identity*. Ed. Stuart Hall and Paul Du Gay. London: Sage, 1996. 1-17. Print.

Haraway, Donna. "Situated Knowledges: The Science Question in Feminism and the Privilege of Partial Perspective." *Simians, Cyborgs and Women, The Reinvention of Nature*. Ed. D. Haraway. London: Free Association Books, 1991, 183-202. Print.

Hasmi, Alamgir. "Hanif Kureishi and the Tradition of Novel." *Critical Survey*, 5 (1993): 25-30. Print.

Head, Dominic. *The Cambridge Introduction to Modern British Fiction: 1950-2000*. Cambridge: Cambridge University Press, 2003. Print.

Hecht, Anat. "Home Sweet Home: Tangible Memories of a Uprooted Childhood". *Home Possessions: Material Culture Behind Closed Doors*. Ed. Daniel Miller. Oxford, UK: Berg, 2001, 123-45. Print.

Holmes, Frederick M. "The Postcolonial Subject Divided between East and West: Kureishi's *The Black Album* as an Intertext of Rushdie's *The Satanic Verses*." *Academic Journal*, 37.3 (2001): 296-312. Print.

Holtzman, Jon D. "Food and Memory." *Annual Review of Anthropology*. Palo Alto, CA: Annual Reviews, 2006, 361-78. Print.

Hooks, Bell. *Art on My Mind: Visual Poetics*. New York: New Press, 1995. Print.

Hua, Anh. "Diaspora and Cultural Memory". *Diaspora, Memory, and Identity: A Search for Home*. Ed. Vijay Agnew. Toronto: University of Toronto, 2008, 191-208. Print.

Huggan, Graham. *The Postcolonial Exotic: Marketing the Margins*. New York: Routledge, 2001. Print.

Hussein, Aamer. "Romesh Gunesekera: After an Odyssey, Paradise Regained". Interview. Independent. 13 April 2002. Web. 09 May 2017.

Ishiguro, Kazuo and Kenzaburo Oe. "Wave Patterns: A Dialogue." *Grand Street,* 10.2 (1991): 75-91. Print.

_____. "The Novelist in Today's World: A Conversation." *Boundary* 2, 18.3 (1991): 109-22. Print.

Iyer, Pico. "Connoisseur of Memory." *Time Magazine* (14 February 1994): 41-45. Print.

Jaggi, Maya. "Interview: Romesh Gunesekera." *The Guardian*. Guardian News and Media, 04 May 2007. Web. 10 May 2017.

_____. "Kazuo Ishiguro with Maya Jaggi." *Conversations with Kazuo Ishiguro*. Ed. Brian W. Shaffer and Cynthia F. Wong. Jackson: University Press of Mississippi, 2008. 110-19. Print.

James, David. "Artifice and Absorbson: The Modesty of *The Remains of the Day*." *Kazuo Ishiguro: Contemporary Critical Perspective*. Ed. Sean Matthews and Sebastian Groes. New York: Bloomsbury Publishing, 2009, 54-66. Print.

JanMohamed, Abdul R. "Worldliness-Without-World, Homelessness-as-Home: Toward a Definition of the Specular Border Intellectual." *Edward Said: A Critical Reader*. Ed. Michael Sprinker. Boston: Basil Blackwell, 1992. 96-120. Print.

Jayawickrama, Sharanya. "Consuming Desire: Identity and Narration in Romesh Gunesekera's Reef." *Postgraduate English: A Journal and Forum for Postgraduates in English,* 8 (2003): 1-19. Print.

Jones, Emrys. "Race and Ethnicity in London." *A New Metropolitan Geography*. Ed. Hoggart, Keith, and David R. Green Sevenoaks, London: Edward Arnold, 1992. 186-203. Print.

Kaleta, Kenneth C. *Hanif Kureishi: Postcolonial Storyteller*. Austin: University of Texas Press, 1998. Print.

Kaul, Suvir. "Book Review: Romesh Gunesekera's The Sandglass. An Immigrant Looks Back", *India Today*. 22 Dec. 1997. Web. 12 May 2017.

Kelman, Suanne. "Ishiguro in Toronto." *Conversations with Kazuo Ishiguro*. Ed. Brian W. Shaffer and Cynthia F. Wong. Jackson: Univ. Press of Mississippi, 2008. 42-51. Print.

King, Bruce. "Abdulrazak Gurnah and Hanif Kureishi: Failed Revolution." *The Contemporary British Novel*. Ed. James Acheson. Edinburgh: Edinburgh University Press, 2005. 85-94. Print.

King, Nicola. *Memory, Narrative, Identity: Remembering the Self*. Edinburgh: Edinburgh U, 2000. Print.

Kivisto, Peter. *Multiculturalism in a Global Society.* Great Britain: Blackwell Publishers, 2008. Print.

Kompridis, Nikolas. "Normativizing Hybridity/Neutralizing Culture," *Political Theory,* 33.3 (2005): 318-43. Print.

Kumar, Amitava, and Hanif Kureishi. "A Bang and a Whimper: A Conversation with Hanif Kureishi." *Transition,* 88 (2001): 114-31. Print.

Kumar, Krishan. "'Englishness' and English National Identity." *British Cultural Studies: Geography, Nationality and Identity.* Ed. David Morley and Kevin Robins. Oxford: Oxford University Press, 2001, 41-55. Print.

_____. *The Making of English National Identity*. Cambridge: Cambridge University Press, 2003. Print.

Kundu, Gautam. "Romesh Gunesekera." *South Asian Novelists in English: An A-to-Z Guide*. Ed. Jaina C. Sanga. Westport, CT: Greenwood, 2003. 93-99. Print.

Kureishi, Hanif. "Hanif Kureishi: Turning *The Black Album* into a Stage Play." *The Guardian*, 29 June 2009: N.p. Guardian.co.uk. Web. 20 June. 2017.

_____. *Collected Essays*. London: Faber and Faber, 2011. Print.

_____. *Dreaming and Scheming: Reflections on Writing and Politics*. London: Faber and Faber, 2002. Print.

_____. *Borderline*. London: Methuen, 1981. Print.

Kymlicka, Will. "Social Unity in a Liberal State." *Social Philosophy and Policy,* 13.01 (1996): 105-23. Web.

Lacan, J. *Ectris*. Trans. Bruce Fink. New York: Norton, 2006. Print.

Lamont, M., Molnar, V. "The Study of Boundaries in the Social Sciences." *Annual Review of Sociology,* 28 (2002): 167-95. Print.

Lane, Christopher. Introduction. *The Psychoanalysis of Race*. Ed. Christopher Lane. New York: Columbia University Press, 1998. 3-37. Print.

Lang, James M. "Public Memory, Private History: Kazuo Ishiguro's *The Remains of the Day.*" *CLIO: A Journal of Literature, History, and the Philosophy of History,* 29.2 (2000): 143-65. Print.

Langford, Paul. *Englishness Identified: Manners and Character 1650-1850*. Oxford: Oxford University Press, 2000. Print.

Laplanche, Jean and J.B. Pontalis. *The Language of Psychoanalysis*. Trans. Donald Nicholson-Smith. London: Hogarth and The Institute of Psychoanalysis, 1973. Print.

Layton-Henry, Zig. *Politics of Immigration: Race and 'Race' Relations in Postwar Britain*. Oxford: Blackwell, 1992. Print.

Leach, Edmund Ronald and Raymond William. *Political System of Highland Burma: A Study of Kachin Social Structure*. London: London School of Economics and Political Science, 1964. Print.

Lee, Benjamin. "Going Public". *Public Culture, 5* (1993): 165-77. Print.

Leese, Peter. *Britain since 1945: Aspects of Identity*. Houndmills, Basingstoke, Hampshire: Palgrave Macmillan, 2006. Print.

Leith, William. "Sex, Drugs and a Mid-Life Crisis." *Observer,* 23 Mar. 1997: 6-8. *The Guardian and Observer Digital Archive*. Web. 27 Apr. 2017.

Lewis, Barry. *Kazuo Ishiguro*. Manchester: Manchester University Press, 2000. Print.

Liquori, Donna. "Texture of Memory: Ishiguro Finds in the Fog of Recollection a Device to Craft Novels." *New York State Writers Institute—Kazuo Ishiguro Times Union Article*. Albany, N.Y., April 17, 2005. Web. 19 Apr. 2017.

Lo, Jacqueline. "Beyond Happy Hybridity: Performing Asian Australian Identities." *Alter/Asians: Asian-Australian Identities in Art Media and Popular Culture*. Ed. Ien Ang, Sharon Chalmers, Lisa Law and Mandy Thomas. Sydney: Pluto Press, 2000. 152-68. Print.

Lodge, David, and Nigel Wood. *Modern Criticism and Theory: A Reader*. Oxfordshire, England: Routledge, 2013. Print.

Lodge, David. *The Art of Fiction*. London: Vintage, 2011. Print.

Loomba, Ania. *Colonialism/Postcolonialism*. London and New York: Routledge, 2001. Print.

Lowenthal, David. *The Past is a Foreign Country*. Cambridge: Cambridge University Press, 1985. Print.

Ma, Sheng-mei. *Immigrant Subjectivities in Asian American and Asian Diaspora Literatures*. Albany, N.Y.: State U of New York P, 1998. Print.

Machinal, Helene. "Kazuo Ishiguro's When We Were Orphans: Narration and Detection in the Case of Christopher Banks." *Kazuo Ishiguro: Contemporary Critical Perspective*. Ed. Sean Matthews and Sebastian Groes. New York: Bloomsbury Publishing, 2009. 79-99. Print.

Massey, Doreen. "A Global Sense of Place." *Makedonetwork* (1991). *THINK/URBANISM*. N.p., 18 Dec. 2011. Web. 05 Apr. 2017.

Malik, Kenan. Preface. *From Fatwa to Jihad: The Rushdie Affair and its Legacy*. London: Atlantic Books, 2009. 1-5. Print.

Malik, Sarita. *Representing Black Britain: Black and Asian Images on Television*. London: Sage, 2001. Print.

Mandler, Peter. *The English National Character: The History of an Idea from Edmund Burke to Tony Blair*. New Haven: Yale University Press, 2006. Print.

Manferlotti, Stefano. "Writers from Elsewhere." *The Postcolonial Questions: Common Skies, Divided Horizon*. Ed. Iain Chambers and Lidia Curti. London: Routledge, 1996. 189-98. Print.

Marcus, Amit. "The Self-Deceptive and the Other-Deceptive Narrating Character: The Case of Lolita." *Style*, 39.2 (2005): 187-205. Print.

Mason, Gregory. "An Interview with Kazuo Ishiguro." *Conversations with Kazuo Ishiguro*. Ed. Brian W. Shaffer and Cynthia F. Wong. Jackson: University Press of Mississippi, 2008. 3-14. Print.

Mathur, Charu. "Home as an Emotional Construct in Romesh Gunesekera's *The Reef* and *The Sandglass*." *Asiatic*, 6.1 (2012): 25-31. Print.

Matsuda, Matt K. *The Memory of the Modern*. New York: Oxford University Press, 1996. Print.

Matthews, Sean and Sebastian Groes. Introduction. *Kazuo Ishiguro: Contemporary Critical Perspective*. Ed. Sean Matthews and Sebastian Groes. New York: Bloomsbury Publishing, 2009. 1-8. Print.

Matthews, Sean. "'I'm Sorry I Can't Say More': An Interview with Kazuo Ishiguro." *Kazuo Ishiguro: Contemporary Critical Perspective*. Ed. Sean Matthews and Sebastian Groes. New York: Bloomsbury Publishing, 2009. 114-25. Print.

McCabe, Colin. "Interview: Hanif Kureishi on London." *Critical Quarterly*, 41.3 (1999): 37-56. Print.

McLeod, John. *Beginning Postcolonialism*. Manchester: Manchester University Press, 2012. Print.

Mercer, Kobena. "Diaspora Culture and Dialogic Imagination: The Aesthetics of Black Independent Film in Britain." *Blackframes: Critical Perspective on Black Independent Cinema*. Ed. Mbye B. Cham and Claire Andrade-Watkins. Cambridge, Mass: MIT Press, 1988. 50-61. Print.

_____. *Welcome to the Jungle: New Positions in Black Cultural Studies*. New York: Routledge, 2006. Print.

Meredith, Paul. "Hybridity in the Third Space: Rethinking Bi-cultural in Aotearoa/New Zealand." *Proceedings of Te Oru Rangahau Māori Research and Development Conference, School of Māori Studies, Massey University, 7-9 July 1998*. Te Oru Rangahau Maori Research and Development Conference, Massey University, Palmerston North. Palmerston North, N.Z.: Te Pūtahi-ā-Toi School of Māori Studies, Massey U, 1998. 1-7. Web.

Mergenthal, Silvia. *A Fast-Forward Version of England: Constructions of Englishness in Contemporary Fiction*. Heidelberg: Universitätsverlag Winter, 2003, Print.

Mihailescu, Calin-Andrei, and Walid Hamarneh. *Fiction Updated: Theories of Fictionality, Narratology, and Poetics*. Toronto: U of Toronto, 1996. Print.

Mishra, Vijay. "The Diasporic Imaginary: Theorizing the Indian Diaspora." *Textual Practice* 10.3 (1996): 421-47. Print.

Modood, Tariq. "Anti-Essentialism, Multiculturalism and the 'Recognition' of Religious Groups." *The Journal of Political Philosophy*, 6.4 (1998): 378-99. Print.

Moore-Gilbert, Bart. *Hanif Kureishi*. Manchester: Manchester University Press, 2001. Print.

Morley, D. and Robin, K. *Spaces of Identity*. London: Routledge, 1995. Print.

Morris, L. "Globalization, Migration and the Nation-state: The Path to a Post-national Europe?" *British Journal of Sociology*, 48.2 (1997): 192-209. Print.

Morrison, Jago. *Contemporary Fiction*. London: Routledge, 2003. Print.

Mulhall, Stephen. *Heidegger and Being and Time*. London and New York: Routledge, 1996. Print.

Murray, Melanie A. *Island Paradise: The Myth—An Examination of Contemporary Caribbean and Sri Lankan Writing*. Amsterdam: Rodopi, 2009. Print.

Naficy, Hamid. *The Making of Exile Cultures: Iranian Television in Los Angeles*. Minneapolis: U of Minnesota Press, 1993. Print.

Naipaul, V.S. *The Mimic Men*. London: Penguin Books Limited, 1967. Print.

Nairn, Tom. *The Break-up of Britain: Crisis and Neo-nationalism*. Champaign, IL: Common Ground, 2015. Print.

Nasta, Susheila. *Home Truths: Fictions of the South Asian Diaspora in Britain*. New York: Palgrave, 2002. Print.

Nora, Pierre (1989), "Between Memory and History: Les Lieux de Mémoire." *Representations*, 26 (1989): 7-24. Print.

Nyman, Jopi. *Under English Eyes: Construction of Europe in the Early Twentieth Century British Fiction*. Amsterdom: Rudapi, 2000. Print.

O'Keeffe, T. "Landscape and Memory: Historiography, Theory, Methodology." *Heritage, Memory and the Politics of Identity: New Perspective on the Cultural Landscape*. Ed. N. Moore and Y. Whelan. Aldershot: Ashgate, 2007. 3-18. Print.

Page, Norman. "Speech, Culture and History in the Novels of Kazuo Ishiguro." *Asian Voices in English*. Ed. Mimi Chang and Roy Harris. Hong Kong: Hong Kong University Press, 1991, 161-68. Print.

Papastergiadis, Nikos. *The Turbulence of Migration: Globalization, Deterritorialization and Hybridity*. Cambridge: Polity, 2000. Print.

Parameswaran, Uma. "Contextualising Diasporic Locations in Deepa Mehta's *Fire* and Srinivas Krishna's *Masala*." *Diaspora: Theories, Histories, Texts*. Ed. Makarand Paranjape. New Delhi: Indialog, 2001, 290-99. Print.

_____. *Writing the Diaspora: Essay on Culture and Identity*. New Delhi: Rawat, 2007. Print.

Paranjape, Makarand. "Displaced Relations: Diasporas, Empires, Homelands." *Diaspora: Theories, Histories, Texts*. Ed. Makrand Paranjape. New Delhi: Indialog Publications, 2001. 1-15. Print.

_____. "Writing Across Boundaries: South Asian Diasporas and Homelands." *Diaspora and Multiculturalism: Common*

Traditions and New Developments. Ed. Monika Fludernik. Amsterdam, New York: Rodopi, 2003. 231-60. Print.

Parekh, Bhikhu C. Preface. *The Future of Multi-ethnic Britain: The Parekh Report*. London: Profile, 2000. viii-xii. Print.

_____. *Rethinking Multiculturalism: Cultural Diversity and Political Theory*. New York: Palgrave Macmillan, 2000. Print.

_____. *The Future of Multi-ethnic Britain: The Parekh Report*. London: Profile, 2000. Print.

Pascual, Mónica C. "My Beautiful Laundrette: Hybrid 'Identity', or the Paradox of Conflicting Identification in 'Third Space' Asian-British Cinema of the 1980s" *Miscelá nie: A Journal of English and American Studies,* 26 (2002): 59-70. Print.

Patchett, Emma. "'Corpus Cartography': Diasporic Identity as Flesh and Blood." *Journal of Post-Colonial Cultures and Societies*, 4.3 (2017): 51-67. Print.

Perera, S.W. "Images of Sri Lanka through Expatriate Eyes: Romesh Gunesekera's *Reef*." *Journal of Commonwealth Literature,* 30.1 (1995): 63-78. Print.

_____. "The Perils of Expatriation and a 'Heartless Paradise': Romesh Gunesekera's *The Sandglass*." *Journal of Commonwealth Literature,* 22.2 (1998): 93-106. Print.

Perez, Eva M. ""As if Empires Were Great and Wonderful Things": A Critical Reassessment of the British Empire During World War Two in Lois de *Bernieres' Captain Corelli's Mandolin*, Mark Mills' *The Information Officer* and Kazuo Ishiguro's *When We Were Orphans*." *Post-empire Imaginaries?: Anglophone Literature, History, and the Demise of Empires*. Ed. Barbara Buchenau, Virginia Richter and Marijke Denger. Leiden: Brill, 2015, 217-42. Print.

Petry, Mike. *Narratives of Memory and Identity: The Novels of Kazuo Ishiguro*. Frankfurt A/M.: Peter Lang, 1999. Print.

Phan, Le Ha. *Teaching English as an International Language: Identity, Resistance and Negotiation*. Clevedon, UK: Multilingual Matters, 2008. Print.

Phillips, Caryl. *A New World Order*. New York: Vintage Books, 2010. Print.

_____. *Extravagent Strangers: A Literature of Belonging*. London: Faber and Faber, 1997. Print.

_____. *The European Tribe*. London: Faber and Faber, 1987. Print.

Pines, Jim. "Rituals and Representations of Black 'Britishness'." *British Cultural Studies: Geography, Nationality and Identity*. Ed. David Morley and Kevin Robins. Oxford: Oxford University Press, 2001, 57-66. Print.

Poon, Angelia. *Enacting Englishness in the Victorian Period: Colonialism and the Politics of Performance*. Aldershot: Ashgate, 2008. Print.

Prato, Giuliana B. Introduction. *Beyond Multiculturalism: Views from Anthropology*. Ed. Giuliana B. Prato. Farnham: Ashgate, 2009. 1-20. Print.

Procter, James. *Dwelling Places: Post-war Black British Writing*. Manchester: Manchester U Press, 2003. Print.

Ramsamy, Shyama. "Island Life: Comparative Analysis of V.S. Naipaul's *Mystic Masseur* and Romesh Gunesekera's *Reef*." *LangLit* 1.1 (2014): 1-9. Print.

Ranasinha, Ruvani. *Hanif Kureishi*. Northcote House, 2002. Print.

Rapport, Nigel and Joanna Overing. *Key Concepts in Social and Cultural Anthropology*. London and New York: Routledge, 2004. Print.

Ratti, Manav. *The Postsecular Imagination: Postcolonialism, Religion, and Literature*. New York: Routledge, 2014. Print.

Renan, Earnest. "What is a Nation?" Trans. Martin Thom. *Nation and Narration*. Ed. Homi Bhabha. London: Routledge, 1990. 8-22. Print.

Richards, I.A. *Principles of Literary Criticism*. London: Routledge, 2003. Print.

Robin, Kevin. "Endnote: To London: The City beyond the Nation." *British Cultural Studies: Geography, Nationality and Identity*. Ed. David Morley and Kevin Robins. Oxford: Oxford University Press, 473-93. Print.

Romanow, Rebecca Fine. *The Postcolonial Body in Queer Space and Time*. Newcastle upon Tyne: Cambridge Scholars Publ., 2009. Print.

Rosello. M. (ed.). Introduction. *Practices of Hybridity*. Norwich: Page Brothers Ltd, 1995. 1-12. Print.

Rushdie, Salman. *Imaginary Homelands: Essays and Criticism, 1981-1991*. London: Vintage, 2010. Print.

_____. *Joseph Anton: A Memoir*. New York: Random House, 2012. Print.

_____. *Shame*. London: Random House, 1983. Print.

Sacks, Jonathan. *The Home We Build Together: Recreating Society*. London: Continuum, 2009. Print.

Sadiq, E. "Postmodernism in Second, Third and Fourth World Literatures: Post Colonial Literary Theory". *Post-Colonial Readings: Essays in Literature and Language*. Ed. W. Mursi and L. Batouk. King Saud University: Al Mutanbbi Library, 2007, 2-29. Print.

Said, Edward W. Introduction. *Culture and Imperialism*. New York: Vintage, 1994. i-xxxi. Print.

_____. *Culture and Imperialism*. New York: Vintage, 1994. Print.

_____. *Orientalism*. New York: Vintage, 1979. Print.

_____. "The Mind of Winter: Reflections on Life in Exile." *Harpers* 269.1612 (1985): 49-55. Web. 05 Apr. 2017.

Salgado, Minoli. *Writing Sri Lanka: Literature, Resistance & the Politics of Place*. London: Routledge, 2007. Print.

Safran, William. "Diasporas in Modern Societies: Myths of Homeland and Return." *Diaspora: A Journal of Transnational Studies,* 1.1 (1991): 83-99. Print.

Sandhu, Sukhdev. "Pop Goes The Centre: Hanif Kureishi's London." *Postcolonial Theory and Criticism*. Ed. Chrisman, Laura, and Benita Parry. Cambridge: Brewer, 2000. 132-54. Print.

Sarah, Pink. *Doing Sensory Ethnography*. London: Sage Publication, 2009. Print.

Schacter, Daniel L. *Searching for Memory: The Brain, the Mind, and the Past*. New York: Basic Books, 1996. Print.

Schoene, Berthold. "Beyond (T)race: Bildung and Proprioception in Meera Syal's Anita and Me." *The Journal of Commonwealth Literature,* 34.159 (1998): 159-68. Print.

_____. "Herald of Hybridity: The Emanicipation of Difference in Hanif Kureishi's The Buddha of Suburbia." *International Journal of Cultural Studies,* 1.1 (1998): 109-28. Print.

Scott, D. "The permanence of Pluralism." *Without Guarantees: In Honour of Stuart Hall*. Ed. P. Gilroy, L. Grossberd and A. McRobbie. London: Verso, 2000. 281-301. Print.

Sen, Amartya. *Identity and Violence: The Illusion of Destiny*. London: Penguin Books, 2006. Print.

Sengupta, Chiranjib. "Romesh Gunesekera Sees an Uncertain Future for Sri Lanka." *Gulf News*. Gulf news, 17 Dec. 2014. Web. 07 May 2017.

Shaffer, B.W. "An Interview with Kazuo Ishiguro." *Contemporary Literature,* 42 (2001): 1-14. Print.

_____. *Understanding Kazuo Ishiguro*. Raleigh: U of South Carolina, 1998. Print.

Sheehan, Kim Bartel, and Deborah K. Morrison. "Beyond Convergence: Confluence Culture and the Role of the Advertising Agency in a Changing World." *First Monday,* 14.3 (2009). Web. 10 May 2017.

Siddiqui, Mohammad Asim. "Politicising Literature and Migrant Identity: A Reading of Hanif Kureishi's *The Black Album*." *Journal of the Faculty of Arts,* 3.1-2 (2004): 106-17. Print.

Silverstone, Roger. "Regulation, Media Literacy and Media Civics." *Media, Culture & Society,* 26.3 (2004): 440-49. Print.

Sim, Wai-chew. "Aesthetic Innovation and Radical Nostalgia in Kazuo Ishiguro's *When We Were Orphans*." *British Asian Fiction: Framing the Contemporary,* Ed. Neil Murphy and Wai-chew Sim. Amherst: Cambria, 2008. 329-50. Print.

Sojka, Eugenia. *Canadian Diasporic Artists and Changing Narrative of Homeland*. Katowice, Poland: University of Silesia, n.d. PDF.

Spivak, Gayatri Chakravorty. "Can the Subaltern Speak?" *Marxism and the Interpretation of Culture* (1988): 271-313. Print.

_____. "Diasporas Old and New: Women in the Transnational World." *Textual Practice,* 10.2 (1996): 245-69. Print.

Stein, Mark. *Black British Literature: Novels of Transformation.* Columbus: Ohio State University, 2004. Print.

_____. Introduction. *Black British Literature: Novels of Transformation.* Columbus: Ohio State University, 2004. xi-xviii. Print.

Sullivan O, Simon. "Cultural Studies as Rhizome". *Cultural Studies, Interdisciplinarity, and Translation,* Volume 20. Ed. Stefan Herbrechter. Amsterdom, New York: Rodopi, 2002, 81-96. Print.

Swift, Graham. "Shorts: Kazuo Ishiguro". *Conversations with Kazuo Ishiguro.* Ed. Brian W. Shaffer and Cynthia F. Wong. Jackson: Univ. Press of Mississippi, 2008. 35-41. Print.

Tamaya, Meera. "Ishiguro's 'Remains of the Day': The Empire Strikes Back." *Modern Language Studies,* 22.2 (1992): 45-56. Print.

Taylor, Charles. "The Politics of Recognition." *Contemporary Political Theory: A Reader* (1995): 269-81. Print.

Taylor, Charles. *Philosophical Arguments.* Cambridge, Massachusetts: Harvard U Press, 1995. Print.

Teo, Yugin. "Memory, Nostalgia and Recognition in Ishiguro's Work." *Kazuo Ishiguro in a Global Context.* Ed. Cynthia Wong and Hülya Yildiz. Burlington: Ashgate, 2015. 39-48. Print.

Thomas, Susie. *Hanif Kureishi: A Reader's Guide to Essential Criticism.* New York: Palgrave MacMillan, 2005. Print.

Tilbury, D., and D. Wortman. Preface. *Engaging People in Sustainability.* Gland: IUCN Commission on Education and Communication, IUCN—The World Conservation Union, 2004. viii-xi. Print.

Tilley, James, and Anthony Heath. "The Decline of British National Pride 1." *The British Journal of Sociology*, 58.4 (2007): 661-78. Print.

Tololyan, Kachig. "(Re)thinking Diasporas: Stateless Power in the Transnational Moment". *Diaspora,* 5.1 (1996): 3-36. Print.

Töngür, A. Nejat. "Hybrid or Misfit? The Brown Man's Burden: Hanif Kureishi's *The Buddha of Suburbia* and *The Black Album.*" *Hanif Kureishi and His Work*. 17th METU British Novelists Conference. Middle East Technical University: Ankara, 2009. 91-102. Print.

Tuan, Yi-Fu. *Space and Place: The Perspective of Experience.* Minneapolis: University of Minnesota Press, 1977. Print.

Tulving, Endel. "Memory: Performance, Knowledge and Experience." *European Journal of Cognitive Psychology,* 1.1 (1989): 3-26. Print.

Turner, Terence. "Anthropology and Multiculturalism: What is anthropology that multiculturalists should be mindful of It?" *Multiculturalism: A Critical Reader*. Ed. D.T. Goldberg. Oxford and Cambridge: Blackwell, 2004, 406-25. Print.

"UK | Race Chief Wants Integration Push." *BBC News*. BBC, 03 Apr. 2004. Web. 14 Apr. 2017. 2002. Print.

Veldeman, Joachim. "Challenges to Theorising Unreliable Narration: An Analysis of Kazuo Ishiguro's *The Remains of the Day* and *The Unconsoled*". Diss. Ghent University, 2007. Web. 22 Apr. 2017.

Vertovec, Steven. "Multiculturalism, Culturalism and Public Incorporation." *Ethnic and Racial Studies,* 19.1 (1996): 222-42. Print.

_____. "Conceiving and Researching Transnationalism." *Ethnic and Racial Studies,* 22.2 (1999): 447-62. Print.

_____. "Three Meanings of "Diaspora," Exemplified among South Asian Religions." *Diaspora: A Journal of*

Transnational Studies. University of Toronto Press, 06 July 2011. Web. 07 Apr. 2017.

_____. *Transnational Challenges to the 'new' Multiculturalism*. Proc. of A. S. A Conference, University of Sussex, Brighton. Oxford: U of Oxford. Transnational Communities Programme, 2001. 1-23. Print.

Vinet, Dominique. "Revisiting the Memory of Guilt in Kazuo Ishiguro's *When We Were Orphans*." *Etudes Britanniques Contemporaines*, 29 (2005): 133-44. Print.

Vorda, Allan and Kim Herzinger. "An Interview with Kazuo Ishiguro." *Conversations with Kazuo Ishiguro*. Ed. Brian W. Shaffer and Cynthia F. Wong. Jackson: University Press of Mississippi, 2008. 66-88. Print.

Walder, Dennis. *Post-colonial Literatures in English: History Language Theory*. Oxford: Blackwell Publishers, 1998. Print.

_____. *Postcolonial Nostalgias: Writing, Representation and Memory*. London: Routledge, 2011. Print.

Wall, Kathleen. "*The Remains of the Day* and its Challenges to Theories of Unreliable Narration." *The Journal of Narrative Technique*, 24.1 (1994): 18-42. Print.

Walzer, Michael. *On Toleration*. New Haven: Yale University Press, 1999. Print.

Wang, I-Chun, and Li Guo. "Introduction to Asian Culture(s) and Globalization." *CLC Web: Comparative Literature and Culture*, 15.2 (2013): 1-10. Languages, Philosophy, and Communication Studies Faculty Publications, 06 Jan. 2013. Web. 19 July 2017.

Ward, Stuart. Introduction. *British Culture and the End of Empire*. Ed. Stuart Ward. Manchester: Manchester U, 2001. 1-20. Print.

Waterman, Molly. "Is the Butler Home? Narrative and the Split Subject in *The Remains of the Day*." *Mosaic: A Journal for the Interdisciplinary Study of Literature*, 37.3 (2004): 157-71. Print.

Weber, Donald. "'No Secrets Were Safe from Me': Situating Hanif Kureishi." *The Massachusetts Review,* 38.1 (1997): 119-35. Print.

Weedon, Chris. *Identity and Culture: Narratives of Difference and Belonging*. England: Open University Press, 2004. Print.

Weeks, J. "The Value of Difference." *Identity, Community, Culture, Difference*. Ed. J. Rutherford. London: Lawrence and Wishart, 1990. 88-100. Print.

Werbner, P. "Essentialising essentialism, essentialising silence: Ambivalence and multiplicity in the construction of racism and ethnicity." *Debating Cultural Hybridity*. Ed. P. Werbner and T. Modood. London: Zed Books, 1997. 226-55. Print.

West, S. *The Victorians and Race*. Aldershot: Ashgate Publishing, 1998. Print.

Weston, Elizabeth. "Commitment Rooted in Loss: Kazuo Ishiguro's *When We Were Orphans*." *Critique: Studies in Contemporary Fiction,* 53.4 (2012): 337-54. London: Routledge. Print.

Williams, Bronwyn T. ""A State of Perpetual Wandering": Diaspora and Black British Writers." *Willia*. University of New Hampshire, n.d. Web. 29 Apr. 2017.

Williams, Raymond. *Culture and Society, 1780-1950*. New York: Harper & Row, 1958. Print.

Winder, Robert. "BOOK REVIEW/Stemed Passions with a Reef Lecture: REEF—Romesh Gunesekera: Granta, Pounds 13.99." *The Independent*. Independent Digital News and Media, 23 June 1994. Web. 10 May 2017.

Wohlsein, Barbara. *Englishmen Born and Bred?: Cultural Hybridity and Concepts of Englishness in Hanif Kureishi's The Buddha of Suburbia and Zadie Smith's White Teeth*. Saarbrücken: Müller, 2008. Print.

Wong, Cynthia. "Like Idealism is to the Intellect: An Interview with Kazuo Ishiguro." Ed. Brian W. Shaffer and Cynthia

F. Wong. Jackson: Univ. Press of Mississippi, 2008. 174-98. Print.

_____. *Kazuo Ishiguro: Writers and their Work*. Horndon: Northcote, 2005. Print.

Yacobi, Tamar. "Narrative and Normative Patterns: On Interpreting Fiction." *Pritoria: Journal of Literary Studies,* 3.2 (1987): 18-41. Print.

Young, Iris Marion. "Polity and Group Difference: A Critique of the Ideal of Universal Citizenship." *Debates in Contemporary Political Philosophy: An Anthology*. Ed. Matravers, Derek, and Jonathan E. Pike. London: Routledge, Taylor & Francis Group, 2003, 215-38. Print.

Young, Robert J.C. *The Idea of English Ethnicity*. Oxford: Blackwell, 2008. Print.

_____. *Colonial Desire: Hybridity in Theory, Culture and Race.* United Kingdom: Routledge, 2008. Print.

Yousaf, Nahem. "Hanif Kureishi and 'the Brown Man's Burden.'" *Critical Survey,* 8.1 (1996): 14-25. Print.

_____. *Hanif Kureishi's The Buddha of Suburbia: A Reader's Guide*. London: A&C Black, 2002. Print.

Zazeel, Tariq. "Unpicking Sri Lankan 'Island-ness' in Romesh Gunesekera's *Reef.*" *Journal of Historical Geography,* 29.4 (2003): 582-98. Print.

Zerweck, B. "Historicising Unreliable Narration: Unreliability and Cultural Discourse in Narrative Fiction". *Style,* 35 (2001): 151-78. Print.

Zinck, Pascal. "The Palimpset of Memory in Kazuo Ishiguro's *When We Were Orphans.*" *Etudes Britanniques Contemporaines,* 29 (2005): 145-58. Print.

Index

K

L

M

N

O

P